ALSO BY SUSAN MINOT

Poems 4 A.M.
Rapture
Evening
Folly
Lust & Other Stories
Monkeys

Thirty Girls

Thirty Girls

SUSAN MINOT

ALFRED A. KNOPF   NEW YORK   2014

THIS IS A BORZOI BOOK
PUBLISHED BY ALFRED A. KNOPF

A portion of this work originally appeared in different form in *Granta* (winter 2012).

Library of Congress Cataloging-in-Publication Data
Minot, Susan.
Thirty girls / By Susan Minot.—1st ed.
    pages cm
"This is a Borzoi book."
ISBN 978-0-307-26638-5
1. Women journalists—Africa—Fiction. 2. Abduction—Fiction. 3. Young women—crimes against—Fiction. 4. Africa—Fiction. I. Title.
PS3563.I4755T45 2014
813'.54—dc23   2013009708

Jacket typography by Esra Oguz / Visual Communication Designer
Jacket design by Abby Weintraub

Manufactured in the United States of America
First Edition

To beloved daughters
Ava
Cecily
Hannah

and the brave daughters of Uganda

Contents

I

They Took All of Us

1 / Thirty Girls

THE NIGHT THEY TOOK the girls Sister Giulia went to bed with only the usual amount of worry and foreboding and rubbing of her knuckles. She said her extra prayer that all would stay peaceful, twisted down the rusted dial of her kerosene lamp and tucked in the loose bit of mosquito net under the mattress.

The bed was small and she took up very little of it, being a slight person barely five feet long. Indeed, seeing her asleep one might have mistaken her for one of her twelve-year-old students and not the forty-two-year-old headmistress of a boarding school that she was. Despite her position, Sister Giulia's room was one of the smaller rooms upstairs in the main building at St. Mary's where the sisters were housed. Sisters Alba and Fiamma shared the largest room down the hall and Sister Rosario—who simply took up more space with her file cabinets and seed catalogues—had commandeered the room with the shallow balcony overlooking the interior walled garden. But Sister Giulia didn't mind. She was schooled in humility and it came naturally to her.

The banging appeared first in her dream.

When she opened her eyes she knew immediately it was real and as present in the dark room as her own heart beating. It entered the open window, a rhythmic banging like dull axes hitting at stone. They are at the dorms, she thought.

Then she heard a softer knocking, at her door. She was already sitting up, her bare feet feeling for the straw flip-flops on the floor. Yes? she whispered.

Sister, said a voice, and in the darkness she saw the crack at the door widen and in it the silhouetted head of the night watchman.

George, I am coming, she said, and felt for the cotton sweater on the chair beside her table. Sister, the voice said. They are here.

She stepped into the hall and met with the other nuns whispering in a shadowy cluster. At the end of the hallway one window reflected dim light from the two floodlights around the corner at the main entrance. The women moved toward it like moths. Sister Alba already had her wimple on—she was never uncovered—and Sister Giulia wondered in the lightning way of idle thoughts if Sister Alba slept in her habit and then thought of how preposterous it was to be having that thought at this moment.

Che possiamo fare? said Sister Rosario. What to do? Sister Rosario usually had an opinion of exactly what to do, but now, in a crisis, she was deferring to her superior.

We cannot fight them, Sister Giulia said, speaking in English for George.

No, no, the nuns mumbled, agreeing, even Sister Rosario.

They must be at the dormitory, someone said.

Yes, Sister Giulia said. I think this, too. Let us pray the door holds.

They listened to the banging. Now and then a voice shouted, a man's voice.

Sister Chiara whispered, coming from the back, The door must hold.

It was bolted from the inside with a heavy crossbar. When the sisters put the girls to bed, they waited to hear the giant plank slide into place before saying good night.

Andiamo, Sister Giulia said. We must not stay here, they would find us. Let us hide in the garden and wait. What else can we do?

Everyone shuffled mouselike down the back stairs. On the ground floor they crossed the tiled hallway past the canning rooms and closed door of the storage room and into the laundry past the tables and wooden shelves. Sister Alba was breathing heavily. Sister Rosario jangled the keys, unlocking the laundry, and they stepped outside to the cement walkway bordering the sunken garden. A clothesline hung nearby with a line of pale dresses followed by a line of pale T-shirts. Dark paths divided the garden in crosses, and in between were humped tomato plants and the darker clumps of coffee leaves and white lilies bursting like trumpets. A three-quarter moon in the western sky cast a gray light over all the foliage so it looked covered in talc.

The nuns huddled against the far wall under banana trees. The wide leaves cast moonlit shadows.

The banging, it does not stop, whispered Sister Chiara. Her hand was clamped over her mouth.

They are trying very hard, Sister Alba said.

We should have moved them, Sister Rosario said. I knew it.

The headmistress replied in a calm tone. Sister, we cannot think of this now.

They'd put up the outside fence two years ago, and last year they'd been given the soldiers. Government troops came, walking around campus with guns strapped across their chests, among the bougainvillea and girls in their blue uniforms. At night some were stationed at the end of the driveway passing through the empty field, some stood at the gate near the chapel. Then, a month ago, the army had a census-taking and the soldiers were moved twenty kilometers north. Sister Giulia had pestered the captain to send the soldiers back. There was never more than a day's warning when the rumors of an attack would reach them, so the nuns took the girls to nearby homes for the night. They will be back, the captain said. Finally, last week, the soldiers returned. The girls slept, the sisters slept. Then came the holiday on Sunday. The captain said, They will be back at the end of the day. But they didn't return. They stayed off in the villages, getting drunk on sorghum beer.

The Jeep had been out of fuel, so Sister Giulia took the bicycle to

Atoile. From Atoile someone went all the way to Loro in Kamden to see if the soldiers were there. No sign of the army. She sent a message to Salim Salee, the captain of the north, who was in Gulu. Must we close the school? she asked. No, do not close the school, he answered by radio. When she arrived back at St. Mary's it was eight o'clock and pitch black and still nothing was settled. Sister Alba had the uneaten dinner there waiting for the soldiers. Sister Rosario had overseen the holiday celebrations and gathered the girls at the dorm for an early lights-out.

The banging had now become muted. The garden where the nuns stayed hiding was still, but the banging and shouting reached them, traveling over the quadrangle lawn then the roof of their building and down into the enclosed garden. Across the leafy paths at the entrance doors they could see George's shadow where he'd positioned himself, holding a club.

I don't hear any of the girls, said Sister Fiamma.

No, I have not heard them, said Sister Giulia. They could make out each other's faces, and Sister Giulia's eyebrows were pointed toward one another, as they often were, in a triangle of concern.

What's burning? Sister Guarda pointed over the roof to a braid of red sparks curling upward.

It's coming from the chapel, I think.

They wouldn't burn the chapel.

Sister, they murder children, these people.

They heard the tinkling of glass and the banging stopped. Instead of being a relief the sound of only shouting—of orders being given—and the occasional sputtering of fire was more ominous.

I still do not hear the girls, said Sister Chiara. She said it in a hopeful way.

They waited for something to change. It seemed they waited a long time.

The shouts had dropped to a low calling back and forth, and finally the nuns heard the voices moving closer. The voices were crossing the quadrangle toward the front gates. They were nearby. The nuns' faces were turned toward George where he stood motionless against the whitewashed wall. Sister Giulia held the crucifix on her necklace, muttering prayers.

The noise of the rebels passed. The sound grew dim. Sister Giulia stood.

Wait, Sister Alba said. We must be sure they are gone.

I can wait no longer. Sister Giulia took small steps on the shaded pathway and reached George.

Are they gone?

It is appearing so, George said. You remain here while I see it.

No, George. She followed him onto the porch's platform. They are my girls.

He looked at her to show he did not agree, but he would not argue with the sister. Behind her he saw the pale figures of the other nuns moving across the garden like a fog. You walk behind me, he said.

George unbolted the doors of the breezeway and opened them to the gravel driveway lit by the floodlights. They looked upon a devastation.

The ground was littered with trash—burned sticks and bits of rubber and broken glass. Scattered across the grass of the quadrangle in the shadows were blankets and clothes. George and Sister Giulia stepped down, emerging like figures from a spaceship onto a new planet. In front of the chapel, the Jeep was burning with a halo of smoke. Dark smoke was also bellowing up in long tubes out of the smashed windows of the chapel. But she and George turned toward the dormitory. They could see a black gap in the side where the barred window had been. The whole frame had been ripped out and used as a ladder. That's how they'd gotten inside.

Bits of glass glittered on the grass. There were soda cans, plastic rope, torn plastic bags. The second dormitory farther down was still dark and still. Thank the Lord, that appeared untouched. Those were the younger ones.

The girls . . . , Sister Giulia said. She had her hands out in front of her as if testing the silence. She saw no movement anywhere.

We must look, George said.

They stood at the gaping hole where the yanked window frame was leaning. The concrete around the frame was hacked away in chunks. One light shone from the back of the dormitory, the other bulbs had been smashed.

From the bushes they heard a soft voice: Sister.

Sister Giulia turned and bent down. Two girls were crouched in the darkness, hugging their nightshirts.

You are here, Sister Giulia said, dizzy with gratitude. She embraced the girls, feeling their thin arms, their small backs. The smaller one—it was Penelope—stayed clutching her.

You are safe, Sister Giulia said.

No, Penelope said, pressing her head against her stomach. We are not.

The other girl, Olivia Oki, rocked back and forth, holding her arm in pain.

Sister Giulia gathered them both up and steered them out of the bushes into some light. Penelope kept a tight hold on her waist. Her face was streaked with grime and her eyes glassed over.

Sister, they took all of us, Penelope said.

They took all of you?

She nodded, crying.

Sister Giulia looked at George, and his face understood. All the girls were gone. The other sisters caught up to them.

Sister Chiara embraced Penelope, lifting her. There, there, she said. Sister Fiamma was inspecting Olivia Oki's arm and now Olivia was crying too.

They tied us together and led us away, Penelope said. She was sobbing close to Sister Chiara's face. They came to know afterward that Penelope had been raped as she tried to run across the grass and was caught near the swing. She was ten years old.

Sister Giulia's lips were pursed into a tighter line than usual.

George, she said, make sure the fire is out. Sister Rosario, you find out how many girls are gone. I am going to change. There is no time to lose.

No more moving tentatively, no more discovering the damage and assessing what remained. She strode past Sister Alba, who was carrying a bucket of water toward the chapel.

Sister Giulia re-entered the nuns' quarters and took the stairs to her room. No lights were on, but it was no longer pitch black. She removed her nightdress and put on her T-shirt, then the light-gray dress with a collar. She tied on her sneakers, thin-soled ones that had been sent from Italy.

She hurried back down the stairs and across the entryway, ignoring the sounds of calamity around her and the smell of fire and oil and smoke. She went directly to her office and removed the lace doily from the safe under the table, turned the dial right, then left, and opened the thick weighty door. She groped around for the shoebox and pulled out a rolled wad of bills. She took one of the narrow paper bags they used for coffee beans and put the cash in it then put the bag in the small backpack she removed from the hook on the door. About to leave, she noticed she'd forgotten her wimple and looked around the room, like a bird looking for an insect, alert and thoughtful. She went to her desk drawer, remembering the blue scarf there. She covered her hair with the scarf, tying it at her neck, hooking it over her ears. That would have to do.

When she came out again she met with Thomas Bosco, the math teacher. Bosco, as everyone called him, was a bachelor who lived at the school and spent Christmas with the sisters and was part of the family. He stayed in a small hut off the chapel on his own. He may not have been so young, but he was dependable and they would call upon him to help jump-start the Jeep, replace a lightbulb or deliver a goat.

Bosco, she said. It has happened.

Yes, he said. I have seen it.

Sister Rosario came bustling forward with an affronted air. They have looted the chapel, she said. As usual she was making it clear she took bad news harder than anyone else.

Bosco looked at Sister Giulia's knapsack. You are ready?

Yes. She nodded as if this had all been discussed. Let us go get our girls.

Bosco nodded. If it must be, let us go die for our girls.

And off they set.

By the time they had left the gate, crossed the open field on the dirt driveway and were walking a path leading into the bush, the sky had started to brighten. The silhouette of the trees emerged black against the luminous screen. The birds had not yet started up, but they would any minute. Bosco led the way, reminding the sister to beware of mines. The ground was still dark and now and then they came across the glint of a crushed soda can or a candy wrapper suspended in the grass. A pale shape lay off to the side, stopping Sister Giulia's heart for a moment. Bosco bent down and picked up a small white sweater.

We are going the right way, she said. She folded the sweater and put it in her backpack, and they continued on. They did not speak of what had happened or what would happen, thinking only of finding the girls.

They came to an area of a few straw-roofed huts and asked a woman bent in the doorway, Have they passed this way? She pointed down the path. No one had telephones yet information traveled swiftly in the bush. Still, it was dangerous for anyone to report on the rebels' location. When rebels discovered you as an informant, they would cut off your lips. A path led them to a marshy area with dry reeds sticking up like masts sunk in the still water. They waded in and immediately the water rose to their chests. Sister Giulia thought of the smaller girls and how they could have made it. Not all the children could swim.

Birds began to sing, their chirps sounding particularly sweet and clear on this terrible morning. They walked on the trampled path after wringing out their wet clothes. Sister Giulia had been in this country now for five years and still the countryside felt new and beautiful to her. Mostly it was a tangle of low brush, tight and gray in the dry season, flushing out green and leafy during the rains. An acacia tree made a scrollwork ceiling above them and on the ground small yellow flowers swam like fish among the shadows.

They met a farmer who let them know without saying anything that they were going in the right direction, and farther along they caught up with a woman carrying bound branches on her head, who stopped and indicated with serious eyes that, yes, this was the right way. People did not dare speak and it was understood.

The sun rose, yellow and bright behind them. Sister Giulia saw the figure of a person crouching in the grass at the far side of a clearing. Suddenly the figure was running toward them. It was a girl. As she came closer, they saw it was Irene. She was wearing her skirt as a shirt to cover her upper body. Sister Giulia embraced her and asked her if she was all right. Yes, Irene said, crying quietly. She was all right now.

We are going to bring back the girls, Sister Giulia told her. Irene nodded with disbelief. Sister Giulia gave her the white sweater and walked back with her a ways till they met again the woman carrying the branches and asked if Irene could go with her back to the village. The woman took her. It struck Sister Giulia how quickly one could adjust to a new way of things. You found a child, you sent her off with a stranger to safety. But then it was simply a new version of God watching over her.

Soon the sky was white. They walked for an hour, then another. By now their clothes were dry though her sneakers stayed wet. The sun was over their heads.

Far off they heard a shot and stopped, hopeful and frightened at the same time. They waited and heard nothing more. The sound had come from up ahead and they started off again with increased energy.

Sister Giulia apologized to Bosco for not having brought water. This is not important, he said.

At one point she spotted a white rectangle on the path in front of her and picked it up. It was one of the girls' identity cards. *Akello Esther,* it said. She was in the 4th Class and had recently won the essay contest for a paper about her father and the effect of his accident on their family. She showed Bosco. He nodded. They had been this way.

When they heard shots again there were more of them and closer. Shouting voices floated through the bush from far off. They'd crossed a flat area and were now going up and down shallow hills. At the top of a higher hill they had a vista across a valley to a slope on the other side.

I see them, Bosco said. She stood near him and looked and could see only brown-and-green lumps with dark shadows slashed off them. She looked farther up the slope, bare of trees, and saw small bushes moving. Then she saw the girls, a line of them very close together, some with white shirts and all with dark heads. Alongside the line were gray and green figures, larger, guarding them on either side. It was too far to see the features on the faces.

For a moment she couldn't believe her eyes. They had found them. She asked herself, What am I to do now? At the same time she set off, but now in front of Bosco. She had no plan. She prayed that God would guide her.

They took small steps down the steep path almost immediately losing sight of the opposite slope. They moved quickly, forgetting they were tired. It was past noon and they moved in and out of a dim shade. At the bottom of the hill they could look up and see the rebels with the girls. It appeared they had stopped. It was one thing to spot them far away and another to see them closer with faces and hats and guns. Then a rebel looked down and saw her approaching and called out. She thought it was in Acholi, but she couldn't tell. She raised both hands up in the air and behind her Bosco did the same.

Other rebels were now looking over. She knew at least she would not be mistaken for an informant or an army soldier. Then she saw the girls catch sight of her. A large man walked down from higher up and stopped to watch her coming. He had yellow braid on his green shirt, a hat with a brim, and no gun. He shouted to his soldiers to allow her to approach and Sister Giulia made her way up the hill to where he waited with large arms folded. She saw the girls out of the corner of her eye, gathered now beneath a tree, and instinct told her not to look in their direction.

You are welcome, the man said. I am Captain Mariano Lagira. He did not address himself to Bosco or look at him. Sister Giulia lowered her gaze to hide her surprise at such a greeting.

She introduced herself and Thomas Bosco. I am the headmistress of St. Mary's of Aboke, she said.

He nodded. She looked at him now and saw badly pockmarked skin and small eyes in a round face.

I have come for my girls, she said.

Captain Lagira smiled. Where were you last night?

I was not there, she said. Yes, it was a small lie. I had to take a sick nun to Lira. She slipped her backpack off and took out the brown bag. Here, I have money.

Mariano Lagira took the paper bag and looked inside. We don't want money. He handed the bag to a rebel, who nevertheless carried it away. Follow me, he said. I will give you your girls. A rebel stepped forward and a fisted gun indicated that Bosco was to remain with him.

She felt a great lifting in her heart. Bosco hung back under the guard of a boy who looked no older than twelve. He wore a necklace of bullets and had hard eyes. She followed Lagira and passed close to some girls and began to greet them, but they remained looking down. She noticed that one rebel dressed in camouflage had a woman's full bosom.

Captain Lagira pointed to a log with a plastic bag on it. Sit here.

She sat.

What have you there?

My rosary, she said. I am praying.

Lagira fished into the pocket of his pants and pulled out a string of brown beads. Look, he said. I pray too. They both knelt down and the rebels around them watched as the nun and the captain prayed together.

It was long past noon now and the air was still. When they finished praying, Sister Giulia dared to ask him, Will you give me my girls?

Captain Lagira looked at her. Perhaps he was thinking.

Please, she said. Let them go.

This is a decision for Kony, he said.

Kony was their leader. They called themselves the Lord's Resistance Army, though it was never clear to her exactly what they were resisting. Museveni's government, she supposed, though that was based in the south, and rebel activities remained limited to looting villages and kidnapping children in the north.

The captain stood. I must send a message then, he said. He had the rebels spread out batteries in the sun to be charged and they waited. She managed for a second here and there to sneak glances at the girls and saw most of their faces tipped down but a few watching her. Would you like some tea? the captain said. She could hardly answer and at that moment they heard the sound of helicopters far off.

Suddenly everyone was moving and shouting. Hide! Cover yourselves, they yelled. Sister Giulia saw people grabbing branches and the girls looked as if they were being thrashed as they were covered. She was pulled over to duck under bushes. Some of the girls had moved closer to her now. Leaves pressed on her. Then the loud helicopters were overhead, blowing dust off the ground and whipping the small leaves and loose dirt. Gunshots came firing down. One of the girls threw herself on Sister Giulia to protect her. It was Judith, the head girl.

The Ugandan army patrolled the area. Sister Giulia thought, They're coming for the girls! But nearly immediately the helicopter swooped off and its blades hummed into the distance. They could not have known, it was just a routine strike. No one moved right away, waiting to be sure they were gone. After a pause heads lifted from the ground, their cheeks lightened by the dust. Sister Giulia saw Esther Akello with her arms over her friend Agnes Ochiti. The girl who had covered her, Judith, was wiping blood from her neck. A rebel handed Judith a bandage. She hesitated taking it. They were hitting them and then they were giving them bandages. There was no sense anywhere.

Orders were given now to move, quickly. The girls were tied to one another with a rope and walked in single file behind Sister Giulia. At least I am with my girls, she thought. She wondered if they would kill her. She wondered it distantly, not really believing it, but thinking it would happen whether she believed it or not. And if so, it was God's will. They walked for a couple of hours. She worried that the girls were hungry and exhausted. She saw no sign they'd been given food.

At one point she was positioned to walk along beside Mariano. She had not dared ask him many of the questions she had. But since they had prayed together she felt she could ask him one. She said, Mariano Lagira, why do you take the children?

He looked down at her, with a bland face which said this was an irritating but acceptable question. To increase our family, he said, as if this were obvious. Kony wants a big family. Then he walked ahead, away from her.

After several hours they came to a wooded place with huts and round burnt areas with pots hanging from rods. It looked as if farther along there were other children, and other rebels. She saw where the girls were led and allowed to sit down.

Captain Lagira brought Sister Giulia to a hut and sat there on a stool. There was one guard with a gun who kept himself a few feet away from Lagira. This rebel wore a shirt with the sleeves cut off and a gold chain and never looked straight at Lagira, but always faced his direction. He stood behind now. During the walk they had talked about prayer and about God and she learned that Lagira's God has some things not in common with her God, but Sister Giulia did not point this out. She thought it best to try to continue this strange friendship. Would Sister Giulia join him for tea and biscuits? Captain Lagira wanted to know.

She would not refuse. A young woman in a wrapped skirt came out from the hut, carrying a small stump for Sister Giulia to sit on. It was possible this was one of his wives, though he did not greet her. At the edge of the doorway she saw a hand and half of a face looking out. Tea, he said.

The woman went back into the hut and after some time returned with a tray and mugs and a box of English biscuits. They drank their tea. Sister Giulia was hungry but she did not eat a biscuit.

I ask you again, she said. Will you give me my girls. She didn't phrase it as a question.

He smiled. Do not worry, I am Mariano Lagira. He put down his mug. Now you go wash. Another girl appeared, this one a little younger, about twenty, with bare feet and small pearl earrings. She silently led Sister Giulia behind the hut to a basin of water and a plastic shower bag hanging from a tree. She must have been another wife. Sister Giulia washed her hands and face. She washed her feet and cleaned the blisters she'd gotten from her wet sneakers.

She returned to Mariano. This rebel commander was now Mariano to her, as if a friend. He still sat on his stool, holding a stick and scratching in the dirt by his feet. She glanced toward the girls and saw that some of them had moved to a separate place to the side.

Mariano didn't look up when he spoke.

There are one hundred and thirty-nine girls, he said and traced the number in the dirt.

That many, she thought, saying nothing. More than half the school.

I give you—he wrote the number by his boot as he said, one oh nine. And I—he scratched another number—keep thirty.

Sister Giulia looked toward the girls with alarm. There was a large group on the left and a smaller group on the right. While she was washing they had been divided. She knelt down in front of Mariano.

No, she said. They are my girls. Let them go and keep me instead.

Only Kony decides these things.

Then let me speak with Kony.

No one ever saw Kony. He was hidden over the border in Sudan. Maybe the government troops couldn't reach him there. Maybe, as some thought, President Museveni did not try so hard to find him. The north was not such a priority for Museveni, and neither was the LRA. There were government troops, yes, but the LRA was not so important.

Let the girls go and take me to Kony.

You can ask him, he said and shrugged.

Did he mean it?

You can write him a note. Captain Lagira called, and a woman with a white shirt and ragged pink belt was sent to another hut, to return eventually with a pencil and piece of paper. Sister Giulia leaned the paper on her knee and wrote:

Dear Mr. Kony,

    Please be so kind as to allow Captain Mariano Lagira to release the girls of Aboke.

Yours in God,

Sister Giulia de Angelis

As she wrote each letter she felt her heart sink down. Kony would never see this note.

You go write the names of the girls there, he said.

She looked at the smaller group of girls sitting in feathery shadows.

Please, Mariano, she said softly.

You do like this or you will have none of the girls, said Captain Mariano Lagira.

She left the captain and went over to the girls sitting on the hard ground in feathery shadows. She held the pencil and paper limply in her hand. The girls looked at her, each with meaning in her eyes.

She bent down to speak, Girls, be good . . . but she couldn't finish her sentence.

The girls started to cry. They understood everything. An order was shouted and suddenly some rebels standing nearby were grabbing branches and hitting at the girls. One jumped on the back of Louise. She saw them slap Janet. Then the girls became quiet.

Sister Giulia didn't know what to do. Then it seemed as if they were all talking to her at once, in low voices, whispering. No, not all. Some were just looking at her.

Please, they were saying, Sister. Take me. Jessica said, I have been hurt. Another: My two sisters died in a car accident and my mother is sick. Charlotte said, Sister, I have asthma.

Sister, I am in my period.

Sister Giulia looked back at the captain standing with his arms crossed. He was shaking his head. She said she was supposed to write their names but she was unable. Louise, the captain of the football team, took the pencil from her, and the paper, and started to write.

Akello Esther

Ochiti Agnes . . .

Judith . . . Helen . . . Janet, Lily, Jessica, Charlotte . . . Louise . . . Jackline . . .

Did I mistreat you, Sister?

No, sir.

Did I mistreat the girls?

No, sir.

So, next time I come to the school, do not run away. The captain laughed. Would the sister like more tea and biscuits? No, thank you. They bade each other goodbye. It was as if they might have been old friends.

You may go greet them before you leave, Mariano Lagira said.

Sister Giulia once again went over to the thirty girls, her thirty girls who would not be coming with her. She gave her rosary to Judith and said, Look after them. She handed Jessica her own sweater out of the backpack.

When we go you must not look at us, she said.

No, Sister, we won't.

Then a terrible thing happened.

Catherine whispered, Sister. It's Agnes. She has gone, just over there.

Sister Giulia saw Agnes standing back with the larger group of girls gathered to leave.

You must get her, Sister Giulia said. She couldn't believe she was having to do this. If they see one is missing . . .

So Agnes was brought back. She was holding a pair of sneakers. She was told she might be endangering the others.

Okay, Agnes said. I will not try to run away again.

Sister Giulia had to make herself turn to leave.

Helen called after, Sister, you are coming back for us?

Sister Giulia left with the large group of girls. They walked away into the new freedom of the same low trees and scruffy grasses, which now had a new appearance, and left the thirty others behind. Bosco led the way and Sister Giulia walked in the middle. Some girls walked beside her and held her hand for a while. They bowed their heads when she passed near them. Arriving at a road they turned onto it. The rebels stayed off the roads. It grew dark and they kept walking. They came to a village that was familiar to some of them and stopped at two houses to spend the night. There were more than fifty girls to each house, so many lay outside, sleeping close in one another's arms. Sister Giulia felt she was awake all night, but then somehow her eyes were opening and it was dawn.

At 5 a.m. they fetched water and continued footing it home. As the birds started up they saw they were closer to the school and found that word had been sent ahead and in little areas passed people who clapped as they went by. Sister Giulia felt some happiness in the welcome, but inside there was distress. They came finally to their own road and at last to the school drive.

Across the field Sister Giulia caught sight of the crowd of people near the gate. The parents were all there waiting. She saw the chapel blackened behind the purple bougainvillea, but the tower above still standing.

Many girls ran out to embrace their mothers who were hurrying to them. As she got close, Sister Giulia saw the parents' faces watching, the parents still looking for their daughters. They searched the crowd. There was Jessica's mother with her hand holding her throat. She saw Louise's mother, Grace, ducking side to side, studying the faces of the girls. The closer they got to the gate, the more the girls were engulfed by their families and the more separated became the adults whose children were not there. These families held each other and kept their attention away from the parents whose girls had been left behind. They would not meet their gaze. In this way those parents learned their children had not made it back. When they came near Sister Giulia in all the commotion, she turned away from them. She was answering other questions. Some mothers were kneeling in front of her, some kissed her hand. She was thinking though only of the other parents and she would talk to them eventually but just now it seemed impossible to face them. Then she wondered if she'd be able to face anyone again, ever.

II

Launch

You have no idea where you are.

You sit among the girls. They're in the shade, talking. It might be birdsong for all you understand or care. You think, I will never be close to anyone again.

2 / Landing

SHE STEPPED OUT of the plane and over the accordion hinge of the walkway to continue up the tunneled ramp. One always felt altered after a flight. There was the pleasant fatigue of no sleep and one's nerves closer to the surface as if a layer of self had peeled off and gotten lost in transit. The change was only on the surface, but the surface was where one encountered the world. Her surface was ready for the new things that would happen in this new place, ready for anything different from what she'd known.

There was a soggy tobacco smell at the gate and loose rugs with long rolls no one had bothered to smooth out. She stood in a line of crumpled people holding their carry-ons and inching forward to wooden tables where clerks slowly stamped passport books after a sliding look from the picture to the face.

She was finally away. She couldn't remember the last time she'd felt the expansion, the air humid, the door opening, dawn light reflected off a hammered linoleum floor as she descended an old-fashioned staircase to the black carousel empty of baggage. There was a long row of bureaux de change with one short counter after another empty and behind them a large plate-glass window with palm trees being eaten by a white sky. Lackadaisical drivers were leaning on the hoods of their cars, half glancing around for a fare. Dark-haired men strolled in short sleeve shirts, women in thin dresses moved slowly. Everything mercifully said, This is not home.

The first time she saw him he flew.

They were in Lana's driveway, unloading alabaster lamps she'd had copied on Biashara Street when a white Toyota truck pulled up and a young man with shoulder length hair opened the door. He leapt over the roof of the truck and landed in a bowl of dust.

Lana gave him a big greeting, embracing him as an old friend, as she embraced everyone. She stepped back to study him, hands on his shoulders. He had on a dirty white hat with a zebra band around the crown. Nice, she said, flicking the brim. Jane, come meet Harry.

Jane set down her crate. Harry, Jane, said Lana. Jane, Harry.

Cheers, Harry said in a flat tone. His chin drew in and he regarded Jane with a strange stoniness, as if she were an intruder who ought to explain herself. The impulse to explain herself was an urge Jane Wood struggled to ignore, so getting a look like that unnerved her. At least that was how she explained the unnerved feeling.

My friend from America, Lana said. She looked back and forth between them. Her bright gaze took in things quickly and let them go, just as fast.

Harry leaned forward and kissed Jane's cheek, surprising her. Karibu, he said.

The phone rang inside the cottage and Lana dove to get it, swerving past the crates crowding the foyer.

We're going for sundowners, she called over her shoulder. You must come.

With Lana, there was always a must.

*

A short time later Jane found herself crammed in the back seat of a dented station wagon driven by a paint-spattered neighbor of Lana's named Yuri. They were headed to the top of the Ngong Hills.

The suburb of Karen flickered by. Its dirt driveways and high concrete walls topped with curling barbed wire hid the airy houses Jane had seen with their long shaded verandas and scratchy lawns. Abruptly the station wagon came to a sort of empty highway, drove on it for a while, then tilted off up a steep rutted road, laboring at a tipped angle. At the top they righted themselves over a lip and arrived at a wide sloping field of tall grass which dropped sharply to a vast smoky savannah banked in the distance with low gray hills.

Striped cloths were spread on the ground and Jane noticed the sunset behind too was striped with grimy clouds. Lana unpacked a hamper and poured vodka and orange juice from a thermos and they drank from dented silver flutes while watching the sky and leaning on each other. A warm wind blew up from the valley.

Jane knew none of them save Lana and even she was a recent acquaintance, met a year before in London on a film set Lana was decorating. If Jane was ever in Kenya, she must come visit. When the possibility actually arose, Jane found Lana and discovered how many guests and strangers took Lana up on her invitation. She was a tall striking girl with a cushioned mouth and flashing eyes. She was also a splendid recliner, as she was demonstrating now, surveying the scene before her like an Oriental odalisque, radiating enjoyment. Her pillow at the moment was a large American man named Don who appeared to be relishing his position of support despite an awkward pose requiring that he brace an arm against a nearby rock. His unwrinkled khaki pants and new white running shoes extended off the blanket into the dry grass. Lana was telling him about a project she had set up where students looked after orphaned wild animals. She must take him there tomorrow, she said, patting his red and white striped shirt, as if knowing money were packed in his chest. Yuri had brought along a dimpled girl in army boots. Jane thought she heard her say she was pre-med, which was surprising. Yuri and Harry were talking about flying. They paraglided here, at a spot farther down the escarpment where the updraft was better. The French fellow wearing a bandana was a photographer named Pierre. Pierre was also staying at Lana's, on the couch in the living room. His low-lidded eyes regarded everything with amusement. He was snapping pictures of the army-boot girl who seemed not self-conscious in the least.

The sky dimmed and the air chilled and they packed up. They took the bumpy road back to Nairobi as it darkened. Harry sat slumped in the back seat beside Jane. She learned his last name was O'Day. He asked her what she was doing here.

What indeed, she thought. Writing a story. Getting away. She could say all that.

Seeing the world, she said.

She's taking us to Uganda, Lana shouted back over Édith Piaf's voice warbling out of the dashboard. Her long bare legs were draped over Don's lap and extended out the window. After drinks everyone was feeling jolly.

Jane told Harry she was there to write a story on the children kidnapped by the LRA in northern Uganda. Lana had matter-of-factly said she'd go with her and that morning Pierre asked if he might come, too. He was in between assignments—there was no famine or war to cover at the moment—and he wanted to try shooting some video, not what he usually did. He mostly shot stills.

It's not really my subject, she said. At all.

What's your subject?

Desire.

It sounded totally pretentious, but what the hell.

And death.

Death should fit, he said mildly.

Death always fits. She smiled.

They both faced forward. In the front seat Lana was whispering in Don's ear. Jane saw her tongue come out and lick it.

Things are hectic in Uganda, Harry said.

Have you been?

Not yet.

We haven't exactly figured out how we're getting there.

I am working on it, Lana said. I might have a possible driver.

Good, Jane said and a for a moment felt a pang of homesickness, which was odd since she did not want to be home in the least. She wanted to be as far away from back there as possible. Clutching at straws, she said.

You'll figure it out, Harry said. You look like the kind of person who does.

She turned her squished neck to him to see if he meant it. Jane was sufficiently bewildered by what kind of person she was, so it was always arresting when someone, particularly a stranger, summed her up. His face, very close, had a sort of Aztec look to it, with flat cheeks and straight forehead and pointed chin. Jane couldn't tell how old he was. There was no worry on his face. He was young. His expression was, if not earnest, still not cynical.

What do you do with yourself? she said.

Little of this, little of that.

She laughed. What at the moment?

I'm thinking about going to Sudan to look after some cows.

Really?

He shrugged. Maybe. Did anyone ever tell you you have a very old voice?

Voice?

The sound of it, he said. It's nice.

Watch out! Lana screamed. The car jerked and swerved. Gasps of alarm rose from the passengers.

Not to worry, Yuri said in a calm voice, straightening the wheel which he steered with one hand. I saw the little bugger. He was trying to get hit.

Lana Eberhardt rented a cottage off the Langata Road. It was green with a rumpled roof where furry hyraxes nested and screeched through the night. In the three days that Jane had been in Nairobi, she had learned the cottage served as a crucial landing place in the constellation of the drifting populace.

Plans were made for dinner. Pierre got into a Jeep for the liquor run. He was tall and slow-moving, as if his attractiveness to women did not require he ever rush. This manner, combined with a French accent, made everything he said sound both frivolous and direct. Don drove off taking Lana in a shiny white rental car to some people called the Aspreys to see if they'd caught fish over the weekend. Their phone was out. Some time later they returned with a large cooler stocked with fish. The Aspreys themselves followed eventually, a short swarthy man and a woman in a shiny green wrapped affair with a plain face who carried herself with such flair and confidence she looked positively radiant. They had with them a beautiful freckled woman named Babette who someone said worked in an orphanage in the Kibera slum. She was dressed blandly in shorts and T-shirt and was all the more beautiful because of it. Other guests trickled in: a man named Joss Hall biting on a cigar and his wife Marina in a long Mexican skirt. There was a silent unshaven journalist whose name Jane didn't catch. Harry O'Day had gone and not returned. Someone said he was sorting out job prospects. Pierre arrived with the liquor and a curly-headed blond woman with a fur vest and bare arms. He spent the evening leaning close to her with merry eyes. At eleven everyone finally sat down to dinner and more people appeared and wedged chairs in. A couple could be heard out in the garden shouting at each other, and Joss Hall came striding out of the shadows, with his head low, as if avoiding blows. Jane found herself glancing toward the doorway to see if that person Harry might reappear, but he did not walk in.

First they were leaving Tuesday, then Wednesday was better, then Friday. Pierre was waiting for some film that hadn't arrived at the dukka in Karen on Friday. Lana had found them a driver, a German named Raymond, but he couldn't leave till Sunday. No one was in a hurry; everyone had a loose time frame. They could wait.

Jane was napping on the Balinese bed in the back garden and woke to Harry's face. He was wearing the white hat with the zebra band around it.

You want to come flying?

What?

Go on a mission. It's only eight, nine hours' drive.

Jane felt away from normal life, sleeping in a borrowed dress, living in a guest room. It was easy to say yes. You just went places here. You went with a stranger. Were you interested in him? Was he interested in you? You didn't ask, even if you wondered. Jane always had so many questions rocking about in her head, it was nice to be in a place where people weren't asking those questions. People here just did things. You just went.

She hardly knew where she was. Some nights she ended up sleeping at other people's houses, missing a ride after the dinner party. The night before, she'd lost her key and Harry had taken her to his friend Andy's adobe cottage, where they slept on the floor in front of a fireplace. Another paragliding guy with a beard was on the couch. Jane had not slept much, feeling Harry's proximity.

What do I need to bring?

Nothing, he said.

But she went to the guest room and put some clothes in a bag. She peeled bills from a wad of cash and hid the rest with her passport behind some books. Her journal fell open and pictures fanned out on the floor. Harry picked them up and handed them back to her, sitting patiently while she wrote Lana a note saying she'd be back tomorrow or the next day. She took a white Ethiopian wrap Lana had lent her and got into Harry's truck with him.

They drove through the Nairobi traffic with the Ngongs' slate-gray peaks zigzagging above and headed west, up hills feathered with crevasses and past scribbled bushes and thin trees, and lit out on a spine-slamming potholed road.

They passed through the crossroad din of Narok, rattling with muffler-less cars. Yellow storefronts sat in a line beside blue storefronts. There were many groceries: Deep Grocery, Angel Food, Ice Me. People walked among goats or sat on piled tires; dust rose up. Then the color-ful blur passed and suddenly the open windows framed a parched beige landscape smelling of smoke and dry grass. After long stretches of unin-terrupted brush and flat dirt they'd find a scattering of huts with people on the side of the road, usually children, turning with slow, aimed faces to watch the vehicle pass.

Harry didn't talk much, but after eight hours in a car she did learn some things.

The main thing for Harry was flying. Work was what you did to pick up a few shillings between missions. He'd had a few jobs, relief work in the north, construction work at a safari camp in Malawi. At home he could usually count on being hired by a German chap who put up electric fences for private houses in Langata. He spent a while too with a bloke trying to save wild dogs in the Tsavo desert. That had been a cool job, he said, nodding.

But mainly he flew. When he first started paragliding he would drive everywhere in the truck till he realized a motorcycle was better for the out-of-the-way places. And out-of-the-way places were the point. The whole continent of Africa was open to him, he'd only scratched the surface. A recent trip to Namibia over the baked desert clay was awesome. Sometimes he went with a mate, usually Andy, but he'd also go alone. His parachute folded up into a rucksack which he strapped to his bike.

She asked him questions; he answered them.

He'd go for days or weeks. Alone, he ate raw couscous, too lazy to cook. By the end of a trip he'd be living on vitamin pills and returned with burnt skin, weighing pounds lighter. His motorcycle got stuck in muddy swamps. Once, deep sand in the desert sputtered out the motor. There was the time he broke his collarbone landing on rocks which made the two-day drive home not so fun. Another time he dislocated his shoulder, but Andy was there and snapped it back.

Many places that he flew he could look in every direction and see no sign of people. Now and then a little cluster of huts was there blending into the brown earth or a thin wire of smoke rose out of the trees. But wildlife was everywhere. Elephants looked like tiny gray chips. Herds of gazelles were a swarm of flies on pale ground when you saw them from above. He looked down on the back of eagles with their stiff wings unflapping as he followed them down the thermal from behind.

Then Harry had a question. Who's the man in the blue shirt? he said.

Jane looked at the unchanging landscape, thinking he meant someone on the road. Where?

In your book that fell out.

Oh. That's my ex-husband.

You were married?

I was.

What happened?

Got divorced? she said brightly. Then, Got divorced. She felt him waiting for more. It was hard for Jane to stay silent if she felt someone wanted more. Two years ago, she said.

Harry rubbed his teeth with his tongue. You still love him? She looked at him, surprised. You keep his picture.

He's dead.

He looked at her to see if this was true. Really?

Yup.

Whoa, he said under his breath. What happened?

OD.

That's hectic.

Happens when you're an addict, she said.

Yes, he said.

No, she agreed. It was bad.

They drove in silence.

How long were you married for?

Three years, but we were together for eight. He was in a clean period when we got we married. She laughed. As if that mattered.

Harry watched the road, tilting his head to show he was listening.

We weren't together when he died, she said. But it was still . . . She didn't finish.

What was his name? Harry said.

Jake.

Harry appeared thoughtful.

That was, Jane thought, all she was going to say about Jake. At least at the moment. Maybe she'd say more later. Some other time, when she knew him better. She might say more, if she thought he cared. But why would he want to know, really, was her first thought. And did she really want to tell him all that? Jake slipping back only a week after the little wedding, the wrenching final break, how she didn't go to the funeral because the new girlfriend didn't want her there. She'd had a hard enough time explaining it to herself without having to describe it to someone else. How do you describe hearing your husband say, I think I made a terrible mistake? And what more can you add about yourself if after hearing this you find that no vow of loyalty could have bound you more fiercely to him than this expression of rejection?

What about you? she said to Harry. You have a girlfriend?

His shoulders rose in a slow shrug. Sometimes, he said. Sort of. His face was placid.

Does she have a name?

He turned and smiled at Jane. Nope.

Open aluminum gates marked the entrance to the Massai Mara and a soft red road led them down a steep hill to the game reserve. They drove onto a flat green plain striped with thin shadows. In the distance a wall-like cliff rose on the western side.

They drove along the eastern edge among leafy trees. There she is, Harry said. To the south an escarpment curled like a giant wave about to break, dwindling off to the west and ending in a hazy bluff.

Harry pointed to some thornbushes which on closer examination turned out to be zebra sitting with ears up in a striped shade. Jane stared fascinated, feeling she was in a storybook, though she was to learn that zebra were not particularly impressive to Africans. Elephant, on the other hand, were by all standards worth driving off track for, as Harry did when he spotted a small herd low in a riverbank. The truck wove its tires through lumpy grasses and stopped, motor off and ticking, giving them a clear view of enormous wrinkled creatures, legs darkened by mud, swaying and bumping against one another. One lifted a trunk like a whip in slow motion and sprayed water. When a large female started flapping her ears, staring directly at the truck and making a throaty trumpet sound, Harry knew to start the engine and back up.

They passed the entrance to a safari camp and its wooden sign hanging on rope with the yellow recessed words *Kichwa Tembo*. Elephant Head. There were a number of commercial camps in the Mara, but Harry was taking her to a private house, owned by an anthropologist who'd married her Maasai translator and so had claims on the land. At the southern corner of the plain the red road tilted up, turning pale and chunky with white rocks. They lurched up a short vertical hill then hugged the side in diagonal slashes of switchbacks. Harry gripped the steering wheel as if he were wrestling something wild. They passed Maasai encampments he told her were called bomas, circular walls of tangled branches containing small huts and cattle which had to be protected from wildlife. On a day's notice the boma would be dismantled and reassembled somewhere else where there was fresh grass.

Are we close? she said. But she wasn't impatient. She felt happy and free. The land was majestic and riding beside him she had the feeling she was where she ought to be. It was not a feeling Jane had often.

Just up here, Harry said, and Jane didn't care if they ever got there or ever stopped.

The white road ran along a naturally terraced area of the escarpment. Down to the right was a tunnel of greenery inside which flowed the Mara River. There was no road at all when Harry turned right down a slope of flattened grass strewn with hulking boulders at the end of which sat a stone house with a tin roof.

They got out. The air was loud with the sound of water rushing by in the river. They went to a door surrounded by a wrought-iron cage with a large padlock on it. No one appeared to be home. Jane sat for a moment in a chair left outside at a green painted table. The river surged by below, the color of café au lait, battering low branches that bounced against the white waves. Above the river a woolly ridge dark as a rain forest rose up against a yellowish sky. It was late afternoon. On the table a wineglass held a coin of red liquid and a dish had the last bits of a tart crust. Harry was digging around in the back of the truck, hauling out the backpack.

They walked straight up, first in the shade then passing the line into the sun. Jane followed Harry's large backpack. They came to a narrow footpath. Halfway up they passed a thin woman, chest wrapped in a plaid red and blue shuka, walking down. Her head was shaved and her long earlobes hung with loops and beads. She was barefoot, probably around eighty, walking without hesitation. Jambo, they said and she nodded, passing by.

It didn't take long to reach the top, and it felt as if they'd gone higher when they did. Soft wind blew and looking over the valley Jane had the sensation she'd never been able to see so far. Perhaps it was true.

Harry dumped out the sack and harness. He took off his shirt and put it back in the sack. As he unrolled the parachute it swelled out like foam. He shook it, then stepped into the harness attached to the thin ropes. His helmet was round and white, making his head look too big for his body. He stood a short distance from the edge with feet planted apart. Past the tall grass at the edge, the plain stretched miles below, brownish green but bleached of color. Behind Harry on the ground the chute flowed out like a wedding train. He pulled at it to free it from twigs and thorns, shaking at a dozen thin lines which all branched out into shorter lines attached to the chute. The likelihood of a tangle seemed immense. A harness of black straps fit over his shoulders and chest and wrapped around his thighs, arranged so that airborne he'd be seated. He stood for a while, staring out, listening. He looked at the clouds, gazing overhead, waiting for a gust. A white mist blew over them, dimming the sun and dampening Jane's face, a low cloud whitening everything. The wind puffed the sheet behind him. His arm kept reaching back to fluff the light fabric, while he stayed face-forward. Wind filled the sail, lifting it, seeming to push him forward. He took a few quick steps. Jane was aware of the absence of the motor roar that usually accompanies a liftoff as Harry stepped off the edge onto air.

The fabric snapped behind him like a boat sail filling with a gust and he shot backward up over her head. He hovered there for a moment then swung back out over the escarpment drop. Jane heard a satisfied sort of whoop. She watched him, holding her hair away from her eyes, as his feet dangled past her and she learned that the person remaining on the ground could also receive a lifting sensation at takeoff. That is, she did. The flying was totally silent. In the air, Harry had said, you didn't hear the sound of wind because you were moving at its speed. You were the wind.

The thermals wound in the invisible shape of corkscrews. She watched his figure soar out over the giant bowl of the world, soon catching the spiral in a wide slow circle as if up a spiral staircase. His sail was long and narrow, puckered like a giant earthworm. Very quickly his figure was quite far away.

To the west clouds were stacked with sculptural definition beside the lowering sun. The clouds, the clouds, she thought. Piled and beautiful, they were both indifferent and inviting. They had that paradox of nature you saw also in the sea, a thing appearing eternal even as it changed every second. Harry was now a miniature action figure under a sideways parenthesis. For a while longer she watched him sail, feeling weightless herself, floating by proxy. She didn't need to fly to feel she was floating. She had a knack for channeling other people's experiences. You left yourself behind and there was relief.

Harry was a white dot.

The vastness of the savannah below reminded her how tiny a speck she was too and yet at the same time offered her the illusion that she could reach across and touch the bluff miles away. Warm wind blew in small gusts against her and the dot seemed to pull her toward it into the sky. In dreams when she was flying she could never make out exactly how it was working. She swooped through doorways, looped over trees, but felt that at any moment the miracle might stop and down she'd plummet. She'd think in the dream, I better concentrate on staying up, but that wasn't necessary. You just stayed up. You didn't know what was keeping you up. It wasn't in your control. It just happened. Like life. She thought how in her dreams she too flew in loops the way Harry was now, riding the thermals, following the shape of DNA.

A white sun perched on the western ridge. When it dropped behind, the light would go. Harry had told her to walk down before dark. Nighttime was the kingdom of the animals. You didn't want to be out there then with them. She entered into the shadow sloped across the hill, taking steps sideways, sliding a little, going down and yet still having the buoyant feeling of drifting over a vast plain. What had taken them thirty minutes to climb took her ten minutes to descend.

On the way down she kept the corrugated roof of the house in sight with the white truck beside it, the lightest thing in the gathering dusk. Darker vehicles were also parked there now. She reached the bottom and walked quickly on a dark road. When she saw a bright little fire going in front of the house it showed how dark it was. Closer she saw piled branches crackling inside a circle of stones. In front of the fire was the round table where two men and a woman were sitting with bottles and a crossed pair of army boots. She was greeted by the people with no surprise at seeing a strange woman emerge out of the dark. A fellow with a thin ponytail stood up and offered her his chair of twisted saplings. Karibu, he said. It was Andy. She sat.

Tusker? Jane was handed a bottle and introduced. The fire was warm on her legs.

The girl named Julia worked at a nearby tourist camp. The one with the boots on the table was Cyril from England.

They asked her where she was from and she asked them and soon they were talking about the baby leopard that had fallen through a torn patch in the roof last week. It landed on Annabel's mother in her bed. Inside the stone house Jane could see more people crossing back and forth making dinner.

It was looking for food, said the girl, her white teeth glowing in the dusk. She wore a safari shirt and a short skirt. But it did freak her mum out a bit.

A bit, Jane said.

What did she do with it? said the fellow with the boots.

Shooed it out the window, said the girl, blowing cigarette smoke toward the fire. Poor thing didn't want to be there either.

Maybe I better go get Harry, Andy said.

He's not back? Jane said. Beyond the fire was blackness and the rushing of the river.

Well, Joss went to meet the plane, he said vaguely. I'll go see. He gently moved off to be engulfed by blackness after which they heard the sputtering of a motor.

Inside Jane met their hostess. Annabel wore a ripped green evening gown and had red hair arranged in a loose triangle on her head. A long table was being set among rocks and feathers and bones. Jane was given the job of picking wax from Moroccan candlesticks and pouring salt into oyster shells, fossils from the river.

Hours later the table was crowded with plates of grilled meat and glistening bottles and candle flames. There were stories of men falling out of the sky, of cars breaking down crossing streams, of mothers running off with young lovers. A steady rain drummed on the roof above them. Jane sat beside a man in a polo shirt who was pointing out the absurdity of monogamy. Look at the animals, he said. Need I say more?

Annabel stood, pouring wine into everyone's glasses, her smile showing wine-stained teeth.

You have someone back home? he asked her.

Kind of, she lied. She thought of the painter she'd liked lately though nothing had gone on between them.

Don't let a man put you in a cage, he said. Ever.

Julia mentioned that it was her birthday as if she'd just remembered it, and everyone shouted and gave her toasts. Some time later Annabel handed her a present wrapped in a banana leaf and tied with a brown Hermès ribbon.

Much later Jane found herself outside in a pitch dark pouring with rain beside strangers pushing a car stuck in the muddy hillside. She gripped the door handle, her bare feet sunk in mud. The car would rev in a great burst, roll forward an inch then rock back down, inert. Try it again! they yelled. Another rev, another group shove, and it wasn't budging an inch. People shouted, insulting each other, laughing. The rain was loud, slapping on the slick grass, but still Jane could hear the low constant roar of the river. The jaunty thump of music played from a tape inside where lanterns shone from yellow windows, casting dim smudges. Otherwise everything was black.

Jane could hardly see her hands. The shirt of the person beside her showed because it was light-colored. They kept heaving and shoving against the car. Suddenly it jerked forward, pulling out from everyone. Jane stumbled, managing somehow not to fall. A headless figure with a white shirt slid by as if on skis and grabbed her upper arm. Harry pulled her along so she skated at his side for a moment on the slick ground before they both toppled over into spattering mud. His arms were cupped around her, and they rolled in this clasp down the slope, somersaulting. The face was close and dark with darker spots where the eyes were and when its mouth came near she kissed it, kissing water and rain and bits of grit on his lips, thinking, *I'm kissing Harry.* She felt his chest warm through his soaked shirt. In her mind were images of the dinner and the faces around the candlelit table, of driving that day on the red snaking road, then of Harry lifting up into the orange air over her. They'd had a lot of wine and her thinking was far off and hazy but one thought did come—this is the way you found a person, crashing into him in the dark, without decision, without knowing where you were going—and even in that abandon she still managed to locate little worn areas of worry pulsing, but with no words to them. Worry didn't stand a chance against this sliding and this person she was holding. The slope of the hill evened out and they stopped rolling and kept kissing and she had a laugh in the back of her throat with the thought, *I'm kissing Harry.* She kept thinking it as worry faded. She saw his hands on the steering wheel, his profile and his placid masklike face.

Wet hair plastered her forehead and his cheeks and their bodies pressed against the length of each other on the wet ground. She felt triply alive, as if delivered from an austere place where it was now apparent she'd been for a long time. How had she stayed there so long? Now she had his warm arms and her back was chilled. The rain kept streaming over them and behind in the deeper darkness the sound of the river was rushing and thundering. Harry was a close new thing which she knew very little about and yet at this moment found it seemed to offer her everything.

3 / Esther

I SIT AMONG the girls in the shade of a tree not so far above my head. It is peaceful with their voices in the air, talking quietly. It might be birdsong for all I understand or care.

I think, I will never be close to anyone again.

We are just now supposed to be drawing pictures of things we would like to forget. You can see why this is strange. We must think, in order to draw them, about those terrible things we would rather remove from our minds. We are told that drawing such things will help us remove them.

Instead I am drawing the tree past the work shed toward the field. It has a curved trunk and resembles a woman twisting to look over her shoulder.

Today I woke with a pressure on my eyes, pulling my forehead. I thought, Perhaps I am getting a cold. Maybe I am.

My mind is uneasy. Since being away, I am used to my thoughts being disrupted. They have cracks in them. I remember in a soft way, as in the distance, how it was to be whole. Nothing. It was like nothing. You just had wholeness, you did not feel it. I would not have known it was there if I had not become as I am now. It has offered me a perspective. It is interesting how one can understand a way that one was only after one is another way.

Beside me the girls' heads are bent close to the paper. They use ballpoint pens and pencils which are better if you want to erase. Red pencils are often used for the blood and the bullets. At night the bullets were red.

Holly is beside me. She leans on a cardboard cracker box. She has drawn a house with a thatched roof and doorway, her house. Soon she will add men with pangas, a chair on fire, and her lute broken on the ground. She was practicing music when she was taken. Holly's from the country near Ongoko, not from the town like me. I am from Lira town, which is not far, just a day's walk.

Past the picnic bench near the shop the boys are together there drawing. I see that one, Simon, with them. His back is to me with his bad leg straight out. When he was shot the bullet was near the bone so his knee is not so good. He swings his foot around when he walks instead of stepping straight. The scar looks like a crack in a window with jagged lines coming out from a shiny pink center against his dark skin. The scars on us are not straight.

Simon is good at drawing so his drawings are tacked up in bicycle repair. One of a car on fire with flames smaller than the smoke, one of a boy with his arm cut off and drips of blood making a puddle. He's skillful at details, doing three shades of camouflage with one lead pencil. His AK-47s shoot clouds and the soldiers have bouffant hairdos and sideburns as in cartoons. Everyone draws them that way, even though they do not so much look like that. They look like anyone.

A high chain fence follows two sides of the property here and there's a wooden fence with pieces fallen out of it along the driveway. The playing field has no fence, but one side goes beside a marsh. We are not fenced in. Here is not a prison and still we are not permitted to leave.

I am not so good at drawing. I would rather look at a thing made in nature. I don't finish drawing that tree.

*

Our camp is called Kiryandongo Rehabilitation Center and we are, during the dry season, a dusty circle cleared in the middle of tangled bush a little ways off the Gulu Road. There are some huts and the office of two sheds connected where Charles our head counselor has an office. The kitchen has a small roof and all sides open to the fire pit and brick oven and there you see Francis cooking. Chickens peck around. We had chickens and when I was small I liked to hold them as pets. They were nervous, but if you keep patient they will calm down and stay in your lap even if their eyes are startled.

We have a parking area for cars. One belongs to Charles and the truck fetches food and supplies. The van is to transport children, but it is broken at this time and has not been used since I have been here.

In the work shed is a shop for making instruments and building chairs and repairing bicycles. Behind in the trees is a large white tent that came from Norway where the boys sleep. The ventilation is not so good and, having sixty boys inside, the air is unmoving and hot. The girls sleep in dormitories with bunk beds so close you can reach over and touch the girl next to you.

Holly is in the upper bunk beside me. She has decorated her area. From the ceiling strings dangle empty boxes of Close-Up toothpaste or fortified protein, an eye-drop bottle, a box of Band-Aids. I have no decoration. Underneath Holly is May, who is very pregnant, due in a month. Her parents do not accept the child coming and have not visited May.

At Kiryandongo we are all united by a thing that also divides us from others. We look at each other and know what we've been through. We also look away for the same reason.

Since my return I meet new challenges of the mind. I have decided to forget everything that happened to me there and so look forward to the remainder of my life. I am not so old, nearly sixteen. My life could still be long.

Before, my life was nothing to speak of. You would not have heard of it. Now, they tell us it is important to tell our story. They have us draw to tell it, but I am not so good at drawing.

We studied the Greeks in school and they had people called rhapsodes who memorized long stories and recited them the way you would a song. The long poems were epics. At banquets or by pools people would sit eating grapes and drinking from goblets and listen to the rhapsodes sing. It was not a song with music, but the rhapsodes still sang. They sang of heroes and of journeys.

When they ask us to speak, I cannot find the words. What I have inside is for me to look at alone. Who else can know it? Not anyone. I cannot say it out loud. How can one tell a story so full of shame?

I listen to the others talk and understand how they struggle. We knew the same things. I stay apart to make peace with it inside myself, if I am able. With the rebels I learned that inside is where it most matters in any case.

I am one of the abducted children. Did I tell you my name? I am Esther Akello.

I have been back about two weeks. The days are strange, I am not used to the peace. I am not used to waking without someone hitting my feet. The first week I slept a great deal and woke with swollen eyes, which in the mirror had dark hoops under them. There is a heaviness in me where gladness does not reach. I know there should be gladness that I have returned. I am free, but gladness does not come to me.

· The boys finish their drawings then get up and kick around a ball on the dusty field. Boys forever like to play with balls. This is better than hitting each other. Simon is running with his bad leg. Charles claps his hands, getting them to go faster.

Here at Kiryandongo they always want you to join in. They say, Come on, Esther, I know you can run. Come on. Get up off your seat.

I prefer to sit. When the ants come I brush them away. If they keep coming back to me I pinch them between my fingers. Maybe I'll get up when I'm ready. Maybe I won't. I hate everyone.

As I said, my town is Lira. At night Lira is quiet and in the day it is not so loud either. We have a pink brick bank and a yellow brick post office and many churches, some with steeples, though most with simply a roof. Goats walk about. The main street is paved from the turnaround at one end and tilts upward past groceries and other shops selling batteries and Walkmans and clothes and stationery to the other end of town where the road becomes dirt and paths squiggle into the countryside. During the dry season the dirt is red and dusty, in the wet season it grows darker and stains our feet like rust.

I was born during the rainy season in April 1982, arriving by way of my parents, John and Edith Akello. I was preceded by a brother, Neil, then followed by sisters Sarah and Judy, and another brother, Matthew. I am told I came out very quickly and my mother who is a nurse said it was the fastest delivery she had seen or heard of. I was anxious to get into the world and to the business of being alive. My eyes opened just then, trying to look at everything even though a baby sees nothing but blurry figures. I was looking to discover things right away. I like to think I came out quickly also to spare my mother pain. From what I have seen giving birth is a terrible thing and I do not know why women must suffer this agony to produce a child. But that is only one of the many things I do not understand. There are many many more things I do not understand than ones I do. Sometimes it seems discovery is the learning of all I do not know. For this reason I am not happy for all the time I have missed school. I want to go back as soon as this is possible.

When we return we first visit the nurse at the clinic. She examines our scars and the sores on our feet. Our soles have become very hard. She checks our bones to see where they might have been broken and looks at our bleeding teeth and chalky tongues. We take medicine for worms and our heads are shaved of lice. The nurse will maybe take a blood test, but she will only do this if you make the request. Most girls do not know to request it because no one has told them. No one wants to frighten them about the HIV virus. They may know a little but choose not to know more. The nurses are advised not to disturb the girls further by informing them to have the blood test.

I ask for a blood test, because my mother is a nurse so I know it is important.

Was. Was a nurse.

The counselors do not like to mention other things. They respect that girls are too embarrassed to talk about the rudeness to which we were subjected. Some things are too private. They do not use the word *rape*. They believe they are relieving us. We may talk about killing someone with a machete, but rape is too private to speak of.

I have decided not to remember, but pictures appear to me no matter. A girl kicked in the face falls to the ground and immediately gets up, because we are marching. If you do not get up they will kill you. I try instead to think of other things: a river in the morning. I think of my best friend, Agnes, beside me, knocking me with her knee, and of the way her face changed when I said something she had thought of, too. I think of the first time I saw my boyfriend Philip on the street in Lira town and the effect it had on my body. I think about sleeping in my tree. But still come the things I do not choose to think of. The boy whom we were made to watch, for an example of what will happen if you try to escape. The rebels surrounded that boy and started jabbing at him with bayonet blades and pangas. Blood spurted where he was hit and black gobs landed on the dust. They kept cutting that boy, who was crying out. I watched with hard eyes. Chunks of skin came off and fell on the ground. I keep remembering his skin in the dirt.

You must not want to hear such things. Who would?

After my escape I was brought to the government building. The first person I was surprised to see was my aunt, not my mother. Aunt Karen smelling of pomade held me in her arms and cried. She was crying hard.

Your mother cannot come, she said, wiping at the tears. Then I received the shock I was not expecting.

She got very sick, Esther. She had the cancer.

What could I say to that? So I said, When?

Aunt Karen sobbed. It was very bad.

And now? I somehow knew the answer.

She could not get better. Aunt Karen squeezed her eyes and shook her head. Esther, your mother has died.

I thought I had gone beyond what I could imagine with the rebels, but it turned out there was more for me to go. Can it be true? I said.

It is funny, the things we say. Of course it was true. I am afraid it is so. But for me, death was not so surprising, even when it was your mother. When?

Aunt Karen kept crying, crying. Three weeks it has been.

I have come too late, I said.

I am not permitted to go home. When you are abducted you are required to stay in the rehabilitation center for some weeks after you return. So it was at Kiryandongo that my family came to see me. Lira is an hour away by car and they would find a ride. They sent word when they were coming so I waited for that day.

When they arrived at the bare yard of the entrance area, I had the feeling of being in a movie when aliens take over a person's body so their eye sockets are yellow, a sign that the people inside are gone. My family looked that way to me. I thought, My mother dying has changed everyone and they are no longer the same inside.

When they were closer they looked as they were before. Neil my big brother lay his loose hand on my shoulder and greeted me by name, but he looked to his fingers not to my face. I greeted my father.

Yes, it is you, he said. I think there were tears in his eyes. I think we all had my mother in mind and were not thinking perhaps of what had happened to me. I am, after all, still here.

We went to sit in the shade of the dorm. They brought me flatbread they knew I liked. My sister Sarah sat on one side. I saw that Judy had changed the most and appeared older—she was now eight—and Matthew was not as plump as before and his front teeth were gone. Aunt Karen sat on my other side and patted my arm. She was dressed up, wearing her wedge sandals. She was not crying this time, just talking. She asked how was it here and was I getting enough to eat. She said our grandmother Nonni could not come, but I would see her when I was able to visit home. Nothing was interesting to me. I saw she was acting like the mother of this family. My mother did not think her sister was a very good mother. Aunt Karen was more interested in painting her nails and straightening her hair. This day she even looked excited to be in her sister's place.

My father stayed still and quiet after they parked his wheelchair. He sat, faced to the side not looking in my direction. When he did glance at me his eyes closed as if it hurt. Was he thinking of what I had been through? Was he thinking of his wife who was now dead? I do not know.

In the family we liked to hear the story of their meeting. On a Christmas holiday my mother came home to Lira and went with Aunt Karen to the army dance. My mother saw my father there. She knew who he was. His brother Robert went around with Aunt Karen, but my mother had become a Kampala girl, working in the hospital there, and wasn't interested in a soldier from Kitgum.

Then, in 1981, with Milton Obote as president, the Acholi and Langi were permitted in the army. Since Idi Amin, the Acholi were not. Idi Amin was against the Acholi. His men had even killed my father's parents, who both died at the massacre in Bucoro.

With Museveni, our president now, if you are Acholi you are not so welcome in the army either. Many presidents do not look after the Acholi and Langi, because we are in the north, and some people believe it is our history to be persecuted.

I asked my mother what my father said to her that night, even knowing the story. She would shrug. My father asked my mother to dance and she said no, and he said, good, he did not want to dance either. My mother wondered if he was nice or mean. He told her he remembered seeing her when she was young but she did not remember that time and he asked her where she lived and what her work at the hospital was like. Most men she knew talked about themselves only. He said he liked the way she was holding her hands. You can tell a lot about a person by looking at the hands, he said. My mother has long hands. What can you tell about me? she said. It is private, he said. She thought he was being rude.

Maybe he would tell her when he knew her better. Maybe you will never know me better, she says. I think I will, he says. Because I'm going to marry you.

My mother laughed and said they had better dance if they were going to get married. So they did, and after they got married he told her what he saw in her hands. They belonged to the mother of his children.

My mother moved back to Lira. They married in June, and my brother Neil arrived six months later. I arrived next. When his army term was up, my father did not re-enlist and instead opened an auto repair shop with his friend Jameson. He'd learned mechanics in the army and liked motors and was good at solving problems. My father likes not talking while he fixes something.

For a while we lived next to Aunt Karen. Sometimes Uncle Robert lived there too, but mostly not. They had a son, Robert Jr., but did not marry. They liked to fight. The brothers were very different. Robert liked being in the army and liked to roam.

My mother and father found a house away from them. Sarah was born, then Judy, then Matthew. We would go to the clinic where my mother was head nurse. Long lines out the door were people from the countryside who would come and wait all day. At home our cousin Lenora looked after us. She started when she was ten.

You see my father in a wheelchair and think maybe he lost his legs in a mine or even from the rebels, but none would be true. When I was five years old, a car fell on him. He was underneath it, making repairs. For a while he was at home, then he got a wheelchair and went back to work. I remember my father standing just once, a time I was on his shoulders. I was high up and scared to hit the doorway as we passed through and he was laughing at me and my worry.

My father does not feel sorry for himself. So if at night when he is home in his chair in the side place in the living room his eyes turn red from drinking this is not so surprising.

When visitors come to Kiryandongo you see how they look or do not look at you. My father does not; my sister Sarah does not stop watching me. If it is your sister you can imagine what she is thinking. I saw her trying to measure if I was wrecked or not. When we were small, people might not tell us one from the other, we have the same shape and face. Looking at her, I have the odd feeling of looking at myself as I was before I was taken.

I ask them about our mother, the ghost hovering there with us. Where did she die? Who was with her? Where was she buried? They told me these things. Did she say anything about me? They said she was worried for me, but believed always I would come home. I thought of my mother's face, with her wide forehead and chipped front tooth. It was hard to picture her sick. As a nurse, she would have understood everything happening to her. Then I thought how at least I missed seeing this thing. I did not have to watch my mother die.

I was relieved when my family left. I wanted them gone. Then I missed them, too. Two feelings come at once and you feel neither of them.

No one here is at ease. We are all troubled.

The boys especially are fighting many times, but the girls are mean also. I saw Holly stomp a chicken yesterday. And Janet, before she would not have hit her baby. When she saw me looking at her as the baby cried she said, What is this compared to what the rebels did?

Nurse Nancy says we are coming out of it. The counselors have us think that after a while you will stop coming out of it and be as you were, yourself again. I think I will be coming out of it forever.

There is a person inside me who has been very bad and does not deserve a chance at life. She has done things no good person would do. I might argue against that and say, No, I am Esther. I am a good person, as good as I can be. But another voice is stronger and that voice says it would be better if I were dead.

They tell us, You are back and things will get better. Again and again they say, You are the fortunate ones. We say it ourselves. It might be so, but—

Holly was made to beat a boy when the rebels learned she liked him. Another girl here found her son's leg up in a tree. No wonder you want sometimes to die. Sometimes your spirit is so heavy you say to it, I cannot carry you around.

Nurse Nancy sits with us talking. She is a wiry woman in glasses who lets her long hair fly around, more concerned with looking after us. She asks us about Kony. What did we think of Kony? Maybe we are mad at him. Some nod. Some girls say he is a bad man. I do not answer. I do not say, I'm not mad at Kony. I do not see Kony. To me Kony is nothing.

Kony took my life away from me, Carol says. She is a St. Mary's girl who has been here a long time. Her parents still have not been found. Below her eyebrows looks filled with sandbags, pressing down her eyes.

Yes, but you have survived, Nurse Nancy says.

I have not, she says. I have not survived.

We have the future waiting for us, Janet says. See, up ahead? There we are. Who knows what is in store.

The future is blackness, Carol says.

Janet says, Do not worry. God will provide.

Christine, one of our counselors, tells us that journalists may come today. Christine was an abducted girl herself, ten years ago. She is about twenty-five and has a square head and round shoulders and wears pearls in her ears. Christine thought she might become a doctor and went to Kampala to go to school, but it did not work out so well, and she came back here and instead became a counselor. The journalists are interested in hearing of our experience, she says. No one has to speak who doesn't want to. Sometimes it can help you. Recently there was a woman from Germany with a tape recorder.

Holly says she would not dare speak in front of such knowledgeable people, and Holly was even at the front of her grade.

Who wants to talk about what happened out there? I say. What good will it do?

I will speak, Janet says. Emily says she also will speak. Emily does not stop talking anyway, though she does not always say the truth.

They want to spread our story, Christine says in her mild voice. It will help all the children.

We think about this. The journalists do not come.

*

After you return, even if the world looks as you left it, you are changed and the world seems changed also. It is new. After my father's accident, my mother said my father did not change. He stayed the same in his new world.

We must find forgiveness, Christine says. We must forgive ourselves.

I am looking for forgiveness, but it is hard to find. What does it feel like?

The fear that I may die any moment is still here. Now and then the fear drains a little from me, but in its place is not a better feeling. There is a hard blankness.

4 / Taking Off

THEY STUMBLED IN the doorway, soaked through. Quiet music played. Jane saw some figures in the dimness past burnt-down candles at the end of the table crowded with bottles and glasses. She felt her way down the hall and found her bag in the dark corner of a room where a couple was laughing in the dark. Returning she bumped into another sleeping body. In the bathroom she peeled off her wet dress and put on underwear and a strapped top. Back in the living room she left the wet dress draped over driftwood bookshelves. Harry emerged behind her carrying bedspreads and kicking cushions to a place on the floor of the living room. Other people were leaning against the wall, some sleeping, some murmuring in a far corner. Harry sat back against a cushion. Come here, he said, his arm straight out, and in the dimness she saw him looking past her, as if a direct look would be too intimate. She sidled against him and put the dry skin of Harry's chest against her cheek and wet hair. He lay still. She was not tired and far from falling asleep. She lay spellbound. People were whispering; another lantern went out, darkening the stone wall.

Some time later she woke, and everything was black and silent and still. The face near her was dark gray, as if in a dream. She touched it and went to kiss the mouth and hands came up on either side of her head, keeping her there. She kissed him, hardly breathing, making no sound. Then he stopped.

Get up, he whispered. He stood and pulled her off the floor, somehow keeping the Indian bedspread wrapped around her shoulders. He steered her through the dark on the soft straw rugs, knocking her into a stool, toward the darker hall, keeping her shoulders in front of him. They came to the door of the bathroom and pushed in. The walls, she'd noticed before, were a rough barn wood stained brown but she could see none of it now.

Too many people around, he said. Keeping her wrapped he lowered her to the floor. Now let me see Jane, he said in the pitch black.

Her breath felt chopped into pieces. Oh, came out—oh. It kept being chopped.

Shhhh, he said, making no other sound. Did he even breathe? His hands in the dark were moving her around, traveling over her. Noises stayed in the back of her throat. That's . . . , she began. Where were the words?

What? he said.

That's. It's. Oh.

But, she wasn't expressing it in the least. Then her breath took over and she went to where words didn't go or matter anyway.

Shhhh, he said.

His hands made her feel small and pliable, and all her nerves were lit. He shifted around and his weight came down on her.

Oh God, she said rather loud. He covered her mouth.

He was there close, but too dark to see. She thought of the rough wood on the walls. She felt his face sort of become her face. She heard the river nearby foaming down the hill and saw the line of the mangled trees she'd seen earlier in silhouette against a pale yellow sky. Then she felt she was in a green forest. Then she was on a porch. It was not a porch she knew, it was a porch in America. There were children playing down the block under leafy branches and it was summer somewhere in the South with beds and white chenille bedspreads and old light fixtures on the walls and railings twisting up the stairs inside. A man and a woman were having sex in the hallway. Then it was Jane having sex with a man in the hallway. Wisteria vines filled the screen door and the door banged shut. Another man was getting out of a truck; he was partly Harry. He came over the threshold wearing boots and pulled open her shirt. No, he came into a side room and threw her on a table and pushed her legs apart ignoring her face. He'd seen her earlier in town, he said. His face gazing at her breasts had only one thing in mind driving him. He shifts her to the side and lifts her against the door, holding her underneath, having to crouch and bend his knees. *I've been thinking of this all day,* Harry said with his legs pressing her knees out and her back against the rough wood, pinning her, legs dangling, toes just touching the floor. One foot has a sandal on, a strap tight on her ankle. He held her from beneath, lifting her against him, pressing his hips so she's on the verge of collapsing but is thrown back, her wrists braced against the frame. He grabs her ass and her feet slip off the floor into the air, with one hand flailing to get a grip on the sink anchoring her, inside the sound of their breathing, and she feels in a sort of tornado as if she's going up a hill powered by wind with gusts rolling dust around and still going up farther and not quite at the top, reaching a crest. Everything starts to shake and unravel with the earth splitting at her feet and the road cracking sideways and air erupting like glass shattering. Her legs flung wide sent off needles of light or song and she had the feeling of falling at the same time rising, of going out and out as she's gathering in, feeling her arms and legs dissolve into a bright bank of dust and finally stillness.

I'm old, you know.
Which means?
I don't know, just I am.
I happen to like old.
Right.
The older the better, he said.
Okay, so—what—you're perfect?

More perfect than you know.

They were twisted into a bound shape on the bathroom floor. They untangled themselves and shuffled, attached, back to the living room.

In the morning they woke next to other lumped bodies under blankets and thin covers, pushed like waves against the stone walls. Jane opened her eyes to see a shirtless man unbend himself from their Indian bedspread and stand in rumpled underwear. He walked slowly toward the sound of the river picking his way over the bodies and disappearing in the light at the door, the back of his head in a rooster's plume of hair. She thought it was the pilot. On the other side of Harry were two heads touching and four arms draped toward each other.

Her head rested on Harry, on the shoulder of this new person. Her mouth was dry and her eyes heavy, but her body felt loose and light. Some people you met and right away knew they were important. Or it might take a while for you to understand how that first moment when you felt taken aback was a jolt not away but to this new person. And if it turned out the other person had a similar thing happen, then it was one of those connectings that happen not often.

She lay on his shoulder and thought that Harry was now important. What *important* meant she could not have said, but the word was there. She pictured the letters carved in wood. She thought of his voice in the dark, saying, *Take this off.* It sounded a little cruel. She drifted on the thought of it, playing it over in her mind.

Later that day they were in the car driving back to Nairobi.

Harry told her about the girl he liked, Rosalie. He saw her at a party, wearing a jumpsuit with zippers. She was small, with skin so pale you could see her veins. Everyone was dancing. Harry had broken his foot and was dancing with a crutch which he threw across the floor and she jumped over. After, they went driving and stayed up all night, sitting on the top of her Jeep and watching the sun rise over Lake Elementaita. She had a boyfriend, so nothing happened. That is, no touching happened, but something had happened. Her hands, he said, looked like an old person's hands. Rosalie told him that she had to give some thought to her boyfriend now, now that she'd met Harry. Afterward he wrote her a letter and she wrote back. She still loved her boyfriend, she said, and didn't know what to do. They kept writing letters to each other. She was still deciding.

What do you write to her? Jane asked.

That I'm waiting for her.

Jane lay across the seat with her head in his lap. Harry pushed back her hair. It had been a long time since she'd touched a person. It made a person feel transformed. Before falling asleep in the bumping truck she thought of how she had come to this other country wanting to disappear, but now felt more vivid than ever. It seemed possible that she might actually be finding herself in some new form.

They reached Nairobi after nightfall. On the Langata Road less than a mile from Harry's, their tire blew and they thumped to a stop. Harry changed it as Jane sat on a dead tree watching in the eerie quiet. A lone streetlight shone amber far down the road like a figure from another era. Harry popped the tire off and cranked the jack, and she watched how youthful his quick movements were and how smooth was the skin of his neck between his parted hair and how nicely shaped were his strong arms, and the perfect contentment she'd felt all day deflated a little with the arrival of her first wish—for more. If only she were that young. She had a keen longing then to be a younger girl whose freshness would make him delirious, the way his was making her.

They were back from their mission, she told herself. *Mission* was what Harry called it. They'd had a nice moment, she explained to herself. So that was probably that. She would be happy with *that,* then. Happiness came in pieces anyway. One had to be happy with the pieces as they came. She was trained in gathering pieces. When you had the bad luck to love a person who cared for drugs more than you, then you adjusted to the netherworld of *Nothing's perfect* and *Whoever said you got what you wanted* and *It will get better.* Those pieces were sharp and cut you, but you still collected them. You justified the cuts.

They went back to Harry's house. He referred to it as his parents' house, even though he'd grown up there. A few spotlights shone outside a garage and at one end of a large roof. She followed him across a dark lawn of stiff tropical grass to the guesthouse. Inside was a wide stone fireplace and heavy wooden furniture and to the side a small bedroom with a mattress of clean sheets in the middle of a cement floor. Harry was under the covers when she returned from the bathroom and she switched off the living room light. She slid in next to him and had the lovely surprise, which always remained surprising, of the first contact with the skin of another warm body which felt, well, like a miracle.

He turned her sleepily. She wasn't wishing for anything then, only this. All right, more of this, then. She felt as if she were on a train, jerking to a start. The slow chugging of the engine was her body coming alive again. As the speed increased, possibilities of the trip expanded. Maybe the journey would not be short. There was hope in the body against her. Maybe it would be a long trip. The Orient Express or the Trans-Siberian Railway. She was riding the shaky rails. She was going faster. Now she was being hurled up against the ceiling.

When she landed in slow motion some time later, her gaze drifted to a blurry window where dawn had turned the sky glass-blue through a pane of lead squares like the windows you see in old churches.

In the late morning, returning to the cottage, Jane found Lana having breakfast in bed with her silver tray. Lana patted the pillow beside her and poured Jane a cup of coffee from a silver pot. Raymond has buggered off, Lana said. He's tossed us for a safari job. Don't blame him, really. But—she used a pointedly hopeful tone—Don wants to come.

Don?

Lana shrugged, as if uncertain whether she was ready to promote the idea. He thinks it might be interesting. He has a car. . . .

Jane looked at her.

Lana bit her toast and studied Jane's face, gauging her reaction. He can always help with the cash flow? she said, chewing.

Later after dinner Lana and Don peeled themselves up off the Balinese bed and slipped away to Lana's room. It was an early night. Jane and Harry stayed collapsed on the pillows, upholstered in hemp and stamped with a black and beige triangular pattern. In the deeper cushions Pierre was asleep.

I'll take you, Harry said out of nowhere.

Where?

To Uganda. I'll drive.

You will?

Sure. I've got a truck.

That would be great, she said. Really?

He looked at her. His face was an inch from hers and his lowered eyes were cool. I just said I would.

What about the cows? she said.

Screw the cows.

Really?

Keep saying really and I'll change my mind.

A warmth spread in her chest.

She couldn't pay him, she told him, but could cover the gas and his room and board. She had a minor expense account from the magazine, she said, actually, hardly believing it herself, since she had no real credentials as a journalist.

It's better if you don't hire me, Harry said. If I'm hired I usually get sacked.

The guest room where Jane was staying had been painted by Lana, salmon and green. Its lantern threw half-moons of light on the stucco wall. Harry got in with her under the pink mosquito net.

He had been with her now three nights and each night in a different bed in a different place. She was in that early lull of physical happiness when going over it was a pleasure, with no real qualms yet. She felt a sinking deeper. And now he was coming with them on her trip. It'll be what it is, she said to herself, as proof she was without illusion, but having no more idea what *It'll be what it is* meant other than a hope against the sinking.

Again departure was postponed so Lana threw another dinner party.

She went into action, arranging what needed to be done, talking to the cook, unruffled and focused. Her energy spread outward and Jane helped her push three tables together and move brass elephants. Lana shook out a long white tablecloth stamped with silver and blue paisley which landed like a sail.

From Jaipur, she said. Lana's things each had a story—linen napkins were from Porta Portese in Rome, gold-dotted plates passed down from her grandmother in Paris, the striped red and green Venetian glasses from the lover trying to woo her back. That worked, she said, for a while.

The cottage had four small rooms packed like a treasure chest. In her thirty-six years Lana had covered a lot of ground. There were the small business ventures: lanterns from Morocco, the alabaster Indian lamps, the belts with Maasai beading. She'd worked as a set designer and fund raiser, started schools for the Rendille in the bush. Her tastes were both extravagant and rustic. A chandelier hung from a water buffalo horn on the terrace. She was generous whether flush or broke. For all the pleasure she found in things, she did not have the hoarding instinct of the materialist. You liked her bracelet? Here. She would unclasp it from her wrist and snap it onto yours.

She held up a conch shell filled with salt. Sweet, she said. She had dressed for dinner in a short satin slip, boots laced to her knees and dark lipstick. Now, she said, most important, the lighting. They lit lanterns and candles which had been placed in abundance around the cottage on stands and floors and tables crowded with silver cups.

How old is Harry? Jane said.

What do you think?

Twenty-six? Jane said tremulously. Five?

More like twenty-three, darling.

You're kidding.

Or twenty-two. What, you care? Age doesn't matter.

It doesn't?

For dinner there was a platter of grill-marked chicken sprinkled with singed herbs, roast pork beside peeled potatoes, stewed eggplant in tomato sauce, green beans shiny with butter and garlic, curried lentils, ribs, shredded cabbage, sliced avocado. Lana's housekeeper and another woman carried dishes in and out of the kitchen, taking orders from Lana in Swahili, without seeming to hear them.

By the time the cook's specialty, coconut flan, was brought out, no one at the table seemed to notice, deep in conversation or having left altogether. Many were out on the concrete terrace, dancing to the turned-up music. By the end of the night however there was no pudding left in the dish. The servants slipped in and out, clearing the plates, leaving glasses and candles and flowers, and a spotlessly washed-up kitchen. The music pounded.

Jane, feeling dazed from drink, from Harry, looked around the room at the people she didn't know, at ones she barely did, in this place where people returned from war zones, from managing famines, from living in tents among the elephants, or being gored by buffalo, a place where everyone seemed matter-of-factly to lead a life of extremity and daring. Harry was with his parents tonight. They'd just returned from a trip vaccinating livestock before they were to leave again. In his absence, her thoughts of him were more vivid. He was young. He was quite young. She kept thinking of him being young. She remembered how easy it had been at that age to take up with a person. It happened all the time—new people came, you were with them. When they were gone, more new people would come. When she looked at it from that point of view she saw they were no big deal. She thought she'd try to adopt that viewpoint. Adopting other people's viewpoints, you could convince yourself you were being empathetic—never mind you were ignoring your self.

More people arrived and the dancing grew wilder. One man took off his shirt and was rolling around on the lawn, a dog barking at him hysterically. In between songs you heard the high squawk of an animal, the hyrax who lived and shat on the roof.

Monday morning, readying for departure at last, Jane sat on a bed piled with linen pillows and watched Lana pack. Lana was tall but seemed larger than a normal tall person. She surveyed her room, eyes narrowed, hands on leather shorts. She was accustomed to packing and moving her caravan, but not having to restrain herself in volume. The room was as full as a bazaar, and indeed she had either bought or sold most of the things in it: piles of vintage fabric, leather-trimmed suitcases, necklaces draped on rusted hooks. She picked up an ancient wicker picnic basket with cylindrical holders for wine bottles.

This we take, she said. She opened the lid to show Jane the relics of the 1920s inside—tin plates with embossed leaves, miniature glass salt bottles fitting in felt holders, a silver-rimmed martini shaker.

What else? she said to herself. The tucks on either side of her mouth deepened in concentration. She strode across the room. Unlike some tall people who try to shrink themselves smaller, Lana strode with the confidence of a giant, jangling when she moved. She hoisted a trunk from behind a stand overloaded with brimmed hats and oilskin jackets and fished out a stack of brand new T-shirts. These we bring for the children, she said, and stuffed them in a canvas bag decorated with beadwork, another one of her ventures.

Jane told Harry that Don was coming with them, too. He shrugged. It struck Jane how lightly people here held on to agendas. She was used to a world of people wielding control in order to have things run smoothly which, she noticed, often caused more tension than peace.

Maybe he'll learn something, Harry said. From Lana.

Jane thought of what Harry had learned from Lana. To fill out the thought, she said, She's an expansive—Jane was going to say *soul* but thought it sounded pretentious—spirit.

You mean she sleeps with everyone? Harry did not say it unkindly.

No, I—

Well, she does. He paused then added, Me among them, you know.

Yes, Lana did say . . . Jane waited for him to elaborate. It seemed that many people here had, if they'd been here long enough, slept with many other people.

Lana's got a lot to give, he said.

It was a surprise to Jane when someone was not cynical in the least.

Lana was now examining a pair of breakable crimson Moroccan glasses with gold designs. She shook her head and returned them to their hammered brass tray. She found a stack of tin Mexican cups pressed in the shape of bells. Yes, she said, these we can use. It was hard to say which gave her more pleasure—having the things herself, or the thought of offering them to someone else.

When they left Nairobi at last, they got caught in the afternoon traffic. Though if they'd left in the morning it would have been the morning traffic, or in the evening, the evening. There was always traffic around

Nairobi, except for late at night when all the cars disappeared and there was no one at all.

Harry drove with Jane beside him. Her body now felt linked to his, and with it came the certainty that his person inside was good and unique and inspiring, regardless of the fact that only a smallest amount of Harry was known to her.

Pierre and Don were in the back on either side of Lana who was tucked into Don's shoulder. Finally they left the traffic behind and the truck hummed over unsmooth road. The passengers fell asleep, bumping awake over potholes. When Jane woke, her window overlooked a valley dropping off the roadside with houses scattered among greenery and Lake Naivasha a purple disc below. The pink lace at the edge of the gray flats was a flock of flamingos. They stopped at a pull-over overlooking the valley when Lana spotted a display of Maasai blankets strung up on sapling branches, and could determine from a distance they were the old wool ones, not the new polyester blend. A woman sat in the shade with narrow shoulder blades and rectangular beaded earrings and was surprised by Lana's speaking Maasai to bargain. Harry hunched down to a blanket spread with collar necklaces and belts dangling arrows and beaded leather bracelets. The old bracelets used gut, the new, plastic thread. He bought one, with red and green diagonal bands. Lana pointed out to Don where they were headed, to the right of the lake, her sister Beryl's house. They were stopping for a night or two. Beryl's husband Leonard was an artist and Lana was keen to show Don his work.

Back in the car Harry handed Jane the bracelet. You need a souvenir, he said. He gave it to her casually, and she felt her face flush. Thanks, she said, as if she were used to having men give her things. In truth it was rare and, snapping on the bracelet, it seemed important he not know it.

In a valley of light green trees they turned off the paved road onto beige dirt. At an open aluminum gate they drove on a smoother road with farmed fields of crops on either side. At a huddle of trees they passed a white barn trimmed in black with wrought-iron windows and a yard of carts with handle pulls tilted to the ground. A long avenue of towering eucalyptus made a roof as high as a cathedral with a white stucco house at the end. The villa had a red tile roof in the Italian style, with a wide terraced balustrade on one side full of potted palms and blooming hibiscus trees.

They piled out of the truck, and Jane felt the thrill of arriving at a beautiful place. At one end, wide double doors were flung open to a gigantic hall with a black and white checkered floor and a great archway in the shape of a spade. French doors were open all along the veranda. An interior balcony rimmed the second floor, with doors behind the wooden railing, some open to windows beyond, some shut. Children came running across from the far end in wet feet and bathing suits, followed by a young woman in a bathing suit top with a kanga wrapped around her waist languidly advancing, shaking out long wet hair. A swallow swooped past Jane's head. Lana picked up two children in her strong arms.

I thought you were getting here for lunch, the woman said, gliding across the hall. She kissed Lana's cheeks.

We tried, Lana said vaguely. To everyone else: This is my sister, she said brightly. Lana stood a head taller though her sister was the elder. Beryl, with her flat stomach and blasé manner, looked more like a teenager than a mother of four.

Well, you're in time for tea at least. Like Lana, Beryl had the Kenyan brand of British accent, but where Lana's was full of enthusiasm, Beryl's was flat. She seemed to be sighing at the boredom of life, particularly incongruous to Jane in this paradise swooping with children and flowers and birds.

Pierre, I knew you were coming, she purred, kissing both his cheeks.

Hey, beautiful, Pierre said.

But Harry, too? Lana doesn't tell me anything. How'd she rope you into it?

Flying, Harry said, kissing her hello.

That all? Beryl raised an eyebrow toward Jane, but she wasn't done with the boys yet. And you . . . are Dan.

Don.

She put out her hand, looking at him straight-on. Welcome, Don. Then she turned to Jane. And you must be the American *writer,* she said, as if another person might find that impressive.

I am, Jane said. It's so nice of you to let us all stay.

Oh God, it's nothing. Thrilled to have visitors. Lana, take them out and I'll get the tea organized.

She pushed through a heavy door and Jane got a glimpse of a large kitchen with a number of dark-skinned people in light blue uniforms standing at sinks or bent over a table dusted with flour.

They crossed the gigantic hall, Jane's nerves still vibrating from the jostling ride. The whitewashed veranda overlooked a garden of spiky bushes and hedges dotted with flowers. Mown paths meandered among more tangled jungle beyond. A sliver of light green pool could be seen at the end of an alley of cedar trees and a gigantic palm tree rose far past the other trees like an exploding firework. Marsh stretched beyond with inky grass markings and black twisted trees. The purple lozenge of the lake lay farther.

On the porch a low table with benches had been set for the children. There were bowls of berries and cookies on plates and pink cups filled with hot chocolate. A higher table of dark wood with brass corners and pale wood inlays was set with a silver tea set and plates of digestive biscuits, lemon slices, brown sugar lumps and a pitcher of cream. Blossoms of jasmine and red hibiscus were scattered among the plates.

Now this is more like it, Don said.

Everyone took a chair but Harry, who sat at the edge of the porch, feet hanging down, leaning against a pillar near the children.

Beryl appeared empty-handed, trailed by a woman in a light blue uniform with a white apron, carrying a tray of more tea and more cups.

Asante, Fatima, Beryl said, and sat. She poured the tea. Her arms were thin and tan. A young boy appeared behind Fatima, rattling a red lacquer tray. A wonderful smell rose.

You have croissants, Pierre said with a happy look.

No, no, Wilson, put it here. And take these to the children. No, these. The boy set down the tray, sneaking glimpses at the guests. So, Don, where are you from?

Los Angeles.

Wait. She looked at Lana. Is this the movie producer?

No, Beryl.

Oh, he sounded interesting. What was his name? She frowned at the children's table. Tessie, stop it. Now.

But Roan's pushing me off.

Then go on the other side. Roan, you know better. She faced back to Lana. What was his name?

Beryl, Lana said.

What?

It was Michael.

Right, he did that movie about the wizards. The children loved it. But you're not in the movies, she said to Don, smiling.

No, can't say I am. I'm in finance.

Right, Beryl said. So you're all off to Rwanda?

Uganda, Jane said.

Never been *there,* actually, she said, surprised. Does everyone have tea? None of us have been either, Pierre said.

So what's in Uganda? She tucked her legs and curled around her cup, sipping it. Something was knocked over at the children's table. Mama! someone cried.

Willa, for God's sakes, ask Tess to pour it. Fatima! Beryl screamed.

That wasn't me. Porter did it, said a little girl with tangled hair.

Fatima appeared and mopped up the spillage. She spoke to the children under her breath, not in English.

Well, help Porter out, then, Beryl said. Tessie, come on, you're the one they're looking up to. Honestly. Beryl decided to stop noticing and turned in the wicker chair, facing away from the children, draping her legs over the armrest. But Uganda has got gorillas, too, I know.

That's in the south, Lana said. We're going to the north. Jane's doing a story about the abducted children.

Oh, right, the rebels. Beryl's attention was already straying. Tess, enough! She spoke over her shoulder. Go on, if you can't behave. The children went running off, except for a boy who stayed to talk to Harry. They appeared to be examining a butterfly.

They call themselves rebels, Jane said, but it's really a roaming band of bandits terrorizing a rural community too poor to defend themselves. They're not getting much help from the government.

Well, that sounds fun, Beryl said.

Lana was looking at the coins on her necklace, hitting them. Fun isn't exactly the idea, Beryl.

No, God forbid fun. No, I'm kidding. Obviously. It sounds good. I mean, good for you to do it. Really. To be honest, I wish I could come.

Where's Leonard? Pierre said.

On safari. Where else? The younger girl came and draped her arm around her mother's neck, observing the guests. Beryl patted the little hand.

Oh, I thought he'd be here, Lana said. When's he back?

Think he tells me?

Lana stood and pointed into a side garden. Some of his pieces are here. Don, come look.

Yes, go look, Beryl said, staying in her chair.

Everyone else rose from the chairs.

Dark hedges enclosed large figures that looked at first to be made of sticks. Then Jane saw the material was bones. Hundreds of bones were cobbled together in hulking forms, one in the shape of a birdcage with a large skull inside, another a tornado with bones seeming to swirl. There was a large foot.

He made practically everything we're sitting on here, too, Lana said.

Don, arms crossed, observed the sculptures with a particular expressive reverence some people display when viewing art. He was frowning and nodding.

My favorite is that one. Pierre pointed down the veranda to a rope hammock strung between two elephant tusks.

Don brightened. That for sale?

God, no, said Beryl.

It's a little controversial, Lana said.

She means illegal.

He found them, for God's sakes, Beryl said. Not even Leonard would kill an elly. Lana, shall we show everyone their rooms?

Let's.

Roy and Damian are flying in tonight, Beryl said offhandedly.

Really? Lana regarded her sister with glittering, knowing eyes. Beryl was absorbed in folding stray napkins and returning them carefully to the tray.

That should be interesting, Lana said. They staying long?

Beryl shrugged. Who knows. I better go see if the children have killed each other. She stood, languidly. Harry, you're in the blue room. Beryl whispered loudly to Lana. Is he staying with—what's her—?

Jane.

Right. You have the blue room. With Jane. And Pierre is in the tower. She strolled off.

Cheers for the tea, Harry called after her, practically the only thing he'd uttered since they'd arrived.

You are so welcome, darling. We'll catch up later. I want to know every little thing.

Lana had a residence of her own on the property, a platform tent out of sight of the house. There was a large bed covered with yellow and orange Ethiopian kente cloth, and a claw-footed bathtub the servants filled with warm water in the evening.

Jane and Harry's room had a four-poster bed painted silver.

After tea she and Harry took a swim in the light green pool beneath the gigantic palm. The early evening was still and quiet. When an owl flew above them it made an eerie *whoosh*. Jane and Harry exchanged a glance, heads above the surface. She dove underwater and held the glance with her as if it had entered a vein.

Back in the house the cavernous black and white hall was booming with Beethoven. The transporting melody seemed to roil in the arching ceiling like thunderclouds.

Jane shut the door to their room on the ground floor near the entrance. The music was muted. She lay on the bed and fell asleep in her wet towel. Traveling, one slept at odd times and suddenly. She opened her eyes to Harry's face with his eyes closed beside her in the soft shadowless light. His face was smooth and inscrutable. In sleep it looked ageless. She looked at the curve of his eyelashes and the dark eyebrows. The thing that frightened her in his open eyes was not there in his shut eyes. When a person was asleep you could ponder his face.

His lip curved over his teeth. The mouth was the same as when awake, composed and calm, a little obstinate. She had the strange sensation that he was a younger version of herself. What was that familiar thing in him? Was it because she had been that age once? She had the odd notion that she'd been inside his head, at another time in her life. But Harry was much further along in self-possession than she'd ever been.

There were no freckles on his face, though his shoulder was sprinkled with them. She kissed his shoulder and, without opening his eyes, he came alive and reached for her and turned her around, pulling her back against him to hold her tight, then lay still again. How many years did she have on him? She hadn't yet counted, but now she did. Sixteen, no, seventeen. Well, that was a record. She guessed the older one got the more records like that one could break.

He slept against her and she looked around the room. There was an armoire whose ivory handles had carvings of bows and arrows, and by the door an iron hat stand with antler hooks. A brass lamp had a colored glass lampshade. She thought how these things would have had to be transported in some bumping truck, wrapped in thick burlap or canvas, to get here. The silver ribs of the bed curved over them, with a white canopy draped on it. The bed looked Mexican with its thick layer of paint shimmering.

She felt far from everything. She often felt far from things in familiar surroundings, so it was a reassuring alignment when she had the feeling when actually far from home.

Here her thoughts didn't dominate the landscape. The landscape and the new people in it, asking to be explored, took over. Far from home, she had less need to answer the questions, Why was she here? What was she thinking? What was the point? Those questions hovered, but did not insist on an answer. Habit was left behind, and with it, the old perspective. Her perspective stayed alert when she was far away. *Back there* was not so important anymore. She dozed off again.

She woke to the deep sputtering of an airplane motor. It grew louder as it descended and seemed to land directly outside her window. Harry was gone from the bed; she got up. She went to the window and opened the shutter to see a small plane in the blue and brown light rolling forward in the field. It came to a stop past where the cars were parked, just another vehicle of transport. The door opened, and a thin metal stair folded down. Two men ducked out and descended. One was pale and fair, the other dark. The pale man went to the rear and opened a door and pulled out some backpacks and a few boxes. The other in rolled-up pants was setting wood blocks under the airplane wheels. An askari with bare black arms and draped in a blanket stood by holding a spear. They exchanged words, and the two men left the plane under his watch. Striding toward the house, they were laughing. Jane wondered which one was for Beryl.

Who was that? came Harry's voice from the bathroom, echoing in the high ceiling.

Two men in a plane, she said. She wrapped herself in a kikoi and went into the bathroom. A lightbulb clustered by glass grapes hung from the ceiling. The sink mirror was stuck with eagle feathers in a fan shape. Harry was sitting in water smoking a cigar. The tub was cast iron with feet, claws clutching balls.

You look happy, she said.

Come in.

She slipped into the water facing him. It was a long bathtub. A part of her checked to see if she felt shy with him. Only a small part did. Then that part was gone. Jane picked up a blue bar of soap and lathered her hands. She was glad to be there with him, but didn't say it. Instead she said, Good cigar?

He blew smoke, nodding.

They heard commotion in the hallway, the two men arriving and being greeted.

On the wall was a framed ink drawing of a naked woman, pregnant, lying on her side. Is that Beryl? she said. They both gazed at the frenzy of curving lines.

Yes, it looks like a Leonard.

She doesn't sound particularly pleased with Leonard, Jane said.

Beryl has a lot of putting up to do.

And four kids on top of it, Jane said.

There was a silence in the tall room. Harry's face was relaxed. Jane felt silence was something which must be filled.

I can barely imagine having one child, she said.

Which was not exactly true. Silence often got filled with things not exactly true. Jane did in fact imagine having a child somewhat often, and rather more often lately. Images of it appeared in various mirages. She was holding a baby in bed just after birth; a child was walking unsteadily across a lawn, arriving to her outstretched arms. Though in the vision Jane somehow looked more like her older sister, Marian, a real mother, and the child was teetering on familiar grass in front of Marian's house in New Jersey.

I'm going to have lots, Harry said.

Really? Lots?

Loads. Their mother is going to crank them out.

That's nice, she said. A breeze swept in the window and she lowered herself into the warm water.

As soon as I sort myself out and start making a living, he said.

Oh, not yet.

No, not yet. He took a puff of his cigar. I'm not ready to sort myself out yet.

So you don't worry then?

About what?

The future.

Why should I worry about the future?

I don't know. People do.

People are idiots, Harry said. He watched the cigar roll in his fingers. At least the ones who worry.

The smell of grilled meat wafted into Jane when she stepped out of her room. At the far end of the rounded hall where music played quietly with a pulsing beat was a sitting area and a fire going in a wide fireplace. Beryl was circling a large table set with red goblets and a turquoise tablecloth tasseled in gold. She wore a long dress from the sixties with an orange and black geometric pattern and cut-out back. Her lips were plum-colored, and long earrings dangled to her shoulders. Jane had on a blue slip dress she had unfurled from her bag and ironed with her hand on the bed and a white flower snapped from the bush outside her window set in the knot at the back of her neck.

Beryl asked her to run down to Lana's tent and tell her to come up. Don't worry if you run into a warthog, she said. That's just Freddie.

Jane followed the narrow path among bamboo trees, watching for animals. Someone had mentioned a hippo appearing the other day in the garden, which Jane thought alarming. Hippos apparently had vicious jaws and could run very fast. In the dusky light she made out bleached white skulls dotting the clearing by Lana's tent. She stopped at a strange noise, then realized they were human noises of an intimate and animal nature drifting through the netting. She turned and retraced her steps. Then from a distance, and out of sight, she shouted that it was dinnertime. She waited for Lana's breathless voice to answer, then heard the laughter following. When she returned to the house, her heart was beating chaotically, as it does after seeing a wild animal.

Once inside she found the night outside had quickly gone black.

An older servant in a white jacket passed her, carrying empty platters to the barbecue pit off the veranda where silhouettes stood before the coals and smoke. Two other servants were lighting candles on the long table. New staff kept appearing; Jane wondered how many there were working behind the scenes.

Pierre was sitting on the couch beside a girl of about twenty who had long shiny hair and wore a crocheted halter top.

Hey, beautiful, he said to Jane with his sleepy pleased look. Pierre looked at women as if he'd already slept with them. Did you meet Lulu? This is Beryl's stepdaughter. Lulu lifted her hand, palm up, unsmiling. Her bad posture did not diminish her beauty.

A couple in their fifties stood at a bar crowded with bottles and an ice bucket. They introduced themselves as Chip and Deedee. The man was in all khaki, and the woman looked as if she'd come straight from a country club with a pink polo shirt and a tortoiseshell hair band. They spoke in thick British accents and were getting drinks for the two men whom she'd seen come off the plane. Jane picked up that Chip and Deedee lived a few farms away and had recently had a run-in with a croc. It had nearly attacked a servant.

What it was doing way up on the drive, Chip said, shaking his head.

Deedee was picking up one bottle after another. Do they have the decent vodka? she said.

The men from the plane were introduced. Roy the fair one lit a cigarette. He shook Jane's hand. Damian, wiry and unshaven, had a surprising smile. They all seemed to know each other.

At dinner everyone drank with enthusiasm. On one side Jane had Chip, whose face grew pink, and Roy on the other side. He turned out to be a doctor, from South Africa. What does everyone think is going to become of that president of yours? he said, but didn't wait for an answer. I think you need more wine. He refilled her glass. You leaving that meat? He started to pick at the food on her plate. You don't mind, do you? I eat nothing all week. I'm starving.

The children appeared in their nightclothes, bathed and brushed, to kiss their mother good night. They frowned toward Damian beside her. Their nanny stood near, then followed their orderly procession up the stairs.

Roy was whispering in Jane's ear. I don't have a wife yet, but I'm working on it. I do want one. I'd be a good husband. I mean it, if I were married to you I'd come home every night and never stop shagging you. Jane looked at him. His eyes were bloodshot and nearly crossed. He seemed to be talking to someone else. So—what d'you say?

I think not, she said.

Why not?

Otherwise occupied, she said.

What, that guy? He pointed down the table to Harry.

Lana had her arms draped over Harry's shoulders and was speaking close to his ear. Harry cut his meat, chewing, listening with a pleasant expression. Lana drew back her face to look at him, as if waiting for an answer. He nodded, thinking. Across the table, Don frowned at them.

That kid? Roy said. His head rolled back in amazement. Some slacker? I bet he still lives with his mother and has a motorcycle and goes hang-gliding. . . .

Paragliding, actually, Jane said.

Exactly! Roy's hands went up. What're you doing with him? Don't you want a man?

Guess not, Jane said, smiling.

Okay, he said. Then his face went stony and he swiveled away from her to Deedee on the other side. Tell me, when was the last time you performed surgery? he said.

Oh God, she said, not for ages.

Released from conversational duties—on her other side Chip was describing generator problems—Jane looked around the table. With everyone engaged she was free just to look. She watched everyone's hands. Some were holding cigarettes, some set down a glass. Lulu fingered a choker with bitten fingernails as Pierre rolled a cigarette, listening to her with low-lidded merriment. Lana gestured as if she were opening a fan. Beryl held a long strand of her hair across her bottom lip, watching Damian draw something with his knife on the table.

The wings are double like this for sexual attraction, Jane heard him say, not for flight at all. Harry's hand lay along the back of Lana's chair. Looking at his hand gave Jane a peaceful feeling.

For dessert out came a layered kiwi tart with strawberries and a silver bowl of whipped cream. Lana, noticing Don's expression, brought him over to the couch by the fire and settled him beside her. She crossed her boots on his knees, anchoring him down. Soon his face lost its frown and grew flushed and merry. His hand disappeared in her clothing.

At the end of the table Jane heard Beryl whisper to Damian, Man is way out of his depth. Low laughter followed.

Jane went back to the room to use the bathroom and found a candle lit on the bedside table and ironed white sheets folded back like in a hotel. She hadn't planned on turning in yet, but it looked so inviting and she lay down for a moment. As she closed her eyes she found herself searching for the place inside her that didn't care whether Harry came in or not.

When she woke it was dark and his body was beside her, asleep. She felt like an animal in the woods watching the lights in a house, waiting for him to come out and look for her. People said that men were the ones who thought about sex all the time. She was like a man then. Except that after sex she thought about it more, not less. It didn't seem to matter that sex didn't necessarily get you where you wanted to be: satisfied with yourself. But you had momentary satisfactions, the beautiful release and a feeling of wholeness. Sex was the wire in the dark, a jolt to the spirit, like the shocks they give people with massive coronaries to get things beating again. His arms around her infused her with calmness and she felt herself shimmering.

In the morning she woke. She pictured him reaching over and pulling her across the sheet or dropping a heavy hand on her hip to check she was still there before dragging her over. She waited for his head to turn and his eyes to open in her direction. The hope felt like a thread whipped in a frantic wind; it was terrible.

He stirred and her heart leapt, vibrating. He rolled to his side of the bed and stood up. His hair stuck out like dark straw. He pawed through a crumpled pile of clothes. The muscle in his lower back was a nice square shape. He found a shirt. He pulled on dusty shorts with an automatic air, then, noticing her there, said, Coffee, in a neutral not unfriendly way and left the room. Her gaze fixed itself on where he'd been and she felt as if she were dangling from a hook high in a tree.

For God's sakes, she said to herself. She was here for a reason. She had a story to write, something more substantial than her pathetic yearnings.

At breakfast the reports of early rains washing out the border crossing to Uganda at Malaba made them decide to stay in Naivasha another day. And Leonard was supposed to return that night. Any reason could change plans; no one objected.

Jane read her book on the veranda among red hibiscus trees. Harry returned from wandering around the farm with directions to a good flying place near Eldoret. A few hours later Jane was standing on the side of a treeless hill in tall dry grass, camera strap around her wrist, looking up the slope where Harry's figure grew smaller as he trudged with his oversized knapsack to the top. The plain below was green and brown brush with wisps of smoke here and there.

Jane sensed movement nearby. Out of the beige grasses three small figures came running up the slope toward her, chests open, arms pumping. About ten feet from her they stopped abruptly, as if hitting a wall. Two boys and a girl stood staring.

Jambo, Jane said. Habari. Hello.

The boys giggled. Hello, they said, covering their mouths. Their T-shirts were in varying stages of disintegration. The girl wore a pink dress with torn ruffles. Her hand kept hold of the older boy's as she regarded Jane with a penetrating frown.

Wewe kijiji? Jane pointed to the cluster of thatched huts farther down the rutted road where they had parked the truck. Direct translation: You village?

The children stared. Maybe she had the words wrong.

Pitcha, pitcha, said the biggest boy.

You want a picture? Jane said. She lifted her camera and they ducked into the grass, swatting at each other and laughing.

Okay. No picture. Jane turned and kept walking up the hill. The tops of the grass brushed her knees. The children followed. She stopped and turned; they stopped too, smiling. She went on and they followed. She arrived at a rock and sat.

The older boy pointed to Harry, now a silhouette on the moonlike curve of the hill. Mzungu?

He's flying, Jane said. She put her arms out and flapped. She had picked up the word for bird. Ndege, she said.

The children stared at the tiny figure with incredulity, then back at Jane.

You English? said the tallest boy, surprising her.

No, American.

America, he said. San Francisco. You San Francisco?

No. I'm New York City.

America, said the boy, nodding. Monica Lewinsky.

Yes, said Jane. That's right.

The three pairs of eyes, close to each other, did not take their gaze from her, sizing her up. No matter where you went, it was always the children who came up to strangers. They were interested.

Ndege? the smaller boy said, and pointed up the hill.

She nodded.

The children dissolved again in laughter.

It doesn't look as if he's getting any wind though, Jane said.

Harry had reached the top and was standing, unmoving in his helmet. The parachute was out of view.

The children sat on the ground, curling around each other. Children had time to chat with strangers.

You married? the boy said.

What? No. Not married. She held out her left hand as if in a Doris Day movie.

Babies?

No, no babies either.

You should have babies.

God, she thought, him too. You think so? she said.

The smaller boy jumped up, pointing up the hill. Harry was airborne, dangling below the fat caterpillar of the parachute.

He's up, Jane said.

They watched him drift along in a straight line, not too high, as if sailing on a calm sea. He wasn't riding a thermal, he was just being blown.

From below in the area of the huts came the sound of pots clattering and a woman calling. The smaller boy cuffed the back of the girl's head and took off running. She didn't flinch but stood, looking a little longer at Jane, as if to memorize her face, then took off, following. Jane thought how little she could envision what their lives were like.

She walked in the direction of Harry's drifting. He was going fast now. She ran, feeling the curve of the hill as if it were the globe she was transversing. She stopped and walked, looking at her short boots, and thought how different she would feel if she were here alone. Even the air was different if someone was nearby and you were following him. Having spent a lot of time alone, she could easily imagine how it would feel if no one else were there, walking in the high grass, connected to the ground and grass. Images of other people would appear at the back of her mind in a sort of random collage. When you were alone, they visited you. With a person nearby, even if he was drifting through the air, you felt the lines attaching you and did not have the same inward gaze.

By the time she reached him, Harry had his sail packed up.

You had an audience, she said. They were impressed.

I think it's safe to say that no other humans have probably flown off that hill.

But they knew about Monica Lewinsky.

Children know everything, Harry said. He glanced back to the hill. If there were more wind . . . I'd like to try again on our way back.

They stepped off the lumpy grass onto a rough road and headed for the truck.

Behind them a woman screamed. Harry put his hand on Jane's shoulder, stopping her. They looked back toward the huts and saw a woman in a yellow shirt screaming from a doorway. A man could be seen scurrying off in an odd crouched position. The woman's arm was raised as if she'd just thrown something, and the hand stayed up, with fingers spread. Harry studied the scene for a moment, then he turned Jane's shoulders around.

Come on. He moved her forward. She glanced back. The woman was bending over to pick up the girl, whose pink dress was streaked with red.

She's bleeding, Jane said. The woman lifted her and carried her back inside.

Family business, Harry said. Not for us.

She trusted Harry, so she went, but thought how children, the ones most needing protection, were perhaps the hardest to save.

On the drive back, nearing Naivasha, the sky lost its ochre glow at the horizon, and the air quickly darkened. No one drove at night if you could help it. You were more likely to be robbed on the road at night. With no streetlights outside of town and only a few other headlights beaming by, it was like driving at the bottom of a dark sea. Out the window Jane saw no signs of life in the blackness. She knew the animals were out there though, awake and on the prowl. The black tunnel of road was lit only as far as the headlights reached. Going down a hill, Harry braked abruptly. In the headlights was a dark lump in the road, a roll of clothes in their lane. Harry put the car in neutral, the motor idling in the quiet night, and peered over the steering wheel close to the windshield, trying to make out what was there. He looked out the black windows to his left and right and behind. Carjackers flagged you down for help, then people hiding in the bushes would pounce out. Flat tires happened all the time, but if you were going to help anyone, you took a risk. Stopping at night at all was a risk. Harry pulled on the emergency brake and opened the door, leaving the car running. He got out.

Lock it, he said, and shut the door.

He strode, not quickly but not slowly either, in front of the dim headlights. He stood over the bundle, looking at one end then the other. He bent down and slid his arms underneath, hoisted it like a sack onto his shoulder and across his back. A head appeared, dangling down. Harry carried the body off the road and set it down. Back in the headlights he had his usual expression—as she'd seen in the five long days she'd known him—internally focused and untroubled. Even carrying a passed-out, possibly dead, stranger on his back. He crouched down to see the person more closely, gave the body a pat, then stood up. Jane unlocked the door.

Just drunk, he said, and shifted into gear.

They weren't far from Beryl's. She thought about the bed waiting for them there. When they got back, there was a delicious curry dinner and a smaller group at the table. Leonard, however, had not returned.

Beryl's guest Damian turned out to be not only a paleontologist but an environmental consultant who flew around East Africa. He and Harry were discussing wild dogs. Jane was surprised to learn that when Harry had worked for a couple of years he'd become rather an expert. The wild dogs were, like most every other mammal on the continent save the human, on the decline. Weeks were spent tracking dogs to locate their dens so they could be coaxed out and transported to areas where they'd less likely vanish. There was a movement among those trying to save them to call them by a less off-putting name—painted dogs.

Either way, Harry said, wild dogs are a lot cooler than people realize. Like all dogs, they are a submission-based species, but it's not to do with sex. Females rule some packs, males rule others. The packs hunt for food together and never fight over it, even when they're starving. When they want food, they beg for it from each other. They don't fight.

Jane looked across the table at Harry. Maybe she looked at him a little longer than usual. He winked, unsmiling.

*

Later they fell into bed like trees and she lay beside him motion-less. She listened to his quiet breathing, asleep. Her leg under the covers against him felt alert. The longing had started. She wanted to wake him but didn't. Mustn't let them know you need them.

Before dawn, he woke her. They were out before sunrise, carrying their bags off the terrace. Beryl was up to see them off, holding on her hip the youngest boy, chewing at her gold necklace. As they drove away Jane watched her figure in the murky light, her brown arms around her son, still standing as they drove down the alley of eucalyptus trees, still unmoving when the truck crossed the fields and turned out of sight.

An unpaved road took them up small hills where in the dawn light the ground looked sprinkled with pale blue sand between ghostly bushes. The sun rose and the road became pink then turned to pavement and the truck slammed the potholes.

On a steep hill the motor started to sputter and buck. Everyone stirred from their drowsiness. The truck strained upward, slowing to a crawl. Harry's expression showed no concern. He stopped, put the car in neutral, revved the engine, then put it back in gear. It popped and stalled. He turned the ignition key. Nothing. The emergency brake screeched on.

Before anyone had even opened a door Lana was out and on her knees in the pebbly dirt. She flung herself underneath the car so her sandals stuck out with their dark red toenails. Her hand thrust out, holding a cap the size of a shot glass, which Harry took, dumped out, and swiped with his shirt. He handed it back to Lana's open palm waiting.

When she slid out and stood, her backside was stamped with white. She rubbed her fingers on tufts of grass to clean off the oil and patted herself down. Now let's give her some juice, she said, and hefted herself back into the truck. The engine started.

Farther down the road, the tire blew.

III

First Days

You are filled with a new intention. Something stretches
beyond you, drawing you along, and as you move forward
in a dark place you can barely make out shapes and your face
feels invisible. No one sees you anymore. You don't think it,
but you have the odd feeling: Maybe this will lead me home.

5 / The You File

You turn new in a new place. Where are you being taken?
You will go further and take the way you have not planned.

You wonder where you belong. It seemed you used to belong
somewhere. Maybe you never did.

Different things matter.

Sometimes, in longing there is a homesick feeling. But when you
picture yourself home, you look out of place, a cutout figure, not fitting in.

You think you have control, but there is no control. Again you are
with strangers, in a foreign place, all far from home.

You wait. What else can you do? You wait, and not so patiently
either, for moments when clarity and meaning visit you. You try to
arrange for their coming, but those moments visit you regardless of—
well—regardless of anything.

You are being taken, yet each step is made deliberately by you. Where are you taking yourself?

Your instinct seeks a right feeling.

In a new place you are surprised to find a feeling of home.

Things you thought lost forever come back. When you add one thing, another is dropped behind.

What will happen. Who knows it.

You hope to bring back something good. Will you ever be able to describe this? This must be described.

Who would have said such a world could exist?

You think, I can't go on. I won't make it. Then you do.

You pray, Help me not turn into a monster.

You sit in the back, watching the driver's hair blow around.

Your family no longer knows you. They do not follow you into your life, but stay at the side of the road, off in their own lives, waiting sometimes, sometimes turning away.

The odd feeling comes which you know may not be right but which still inhabits you: I belong below people.

Most people when you get up close are not more in focus, but less.

We cannot avoid wounding another. We do it by being ourselves. Stay away from people and you avoid brutalizing each other.

Easier if you need no one.

In the freedom alone you have a beautiful feeling then think, I wish someone were here to feel it with me.

Without someone beside, what's the point? You think, *Stay with me.*

You keep on. It doesn't help to think of how they are treating you. It doesn't help to think how others are being beaten.

What good does it do to think of it?

Someone hurt because of you may be the hardest thing to bear.

You think your life is your own, but we all belong to others.

Life is the same everywhere.

There is nowhere like this.

These things must be told. You wonder if the world knows of such things. They must not. Surely such things would stop if they knew.

You care, then you are drained of caring.

You missed the time of growing into a woman. You became one too quickly. You are still a girl.

You pretend you are not watching him. Dry grasses blur along a crumbling road.

You might have found yourself anywhere on the planet, but here is where you end up: with people, fighting.

You belong where you are. You are possible.

You think that if you share what is in you, you will be exposed, so you keep it to yourself. It is right to feel in pieces.

Will you ever be free?

The tangled brush abruptly ends and the land zooms out to a wide savannah with flat-topped trees in the distance and a hazy horizon.

In the morning you wake to roosters crowing. Where are you? Then you remember. In this other life.

6 / Recreational Visits

THEY STOPPED IN Nakuru. The week before, the town had been in newspaper headlines as having the worst rioting after the January elections. The Kikuyu, Kenya's largest tribe, were targeted, houses had been burned, and eighty people killed. Other reports said there were more. The white truck pulled into a peaceful gas station. The only sign of violence was hundreds of flattened dragonflies plastered across the parking lot like green satin confetti.

Lana disappeared into Desire Grocery. Jane strolled past storefronts, notebook in hand. On assignment one could be official in looking for things to notice. A large tree made shadows out of men who sat on a circular bench, observing. A boy passed Jane pushing a warped hubcap.

Jambo, she said.

The boy lifted his hand, looking hard at her.

The town consisted of a small line of shops. In one window burlap cks spilled beans, tea bags were stacked like dominoes and a few belted dresses hung from hangers. In a restaurant doorway a blue and green beaded curtain hung showing a diamond-patterned snake and behind was a shadowy room with a couple of tables and a menu painted on the wall for goat, chicken, rice, chipatas. The establishment next door was a window with a narrow shelf selling cigarettes, batteries, and aspirin. No one appeared anywhere within.

Lana came out of the grocery carrying paper bags stained with oil and a handful of clinking glass bottles, laughing over her shoulder to the friends she'd made inside. A white van with a red cross on the side had pulled into the gas station on the other side of the pumps. A tired-looking woman and man were getting gas. A black circle logo on the back had a machine-gun silhouette with a line through it. Jane stood nearby, about to ask them where they were going, but saw that her fellow travelers were decidedly uninterested in the Red Cross workers. Apparently NGOs occupied a parallel world of their own.

They drove on through the farmlands of Molo. Tea fields tilted on hills were electric green against a sky of gray storm clouds in the distance. Women in kerchiefs were bent over in narrow paths of black shade, picking leaves into baskets. Along the road schoolgirls in blue uniforms walked in groups or alone. The road straightened and fields of sugarcane spread on both sides, its stiff shoots rocking side to side in the breeze.

The road was a demolished tar surface pockmarked with red gashes. Few cars appeared. Now and then the surface changed back to dirt with deep railroad-track ruts then back to the corroded blacktop with potholes big as sofas. The truck slammed into them and you felt it in your spine. When Jane cried out, Harry said, You're going to have to be tougher than that.

She learned to stop bracing herself, it made the slam worse.

They got used to being thrown up and down and jerked forward.

What day is it anyway? Jane was in the back seat, attempting impossibly to write in her notebook. The pen stabbed the page, then was thrown off.

February? Pierre's eyes were closed, but his head magically lifted off the backrest before they banged down.

Thursday or Friday, Lana said, proud to know.

Don consulted his watch. February the eighth, he said.

My brother's birthday, Lana said sleepily.

I didn't know you had a brother, Don said.

Yes. From my father. Different mother.

Where is he? Don said.

François? Who knows. I haven't seen him in years. She was in the front seat, leaning against the passenger door, facing the back.

Pierre's eyes opened. I saw him a couple of years ago in Cape Town.

That's right, you did. Still in Cape Town, then, I guess, she said. He got a girlfriend pregnant who wasn't really his girlfriend. So he married her. Then he was trying to get his pilot's license but had high blood pressure and was barred from applying and ended up dealing drugs.

More lucrative, Pierre said.

He must have the baby now.

Yes, a boy.

Another nephew, Jane said. Being an aunt was a thing you could be proud of, without having done a single thing. Her sister's three children gave Jane that feeling.

I guess, Lana said.

Wow, said Don. I don't have a brother, but I honestly can't imagine not knowing where he was or if he had children.

Lana regarded him with a cool glance, considering a response, deciding something about Don. She said nothing.

Don had two children, Jane knew from Lana, though she hadn't heard him mention them himself. He'd recently gotten divorced from his college girlfriend, a woman who ran a successful children's clothing line. When his wife caught him having an affair with her assistant they split. According to Don, it had been coming for a long time. That's why he was here, he told Lana, seeing something of the world and not working for a change.

No one knows where I am, Jane said. Not specifically.

Her sister, Marian, had complained of it last summer, when Jane was visiting in New Jersey. They were with the kids at the town swimming pool, a compound with yellow bathhouses enclosed by a chain-link fence where Jane was mesmerized by four different pools, all crowded with people. The vast wading pool where they set up camp looked like a feeding frenzy of sharks. Children shot out of the water, gasping for breath, splashing into each other with stiff arms. Some ran in slow motion through the choppy waves. Marian's children had been shy about learning to swim—nervous in the surf at the seashore, clinging to the side of a neighbor's placid pool—until they came here. After the first few moments observing the mayhem, they jumped in and were happily dunking underwater. Chaos was apparently less intimidating.

Marian spread sunscreen in brisk strokes over her son's shoulders, then applied what remained to her own face. How am I supposed to know where you are? she said, looking at Jane with a worried expression which Jane had grown accustomed to seeing when she was the subject of discussion. Jane found it genuinely hard to believe she mattered enough for Marian to care. She would come back. Jane was still young enough to think people always returned and the people left remained there where you'd left them.

People know where I am, Harry said. If they love me. Harry seemed to be visiting the conversation, rather than joining it, as if he had other, more interesting things to occupy himself. Jane wondered who Harry's people were and how many were women.

My family never knows where anyone is, Lana said. Unless they're dead.

I know precisely where my parents are, Pierre said. I could tell you what chairs they are sitting in depending on the time of the day.

Do they keep track of you? Jane said.

Pierre looked at her with his bedroom eyes. They think so.

Harry, forward on the steering wheel, was studying the sky through the windshield. The sun was white in a white sky. The land now was a flat floor of sandy dirt with dry brush and farther off gentle hills curved into small peaks like meringues and dark-gray clouds hovered like torpedoes. A humid wind blew in the open windows making whirlpools of everyone's hair.

Harry downshifted, and the truck bumped to a stop.

Now what? Don said, disapproving.

Stopping, said Harry. Jane saw he had his eye on the peaked hills.

Lunchtime, said Lana.

They unbent themselves and stepped into wildly quiet air. Jane walked along a dusty strip butted up against a glassy marsh and crouched behind a bush. Thin grasses trembled in the heat. On the other side Pierre stood peeing behind some spindly trees, gazing out. Lana spread out a red and black Maasai blanket on the ground and in moments had cheese set on a rock and the top unscrewed on a jar of chili paste. We've delicious chipatas, she said, and pickles. She laid the beer bottles on their sides. She stood up and retied the yellow and crimson kanga around her waist, then settled back down. I'm going to eat and nap, she said. Thank you very much. She patted the blanket beside her. Come on, Don. Picnic.

I'm going on a recky, Harry said. He bit into the triangular dough of a chipata and set off toward gumdrop silhouettes of rocks. Maybe he could fly here on the way back.

Can I come? Jane said. Her legs felt rubbery, her body still vibrating. A walk would be good.

Karibu anyone, he said, jumping a wet ditch.

Moi aussi, Pierre said. He bent over the blanket, carefully selected a chipata, and followed, camera against his chest.

We should be going in half an hour, Don said. If we want to make it before nightfall. Don had been studying the maps.

No worries, Harry called back.

Lana put her hand on Don's back and smiled. The smile seemed to confuse him. It made her smile harder. As Jane walked away she heard, Apparently I must make you relax again.

The bumps of grass were wet and Jane's sneakers were soon soaked. Patches of water whitely reflected the sky. She followed Harry toward a cluster of rocks which up close looked like a wall of mangled teeth jumbled together. After ten minutes they reached the rocks where it was drier. Smaller rocks were scattered as if a fortress had been toppled. They followed Harry up the side and at the top found themselves on an escarpment of rocky towers that made a cliff stringing off to the east. The formation was not visible from the road, but Harry had detected it. The cliff dropped steeply to a plain below, disappearing in haze.

Harry walked, and now and then jumped, along the ruined ramparts. Pierre gave Jane a leg up to the ridge, then stepped down to a lower pathway, pensively unscrewing the cap of his camera. Harry looked back at Jane.

It's like climbing a stone wall sideways, she said.

They pulled themselves up each high tower, topped with a smooth lidlike slab of rock. From one, they looked back to the road.

I don't see them, Jane said. Only the car was visible.

Maybe she's eaten him alive, Harry said. But he was studying the sky.

Is it a good place to fly?

Might be.

He leapt across to the next rock. Jean stepped down, then climbed up to the next slab, perfectly round and gently concave like a saucer. Below, Pierre was a face behind a camera. She stood at the edge, facing the plain, looking past her wet sneakers. Looking at a wide space you felt something wide also expand in you as if your chest were a mirror. On one side of the saucer was a pile of flat rocks, a sort of miniature tower. In nature things reiterated themselves. She crouched down and reached for the lid on top and her arm was suddenly jerked back.

Watch it. It was Harry, holding her arm in a tight grip. Drop it, he said.

She set the rock down. He had her step back, holding her wrist. He balanced on one leg and flipped the rock off with his toe. Curled inside, as if in a jar, was a coiled snake, the bright blue color of Windex.

Never pick up rocks around here, Harry said.

Jesus. What is it? Is it dead?

I'd guess sleeping. But let's not find out. It's a viper. Nasty little buggers.

Yikes. Thanks.

No worries. He let go of her wrist and gave her a look that she felt in her knees. She turned away. Whatever it was her face might show she felt was also dangerous for him to see.

The bridge was still out at Malaba, so they chose the southern route to cross the border. They knew it was near when more people appeared on the road walking. There were not more cars, only more people, till a steady stream lined the road. By the time they arrived at the gates and booths, it was a bustling crowd. Some people were dressed in sharp, clean clothes, buttoned up, belted, women in dresses. Others wore tattered shirts. Everyone, Jane noticed, was lean. People pushed bicycles. Children ran, women walked slowly with a stately air. Jane noticed the women rarely moved quickly. They were not hurriers. An emaciated Maasai man rearranged his plaid shuka over his bony shoulders. He might have gotten here after walking nonstop for days, the way the Maasai traveled.

Tension gathered in the car. Lana and Harry said that border crossings were only an opportunity for officials to mess with you. Everyone got out with their passports and stepped stiffly onto the scruffy green porch of a wooden building. They filled out passport cards, writing against the wall. Harry took the clutch of passports and cards and various papers involving the car and pushed them through a window. Jane stood beside him and watched as the papers were carried by a young man in a white shirt across the room to another man in a white shirt, sitting at an empty table chatting with a shapely woman in a skirt. He did not acknowledge the arrival of papers; he and the woman were laughing. After a while he looked to the desk in front of him, still talking, and eventually picked up some of the documents. The woman opened a file cabinet behind him, so he had to crane his neck to keep speaking to her, holding a passport in the air. He shook his head and faced back to the papers. She kept talking and he nodded, making slow marks on the papers, smiling. He did not once look toward Harry, waiting at the window beside Jane.

Pierre was out on the porch, talking to a little boy. Don handed some coins to another child, who looked at them eagerly, then hurried away, trying to hide a satisfied expression. Moments later, he returned with a half-dozen children who swirled around and mobbed Don.

At last the passports came back through the window. Quick, Lana said in the doorway. Let's go.

They walked across the dusty lot, finished with Kenyan customs, to customs on the Ugandan side. Things there were decidedly more spiffy. The building was new, made from cement blocks. A uniformed man singled out Lana and Harry for their Kenyan passports, and escorted them to a room where they sat before another uniformed man at a desk. Here they were questioned with a decided lack of urgency.

Why, please, were they traveling to Uganda? What sort of holiday? The man patted the desk quietly. Who were they staying with in Kampala? Lana gave him the names of her friends on Lake Victoria. What sort of work did the McAlistairs do? They are not Ugandan? No, they are Scottish, Lana said. They work as sound engineers for parties and are starting a computer consulting company. The word *computer* made the man's mouth turn down. Some things were suspicious. They knew not to announce themselves as journalists or photographers.

When Lana and Harry came out, they hurried toward the truck where doors were open, the others drinking Fanta and collecting interested glances.

They crossed the border. As soon as they entered Uganda the landscape changed. The roads were sturdier and the vegetation lush. Blue hills in the distance became lumpy silhouettes as the sky brightened before the sun set. In the car a silence collected, as if the new country was already alerting them to the differences they might find in themselves here.

They drove through darkness. It was late when they reached the streetlights marking the outskirts of Jinja. They spotted a pink neon sign and stopped at a Chinese restaurant. The deserted parking lot was tinged pink, and the truck was bathed in pink when they got out. They entered an empty restaurant. A large silver fan covered one wall, and on a mantel running the length of the room were inch-high soldiers fighting each other.

They sat down and were given menus by a stooped Asian man. Everyone looked tired. Pierre held his camera in front of his face and was panning the room as if it were a periscope. Don observed the menu, chin tucked in, noting the large selection of chow mein. Well, Fung Yu, too, he said.

Jane had taken her notebook out, but was writing nothing.

Pierre lowered his camera. So, Don, what's your story?

Don looked at him with an insulted expression. What do you mean?

Pierre seemed pleased.

Don is what you would call a successful businessman, Lana said.

Are you?

Some of us have to bother with the practicalities of the world, Don said. I know it's boring. He was looking for the waiter.

The waiter came and took their orders. He did not meet anyone's eye.

What business exactly? Pierre said.

Don took a deep breath. It's not creative like you all. Then he began to explain. Harry drank his beer and regarded him with interest.

Jane compared what he said with what Lana had told her, that he bought failing companies, fixed them up, then resold them. Don was describing it rather differently with more technical terms. He did say he was here taking a break from the grind. Jane started writing in her book. The thought of Jake appeared, altered at this distance. She remembered how he had signed up for a business course at night, then it turned out he was spending the Tuesday nights at high-stakes poker games in hotels around New York. Soon came phone calls from strange men asking for payments. Then another image of Jake came to her, one that came often, of the day he sat slumped in the chair reserved for him, in the middle of that empty room, facing the semicircle of family and friends, as they itemized one after another their disappointments and grievances against him. He was wearing his motorcycle jacket and a tie. His chin dropped down further with each strained utterance from the mortified family and friends who were being made to speak. Among them, she remembered, was the boss who studied bats, with pointed ears resembling a bat himself. Jake looked at none of them, and it seemed unlikely he was going to. His head remained bowed with humiliation; then she realized, of course, that he had fortified himself with an injection before arriving at this appointment with his older, disapproving brother. An intervention it was called. It still gave Jane an odd, fluttery feeling to remember it. The facilitator, a very thin man, put the question to him: Was he willing to get help, or have everyone here cut ties with him if he did not? There was a great silence. Jake, his mother said. A lawyer with a gray bob, she had long given up on him. What? he said. He looked at everyone with hatred then stood up like a weak wave rising. Anything else? he said, and walked out of the room. His dismissal of them was so breathtaking and absolute it still shocked her to think of it. She was divorced from him by then, though they were still meeting in secret and having sex. But none of the others knew that.

Harry's eyes were closed, resting. Everyone parsed out the bill. Jane unfolded a fortune from her cookie. *You will find yourself wherever you go.*

Traveling, she thought. You could outrun yourself for a while, but it didn't last. Your self always caught up.

They drove in circles around an empty rotary in a topaz light, unable to choose a turn. Everyone was perched, watching.

That looks as if it goes back to the highway, Lana said.

Let's just find the nearest motel, Don said.

There're no lights down that road.

Just pick one for Christ's sakes.

Harry turned at the next road.

Easy there, Don said.

All tired eyes were on the lookout. A string of lit motel signs appeared. A number of them had *No Vacancy* signs.

Who would come here? Jane said.

Tourists, Lana said. We're at the foot of the Nile.

One sign said *Happy Aches Motel.*

Sounds promising, Jane said.

They pulled in. A deserted building had no lights in any windows.

Now what? said Don.

They continued on. Streetlights disappeared.

What time is it?

Don reported that it was ten-forty-seven.

There were no signs of life on the black, well-paved road.

This all looks new, Jane said.

The road forked, and Harry turned onto more newly paved tar and wound along the shorn lawns of a suburban development. Suddenly they could have been in Ohio. Occasional streetlights threw down milky pools onto curbs with garbage cans at the ends of short drives. A white sign near a clipped hedge said simply *Hotel,* and they turned up a drive.

Eureka, Don said.

The house looked like a country club with a long white porch. Lana got out and banged a brass knocker on the door and entered. They waited.

Come on, Don said, and was ignored.

After a while Lana returned, bringing energy into the lethargic car. No, she said. Let's go.

No vacancy?

It's a brothel.

Really? Pierre said. Great. Let's stay.

There are some beauties at the bar, Lana said. But single white girls are definitely not welcome.

Please, Pierre said as they drove off. Can't I find you all tomorrow?

This is ridiculous, Don said. Where the hell are we going?

No one answered him. They continued along curving roads. At the base of a lamppost swarming with moths they spotted a pale girl in a halter top smoking a cigarette on a tilted lawn. Beside her was a knocked-over bicycle, a yellow inflated canoe, and a white dog. Harry slowed down.

Hey, he said.

Hey. The girl looked up with no surprise.

You don't know a place we could crash around here?

The girl looked left, then right, like a cartoon. Not really.

No motels?

Not around here.

The truck idled. She took a drag of her cigarette and glanced behind her. You could probably stay here.

Really?

Maybe. She tapped her ash and stood up. I'll ask.

Cheers, Harry said, and pulled the truck into a short driveway cluttered with more bicycles and paddles and rubber tubes.

A bare-chested fellow with orange tufted hair strode out in bare feet. We've got a spare floor, he said in an Australian accent. Where're you all from? I'm Brian.

He ran a rafting outfit with a couple of guys from Sydney.

Inside the prefab house there was no furniture. On concrete floors were strewn sleeping bags and cardboard boxes. A few candles glowed in corners beside shadowy figures. There was a man leaning against one wall with his eyes closed. Deeper in the house, a tape player was gently pounding rock and roll.

Everyone accepted a warm beer to be polite, but even Lana was looking wan after driving all day. Business hadn't been so good lately, Brian told them. Recreational options on the Nile were short-lived. The government was planning to build another dam.

Jane laid a blanket down beside a pile of lifejackets and went to find a bathroom. Feeling her way along a dark hallway, she ran into a couple kissing; it was Don and Lana. She found a toilet in a sort of open alcove near a loudspeaker. It was like being inside a giant beating heart. When she got back to Harry, he was asleep.

She lay beside him awake. After a while the music clicked off and there was some shuffling around, then it was quiet, a quiet house with floors covered in bodies. It reminded her of college, and for a moment images appeared of *things back there*. Faces appeared. She saw her old friend Stacy, in Congress now with a girlfriend, then her sister, Marian, pressing petunias into window boxes. Just before she'd left for Africa, Marian had told her she was having another baby. She saw her friend Penny in London, waving from her doorway (three boys and a husband) as Jane drove off in a cab. Then she saw Jake teasing Penny one time in New York as elevator doors closed, and she and Jake were left alone. It was odd to be thinking of Jake more today than she had in months. The others in the world *back there* seemed so embedded in their lives. Except for Jake—he wasn't in his life anymore. Though he felt no more distant from her than the ones still alive. Then she thought of watching Harry take off from the escarpment, and of his face expectant as he waited for the wind. Next to her his face smelled of soap he'd washed with before going to sleep and his shoulder was salty and dusty. He was younger, but as a man he was bigger. Harry was her best new thought, and she stayed with that till she fell asleep.

She woke to something leaping on her forehead. A black furry thing scampered off. It was grabbed, and a monkey was placed on Brian's shoulder. Name's Bastard, he said. Everyone rose, rumpled.

The Australians offered them a discount rafting trip, so later that morning they found themselves on a dirt road with spindly bushes encroaching like umbrellas. At a put-in they removed rubber boats from the tops of their vehicles and launched them onto the Nile. The surface of the river was like melted glass, swirling and dimpled with current.

Sitting in the rounded bow, Lana dragged her arm in the water. It's so warm. Too bad we can't swim.

Brian stood up in the stern. Why not? he said and dove overboard.

Everyone followed. The water was dark green and they floated in it, arms out, toes breaking the surface, letting the current carry them. Twist one way and the water would spin you that way. It would turn you the way you bent. The bank was an unbroken wall of mangroves with knobby trunks and bushes jutting out in shelves over the water. Hulking birds perched still as mummies, watching them drift downstream. Suddenly wings would lift, and, crooked and bent and thin, they would fly into the blank sky, uninterested. The Australians pointed out the species: open-billed heron, fish eagle, darter, the ancient cormorant. Harry grabbled Lana's feet to swirl her over. He reached for Jane's arm and held them together so the three of them were linked shoulder to shoulder moving down the river. The water was warm and thick. Jane kept thinking, I'm in the Nile, aware of the romance in the word. The source of the Nile. It was part of the bigger world, of history.

Then she thought of how in history at that moment, three hundred miles north of this peaceful gliding river, children were being yanked out of their homes, held captive, raped, infected with deadly disease, and made to kill. The sun shone down as the river carried them along.

Signs for Kampala appeared on the road late in the afternoon, and short of downtown they stopped at a place called Al's Bar, where Lana had been instructed to call their hosts. Al's Bar had an enormous thatched roof and was vacant at five. Boz Scaggs played over an empty bar. Lana borrowed a phone to call the McAlistair brothers.

An hour later Pat and Rodney McAlistair arrived, blasting techno music from huge speakers mounted on a roofless Land Rover. The windshield was folded back, and it had enormous jacked-up tires. Pat, the older brother, was dark and barrel-chested with a booming voice; Rodney was narrower, with beige eyebrows, silent.

Follow us back to the house, Pat said. Giving directions never works. Nothing here is marked anyway. Get in, girls. You're riding with us.

The sun set as they drove south of Kampala to the Gbaba Road. The headlights of the Toyota behind them lit the stirred-up dust. They drove past lines of shacks lit with candles stuck on counters or inside tin cans on the ground. They were selling bags of chips, breadfruit, dried meat, and cans of soda. Stiff kangas hung over rods, flip-flops were wound around poles like rose vines.

Jane and Lana stood braced against the roll bars, blasted by warm wind and throbbing music. The road turned dark, and the land seemed to become greener and deeper. The farther they went, the softer the road became.

Eventually they arrived at an aluminum gate glinting in headlights among the trees. A dark-skinned man appeared out of the shadows. This askari was a Samburu in a long greatcoat who unlatched the lock and let the cars through. Jane looked back and saw him close the gate. He would be, as all the askaris were, at the gate all night. The Land Rover came to an open black space with far-off squares of lights in a cement block house with no curtains. They neared the house and parked on the grass. It was a rental, Pat said. They'd been there two weeks.

To the north on a hillside dotted with yellow lights was Kampala's suburb, but down here there weren't many houses nearby. The black space was a huge lawn at the end of which, they were told, were the shores of Lake Victoria. The silhouette of a woman stood in the open door with a baby in her arms. It was Pat's wife, Daphne.

Here, please, take her, she said, pouring the baby into her husband's arms. Her hands lingered over his big hands, and her large liquid eyes gazed at him with a manic hope. She had dark bangs and a fresh face. Come in, she said. Her quick gaze moved up and down her guests, as if to see what they'd arrived with, what news of the world. The house is in shambles, she said. We just moved in. Who wants a beer? Unpacked boxes were piled against the walls; a plastic tarp covered a big lump in the hallway.

Lana put a firm arm around Rodney and strolled him into the darkness of the lawn, her chin raised in profile, saying, Tell me everything. He was another of Lana's old flames. The brothers were starting up a computer business, but still getting hired out for concerts and parties. During the next few days, music was always playing from speakers lodged in the windows, sailing across the bristly lawn.

Again, Jane noted, they were being hosted by a mother with child. Daphne was in her mid-twenties, and later, as they sat around candles on a makeshift door propped on cement blocks, Jane learned that being a mother had happened earlier than planned. Daphne had been working with trauma victims, first in London, then in Bosnia. Already that seemed like a long time ago. She was from Scotland also; she and Pat had known each other since they were kids.

Harry and Jane were given a room that just fit a double bed, leaving a few inches of space beside one wall. They got under the mosquito net and found each other's tacky skin in the heat. Jane felt a little drunk and thick as she rolled around with him. Though she was taken up with his body, images still appeared in her mind of the drive that day, of the candle flames on the counters of the shacks, of Pierre flicking Lana's anklet, of the morning already so long ago, of Harry pulling Jane over in the waters of the Nile and letting her go.

Later she lay awake in another new bed, listening to his quiet breathing. Already she could review their other nights together in other beds. She felt more with him when he slept and rode the feeling as if it were a raft on the sea. His mouth was near her forehead, as close as it could be without touching. Her arm was draped across his waist, and her leg was hooked heavily over his hip. Their bodies could not have been closer, and yet Jane felt what she so often did in precisely this proximity: how very far away another person was, and how immense and unknown his mind. Her hand flat on his chest felt the sweat on his skin and still she had the longing to be closer. Would it ever stop?

After having music thumping all night, silence was profound. Everyone in the house could therefore hear the woman with the Scottish accent screaming, *Goddamn it, Pat, you should have told me!*

She woke early. There was the milky cast of a mosquito net. Where was she? That's right, a new place. To avoid the waiting again for Harry to roll in her direction or not, she got up. The house was quiet. Someone had made coffee and she followed the smell to the kitchen. There were dishes in a tiny sink. A narrow window looked on a gigantic lawn to the lake reflecting an orange sunrise across the horizon. The kitchen was a welcome disarray, the counter crowded with plates and wrappers, mango skins, the ubiquitous carton of Parmalat. One mug was stamped with the face of Nelson Mandela.

She heard Daphne's voice out the back door and saw her talking quietly to the baby as she hung laundry on the line. She had probably been up for hours. The new mother led a life parallel to others. Jane thought of her sister back home who inhabited her role with a placid, focused air and of her husband with a manner to match. She saw that Marian had a capacity for attachment and had tried to mimic it, but did not feel it penetrate some hard core. Jane's attachments to people turned out to be more intermittent, not entirely there. Perhaps it was herself never entirely there. Jane took her book and cup of coffee out to the front lawn and sat on a dewy chair.

She stared at the water beyond the grass. The lake drained of blue as the sun rose and the color was pulled into the sky. Behind her were gentle kitchen sounds and the smell of toast. She pictured Harry still sleeping. He was making beautiful moments. And wasn't that all one got anyway, moments? She had a shameful awareness, which she managed mostly to hide from herself, that her connection to the world came only in a string of moments. Might she hope for more? She opened her book to read about the Lord's Resistance Army.

Jane felt like a white plastic chip in an ancient forest and asked herself again just what she was doing here, in a place she'd never been, going to report on a place she didn't know about, with struggles she could only begin to imagine. How did she find herself here? Fact is, she'd made a choice each step of the way. It was how a person arrived anywhere: with one deliberate step after another. She read about Uganda's recent history, about Idi Amin having people buried alive at Bucoro, about pregnant women being disemboweled.

She read on. The Lord's Resistance Army was led by a nut named Joseph Kony.

Attacks associated with the LRA had been around for nearly twenty years. Everyone found it astonishing that no one had stopped them. The statistics, as always, were difficult to digest, much less fathom. Just a year ago four hundred civilians were slaughtered in Kitgum. She saw on the map this was where they were headed to visit.

Hey, said a voice above her, and she felt a hand on her shoulder. How goes it?

Past the brim of her hat she saw Pierre's crumpled khaki pockets.

She felt the transformation that came when a person was near. His hand on her shoulder grounded her. I'm discovering new and inventive ways people have of brutalizing each other, she said.

That's our Africa, he said.

He was holding a book. Here's more, he said. The raid on Entebbe. It happened right nearby, you know. She took the book and read about the famous hijacking. Could that have really been more than twenty years ago? She was in college then. Jane remembered the story but not the details. Some world events made an impression then, while others seemed to slip by.

An Air France plane had been hijacked by Palestinians, and Idi Amin offered them asylum. His precise words greeting them at the airport were: *I am His Excellency, Field Marshal Doctor Idi Amin Dada, appointed by God Almighty to be your savior.* Then Jane thought, Was Harry even born then?

Uneasiness came over her. She felt nauseated. Maybe she wasn't getting enough sleep. Maybe they were drinking too much. Maybe she liked him more than he liked her. What was happening to her? Here she was reading about hostages and terrorists while wondering like an idiot if a boy she liked liked her back.

But she did not drop the thought. He'd lost interest in her. Boys always did. She was too old. Too needy. He was put off. He was a healthy, self-possessed *young* person who didn't have a neurotic need to merge with someone else. She observed herself, humiliated to be entertaining these thoughts, much less to find them true. In stunning relief rose the shadows, as if lit by the sun off Lake Victoria, of the contours of all her unappealing attributes: impatience, dissatisfaction, age. She lacked a calm, inviting interior.

She regarded her legs crossed in front of her, her skirt to the knees, feet in flip-flops, chipped red-painted toes. She wished she had a different body, with long legs, and a different face, with full dark features, and a spirit that spread joy around her. What she saw instead was a person with no real home, a woman without a child, an idiot girl whose mind despite being full of hijackers and anti-Semitism, SWAT teams and demented dictators, was nevertheless still preoccupied with a man fifteen years younger who at eleven in the morning was still sleeping.

How to stop the spiraling of the mind? Tumult led to restlessness. She got up from her chair.

The door was open to the front room. Daphne was sitting on the floor against the couch, nursing the baby. She looked at Jane with searching in her eyes.

How far away is the airstrip at Entebbe? Jane asked.

It's just here, Daphne said. Twenty, maybe thirty minutes. She had a level gaze with dark defined eyebrows. The eyes said to Jane: I am trapped with this baby. You all still get to do things and go places.

Jane, however, regarded Daphne with admiration. She had strength and maturity, a robust man, and had managed to have a baby. Daphne was ten years younger than Jane, but doing far more grown-up things than Jane had managed.

I'd like to check it out, Jane said, holding up the book. Now I'm brushed up on it.

It's completely abandoned, you know. Nothing much there but a lot of weeds.

Historical, though.

What is? Harry said, coming into the room. He sat on the couch by Daphne. Jane got a pang at how near his leg was to Daphne's bare shoulder. The pang was mortifying.

Entebbe. Want to go see it?

Sure, he said automatically, and she was grateful for his quickness. He rubbed his forehead with the heels of both hands. But coffee first.

Daphne rose like a dancer, balancing with an extended arm, not disturbing the nursing baby. I'll make more.

No, Harry said, helping her up. No worries.

It's fine. Really. I'd like to do something other than feed this monster.

They walked toward the kitchen. Harry let Daphne go before him through the doorway, and Jane imagined them as a couple with their baby. They looked more suited to each other than she and Harry could ever be.

Her mood did not improve in the car. She felt impatient, tired of being a guest, mooching off people. She should have been in the north by now, working on the story, occupied with more substantial things.

The truck was on another crude road, bumping as always. A jagged cliff rose up on her side in pale cubistic rocks. She watched Harry driving. He had on his hat with the zebra band and sunglasses, and his closed mouth looked sealed off.

Did you want to come? she said.

He glanced toward her, to check if he'd heard her right.

You don't seem as if you want to be here, she said.

He drove on, staring like a stone person.

Because you don't have to be here if you don't want to. We don't *need* to go.

What are you talking about? Harry said. He faced the road, doing his best to ignore this.

You seem irritated.

His head sort of reared back. What?

She felt as if she were being sucked under by an uncontrollable force, and if that's how it was going to be, then she might as well revel in it. She pressed on. You seem like you don't want to be here, she said.

You're sounding crazy, he said mildly.

They continued to bounce in the car, driving in silence. She felt as if loose wires were flying about in front of her face, each a different thought or thing she might say, with none being the right one. The silence felt unbearable.

The cliff ended, and the road crumbled down to a wide unkempt field of weeds. The lake reappeared beyond lush tangled bushes. Far off, a tarred area encroached with grass surrounded a low white building whose windows were smashed out.

There it is, Jane said, relieved for something outside of herself. Were you even born when this happened?

Just, he said.

She told him what she'd read, how in the end the Israeli commandos got the glory, not the Air France crew—who had chosen to stay with the hostages when they could have been released.

They did their job, Harry said. He stopped the car.

They got out on their opposite sides. The midday sun was strong and thin with the high elevation.

I don't even think that's the original terminal, Jane said.

They walked around the building, then strolled away from each other. Tarmac fissures sprouted grass. They met again in a shallow riverbed where puddles of water lay among white rubble and stones. Harry faced away from her; she deserved to be ignored. What was wrong, really? Nothing. Herself. If only she could observe the world with amusement and be inviting and light. If only she were ageless.

One of the hostages had been an older woman with a medical problem who'd been allowed to go to the hospital in Kampala, leaving her adult son at the airport with the hostages. When the hostages were freed, her son had to decide if he would stay. He ended up flying back with the others, leaving his mother in Uganda. Idi Amin, infuriated by all the events, had the mother dragged out of the hospital and killed. Jane told Harry this as she balanced on the rocks. The poor woman, she said.

Harry's back was to her. It's the son I'd worry about.

The white stones buzzed with flies. Of course, he was right. Worse for the living. This riverbed felt like a bottomless pit of engulfment. She was thinking too much, and too much about him. Despair increased with this reflection. She made herself breathe, and an overwhelming hunger seemed to spread dark wings in her, and she longed to feel both everything and nothing.

Let's go, she said and turned. She could turn away from him, too.

In the car the gaping thing expanded into something palpable, pressing on her lungs. What would become of her? The future loomed. Contemplating the future always guaranteed more worry. She asked Harry if he knew what his plans were when they got back to Nairobi, after the trip. This was a subject certain to hurt her, and apparently she wanted to be hurt.

I'm not thinking of the next thing while I'm here, he said. People spend too much time thinking about what's going to happen next. His face was calm and his voice sure and uninsistent. He did not seem to be fazed by her appalling behavior. This immediately calmed her, and all the whirling thoughts seemed to land, flattened out.

Life could shift that way. You could be suddenly hijacked and the terms of your life would change. Someone outside of you could alter everything. By the same token you could be bereft and alone to the core one moment and with nothing outside in the world changing, and the next moment because someone spoke feel your existence united and whole. Things could change that fast. They had just now.

I'm sorry, she said.

He shrugged.

I've taken out my bad mood on you. Really I'm sorry.

It's okay. He gave her a quick, kind look.

Will you forgive me?

No worries, he said. They were back at the driveway.

Her relief was tremendous. I don't know what's wrong with me. Really, will you forgive me?

Jane, I said it's okay. This time his voice had an edge to it.

Kampala was swirling with white dust and the sound of jackhammers. Rodney volunteered to drive Jane and Pierre in on Friday afternoon, through streets banked by sawhorses and pyramids of rubble. The city was enjoying a boom. Plastic flags decorated the awnings of new businesses, foundations were being dug for banks. At a roundabout, cars were at a standstill, and Rodney told Pierre to get out and ask a matatu to move so they could turn. Through the dust around a white clock tower they saw a bobbing line of helmets—*hup-two, hup-two*—jogging toward an unseen disturbance.

I thought it might be something like that, Rodney said, unimpressed.

What was that? Jane felt she was watching a newsreel.

Rodney shook his head. Who knows. Some little riot being crushed.

They wound their way out of downtown and up a hillside into trees on curving old streets with leafy canopies, past the quiet embassies barricaded behind electric gates, and the converted colonials that housed the nongovernmental organizations, the ubiquitous NGOs.

At each short driveway was a sign: Oxfam, Save the Children, GOAL, Set Them Free International, Friends in Service, SMACA (Save Mothers and Children Association), Humanitas Foundation, Plan Uganda, EACO (Empower and Care Organization), Greater Life Mission, Action for Community Development. They passed more: Centre for Treatment of Rehabilitation of Torture Victims, Helpers International, Uganda Coalition for Crisis Prevention. Suddenly Rodney McAlistair's silence broke, and out came a steady monologue about the ineffectuality of these so-called humanitarian organizations. He spoke as if he'd been talking all along and was not the silent brother. The effect on the country's economy was parasitic, not to mention the psychological effect on people who as recipients of charity were only encouraged to remain helpless and dependent. . . .

Jane and Pierre listened, nodding.

World Vision, Jane interrupted. In here.

They turned in to a parking lot.

Concrete steps led up to the wide wooden veranda of a yellow building. They crossed a long hallway of walls painted brown halfway up in imitation of wainscoting, and came to a quiet reception area where an old black telephone sat on a high counter and the top of a receptionist's head was visible behind. A few people waited in chairs around low tables scattered with pamphlets. Jane told the receptionist they were there to see Bobby Kiwanuka. She nodded. Please, you wait just here, she said.

They sat on a bench. Pierre held his camera in his lap with the red light on, filming. Jane looked through the pamphlets. Fact sheets about sexually transmitted diseases, press releases on the battle against AIDS—Uganda had one of the best track records—booklets on agricultural development. And pamphlets about the children, with which she'd recently become familiar. She thumbed through. It was difficult to look straight on at the accounts written by the children: *I tell you, a sword of sorrow will pierce your heart. . . . I have much more to tell you, but the more words I write, that is the more sad I become. . . .* A woman strolled by carrying a box. Her heels slapped tan wedges, the only sound in the light-filled building, until the slapping faded away.

Pierre said, One learns to wait in Africa.

At last Bobby Kiwanuka appeared. Welcome, he said.

He was a small, round-faced man with a walleye. He led them down steps, out through a courtyard, then back upstairs along a hallway, past small school desks shoved against the wall and World Vision calendars hanging and old file cabinets. Mr. Kiwanuka's office was in the corner of the wing. It had wooden armchairs, a desk with a green blotter and a yellowing map of Uganda. He sat in a chair higher than his guests, as if to compensate for his short stature. He described how the children usually escaped during battles with the government troops and were brought in by the army to one of two main trauma centers.

Jane was struck by his cheerful tone. Perhaps familiarity with such horror required an upbeat attitude if one was to maintain one's spirits.

When they come home, he said, making a gesture of encouragement, they are lost.

First they receive medical treatment and their families are located. Many are rural village children who until now have never been away, he said. Often their villages have been destroyed or evacuated, so their families may be dead or relocated.

Jane glanced at Rodney to see what he was making of this. His light-colored eyes were intent.

Often they are unable to return to school, Bobby Kiwanuka said, clasping his hands. In the camps they receive therapeutic counseling and vocational training. In addition to everything they have a lot of guilt. They have killed, they have beaten. They may even have attacked their own village. You ask them what are their hopes for the future? He shrugged. They have none.

So spoke the man heading a program of rehabilitation.

Jane asked him why the Ugandan army was not more successful in stopping the rebels.

It is a bit confusing, he admitted cheerfully. There are rumors that the UPDF disguise themselves as rebels and are the ones perpetrating these things. So, you see, it becomes complicated. He frowned, giving it more thought. Then he brightened up. But just recently, after a skirmish, seventy-one clients were brought in.

Vocational training, Rodney said as they got back in the car. That means they repair bicycle chains.

Better than nothing, Pierre said, and slapped Jane on the backside. Get yourself in there. Pierre couldn't go too long without a flirt.

They came to their next stop. Maybe it was always this quiet at the Ministry of Information, or just late on a Friday afternoon. An empty yellow and blue hallway led up a wide flight of stairs to more empty halls and more wide stairways. A large woman in a yellow dress glided past them, dreamlike.

In the small room where the press passes were handed out, a goateed man in a tweed jacket said he had run out of glue. He asked Jane the name of her sponsoring organization and left, to return some time later with a small white tub. He scooped the paste onto photos of Pierre and Jane into small pink booklets.

So, he said. Now you pay.

Jane was handed her press card. *Jane Wood. Herpes Magazine.*

Last stop was UNICEF, a slender white building surrounded by a fence of white iron bars in a chevron pattern. The one-car driveway was occupied, so they parked on the street. Rodney elected to remain in the car. I've seen all I need to, he said. The door and windows were covered with the same white bars. Knocking by Jane and Pierre produced no response.

Maybe it's too late. Jane peered through a chink in one window. Wait. I see a light.

Pierre banged again. They waited. The street was quiet; no cars passed. The door opened.

Yes? An unsmiling Indian woman with shiny hair opened the door. She wore a narrow skirt with a crisp tailored shirt tucked into a tidy and professional waist.

Hey, yes, Pierre said, and started to move forward. The woman did not move. He stopped near her, smiling. Can we come in?

Who are you?

Jane told her. I called the other day? Jane said. Are you Rahna Puar? Jane had gotten her name from a human rights organization back in the States. Her title was Advocacy Officer, whatever that meant.

I am. The woman's eyes, lined in kohl, were sizing them up. Jane felt she was transparent as an amateur. Come in, Rahna Puar said flatly. It was hard to tell whether she was acting the jaded professional or being simply unfriendly.

She led them up a narrow white stairway to a small room with one wall of windows and a round table filling the space. No one else appeared to be at the office. Covering two walls was a honeycomb of files and binders, and a large whiteboard in the center scribbled with indecipherable diagrams of initials and numbers. She left them and returned with four large black folders, which she dumped with a smack on the table. She was the staying-late girl, the expert, and looked unimpressed with her visitors.

So what can I do for you? she asked, long-suffering.

We were hoping for some advice, Jane began. We're headed to the north this week and wanted any, you know, tips you might have.

Tips? The woman nearly spat it.

Warnings, suggestions . . . Jane's hand stirred the air, as it did when she was at a loss for words. She brought the hand back to the table and felt the metal edge. Any foreigner passing through, Jane thought, ran the risk of scorn by those rooted and committed to a place, the ones who stayed, who knew the ropes.

Pierre stepped in. We were wondering how dangerous it is.

The woman didn't roll her eyes, but her tone conveyed the same thing. It is a war zone, she said. It's dangerous.

So . . . driving would be—? Jane said.

You'll be fine, she said, enunciating her words with a musicality which somehow conveyed hostility. People do it all the time. She might as well have been saying, Good luck, suckers.

I'm sorry if we've interrupted you, Jane said. We don't want to impose. While we're there, is there anything we could do for UNICEF?

The woman looked unpersuaded.

Wait, Pierre said. Do you think it's too dangerous?

The woman spoke coldly. I go up there once a week. Then perhaps Pierre's charm made a tiny impression on her. She sighed. Okay, she said, looking away from him as if that was dangerous. Don't travel at night. Make sure you see people walking along the road. If you don't see people walking, then the rebels have been nearby.

Isn't the military there, patrolling? Pierre said, with a melting look at her.

The UPDF? She looked at them with pity. Sure, they're there. But this apparently was another thing about which they'd have to learn themselves.

When they got back to the lake, Jane found Harry helping Pat build a shed. They were both bare-chested, wearing hats. Harry waved and kept working.

That night they barbecued fish. An English doctor named Arthur Saxon showed up for dinner. He'd just started working in Kampala and had a terrible sunburn. He blushed a deeper pink when he saw Lana, surprised she was there—they'd met, did she remember, at a wedding in Dorset?

I think I do, she said, eyes flashing. I think I remember your brother, though. Vere?

Yes, Arthur said. You would.

Arthur also said he had read one of Jane's books and told her that he liked it very much. Everyone appeared surprised to hear it and looked at Jane as if she'd undergone a transformation.

I thought you were a journalist, said Pat McAlistair. Jane hadn't thought Pat noticed anything. He seemed one of those men propelled forward by unthinking exuberance. So now she was surprised.

No, she said. I'm just faking it.

Later they danced on the lawn. At one point Pat picked up his wife in his massive arms and carried her, running out of the circle of light made by the fire into the darkness toward the lake, and that was the last they saw of them.

*

Daphne had worked for a professor at the university in Kampala. Helga was an expert on trauma in children. She thought Jane should talk to Helga. Lana and Don begged off and went instead to the flea market where Lana had heard there were great deals on fabric. Harry and Pierre took Jane. They sat in front and Jane found that sitting between two men in a truck driving new roads gave her a splendid feeling in both body and soul.

Kampala was a city of hills, and they wound up the southern residential area on a bleached switchback alongside whitewashed walls interrupted by metal gates. In the distance was a green plain, then the lake, a soft navy blue which grew larger and mistier as they climbed higher. Near the top they turned at the appointed number up a short vertical driveway paved with a grotto of rocks, to a modern house perched at the edge of the hill.

The doorbell was answered by a woman with cropped gray hair and a square, handsome face. Helga wore no jewelry or adornment, presenting herself as simple, unfussy and efficient. Her lidded gaze suggested arrogance.

Tea is coming, she said in a German accent. Come in. Like many people in the healing profession, Helga had an unsmiling expression and a neutral tone of voice.

A large window took up one side of the house, framing the hazy air and ruffled lumps of trees. The lake beyond sparkled from this height like broken glass. They sat on a low sofa around a low table. Jane saw not one thing of color in the house. A young Asian woman appeared with a tray. She set it down, swinging a thick shiny braid off her shoulder.

This is Sunali, Helga said. When she looked at the girl, her face changed, softening into something private and warm. Sunali nodded, barely glancing at Harry and Pierre, and set down cups and lined up spoons and put out paper napkins with her small hands.

Helga turned to Jane, businesslike. So, you are going to see the children? Sugar?

Jane told her what story she hoped to report on.

Yes. The nuns, of course, We've all heard that story. It's gotten a lot of attention. It travels well. Everyone likes it because it's dramatic. I suppose it captures people's imagination.

Well, it captured mine, Jane said. She wasn't sure if she was being insulted.

You, Helga said, turning to Harry. What do you do?

Drive.

Helga nodded, looking at him solemnly. This was acceptable.

Helga hadn't been back to the north in over six months, she said. She was too busy here, teaching. But things hadn't changed up there, as far as she could see. She'd been in Uganda for eighteen years, but Kampala was changing. They saw all the construction going on. Then she talked about the disaster of Idi Amin. Did they know he deported most of the Indian population, who were, she pointed out, the economic strength of the country? And now, she said, we have Museveni. She shook her head. This apparently spoke for itself.

Are you from India? Pierre said to the beautiful girl.

No, Helga answered for her. She's Samoan.

There was a long pause and Jane asked more about the children.

When you talk to them, Helga said, ask about their escape. They are able to speak of this with enthusiasm. The escape is the first time they are able to act on their own behalf after having been powerless for so long. The period of captivity they feel as a blur, it is how they manage it. You can ask them about the small bits of their daily life with the rebels and a bafflement descends.

I suppose they want to forget it, Jane said.

They still have a lot of violence in them, said Helga. It's hard to dispense with such things. Not many of them get over it, you know.

May I have more tea? Pierre said, holding his cup up to Sunali.

As Sunali poured tea, Helga placed her braid on her back, holding it like a leash.

Of course one is not allowed to say it, Helga went on. One mustn't even believe that there's little hope for them. But it's true.

Do they know you think that? Harry said.

The children? Oh, no. I just study them. The more we learn, the more we hope to help them. She left the braid on Sunali's back and admired it there. Sunali kept still, accustomed to being admired.

Did you grow up in Uganda? Pierre said, taking his cup of tea. Sunali appeared deaf.

Helga spoke for her. She doesn't speak English.

Swahili?

She speaks Samoan.

You speak Samoan? Pierre said to Helga.

Certainly. Sign language would have gotten a little tiresome after ten years.

The girl didn't look more than twenty-five, Jane thought. She pictured them, as she was compelled to do whenever she saw a couple, in bed with each other.

As if sensing Jane's observation, Helga tucked the hair behind Sunali's ear and spoke in German. Sunali smiled. Of course she speaks German, Helga said.

Driving home, Harry said, Looks like Helga is doing a little child abduction herself.

That girl was giving me the eye, Pierre said.

Really? Jane said. She was so out of it. Things opened in one place and shut in another. Girls with allure had secrets. Was Helga kind or cruel? What were the secrets of girls with allure?

As they wound down the powdery roads, Harry took Jane's hand and held it against his stomach. The world felt fine.

It was Sunday, and water skiers were drawing white Vs on the purple waters of the lake. Next door, coolers were being carried down to the yacht club where people had gathered for a barbecue. The men were pink with sunburn, and women in large T-shirts sat cross-legged in shorts, their painted nails relaxed on armrests, visors on their heads. The talk was of the buyer of Idi Amin's compound around the corner and how he was planning to turn the land into a resort.

Behind the cows grazing at the far edge of the lawn, Harry could be seen practicing with his glider. Jane watched him. He stood on a low crest with the ribbed chute puffed out behind him. Now and then he took a step and would be lifted into the air, then land in slow motion, as if he were walking on the moon. From the screened window the Ink Spots were crooning *Someone's rocking my dreamboat . . .*

Aren't you coming? Pat McAlistair strode across the scratchy lawn, bare-chested and barefooted. People always wanted you to join in.

So, some time later Jane found herself riding in a chipped outboard, where people one at a time were dragged tilted on a creamy wake. The thought came to her that this area of the lake was once full of bloated bodies floating downstream after an Idi Amin massacre.

It was her turn; she jumped in.

The water was warm and thin and dark like tea, with no salt taste. She struggled her feet into the cut-in-half rubber slippers attached to the water ski and crouched, white knees showing in the brown tea water. Hold your arms in, they yelled as she braced herself. The boat burst forward with a high rev and she kept stiff and was miraculously pulled up. The bottom of her feet skimmed the water surface as she followed the deafening noise of the motor. Water sprayed in a plume when she turned, the wind was hot on her wet skin. After a few spins, she released the wooden handle and sank slowly like a statue lowering in quicksand. The boat cut a sharp turn and returned to her, idling. Lana, in a black bathing suit with a neckline plunged to her belly button, jumped in. Jane slid her the ski.

The boat had been driven from a driftwood dock on the other side, but Jane could see the house from here. Can I get back this way? she said.

Sure, said Pat McAlistair, coiling the rope, looking with intensity at the other boats.

Jane swam toward what looked to be a bed of thick growth. Up close she saw it was the water hyacinths they'd been talking about, the vegetation clogging the shore and threatening to choke the inlets. The leaves of the water hyacinth were large and rubbery and the stems thick dark cords winding around each other. She began to pull herself through the tangle, unable to touch bottom. As she penetrated the bog, she had the odd sense, which came to her when traveling, of being slightly behind herself. It was as if the person thrashing through this woven marsh was ahead of her in the future and she, her real self, was watching and hadn't quite caught up. She wasn't far behind herself, she was within sight, but she wasn't quite arrived at this new unknown place. She wasn't, as the phrase went, in the moment. The sensation was unsettling, but also stimulating. There was relief, as if a chance were still there for her, before she caught up with herself, to gather parts still at odds with each other and in the lag time to allow the scattered bits to be pulled together and nearer to being whole.

Her thoughts turned from herself to Harry. How odd it was that once you kissed a person he infiltrated you. After lunch, while she painted the view with Daphne's watercolors he'd sat behind her on the concrete deck, his legs straddling her, encasing her. Her body accepted the occupation of him, whether chosen or not. Apparently being occupied by a man did not have to do with suitability or personality. The body decided and the mind followed, helpless. This usurpation seemed to be, she noticed, relegated to females.

She thought of Harry saying his mother was the coolest person he knew. It was better than his mother being a nightmare. A nightmarish mother was something to contend with, though adoration was another hurdle. Jane had met his mother, Sheila, the night before they'd left Nairobi. She was a trim woman with short hair and an intelligent expression, standing at the fridge, looking for supper. Karibu, she said to Jane, neutral. Good trip, she said when they were leaving. She and Harry's father were scientists, specializing in livestock. Harry's mother was clearly not the sort of woman to let her body override her mind. That is, she appeared to be an adult.

The weeds were hard to haul through. The stems were strapping across her chest.

She heard Lana shout and turned around to see her following, her broad shoulders visible above the rug of growth. Looks like you picked the easy way back, Lana called. She appeared, however, to be making effortless progress through the tangle. Her body twisted side to side as if she were dancing a rumba. Lana looked to be very much where she was, and always did, unbowed by obstacles in her way.

The last night with the McAlistairs, they went out to dinner at an Indian restaurant off the Gbaba Road. It was in a house on the second floor with a screened-in porch perched in the trees. A Bengal wall hanging covered a fireplace. At most of the tables sat people with light-brown skin. Many Indians had returned to Uganda after Idi Amin's banishment in the eighties.

The rice arrived beside the vegetables upside-down in scoops.

At the next table were two handsome men with whom Lana soon made friends. They were doctors. One was an Italian who not only was a paraglider but had just returned from years of working in the north. He told them they had to go to the hospital at Lacor. It was run by a man named Carlo Marciano and was the best hospital in the north, no small achievement given where it was. He scribbled a note on a paper napkin. Tell him I sent you, he said. He was retiring for a while. You can't work there forever, he said. You begin to go mad. Jane looked at his young face, ragged around the eyes. He and Harry fell into an intense discussion. He was headed to Ethiopia to paraglide.

When Jane was ten, she had decided to be a doctor. She liked dissecting animals in science, and healing sick people seemed like a good thing to do. She pictured herself touching the glands by children's ears and walking purposefully down a hospital corridor, the way doctors did on TV. But it turned out being a doctor required a lot of reality and a lot of being in the world and Jane found herself drawn more and more into the world of dreams.

Don picked up the torn piece of napkin. This ought to be a big help, he said.

Everyone was learning to ignore Don. Jane folded the note and carefully jammed it into her stuffed wallet.

So, Lana said to her new friends as the check was being examined. She slapped her thighs with gusto. Where can a girl around here go dancing?

The next day they set off for a war zone.

7 / Independence Day

AFTER WE TURNED OUT the lights in the dormitory we could hear the wrappers crinkling from the sweets the sisters had given us for the holiday. Agnes was in my bed with me. Agnes and I usually slept together in any case, not just because the rebels were nearby. We hugged each other, pretending to be worried, but we were not really. We had locked ourselves in with the steel bolt. We were safe. We knew about the LRA cutting people's mouths off and stealing from the villages, but I myself had not seen a rebel. They did not show themselves and hid in the bush. One girl at St. Mary's, Alison, had an uncle taken when he was fifteen and a week later he was found, not alive, tied to a tree. Margot's brother had been taken during Easter week in Nebbi and had not come back. You would hear these stories.

Then you find you are in the story. The story is happening to you.

Agnes fell asleep first, as she always did. I heard her breath turn thick, but I stayed awake. I had a math test on Tuesday, and I was thinking how after Tuesday I would be glad that math test was over. I went to more interesting thoughts. I thought about Philip, the boy of mine. I thought about his hands. His hand was two inches higher than mine, we'd measured. I thought about the last time home in Lira, when we kissed behind the library. He said to me I was different from the girls he knew, but he meant it nice. I remember that night having a safe feeling I was not to have again.

We woke to the banging.

Across the ceiling, lights bobbed like car lights on a bumpy road. We heard shouting, then a large thing banging, banging on the outside wall. They were stoning the glass in the window past the bars. Girls started to cry and others quieted them, putting their hands over their mouths. Maybe they would not know we were inside if we remained quiet. I sat up, with Agnes squeezing her arms around my waist. I kept my eyes in the direction of the banging. They know we are in here, I was thinking. About a hundred and fifty girls slept there. They know the building to find us in. Other times when the rebels were near, we were taken by the sisters to town to stay with different families in small groups. But this time we did not go and this time they had come.

Quick, I told Agnes. Go under the bed.

Other girls were there also. Then noise flooded in. From below the mattress I saw flashlights and the shadows of the rebels climbing in the window. They had pulled out the bars. They came stomping in. Electric lights were switched on, and the first sight of them was frightening. We saw them now. We saw their faces. They had on brown berets and red berets and baseball hats. Some had braided hair and dark glasses. Many wore camouflage shirts. Everyone was screaming. The rebels hit us.

Do what we say or we kill you! They spoke in Acholi. They spoke English also. Line up here! Now!

Agnes was frozen beside me. I held her ankle. She started to move and I gripped her to stay.

Then they pulled the mattress off the bed. I let go. Okay, I thought, we cannot escape them. Agnes was crying. Stop, I whispered. Do not let them know it. I saw Agnes's face try to keep this idea. We were pushed together roughly. Girls tried to put on their shirts or dresses. The rebels held pangas and guns and with a free hand picked up things, shoes and clothes and blankets, throwing piles on the beds. They told us to carry these things. Some of us found suitcases. Others made bundles with sheets.

We were made to stand in a line, and they collected us in groups of five or six and wound a rope between us at our waists. When a girl cried, they shouted, Quiet! Maybe they would hit her. Abigail was taking her shoes from the floor and a rebel hit her back, making her fall down. His sunglasses reflected the lights. He was not old; he was young, fifteen or sixteen.

The rebel tying our rope had a chain around his neck with a light-blue oval charm of the Madonna. He tied our hands. I tried to press out my stomach to make extra room but only managed a little. The rope stayed tight. I did not like it, but I found no choice. We had to do as they told us.

Agnes at least was behind me.

In front I had Louise. Louise was tall for fourteen and our best football player. I looked at her strong back, and when she turned I was glad to see she was not crying. We looked at each other without speaking.

Pick up your luggages, they said. I took my backpack. I managed to put my feet into sneakers. Agnes had found only her sandals. I had the thought she'd be sorry to walk in them, a thought next to more important thoughts such as, Am I going to die? I noticed Louise had no shoes either, so I kicked her leg. She understood and starting looking around.

They unbolted the door, hitting it with their guns instead of just sliding it to the side, and we were led across our courtyard. The light from the dormitory reached a small distance across the grass. Smoke blew over us and we smelled burning. The lights at the entrance to the sisters' area were bright and shone on the white gravel. Out of the corner of my eye I saw the figures of the children crouched against the cafeteria building, hiding. I looked away to protect them.

We walked together, attached by that rope.

Then across the grass I saw a shadow running small as a dog toward the music rooms. A rebel ran and caught up to the shadow. He picked it up. It was a smaller girl, I think Penelope. He didn't bring Penelope back, but pulled her over to the trees where it was dark, and I did not want to think what he was doing to her over there. She was only ten. Only the other day I was sweeping the sorghum platform when Penelope came and said, I know you. You are Esther. Her six pigtails were held at each end with a different plastic barrette. I am a good sweeper, she said. Want to see? I gave her my broom and Penelope swept for me, concentrating hard. She asked me how old I was. I said I was fifteen, though my birthday was not for a while.

Where are we going? Agnes whispered.

Into the bush, I said. But what did I know?

Near the chapel we passed through a thick band of smoke and I heard glass breaking. Rebels were hitting the windows with clubs. Smoke streamed out of the chapel door but I saw no flames. Maybe they will not burn it down, I thought. Nearby the Jeep was also burning and we worried it might explode because flames were there.

We walked out of the school gates onto the drive. But soon we veered off that road. We walked and walked in the night without a path, then we would find a path again. We got used to seeing in the dark. I made out the long line of girls. Later I learned there were about one hundred and forty of us in that line. We came to a place of marshy water and were made to walk through and became wet up to our chests. The smaller girls held on to the chests of the others or were carried. The water would be over their heads. When we emerged from the water, Agnes pointed to her feet and one sandal was gone. Agnes was always this way, losing hair clips, losing her papers.

We did not know where they were taking us. We did not know if we would live or die. You now have a new perspective. You do not care so much about the thorns scratching your legs or that your shirt is wet. You notice other things. Above the trees dawn was lightening from dark blue and it made me think of my family in our house in Lira, all sleeping. My mother was the one who decided I should go to school at St. Mary's in Aboke because I would learn more there. You might make something of yourself, Esther, she said. The ground was still dark, but I could see my light-colored sneakers.

Then the sun rose and spread behind us in a bright band lighting the scraggly branches gray in front of us, and I felt it as if my mother or sisters were offering their hands in help. That light appeared quietly. For an instant I had the feeling I would sometimes get of the world being a sweet place and how lucky I was in that life, then immediately saw that I might not be so lucky now. Inside us were new feelings of fear. The good world was overlapped by another one. We walked on the road again, then turned for the last time off into the bush.

The rebels had not been so visible to us, walking with guns strapped across their chests, thirty of them, maybe forty. As it lightened, their faces appeared. Kony was not there. We did not know then, but Kony would not go on raids. The man leading us was named was Mariano Lagira. He was a fat one. But he walked as if he was not fat, he walked quickly. Always two or three soldiers walked near him. Some soldiers were very young, younger than me, eleven or ten years old. Even they were carrying machine guns with necklaces of bullets. The young ones looked the hardest. One tall rebel had two scars, one down his forehead and across his mouth and then one going the other way, as if someone had crossed him out. I heard a girl scream then a gun shoot.

Some of us had broken off to escape. Some were brought back. Later we learned that Irene had escaped at that time.

A rebel shouted, If you do like this again we will kill you. Everyone heard.

We went up and down hills. The sun rose and it was morning, but unlike any morning we had ever had before. It was the same thin sun and there were the usual thornbushes with flaking bark we see every day of our lives and dark green leaves like narrow beans along thin branches. One girl, Patricia, she would not stop crying and two rebels hit her on the back and shoulders till she stopped. If we looked to watch, they would raise their guns till we looked away. We learned quickly how it was to be.

We were tired but still we walked. We crossed another swamp and again got wet. We were made to crouch down which was supposedly resting. It was muddy there and I held Agnes's hand. She had on the white nail polish we put on two days before and it was good and bad to see it.

I mouthed to her, It will be okay. She nodded. Her mouth was open in a round shape, wanting to believe me, but not so sure.

We went farther, down in a valley. We climbed a hill.

The commander Mariano Lagira said, We will stop here.

It was about one o'clock. There was some shade and we were made to sit.

It was then that we saw her thin figure coming up the hill. It was Sister Giulia, our headmistress. She had come after us, having followed in the night. Mr. Bosco our math teacher also was with her. Mariano Lagira saw them. He said to us, to all the girls, You stay here. If you do not stay we will slaughter this nun before you.

We kept down our heads, but were able to see what would happen. Sister Giulia was not wearing her habit so we saw her light brown hair we had not seen before with a kerchief over it. Sister Giulia, she is very small, with thin arms and skin so light her nose becomes pink in the heat. She is nice to everyone and a fair headmistress and gives soft handshakes to her girls.

We watched with worry and hope when she went to sit with Mariano Lagira. We could not hear her voice, but we saw her take out her rosary. She bowed her head and kneeled down. At least Mariano Lagira was not slaughtering her. Then he was kneeling also, praying beside her. Afterward he took her hand to stand up. They had tea. In another place some soldiers spread batteries on the rocks to charge them in the sun. Sister Giulia had a piece of paper and was writing something, leaning on her knee. Then she was gone from the chair. Then she was by a small hut, washing her hands from a plastic jug.

The afternoon passed in this way, watching Sister Giulia.

The sound of the helicopters came then, growing louder, and soon they were close and all was confusion. Rebels moved everywhere. Quick, they said, pushing us to the ground and pressing branches on our backs. Take branches this way, they said, and covered our heads, as if we were in a school play, acting as trees. Bullets came flying. We kept our heads down, praying. Dust swirled.

When the sound faded, everyone stood. I had scratches on my arm from a tree and Agnes's face was half pink dust from being pressed on the ground, but we were not hurt. Judith, our head girl, had blood on her neck. A bullet had passed over her skin. She had been shot. A rebel handed her strips of cloth for a bandage. Was this the one who had been hitting someone moments ago? Judith shot. Yesterday this thing we would have never known.

We were made to line up again. At St. Mary's we might be made to go in a line, but now we were here to be counted if we were all there. During helicopter attacks an escape could happen. Some ran to find us. We who remained prayed for them. In any event, no one was brought back.

Later we were given cassava leaves which we ate, being hungry. It was not our usual supper. Then they began to select some girls to move to a place apart. Louise was pointed to, I was pointed to. Also Janet and Charlotte and Jessica. I saw they were picking strong-looking girls. They pointed to Agnes. And Lily and Helen, also picking the pretty ones. We did as we were told and went there.

It was evening, perhaps around seven o'clock. Insects had started their song, coming out in waves from the trees. Mariano Lagira was by the hut, sitting with Sister Giulia. He had taken off his beret and his head was without hair.

What are they doing? Agnes whispered. He was drawing with a stick in the dirt.

Hush.

In this way we watched our fate decided.

Sister Giulia stood. She approached us where we sat. When I saw her face and its unhappiness I knew it was bad news. She was being permitted to speak to us.

Be good, she said. Girls began crying and reaching for her sleeve. She shook her head. You must not cry. You must be strong.

We tried to do as she said. But some of us had things to say and this was our last chance to say them. Sister Giulia looked down, listening and nodding, then shaking her head, then nodding again. She was too upset to write, so Louise took the pencil and listed our names as Sister Giulia watched us. She looked at each one, telling us she would not forget us. She looked me in the eye and I held on to that look.

Then we saw that Agnes had slipped aside to the other group, and when we whispered it, Sister Giulia closed her eyes and said she must come back. Agnes did as she was told. It must be this way, Sister Giulia said, shaking her head, not believing it.

She kissed her rosary and gave it to Judith. She handed her sweater to Jessica. As she walked away, Helen called after her, You are coming back for us? but Sister Giulia was unable to turn and answer.

Sister Giulia left, taking some of us with her while thirty of us remained.

That first night lying on the ground before sleep I asked myself, How did we get here? Your life is your own one moment then suddenly it changes and belongs to someone else. In the past I have felt as if my life belonged to someone else but that was for love. I felt my life leave me and belong to his life. I liked that belonging; I chose it. Later however I learned it might not be so good to belong that way either.

People interfere with your life and decide things for you then your body develops an angry feeling unsettling to your stomach.

The first days are still vivid for me. I would not be sorry to forget them, but so far they stay. Things latch on to you and are not so easy to unlatch. You may try to forget, but forgetting happens without your trying, when you no longer care.

None of us knew how long we might be with the rebels, if we would live or die. For myself I tried to keep a calm place inside me. This place I thought of as my soul. I pictured it in the shape of a white marble bowl. No one could disturb that bowl, it was old and curved and the one and only property only mine. I would keep that white bowl in my mind. I used to think God sat in that shallow bowl. Now I do not know it.

The day after our abduction, again we footed it through the bush. They kept us together, the girls from St. Mary's, making us carry what they had stolen from the school. The rebel with the scar of an X walked near us, wearing boots with no laces. He was tall like a Dinka, but I do not know if he was from Sudan or not. Later we learned his name was Majok. Agnes and Louise were with me. Agnes wore the sneakers of Alison, too big for her but they were shoes. She wore a nightshirt with her skirt. I had on our school uniform, the white shirt with a collar and our blue skirt.

The rebels did not allow us to speak with one another and so we learned to whisper, or wait till they were away. It was very hard not to talk. I used to feel, If I do not speak, I will burst. I looked to Louise. She did not always talk so much before, but when she did it sounded natural, as if she had been speaking all along. Her words were not soft or shy, they just did not happen all the time. While others were talking, I used to see Louise watching them sidewise, listening, and feel she was listening more than others, learning something more about what they were saying than they even knew. With Louise you would get the feeling you talked too much.

Louise took the role of our protector. She was that girl who knew what was going on. If you wanted to know what to do Louise was the one to look to. She was tall and you had the feeling she could see over our heads farther into the surroundings and warn us if danger was coming. Indeed, this is what she did. Louise had a mournful containment. She had shallow eyes and a long chin and looked like a picture the nuns had shown us of St. Lucy holding her eyeballs in a plate. She knew which rebels you might talk to and which ones to stay away from. She was brave, but cautious. Perhaps this is why she has still not escaped. She will try only if she is sure of it.

At the end of that first day we came to a village where we found another group of children who had been with the rebels for some time. Their feet were swollen and their clothes dirty. From the huts women brought bowls of food. Mariano Lagira sat on a stump with other officers and ate with women who sat nearby or fetched him water.

We learned, in whispers, that for weeks these other children had been just walking. Look at the skin worn off my feet, one girl said. They do not provide us with enough food.

Have you tried to run away? I asked. In the first days you kept thinking of escape. A voice in you said, I may get away soon. Another voice also said, You must not run and endanger the others. You must not be killed. Those two voices came to us at the beginning and never left.

The girl shook her head. Tipu Maleng can see where we will go, she said. Then we will be killed. This girl was like a trembling animal in a bush.

Louise frowned at me. She knew the Holy Spirit would not be trying to stop them. I saw also a girl there I knew from Gulu. She wore a yellow dress with spots of muddy water dried into dots. She stared at me. She would sometimes come to our church in Lira. We did not speak, because she was sitting alone far away. She smiled at me, but I did not smile back. I did not dare.

Later we left that place and were taken not far to an area that had been cleared. We heard shouting from the place we had left and soon rebels joined us and they had with them this girl from Gulu. They told us she had tried to escape. A rebel with mirror sunglasses gripped her arm and others were hitting her to move.

Now you see what happens when you try to run away, the rebel said.

Then they tell us, Gather firewood. We look around for sticks. No, they say, bigger ones. I pick up a few and put them in the pile. The rebel with the sunglasses takes the sticks and gives them to us.

They say, Stand here. We stand in a circle where they point. In the middle is the girl from Gulu and we watch this rebel kick her with his boot. Then he hits her, his short arms holding a stick.

You. They point to Louise, tall and strong. Sunglasses hands her his stick. You kill that girl, he says.

The girl from Gulu is now on the ground curled on her side holding herself as if sleeping. Her eyes are squeezed tight and her mouth is bleeding. Louise stands there.

If you do not do this, instead we will kill you, says Sunglasses. All of you.

All of us? I think.

Louise holds her stick, dangling. She hits the girl on the leg but not hard.

Majok the Dinka steps over. No, he says. He takes the stick, turns it around and hits the girl with the bigger end. She lies on her side with her knees up and jerks a little.

Louise hits. The stick makes a sound.

Everyone must do this, Majok says. The Aboke girls will learn the example.

All of you will kill this girl, Sunglasses says.

A prickling feeling spreads on my forehead and the air crowds me, making me feel smaller. It is hard to breathe. With an effort I keep breathing. Maybe I am going to faint, I think. But I keep standing. I do not want to hit the girl, none of us wants to hit her. But we are not allowed the choice.

We are each made to step forward. Agnes has tears wetting her cheeks. The rebels push her with their guns. I hold a stick and do not move forward and am pushed from behind by a hard hand.

You hit, says the voice behind me.

One time in our garden a hedgehog came charging out of the trees, being chased by something. I grabbed a shovel and hit his neck when he came close. He jumped back and ran off. I did not like hitting him. Up close I saw his skin with the rough hair over it and it seemed as real as my skin and the thud was a terrible sound.

Everyone is hitting now. My stick comes down and the girl no longer jumps. Maybe she does not feel it anymore. One hopes this, and to hope this is a terrible hope. Most of the sticks beat only the legs. Everyone fears to beat the head.

My gaze looks at what is happening but a small gate in my brain makes a space and I leave through it. What I am watching continues on, in a separate place glassed off, in a universe of its own. The hands holding my stick are no longer mine.

By now the girl's face did not appear to be sleeping, it was covered with blood. In this way that girl was killed.

She was not the last dead person I saw. The girl from Gulu was the first. Later I learned her name was Susanna. She is now one of the tipus who come in my dreams. Many dead people come, and when Susanna is there, she comes in her yellow dress and says, I am the girl from Gulu. You have killed me.

I say, I did not mean to kill you. They made us do this thing.

She looks at me.

I say, Please, will you forgive me?

And the girl from Gulu shakes her head. She says, No.

After that day I am a new person. I am no longer a person who has never killed. I am now a person who will always ask herself, Could I have not done that thing? At the time I thought, This is the worst thing that would ever happen. Later I stopped deciding what the worst things could be.

What if, when they told us to hit her, one of us did not pick up a stick and one at a time everyone refused it? What if instead they had killed us all? Would that have saved the life of the girl from Gulu? I think the answer is no. I must believe it.

Should I have refused in any case? I have only one answer to that: I do not know. I did not refuse, so I must believe this was the thing I must do. But I am never sure.

In the morning I wake here in my bunk feeling a thumb is on my throat. It feels like a bruise, but I have not been hit. Sometimes the ache travels up the back of my head and I feel a strap tightening. Perhaps I am getting sick.

We walked many miles those first days. You might think you were headed to a new place, then realized you were again where you had been. The rebels, they do not move in a straight line.

Once, crying, Agnes said, Let us ask God to kill us. Louise said, No. Let us tell him as long as we are alive to keep us this way so we may see our parents again.

On the fourth or fifth day, we walked all morning. Agnes stayed beside me. It would have been worse if we had not been together, we had ourselves at least. We came to a place with huts and a cleared area marked with branches and rocks around it, a rebel compound. Near the center of the circle was a cross of thin trees. On the ground, drawn in the dirt, they had made a map of Uganda.

A soldier approached us. He was wearing a green hat with flaps over the ears and tiny braids in his hair and had a bone necklace. So you are the girls from St. Mary's, he said. Why do you make so much trouble? We learned our abduction had been in the newspapers and also on TV. Why are you so special? he said. He hit Janet with the back of his hand. Why are you on the radio?

The rebels had been taught by Kony to be against anyone being special, except for Kony himself. Lagira was there, talking with some other officers.

Sometimes they gave us sorghum in a bowl to share between us, but today they said, You do not eat today.

A rebel wearing an oversized white tank top and a blue velour bowler hat drew a big heart beside the map of Uganda. Inside, he traced a grid with squares, as if for a game.

They told us to stand in each square and remove our blouses. We did as we were told. This was life now. No prayers at breakfast, no weeding in the sisters' garden, no being at our desks staring out the windows while swallows flew into the classroom.

Lagira and the rebels drew white hearts on our chests with a paste made of egg and powder, and drew another heart on our backs. With shea oil they made crosses over our mouths and our foreheads.

Lagira poured water one at a time on our heads. This will protect you, he said.

I thought, Protect us? We are already abducted. What more can we fear? He told us he was doing as the Bible instructed him. If some girls believed this, I did not. I saw Agnes watching, uncertain.

The rebels told us many things. They said they were trying to overthrow the government of Museveni, but we never once saw them make an attack on the army. If there was a battle it was because the army had come. The rebels ran if the army appeared. The rebels only attacked villages and people unable to fight back, such as old people and children. If a person was strong, they would gang up and kill him, but they were not fighting Museveni's government.

We stood in that yard the whole day. Then for two days after, we were made to go without a blouse. Three, they said, for the Holy Trinity. After the three days we were permitted to cover ourselves. I was given another shirt. This one had buttons, but it was not my own.

At this camp were many officers. Their shirts had purple and yellow braid in their shoulder flaps. A fire was going through the day and the officers sat around it. The girls of Aboke were brought for them to see. They stood across from us or sat on stumps and looked.

Then they started to pick out girls. An officer wearing a red baseball hat pointed to us, and a guard with his gun on his back came over to Lily, one of the prettiest girls, and took her arm and made her stand. He led her to the man in the baseball hat who led her away from the circle. A man with gray and white hair puffed around his head pointed to Louise. When she was pulled up she tried to take her arm back, but not too hard.

She stood straight when the rebel pushed her. The man with the puffed hair shook his finger at her, smiling, and said to come with him. Then Janet was told to stand. She started crying. An old man came forward, limping, and took her. We were taken one at a time.

An officer with round cheeks pointed to me. He was old, in his thirties. You, he said. Stand up.

Now I was the one we watched. I got to my feet.

What is your name?

I told him Esther.

You come with me.

He turned, waving for me to follow, but did not move. Agnes's face said, What will you do? I wanted to show that even if I went I did not have to be frightened. Her face said, Esther, you better go.

The round-faced officer looked back and shouted to me. He waited with arms crossed. His eyes were hidden by the reflection of his glasses but his mouth showed that he was frowning. The guard nearby butted my shoulder. I moved a little. The other officers laughed and spoke to him in Lor. I did not know Lor so well at that time. I only knew Acholi. I felt their faces watching when the round-cheeked man turned, as if to say, Your fate is up to you. So I went, watching my feet moving over the light and dark earth. He stopped again and waited and made me to walk in front of him. Soon we were out of sight of other eyes. We came to a hut.

After that the days were the same and I lost my sense of time.

It is strange to be back. When I was with the rebels I stayed calm inside while there was much suffering around me. Now where it is safe here I am full of anger. Maybe I will nearly explode. I could even pick up a gun and kill someone, I think. I would not do it, but I still do not so much care if I am good anymore or not. In these times it feels good to hate.

When we were out of sight of the others, the man with the fat cheeks pointed at a hut among the trees. Go here, he said, his voice deep at the back of his throat. He had me pass before him. I entered. Two cots were there, one with a purple and green kanga covering, the other with no cover. Sapling trees in mud striped the wall.

The man entered after me. He closed the door but it would not shut so he kept tugging it till it was going to stay closed. There, he said. His chest looked puffed out, like someone about to fight. His shirt had a collar with gold embroidered patches on it in the shape of wheat. I noticed inside the hut his chest sank down. The voice also changed, trying to be gentle. His face was shiny. Come here and sit. He sat on the green and purple cot. I sat, but not close.

You are not the prettiest one, he said.

This I did not need to be told.

But Lotti chose you.

He stood and undid his pants and pulled them down. One foot got caught and he hopped around almost falling over. He sat back on the flat bed with his round white underpants showing in the gloom. Come, he said and grasped my arm. He pulled me over and I vacated my body.

My body is not weak and has always taken me about well. My arms carry water buckets, my fingers pull stems off fruit. I like to eat and feel satisfied. I like to hold animals to my chest and feel their fur and nerves. My legs run me from place to place and my heart hits inside me when my feet hit the red earth running. But this body only carries me, it is not me. When that body is being hurt, I will go from it. My brother liked to whip us with a switch when we played. He was not so mean, just being a boy, but it would hurt, and I could not always fight him off. I learned to concentrate so it would not hurt so much. I made my body not belong to me.

So now I watched from a hollow place apart when this man lifted my shirt off my head and pushed me onto the mattress. His hands would touch me there and there. I did not think of where he was touching. I thought of other things. Even so, his body was heavy. Maybe it was hard for me to breathe, but I had risen up close to the corner of the thatched roof where it slanted, and was turned away from what was happening below. I did not see the eyes of this man close to me and the pressure behind them as he looked downward making them swollen. I did not hear the mattress thumping against the cot or hear him tell me to put my finger in a certain place but kept myself tucked close to the straw. It occurred to me the girl under him was not pushing him off or laughing at how stupid he was but was only doing what she was told. I did not like this, so I let it go. It does no good to keep with thoughts that make you feel bad. I did not smell his breath or the smell which came off his body or from his arms.

I did not watch, apart in the air. I did not think how I would not be suitable to marry now. I thought that later. I thought other things later, but now I stayed facing a small window with leaves and white spaces beyond. The window was edged with dry mud, not square or round, but in between. I did worry it might hurt. I closed my eyes.

I thought of Philip, the boy I love. This helped and did not help. What would he have done if he saw this man on top of my body? Philip was strong enough to pull this man off, this loud-breathing body. For one second I forgot and saw the man's glasses pressing my cheek, making a mark. I closed my eyes again to wait till it was over. It would be over. The breathing went on, what he did to me went on. I cannot think how long. Finally he made a strange cough in his throat and it was quiet. He lay there. The air kept shaking, though it was still. I was another person again, another new person.

He cleared his throat and moved off me and I lay there and after a while floated back down into myself. I could feel then where I hurt. My face hurt and between my legs. Some of the pain was sharp, some was dull. I kept my eyes closed.

Look at me, he said.

I didn't speak.

Why don't you look at me? he said. Don't you like my face?

For a moment I did not want to save myself. I opened my eyes, not looking at him. No, I said.

He bent his elbow as if he would hit me, then dropped it. He laughed. No, it's not a pretty face, he said. I don't like my face either.

His face came down near me, closer. You have a resemblance to my wife, he said.

That made me look at him, but only for a second.

She was called Flora, he said.

I looked again. She's dead. But in you I am seeing her again.

I lay on my side while he dressed. I am Greg Lotti, he said. You will be mine now.

So I was wife to that Greg Lotti. When we were alone he might call me Flora. I did not mind answering to it. It was like having another person there and being another person. At night his heavy body came onto me. I did not stay the night always with him and then could sleep with the girls in a smooth ditch or on leaves where I might find Agnes or Louise or Janet. Agnes said maybe Flora's tipu would come to me. Maybe she would be mad. Maybe she would help me. I don't believe so much in tipus helping or not.

Greg Lotti was not as cruel as others. Agnes, however, she got a bad one. I am lucky I did not get that one of Agnes's. Greg Lotti only beat me one time. Two boys had escaped, and the rebels looked for others to blame. They said the boy was carrying water with me and told Greg Lotti, You must punish this one. They watched so he would hit me with a stick. He did not hit my face, just the back of my head. When I fell he hit more on my shoulders. When you are beaten the world disappears and you become only pain.

Afterward he told me he was sorry to do it. I will kiss your tears, he said. He says he loves me.

This man Lotti, he was not the worst man. Even so I do not like to think of him. He carried his body with extra flesh sloshing around.

In my first week back I have another visitor at Kiryandongo. Louise's mother comes to look in my eyes.

While we were gone, Grace Dollo became famous. The parents of the girls of St. Mary's had formed a group called We Are Concerned and Grace advertised their cause to the world. She traveled to the United States, to New York City and another time to Washington, D.C. She met with famous and rich people who listened to her story. She shook hands with Hillary Clinton. She spoke at banquets and collected money which the group used for writing letters and making themselves known. We had been told of this in the bush, but you can never be certain if what you heard in the bush is true or not. We were also told that our parents did not want us anymore. We were told Sister Giulia had returned to Italy and forgotten us. I wait to believe something till I discover it myself.

Grace Dollo sat with me near the hut of Nurse Nancy. She stroked my hand with her cool one, sitting with one hip on the ground beside me. Her loose curls blew around her cheeks.

We are so glad you've come back, Esther. Her voice caught on the words and we waited till it was smooth again. If your mother could have seen you she would have been very happy. She told me my mother had gone to their meetings till she got sick.

I feel she is still here, I said. I meant that I pictured her at home, but it did not come out that way.

She is here, Grace said.

We sat in silence. Then she said, You know who I want to hear about. She was looking at my face as if it were a map, trying to locate where X marked the treasure on it.

Louise. I nodded. I have even seen her the day of my escape.

Grace looked away, picturing this. Yes, I have heard it.

How could she know it? News here travels on air. I told her I had asked Louise to come with me, but she did not believe we could make it.

Grace nodded. How is her health? She looked deeper into the map of my face.

Not bad. She is thinner. They do not feed us well.

We spoke of this for a while, then Grace said, I have heard Louise is going to have a child.

Yes. I could not know if she knew of the first child or only of this other on the way.

It will come when?

In many months.

She frowned, watching her lap. I was relieved she was not crying, like some parents. Esther, the other child of Louise's. It is a boy?

He is George.

She flinched when I said this. I would not tell her more than what she asked.

George stays with her?

No. The children are kept near the father.

He is the same father of this child?

Perhaps, I said. His name is Ongaria. Before that Louise was wife to one called Atubo, but Atubo had died, so why tell her this?

Sometimes when I am talking I feel a blank wall come down in my head. With the rebels we were not permitted to talk, so now speaking I feel a robot person speaking in my place.

Tell me about the other girls, Grace said. The other children. Before she left she said, Thank you, Esther. The closest thing to seeing her is seeing you.

IV

To the North

8 / On Location

THEY STOPPED AT Karuma Falls where the White Nile separates the north from the south. A flat bridge spanned the river with a low concrete wall striped black and white and a steel railing burst into a tangle halfway across. They all stood in the sunlight, looking down at the rushing white water where Idi Amin had had people thrown in to be eaten by crocodiles.

Pierre nudged Jane. In the shade of a nearby rock two soldiers sat unmoving in successful camouflage uniforms. Then out of nowhere an army vehicle appeared, tires stirring up dust, and two soldiers got out.

You must move from here, one soldier said, shooing them off with an arm. The other soldier held a gun at his chest, expressionless.

Don immediately pulled Lana toward the car, having respect for authority. Pierre and Jane stepped back from the railing, hesitating. Harry, however, did not move, and continued to gaze at the frothy water, hands deep in his pockets, pretending he didn't hear. Having kayaked, he was probably assessing the white water.

The soldier with the gun frowned at Pierre. No pictures, he said. Pierre held his hands away from the camera hanging from around his neck, as if he'd never had any intention of using it.

Away from there, the soldier called to Harry, who turned with a blank look.

For God's sakes, Don called. Come on.

Everyone, including the soldiers, regarded Don with surprise.

Harry turned slowly and sauntered back to the truck. Jane watched the way he walked. Don't like being told what to do, he said, starting the truck.

Don said, When a guy has a gun—

Haya. Twende, Lana said, shutting him up. Pierre rested his camera on the window and started clicking pictures as they drove away.

They crossed the bridge into the north.

Immediately the road deteriorated. The land got hilly. The bush seemed to lose its green density and become pale. An occasional acacia tree appeared, umbrellalike, out of the ruffled trees.

Slowly was not how Harry was driving. The truck slammed deep in the potholes, the passengers flew up and landed. Don asked him to cool it and Harry mildly responded that they'd make shit-time if he did. Techno music pulsed from the dusty dashboard.

The side of the road crumbled like pie crust, and on either side on the smooth red paths people traveled, women with huge bushels of sticks on their heads and babies on their backs. Only men, it seemed, rode bicycles, sometimes with a passenger side saddle on the bar in front of the seat or balancing a mattress across the handlebars. Faces turned in slow motion to watch the truck go by. Goats pulled at leashes or ran free. Small children held the hands of even smaller ones. A screen of haze infused the air with a silver light. No other cars appeared.

Can you turn this the fuck down? Don said in the front seat. My eardrums are being destroyed. He reached for the dial and Harry stopped him, grinning.

Don't you want the driver to be happy? he said.

I'll drive, Don said, if we can listen to something decent.

The light is strange, Pierre said, head tipped at the window. No shadows.

It's the smoke, Jane said. Puffs rose out of the trees like dialogue bubbles from villages hidden from sight.

They're burning down the forest so they can cook their food, Harry said.

Please, Don said, and reached for the dial.

But this is the good part. Harry shifted gears climbing a hill. He turned up the volume.

It's all exactly the same, Don shouted, covering his eyes.

Poor Don. Lana ruffled his hair. Missing so much, she said. He looked at her; they held a gaze.

Jane watched out the window. A woman in a fancy green dress with bare feet looked to be in a sort of trance, walking with empty hands. For a moment Jane felt the aura of her world then they were gone, leaving her behind.

They drove on; the streams of people thinned. Lana fell asleep, unfazed by bumps or noise. Her head was flung back, chin raised, against Pierre's shoulder. Her dark hair swirled around her face like an anemone. Don kept looking back at her, uncertain. The music changed, becoming slow and melodic. Jane recognized the music, but couldn't have named whether it was Beethoven or Mozart.

Don appeared relieved, then found something else to worry about. Should we still be here on this road? he said.

The paths were empty of people.

We're where we should be, Harry said.

Jane looked at the back of his head in front of her, driving. He had on his hat with the zebra band, his dark hair blowing around at the brim. She could see his hand on the steering wheel and past it the road in front, red-rimmed, making a triangle up the hill ahead.

His head turned to the side, and she saw his profile from behind, his dark sunglasses hiding his eyes and his flat cheek below and the swell of his mouth and something leapt up inside, startling her.

*

She stared. The humid wind blew, the red path blurred by. A shocked feeling moved liquidly through her arms. Harry, she thought, Harry. Silver leaves flickered in the bush, the world out there seemed to go on forever.

She felt she was floating. The music added to the pleasant feeling of disturbance. Then, as if sensing something in the shadows, she felt a fear. Harry was not the right person for this feeling.

She stared out the window, spellbound. The truck shifted into low gear, revving up another hill toward the white sky.

She must prepare herself. There would be an end and pain coming. Everyone always said that: Prepare yourself. They also said, Protect yourself. How one protected oneself she hadn't a clue.

She thought of seeing Harry standing on the lawn outside his parents' house, legs apart with his pants rolled up, arms crossed, looking intently at the sky. She felt the hit of him and at the same minute saw the end. They had hardly started.

Maybe she was wrong, maybe it would be okay. Something might happen about which she had no idea, something good. It was possible. The music stopped when the tape clicked off, and it was quiet. One could hope.

They arrived in Lira at dusk. Flower beds filled the circle of a small rotary at the bottom of Main Street. They pulled over and asked a man wrapped in a blanket if he could tell them where Chain Market was.

He stared with wonder at the passengers inside. Just there, he said, pointing vaguely up the road, possibly at a blue building. Main Street sloped up a hill between low buildings with dark trees encroaching at the end. They drove up and turned onto an unpaved alley alongside the blue building. In back was a long concrete porch where a group of people sat together, making one dark shape in the dusk.

This is it, Jane said.

A woman's silhouette detached itself and came forward down the concrete steps. She wore a long dress and had loose curls to her shoulders. She stood waiting as everyone unpiled from the truck.

Jane approached the woman who held out her hands. So you have come, the woman said. She said it as if she had not been sure.

Jane grasped her hands.

We have been waiting for you, the woman said.

I hope not too long, Jane said.

No. Just five hours. She said this with no irony whatsoever.

A few months earlier Jane had gone to a dinner party in New York. She easily might not have gone. She was in and out of the city. In fact, she tried to be out of town as much as possible, en route somewhere. She preferred not to be in the familiar life.

The dinner was in a downtown loft of a couple she knew, a journalist and a filmmaker. Large windows looked out on the cold autumn night where steam rose from grates in the street. Inside the candlelight pooled in the glasses of red wine. The dinner was being given for a woman from Uganda. Her name was Grace Dollo. Her trip had been sponsored by a human rights organization, some members of which also were sitting at the table. The next night she was being honored at their annual fund-raising benefit. She'd come to advertise her cause. Grace Dollo was in her early forties. She had a handsome face with deep dimples. She wore a brown and yellow flowered sundress reaching to her ankles and looked more relaxed than everyone else there.

At the end of the dinner everyone's attention turned to the woman. Forks were put down. People sat back in their chairs. Some looked at her. Others stared into their laps, perhaps finding it hard to face her as they heard the story she told.

Grace spoke with a calm self-possession, not trying to convince these strangers of anything, but instructive and bright, telling them in a matter-of-fact tone about children being abducted from their boarding school in the north of Uganda. Her daughter was one of these children. Jane was mesmerized. There was a silence when Grace finished.

Finally someone said, Do we know about this?

Grace Dollo regarded the person with a blank face, unable to answer the question. The thought took hold of Jane: Something must done about this, maybe I can do something.

That night as she walked home she had moved on from *Maybe I can do something* to *I will do something*. She pictured the girls being led away from their dormitory in the night and imagined the thirty girls the nun was forced to leave behind. . . . The image did not leave her. She crosssed Canal to the empty region of lower Sixth Avenue, walking up to the busier stretch in the West Village where people filled the sidewalks in Saturday night clusters. Grace's story stayed before her like a great bonfire making small shadows of everything, including her small troubles.

It had been a long time since she had been penetrated by something like this. *I will do something,* she told herself, *I will help.* She could feel the wine she'd drunk, both thickening her mind and also focusing her. She knew how easily these resolutions slipped away. One made promises to oneself; then in the morning, off they slid to that place where good intentions went. She was determined not to let that happen and to hold onto this one, to someone else's dilemma, not her old tiresome ones. The impulse registered deep within her and seemed to become solid. Her usual habit of undercutting a new thought—really, what difference does it make?—did not break it. *I will,* she told herself. *I will.*

She walked home in a kind of hypnotic state, feeling more calm and directed than she had in a long time.

I am so sorry you've been waiting, Jane said. It took longer than we thought. She followed Grace up the steps, turning back to the others to show a mortified face. That's terrible you were waiting so long. Really I'm so sorry.

Come meet the parents, Grace said.

Yes.

They are here.

There were about ten women and one man. Jane shook each person's hand. They offered her a crate and she sat. She saw Don's figure wander off toward Main Street; he was either not interested or unsure if he was being invited. Lana, Pierre and Harry sat on the edge of the porch and listened.

A silhouette said, First you are wondering if your daughter is alive or dead, then you worry, if she is alive, does she have enough food? Is she being beaten?

It is hard to enjoy your food when your daughter is starving, said another voice.

Imagine not seeing your daughter for months, another woman said. It causes sickness in you. I am the mother of Helen.

My daughter is Agnes, said another. It was her birthday just now. Each year I would make the same cake. I made it this year, but she could not eat it.

There was a murmur of understanding.

Only last year, the woman beside her said, my Lily was unwrapping dolls under the Christmas tree.

Now our children have children themselves, Agnes's mother said. Rebel children.

Louise is expecting, Grace said. Jane was surprised to hear this; she had not mentioned this in New York. I know that if she brings this child home I must not hate this child. This is hard for me.

Jane and Lana exchanged a look of alarm.

The man, sitting upright as a schoolboy, had gray spots at his temples. This is Pere Ben, Grace said. His daughter is Charlotte.

The week before, I lost my mother, he said. Then I lost my daughter, and five months later I lost my job.

He and Grace laughed.

We made a trip to Sudan to find them, he said. Grace nodded, eyes closed. He would tell this story.

Arrangements had been made for the parents to meet the rebels. A doctor who had treated Kony—for a urinary tract infection—organized the meeting and received payment, though he assured the parents he was not on the rebels' side. He would have done such things for free, he said, but these matters took time . . .

The only reason Kony agreed to the meeting, he said, was because St. Mary's had gotten the attention of the world and Kony might defend himself and say, You see? We are not the monsters they say we are.

Two of the sisters, Giulia and Rosario, went in the group with Pere Ben and Grace. They flew by airplane to the border of Sudan. The first time, they waited there, but the rebels did not come. Another time later, they made the trip again, and this time the rebels arrived to meet them.

Jane was struck once more by how mildly people accepted when plans were thwarted.

The parents were brought to a deserted compound. See? the rebels said. No children here. This camp is abandoned for a long time. Fires, however, were still smoking, and wash hung on lines and bushes.

When the parents asked to see Kony they were told the next day. But Kony never met with anyone and he was not to meet with them now. The next day, returning to the same camp, they found it swarming with people. There were hundreds of children. They were sure the girls of St. Mary's must be among them. When the parents came near, the children would run. Each parent was also trying to slip away from the guides. Pere Ben followed some children hurrying down a path.

Jane was writing in her notebook, unable to see the words on the dark paper. Don reappeared and sat leaning against Lana. Pere Ben's voice came out of the dark now, unattached to a person, the voice of the group.

One girl about nine kept looking back at him. She stopped with a few other children and he squatted down to her. She put her hand over her eyes, the others turned their faces. A rebel came up and started kicking the children. Stop, Pere Ben said. Let me speak to these girls. The rebel glanced to the doctor who had arranged the meeting. He was saying to allow it. The rebel stepped back, angry.

The children stood before me, Pere Ben said. Do you know the girls of Aboke? I asked. Each refused to talk. Their eyes said they had been told to remain quiet. If you tell me what we are asking you I promise we will take you away with us, I said. It was because I felt Charlotte was nearby that I said this. The children glanced to the commander standing with the sisters. Other rebels were around but not near. Another face showed some interest in me, a girl maybe eleven. I focused on these two. The youngest still would not speak, but she looked as if she might try. She stared at my shoes. The older one looked straight at me. The boldness in her face made me think she had not been in captivity for so long. Her eyes say, Are you sure? Before God, I tell her. I commit myself to freeing you if you tell me this thing.

It was enough. This girl moved her lips, whispering. I could not hear. Then I hear it. Last night they came back, she says. They were here this morning, but now they have moved to Camp Fourteen. They have gone in a lorry. This was the first information we had found. I felt hope. Is this true? I said. Yes. Just this morning they were here.

So Charlotte was nearby. *Just this morning they were here.*

Then the girl's expression changed. The doctor and the same rebel were just there. Pere Ben stood.

What right have you to promise these things you cannot give? the rebel said.

Pere Ben pulled a camera from his pocket and quickly took pictures, one of each girl. I have pictures of these girls, he said. So no harm must come to them.

The rebel looked at him with cold eyes. Two more rebels came over and pushed the children away. It was time to go.

Later they learned that after the visitors left, the girl was killed, hit with a piece of metal on the back of her neck.

Yes, Grace said. This has happened.

Swallows dipped under the eaves of the porch like black rags.

Already it is more than a year, someone said. We will not soon forget that day.

No, the voices mumbled together.

The cicadas filled the night air. Jane felt everything drain from her and thought, I will never complain ever again. At the end of the porch was Harry's white hat, the only thing showing in the dim light.

They checked in to the Lira Hotel. There was a reception desk and a few feet away a number of tables set with place mats. They put their bags in their rooms then came back for dinner.

Everyone was tired and barely looked at the menus, thinking of the stories they'd heard.

That was heavy, Don said. I felt a little like I was butting in.

Everyone nodded, united by the awareness that their usual concerns looked awfully trivial.

It is amazing what people endure, Pierre said.

They don't have a choice, said Harry.

They ate curried vegetables and the stew special. Across the dining room was a bar with stools where music suddenly started pounding. Lana pushed away at her plate. Did anyone want her eggplant? No one answered. No one ordered dessert. Harry and Jane said they were going to turn in.

I think some of us need more drinks, Lana said, and stood. She squared her shoulders toward the pounding music. Don and Pierre stood and followed.

Jane and Harry took the white gravel path of an interior courtyard. The music grew fainter, though the bass continued to thump the air as they turned a stucco corner into the shadow of door number 7. Jane inserted a rusty key.

I can't believe they were waiting for us for five hours. The people here are so much more— She felt for the light switch inside.

Stop talking, he said.

I was just—

Hands gripped her shoulders, holding her arms down, steering her into the room where the light was striped and dim, coming through a lattice shade. He turned her around and lifted her onto a small table by the window. Her long dress was pulled up to her hips. Sometimes Harry seemed tall and other times smaller, maybe if he was beside a tall man, but now he seemed tall. He pulled her close, socking the air out of her. This is how I like you, he said so faintly she could barely hear.

Then he said, more clearly, Tell me.

Yes.

Yes what?

She didn't answer.

You like that? he said.

Her breath was all irregular.

Tell me, he said.

No.

Tell me.

She smiled. No.

The light from the window was sharpened on the floor into checkerboard squares. He held her draped over him and staggered her, collapsed on his shoulder. There were two single beds, each against the wall, with a narrow space in between. She felt her body all mixed up with his. His breathing sounded asleep, then he spoke.

We don't do that enough, he muttered.

He said it as if they were a couple with a long history and not people who'd known each other less than two weeks. Then, at the edge of sleep, she wondered, because wonder never stopped even when gratified, if he'd meant the world in general and not specifically the two of them. She wouldn't ask. Sometimes the answer could snap you in half.

Entering a person's private terrain was dangerous. You never knew where another person's tender places were and chances are they were different from yours. You didn't know the damage you might cause. Maybe the person didn't even want to be explored. Most people she'd found wanted to be left alone.

But tonight Jane was not feeling how apart she and Harry were.

The throbbing music stopped and the room was extra quiet.

She saw again the parents on the porch, and heard their soft voices under the roof. Each day your child was gone you must think you couldn't bear it another then the next day comes, and you do.

How far away were the rebels now? What children had been hurt that day or killed?

She was aware of being in a place where others were so much worse off than she, and yet felt content lying against Harry. She would have liked to tell him of her happiness. The feeling rather astonished her. But happiness was hard to express. When happiness was over, she found plenty to say. When it was in you, you felt mute.

Tomorrow they were going to St. Mary's. She thought how maybe Pierre could film Grace in the car on the way. She didn't want to miss a thing.

In the morning they drove back into town. There seemed to be a church every third building, some with steeples, some bunkerlike with signs on the front lawn. Jane bought some notebooks in a store selling coffee and ribbons. In a bank of sharp new bricks they cashed travelers' checks. It took forty minutes, as strips of paper were carried lackadaisically from one desk to another, scribbled on, transferred to a ledger, brought back to the same desk, then sent off to another quarter. In Jane's wallet she noticed she had bills from five different currencies.

When they came out the truck was dead. Lana and Don were nowhere in sight. Some people standing by helped Harry and Pierre push the truck down the slope while Jane steered, but they couldn't get the engine to turn over. They were shown a repair shop off a side street and conveniently glided to it without a sound.

We Fix It Garage was a small concrete building painted yellow with a green stripe around it beside a wall-less garage with a corrugated tin roof. Parts of automobiles lay scattered about in the weeds, and in front sat a man in a wooden wheelchair beside another man in a chair. They watched the truck slide in. The man in the wheelchair lifted his chin in greeting, and sat forward from the tasseled cushion behind him. He had a wide chest in a crimson T-shirt and strong arms.

Harry got out. Jambo, Bwana, he said. He stood with his hands in his pockets. Through the windshield Jane watched them talk.

Karibu, Kenya, said the man in the wheelchair. I know Kenya. My aunt, she was living in Kenya.

No more? Harry said.

No, she is no more.

They continued chatting, nodding, pausing. Eventually Harry pointed to the truck and the three of them looked at the truck for a while. Then the man in the wheelchair rolled toward the Toyota and, bending to look underneath, tipped his wheelchair nearly on its side, bracing himself with one of his strong arms. Neil! he shouted.

An orange wool hat appeared behind a barrel in the garage and a young man emerged pulling the hat over his ears. He listened to his orders, then ducked out of sight. The man wheeled over to a small yellow vehicle with no doors and no hood, and hoisted himself with a jerk out of the wheelchair into the passenger seat. He started the yellow car and drove it to the truck. Jane got out as the young man appeared with jumper cables.

She walked back up the road to where she'd seen a woman selling fruit. A few pyramids of onions and bumpy breadfruit lay on a cloth in front of the woman, who was looking down, showing the top of a wide-brimmed straw hat. Jane spotted a basket of lemons. Upon closer examination she saw they were oranges. Yellow oranges.

How much? she said.

The brim of the hat tipped up and the woman faced her. It was not a woman, but a young girl. Where the girl's mouth should have been was a hole with a thick rim of scar around it. Jane kept her gaze on the face, trying to hide her shock. The girl held up four fingers.

They look really good, Jane said. I'll get some for everyone. The girl did not seem to understand her. But Jane kept talking. I'll take all of them. Why not? She picked up the oranges and gestured.

The girl regarded her with a slow blink. She reached to a plastic bag beside her bent knees and removed a crumpled piece of paper which she smoothed out on the ground. She indicated that Jane put the fruit there. Oh thank you, Jane said. Asante sana. The girl piled oranges on it. Some rolled off. That's okay, Jane said, I can just carry them. The girl stopped wrapping, thinking Jane did not want them. No, no, I want them. She held up her wallet, embarrassed to be an American waving money. Ndio. Asante, she repeated. The girl handed her the wrapped oranges and took the folded bills. She put them in a box and selected coins for her change.

Hapana. No, that's for you. You keep that. Asante. As she strolled back down the hill, she checked herself to slow down, aware of being like the other white people who moved fast, always hurrying away.

The truck was running again and they stopped to pick up Grace. Jane knocked at the open door frame as Grace appeared from behind the house with a handful of eggs. Behind her, chickens fluttered. Come in, please, she said. Jane looked back to everyone sitting in the truck, idling to charge the battery. They'd wait.

A man sat in the living room. My husband, Milton, Grace said, pointing the eggs in his direction as she continued past him into the kitchen.

Hello, Milton said. He stood, a trim man in a white short-sleeve shirt.

Jane moved forward, putting out her hand. Nice to meet you, she said. He offered his left hand, there being no right arm.

Please, he said, you are welcome.

Jane sat down on a hard orange sofa. On one wall, hung high, was calendar with a photograph of Victoria Falls, on another a tapestry in a velvety weave of red, gold and brown depicting the Holy Family. Grace is taking us to St. Mary's, she said.

So you will meet Sister Giulia.

Yes.

Then you will see, he said mysteriously.

A little girl appeared in the doorway, staring.

Hi there, Jane said. Who's this?

My daughter Hannah. Come say hello. The little girl approached Jane with trepidation and bent on one knee, curtsying. The lady is from America, Milton said. The little girl looked up, startled.

Yes, I am. How old are you?

Five.

You must be Louise's sister. The little girl looked back to her father to see if she should answer. He nodded. We pray for Louise every day, he said. He picked up a photograph in a flowered cardboard frame from the table beside him. Here she is. The girl brought it to Jane. It was a studio portrait of a girl standing sideways in front of a painted turquoise ocean with islands and palm fronds. Her white shirt was tucked into a long purple skirt, and one hand held her hip in a sort of bathing beauty pose, but her face straight to the camera was not flirtatious. It was innocent and clear. Her hair had been done in two shiny rolls above the temples.

She's beautiful, Jane said. Seeing Louise's face added a layer.

Grace came in with a boy and a girl beside her. Children, she said. You come now and tell our visitor your name.

Dorothy. The child curtsied. Harold. A boy bowed his head.

He is tall for nothing, Milton said. He's gone past the others.

This one, Grace said, and another girl peeked out from behind her, she is called Martha. Martha whispered to her mother.

Hi, Martha.

She would like to touch your hair, Grace said.

Certainly, Jane said. Louise is beautiful, she said, handing Grace the photograph.

It is old now, she said, putting it back. All right, Martha, come.

Grace sat in a chair with wooden arms. It was six o'clock in the morning when we heard, she said.

Jane recognized the beginning of a story. Yes, tell me, she said. The others can wait, she thought, hearing the truck's motor still going. This is why we are here.

Someone came banging on the door. *The rebels have taken them, all the girls of St. Mary's.* My God, I lost my head. I screamed. I felt helpless. My husband was confused.

Grace didn't look at Milton, but he was nodding.

He even didn't know what to do. Another neighbor heard me screaming and came in with her husband, saying, What is the problem? My husband had the courage to tell them. They comforted us, we prayed with
them. Then I thought, Why sit here? Let me get to Aboke. My husband
was still looking for a means of traveling, but I got out of the house. I was
dressed shabbily and I took off for the bus park and got a pickup. I was
dropped at a juncture and caught a ride on a bicycle. The road by then
was muddy. Part of the way we walked. I was at the school by seven.

I saw Sister Alba there first and some teachers and other people from
nearby. By eight o'clock the schoolyard was filled with parents. It was
like a funeral. It was like a graveyard. People were weeping. I was with
my friend Serena whose daughter Jackline was taken, and we thought,
Should we walk and find Sister Giulia? Some of us mobilized and said,
What do you think? Then we said, Let us wait till Sister Giulia returns.
So we waited. All day. That night some of us stayed at St. Mary's and
some went home. I went back, because I had the children.

The children sat quietly in the living room, not appearing to listen.

But there was no sleep, Grace said. I returned at seven the next morning. That friend of mine, Serena, she has since died. She died of sorrow.

There was a pause; she continued.

Then we heard that Sister Giulia was returning with the children.
We decided to follow in that direction. We drove there with a man from
Gulu, a manager of the electrical board. We met them five miles up the
road. The first girls were on a tractor. Others were coming on foot, some
on motorcycles. There were many girls piled on that tractor. I looked
through quickly and of course did not see my daughter. I screamed.

Grace spoke so mildly it was hard to picture her screaming.

Those children's faces on the tractor told me. They didn't speak, their
faces did. Mama Louise, their faces said, we have nothing to give you.
You have nothing to hope for.

Everyone sat silent. It must have been horrible, Jane mumbled.

Grace stood up. The sisters will be waiting, she said.

Jane stood. She said goodbye to Milton and the children. Grace, how
many children do you have?

There are six, she said blandly. Let us go.

9 / In the Bush

In strange places new thoughts come to you.
What has been true no longer is.

WE SOON LEARNED things. You would always be tired from walking and your feet always sore. You would always be hungry. You did not
forget your life before, but it was like a movie you saw, not believing you
were really there in a bed with sheets or eating chicken from a plate or
putting on your purple skirt for Mass.

The rebels told us in any case our families did not want us anymore.
They would teach us to be in Kony's family.

What they taught me was to hide—my fear and myself. Sometimes it
was like dragging a dead animal behind me. Sometimes I felt a thick pad
of cotton come over my head.

How were our days? We searched for food. We gathered vine leaves
and cooked them. We ate cassava leaves, simsim, boiled sorghum. We
carried the radio, carried water and were always thirsty. We cut grasses
for thatched roofs and collected firewood, dug for potatoes and planted
maize beans. Our blouses were filthy. We washed clothes. We would

walk from place to place and find other groups of rebels in deserted villages or sleeping in dry riverbeds.

Some days were worse than others. You walked past children sleeping on the ground then saw they were not sleeping, they were dead.

The rebels had many rules. There were certain rocks you must not step on. No farming on Fridays. You could not eat pig, but could eat warthog which others might say is a kind of pig. Some fish was okay, if it had scales, like mudfish. But eat lazy fish and you become lazy. No pigeon was allowed, or gazelle. They once ate gazelle till the time Kony was detained in Khartoum and a gazelle was sacrificed to cause his release. After that, gazelles must be respected.

Rebels were not to eat with strangers. The Greeks we studied in school believed the opposite. Sister Alba showed us that welcoming strangers was the sign of an advanced civilization. The rebels were not an advanced civilization.

They prayed many times a day. First you must set down your gun. Sometimes they prayed with a rosary, other times bowing to Mecca. Before a battle you must prepare. You would not eat that day. They clapped and sang. One time an angel instructed Kony that rebels must not sleep with a woman before battle, but this was not always observed. You would draw a cross in oil on your forehead and chest and shoulders and also on your gun. The Holy Spirit in the oil protected you. If you had not offended the Holy Spirit then you would not be killed in battle, otherwise you would be. Clean water flicked from a stick onto the path in front of you was also protection; it would drown the bullet coming. Or a stone sewn inside cloth worn around your wrist would also stop a bullet. The bracelet turned you into a mountain, so the person shooting saw a mountain, and how could he harm that mountain? If you wore a cross on a necklace you would remove it and place it around your wrist to grip during battle.

Orders came from Kony. Destroy all the white chickens. He had twenty of his own soldiers killed by firing squad because he said they had killed innocent people. It was not explained how those people were more innocent than others killed. He also killed soldiers who slept with someone else's wife or men sleeping with other men. One rebel died for practicing witchcraft. If you died in battle it was because you had broken a rule. If you were shot in the penis it was because you had sex on duty; in the stomach, you had eaten in the wrong order.

Some children believed what they told us. Some of us became rebels. When you were given a gun you started to kill and after a while you would look at yourself and say, I am a rebel now.

Here at Kiryandongo the children are still cruel. We often have bad behavior. Girls and boys are always fighting, so it is fortunate we no longer have guns. The boys are perhaps more cruel. The rebels got us in the habit of cruelty. We may be grateful and wish to leave cruelty back in the bush, but it is not so easy. They gave us the habit of hate.

I noticed then how maybe I was becoming hard. You watch a rebel in battle use a boy as a shield, with a rope around his neck to keep him from crying out, and after seeing such things your heart changes. The heart turns to the side and looks away.

In the bush it was not always easy to remember people might be full of love. If you were stubborn you could hold on to the view. My mother said I was a root hard to yank, so being stubborn perhaps helped me in this case. I would think of home and what was good there. I would sit in my father's lap with my sisters, smelling the beer in his mouth. I would think of Philip and what swam through me when his skin touched my skin. Those things existed in the world even if they were not before me.

I had odd thoughts. I have not seen a curtain in a year. I have not had ice cream or worn a belt. I have not done my homework or sat at a table. I have not hugged my mother or father.

Slivers could take me away. I would sit with my knees on the kitchen table while my mother cooked at the stove. Is there not work you could be doing? she says. She wants me to be like her, always doing something. I like doing nothing. There is our yellow table, the smell of rice boiling. No one else around and I have my mother to myself.

I held these twigs in my hand. If I did not, a cloud would fill my head and I would feel lost. I would say to myself, Remember those good things.

Some people call those twigs God. The rebels did many things in the name of God, but I did not see that God of theirs. I saw only my twigs.

There was a tree by our house in Lira I used to climb. The bark was smooth with scars where it split and grew back. I would lie on the thick branch like a cheetah and in rain the roof of leaves kept me dry. Before falling asleep with the rebels I might imagine that the leaves I heard rustling in the bush were instead the leaves of my tree and would feel the same way I had at home.

Each month we would receive haircuts. We sat on stumps and were shaved with an electric shaver. Closing my eyes I pretended it was my mother's hands on my head and would receive the feeling of being cared about. But sometimes thinking about what you no longer have would not help. A sharp pain told you, Think of something else, not so important. You said to yourself, For now this is the life I anyway have. You thought instead of a folded skirt your mother left for you on your bed. So that is okay. You thought of music class at St. Mary's, when birds flew in the windows and how everyone would sing loud near the end.

Philip I waited to think of at night. I would think of his arms. I would think of him pushing me over swimming in the river. I would think of him saying, You are the right size, and the feeling near my soul which I got only from his voice. I'd think of kissing.

You can love a person right away from seeing him. This happened with Philip. I saw him and my body immediately felt it was so. Louise and I were passing by a group sitting on the veranda outside the grocery, and there was a boy I didn't know with wide shoulders and his T-shirt hanging loose. When we came near he looked at me, with his chin held up and eyes sort of sly. I looked away, shocked. I felt I had run up a hill and was not at all tired. We stopped with the group and I looked everywhere but toward him. Why does a person do that? Soon he was standing beside me. He said, I have met you before. It is not so, I said. Yes, you had ribbons coming off your hair just here, he told me, and touched my head. It was not me, I said, but he was describing a hair band I once had. Philip noticed these small things, and noticed them in girls. That is the good news and the bad news.

Sometimes he would laugh out loud for no reason. What is it? a person would say.

You, he says. You are funny.

I know some things about myself and one is that I am not so funny. But to Philip I was.

Even if I liked Philip soon I was finding things about him which might bother a person. For instance, he talked with his face very close to other girls, smiling and finding them funny also. I was not being jealous. I was just thinking, Why does he have to be so close?

And he does not come when he says he will. He will only do what pleases himself. Once, I was plucking a chicken while he sat beside me and I asked him why he did not help me and he said, I am happier watching you and your fingers moving.

There was the time we parted when Philip went with Jessica. When it happened my body felt split down the middle by a claw. I cannot tell you what pain spread through me. You must feel it yourself to understand such hurt in your heart.

When I heard the news is frozen for me like a painting. It was after English before geography on Monday morning and I was crossing the grass. I remember which trees were in the shade and seeing Janet and Agnes and Louise coming from the sisters' building. Esther, Louise said, walking up, her notebook over her chest. The hem of her uniform was far above her knees, because she was growing faster than her clothes. Philip was here yesterday.

Yesterday was Sunday, and I had been with Louise and Agnes, and she knew we had not seen Philip. No, I did not see him.

I did, Janet said. She did not like saying this.

Tell her, Louise said.

I saw him go with Jessica.

Jessica? I said, not believing it, but my body believed it.

For a long time just the word Jessica was that claw splitting me. Then I learned if you love a boy you are no longer free. The boy may become more important than your own self and if it is so, you will find trouble there. The first time you are hurt in your heart, you do not forget the lesson. It stays forever.

When Philip went with Jessica I had to ask why it was so. I saw she was a happy girl. She wasn't always asking, Why do you say this? Why do you do that? Maybe he did not like those questions from me. I asked because I wanted to understand him. Maybe I wanted him to understand me also. Maybe I did not smile a lot. Maybe I did not feel like smiling all the time. People smile sometimes for no reason. I save smiling for when I feel like it, okay?

When Philip joked with me I liked it and I got the feeling he was tipping me over onto a bed of feathers. Do not be so serious, Esther, he said. Your face will freeze that way. When he came back, it was after I had stopped hoping for it. We sat in the garden and I knew why he had come but I still had the hurt.

I know you are mad, he said. He was not joking for a change. But I want to come back with you. I do not know why I went with her.

You just want to come back because I am the one beside you now.

No, Esther. You are the one.

I kept my face hard.

Esther. Do not be this way.

You used to like the way I am.

I still do. He tried to touch my hand.

Stop.

All right. But I will come back tomorrow. Maybe you will want to hear this tomorrow. He threw a stone at a chicken.

My friends say, why should I even let you in the door?

He nodded, his head between his shoulders showing his long neck and the muscle like a smooth trench. But here you are, outside the door talking with me, he said, about to laugh with his eyes squinting, and the old thing happened. I looked away.

Esther. He pretended he was staggering around while still sitting beside me. But I was the one falling over. I was falling back into that pile of feathers.

What you did with her, I said, I do not want to know it.

So I was with him again, and my feelings had sadness in them which they did not have before.

For no reason I will get dizzy. It happened in the bush and still happens here at camp. Bright spots and dark spots appear in the air close to my face. In the bush this was dangerous. If you were walking you might fall. You hoped someone would catch you then. We helped each other. Now I wake in the night, the ceiling is spinning.

Last night my mother appeared to me in my bed. Her face looked down at me from a ripped-out corner of the roof. Her face was calm, but my heart beat with wildness to see her. I was frightened.

Today I got my blood test back. I do not have the virus. I think that is why my mother appeared, to offer me this news.

In the bush I sometimes dreamed I was at home, then waking up would make home disappear.

Here in the camp girls wake screaming.

V

It Is Possible

10 / At St. Mary's

ON THE DRIVE to Aboke, Grace reported the rebels had attacked a grocery nearby in Atipe and there were three abductions.

How do you get this news with no phone lines? Don said, hungover, with pink eyes.

Grace shrugged. One hears it.

A dented van packed with bodies careened past them, its back doors swinging open, and people hanging off.

This past Christmas, Grace said, here on the Lira-Gulu Road, a woman was shot riding one of those matatus. She was on the luggage rack and just flew up and was dead before she hit the ground. You can tell a dead body even flying through the air.

Pierre, sitting next to her, gazed at her with admiration. Her face was calm, curls blowing around.

They drove in the hot morning. The road narrowed to dirt and Grace directed them over a rickety bridge of bleached boards warped with gaps. They proceeded slowly, fearing collapse. Children wading nearby in the rushes spotted them and came splashing over. Their hands reached up to the windows.

Behave, Grace said. When they spotted her inside, they backed off.

After a field of sunflowers they turned onto a driveway that crossed a large unplanted field of fried grass toward a stucco wall hiding half of a church painted in an Italian Mannerist style, chalky pink and yellow and green.

A white-haired mzee opened iron gates and they entered a sort of Eden of high leafy trees and purple bougainvillea spilling from roof eaves. Flower beds encircled tree trunks and hanging pots of fuchsia dotted a turquoise veranda with crimson trim. Four nuns in wimples and dressed in pale blue nurselike uniforms stood on the porch.

Greetings came in English, Italian and Swahili. The guests were invited inside for lunch. A soldier, gun strapped across his back, strolled by, crunching the white gravel path, ignoring the people and being ignored.

A long table stretched from the entranceway to an inner courtyard where an enormous sunken garden was laid out in square beds of flowers and vines and rows of lettuce. The table was crowded with dishes of food the nuns had prepared themselves: meatloaf, macaroni, chicken, potato salad, corn, green beans, rice, stewed tomatoes. All the vegetables had come from their garden, they said, even the coffee beans. Jane scribbled notes, every detail important.

They sat and said grace and passed the bowls.

Grace had known the sisters for a long time; she had gone to St. Mary's herself. There were no rebels then.

They are not too far from us today, said one sister with the long face of a primitive Madonna carved in wood. Her name was Sister Fiamma. They are looking for food and people.

Jane's attention was half taken by the silent Sister Giulia. She was the size of a small boy, with wide-set eyes behind large peach-rimmed glasses. Her wimple was tucked over her ears and she ate and listened with an open expression.

Sister Rosario, a hefty woman with a no-nonsense air, was talking about a local boy: He was seven when the rebels took him. He is fifteen now.

The nuns nodded. Sister, it is possible.

They talked about the night of the abduction.

There was a path beaten across the grass, Sister Alba said. Robust, with red spots in her cheeks, she was the oldest nun, here fifty years. It went from the gate directly to the dormitory. They knew where they were going.

Don't you worry you're going to be attacked again? Don said.

The nuns looked at him with alarmed expressions.

We have soldiers now. Sister Rosario squared her shoulders.

We did not always do anything before, Sister Giulia spoke finally. Before this we were afraid to talk. She had a hushed voice, full of wonder. The visitors all looked at her, waiting for more, but nothing came.

We thought it would hurt the girls to speak, Sister Alba said. Then we decided we must speak.

Now we will not stop, said Sister Giulia. She spooned yogurt from a small bowl.

I admire your strength, Lana said.

Is it strength? Grace said with an impatient look.

On top of this you have your own personal problems, Pierre said.

No, Sister Alba said. I have no personal problems. The people's problems are my only problems.

They talked about going to meet the rebels in Sudan.

Sister Rosario had some discomfort on the flight, Sister Giulia said, smiling.

Yes. Sister Rosario agreed to smile, but it was conceding. We were to land in Khartoum, but near our destination the pilot said it was not possible.

Tell the reason, Sister Giulia said, still smiling.

He was told it was too sunny. The nuns all chuckled.

After lunch Pierre set his tripod up under a towering camellia tree in the middle of the quadrangle. At the other end of the yard students in blue and white uniforms crossed in and out of fig trees near the school building, going to class. Nearby a platform used for sifting maize was watched over by a painted plaster Virgin Mary.

Three girls were brought to them. They slid down in curtsies and extended their soft hands. Sharon, Beatrice and Theresa sat in chairs set up side by side, hands in laps, mouths closed, unsmiling. They wore clean T-shirts, two white, one light blue. Their hair was in the style of nearly all the girls, cut close to the scalp. Sharon wore pearl earrings. She'd been with the rebels for a year. Beatrice and Theresa had escaped together after a month.

Lana leaned forward and took a thistle off Beatrice's shirtsleeve, smiling. Beatrice flinched, then tried a smile. Jane sat on a low stool in front of them. She told the girls they were interested to hear their stories. Don stood towering in his crisp jeans, arms crossed, waiting to see what to make of it all. But even he seemed to be under the spell offered by a set-up camera.

Film offered the promise of permanence. This light, these words, these shadows, would all be preserved. The day would end, the season change, the tree topple, the people here grow old and die, but their images and the stories they told on this afternoon would last, as long as the images stayed recorded. Harry sat on the ground, slumped against the trunk of the tree, hat brim over his eyes.

Pierre nodded he was ready and pressed the red button.

The girls kept very still as they talked. They didn't move their arms, they barely moved their faces, only their mouths moved. A camera aimed at you can turn you back on yourself. Their voices were very soft. Did they seem especially gentle in contrast to what they were saying? No, people here spoke with a sweet softness.

They described the night of the abduction. *For us we hide under our beds.* When one girl was speaking the other two looked off, not glancing at the one speaking. The sun dappled the grass in shadow. Now and then a soft wind pushed the air. Jane asked about their escapes. *In the day it is not possible to run. It is only possible at night or if you make your toilet. Some try then. Some make it, some do not.*

Then the girls grew more relaxed. A forehead was scratched, a shoulder hugged an ear. They began to nod to one another. Suddenly an eager

look brightened their faces, surprised by something said not acknowl-
edged before, something they too had felt.

After her kidnapping, said Sharon, her left arm became paralyzed.
Even if I could lift it, it would fall like so. She hoisted her arm with one
hand, then let it drop like a sack.

Don had moved to a chair nearby and sat with a deep frown, watching his sneakers, glancing now and then at the girls, almost suspiciously.
Harry was close enough to hear the girls, but was he listening? Jane
couldn't tell. Pierre stood bent at the tripod, sweat on his face.

Jane had put her sunglasses in the collar of her T-shirt, not wanting to
hide her eyes from the girls. She gazed at them, listening. Even absorbed,
she had a voice inside murmuring, *You do not know what it is to be pulled
from your house in the middle of the night, what it is to be marched through
the bush with blistered feet, to see babies thrown against trees, you've not had
a daughter taken from you, you've not even had a daughter* . . . and another,
continuous voice at the bottom of her mind like subtitles: *Why did this
happen to them and not me?*

Soon the girls were relaxed and interrupting each other. *In some villages, they do not want the children back . . . so then where are we to go? My
family would take me back. I am fortunate.*

Fortunate, thought Jane.

By the time the girls got to the end they were hitting at each other and
laughing, the white people before them looking pale and shattered.

The sisters and Grace stood on the veranda, near the parked truck.
Jane felt a strong urge to be alone and offhandedly mentioned that she
wanted to check out the classrooms before they left and started across the
quadrangle. One of the sisters moved forward to accompany her, but Jane
waved her off—No, no, just a quick look, please don't bother. She was not
ducking out gracefully, but there you go. She needed to get away. Or get
closer, or something. Maybe one was less likely to notice a quick getaway.
Quick getaways were a specialty of Jane's. You had to be sure not to look
at those you left, or you'd see how badly you had done it. She strode across
the springy grass, to relief in the silence.

The stories told by the girls were engulfing her. She was filled to the brim with the images. Other realities exist, she told herself, but at the moment, this one of rape and killing and looting was crowding them out. Why was horror more vivid than tranquillity? Other realities were layers away, like overlapping screens, located far off, somewhere on the other side of the bridge at Karuma Falls. Even the soft air fanning her damp neck was a layer away from where she really was. What was the line? To learn of another's suffering is to confront one's own shame.

She came into the shade of a line of fig trees and arrived at the one-story building. The students were gone, the school day was over. Classrooms here were lined up one after another, with open doorways, to interiors painted half blue and half white. She walked into one and saw empty desks with attached chairs, while in her mind's eye she saw machetes slicing into skulls and men kicking children with their boots. One minute, these girls had been sitting at these desks, curious, bored, and the next minute in a hut under a man raping them. Children . . . The high windows on the other side of the classroom framed yellow and green foliage outside. She thought how far removed it was here from cities or seaside towns or suburbs. Those were the places one conjured when picturing normal life.

She noticed without really seeing them leaves scattered under desks, blown in the window.

She thought of news and of TV, where these things were supposed to be reported, and how no one wanted to see such things and no one wanted to show it and certainly nothing she had learned before had conveyed this hell as vividly to her as it had been by these three girls. Even that view was one step removed. She had only heard a story.

Jane?

She jumped. A hand touched her arm.

Hey.

She turned. We've been calling you.

Harry's face had its own reality. I just— she began. Those girls—

I know.

He turned her around, steering her like a child, out of the classroom.

I was just thinking, she said.

You should stop that, he said. Come. Time to get out of here.

She walked beside him across the rectangle of grass. Above the white truck where everyone was waiting was a wide ruffle of purple bougain-villea like a low cloud.

It's so pretty here, she said.

They were intersecting the path made by the rebels to the dormitory. She did not say what she was thinking: How am I ever going to get out of here now?

They drove back to Lira in the dusty light. No one spoke.

By the time they arrived at the roundabout at the bottom of Main Street darkness had fallen. Streetlights lit the red and orange flower beds arranged like frozen-food trays. In the town a few lights wavered in the darkness. Grace wanted to be let out here to walk home. Jane got out of the truck to say goodbye. The next day they were headed farther north, to Gulu and the rehabilitation camps.

At Kiryandongo, Grace said, You will find St. Mary's girls also there. This one, Esther Akello, is returned just now. You see her. She is a friend of Louise.

Jane said she would.

God bless you on your way, said Grace Dollo.

Jane had the feeling in that moment she'd been there before, in a dream on that red dirt road beneath the streetlight. The women kissed one another goodbye.

No matter how vivid, the first impressions vanished if you did not write them down. Jane had learned not to trust anything left on its own to last. She could look back to a journal years old and find that, not only did she not remember writing it, but she would not even remember what it was she was describing. She sat in the back courtyard of the Lira Hotel near the one outdoor light, her back against the concrete wall, writing.

After their short dinner Lana had said she was going to bed. Don and Pierre both gazed after her as she walked off with long strides.

Harry appeared, carrying an oversized beer bottle. He sat a step down in front of Jane and leaned against her, so her legs were straddling him. They faced the white pebble path.

They handed the bottle back and forth and spoke of the girls.

I don't need to hear the details, Harry said. You get the idea pretty fast.

But it's important to know. Isn't it?

It's important to try to stop it. No one needs to be convinced of that.

But it isn't being stopped. Her arms were around his shoulders and she felt the swell of his back. People should know about it.

I never liked *should,* he said.

If they know about it, they will be moved to do something.

Have you ever considered turning some of the attention you give to others to yourself? Harry said.

Jane laughed. No. Much easier to stick up for other people.

Children have no economic value, Harry said. African children even less. This has been going on for, what, ten, fifteen years? And who has noticed? She could feel his voice through his back vibrating in her chest.

It's important to speak for the children.

Yup, Harry said. He finished the last swallow of beer. I hear their stories and feel bad. How does it help them if my head is filled with horrible images?

It helps them if you listen, she said.

But I just want to block it out, he said.

I would like to be able to blocks things out, Jane said. Did you know that it's a myth that trauma victims block things out? It's actually the opposite of what happens. It remains engraved.

You do, said Harry.

What?

Block things out.

I do?

I watch you go away when you're right here.

Really? she said. Sometimes she felt any other version of life would be preferable to the one she had. It's hard here, she said.

You expect something different?

No.

People here have luck against them, he said. You can't lend people luck.

You can try.

Trying is good, he said. He took her hands off his shoulders and stood up. I'm going to bed.

I'm going to write down a few more things.

You do that.

Some time later, she returned to a dark room. The bathroom light threw a white stripe to the corner where Harry's body lay on its side in one of the beds, motionless, a band of light curved up over his shoulder.

She switched off the light and got into the bed opposite. She lay on her back and against her closed eyes saw the faces of the girls, the frowns creasing their smooth foreheads, their demure eyes at one moment, drooping with heavy lids, then the next moment lifted, with a bright shine in them of something good, of relief. She heard their soft voices speaking of unspeakable things. Tears leaked down her temples. She would never forget them, she thought, then immediately wondered how long it would be before she did.

In the middle of the night she woke to sharp snapping sounds outside. Harry stirred in the other bed.

You awake? she said.

Yes, came his voice out of the black.

What was that?

Gunshots, sounded like.

Were they close?

Not too.

They sounded sort of close.

Well, they've stopped now. They both listened. After a moment, he said, What are you doing over there?

Sleeping.

You should be over here.

I should?

Yes.

She felt her way over in the dark. He was nearer than she thought.

11 / Was God in Sudan?

IT TOOK DAYS of walking to get to Sudan. We traveled in a small group, about fifty of us. The rebels were about twenty. Most of the girls of St. Mary's were with us. I walked by Louise. Agnes, she was near Charlotte. One boy with us, very thin, died on the way. You think by then you would be accustomed to long journeys but we never got accustomed to it. We filled the splits in our feet with mud then walked then filled the splits again.

At night we collected leaves to sleep on. Sleeping, the girls stayed close. In the morning before opening your eyes, you might hear a rooster and be sure that the walls of your room were around you with your cross on the wall and your jacket on the hook and then opening your eyes had a moment before you understood the ceiling above you was branches and white sky and leaves like shriveled paper. Then you would remember: I am in this other life.

One day we passed through my grandmother's village. The rebels did not know I knew this village. Fortunately we did not stop there.

You are thinking about home when you are crying.

In Sudan we stayed in a riverbed. A trickling stream ran through it, enough for doing washing. One day I was draping bedclothes on a bush when a rebel came to me. He had on a brown wool hat covering a puff of hair and wore a blue shirt with white stripes on the shoulders. He was not so tall, only a little taller than me. He did not carry with him a gun, there were other rebels nearby with guns.

There are thorns on this bush, he said. You will make holes.

My mother uses this bush at home, I said quietly. The points are not so sharp but keep the washing from blowing away.

Even so, I began to take the sheet off. Speaking of my mother brought her near me then made me feel how far from me she was.

This rebel had eyes wide apart and a round forehead. He looked at me. All right, you leave it there. He kept looking. You are thinking of your mother now, he said.

You are never certain if it is okay to answer. I lifted my shoulders a little.

He shook his head, smiling as if I know nothing. But she is not your mother anymore.

I looked to see how he was meaning it. His forehead slanted to his hair. You have a new family now, he said. Kony's family. Your mother does not want you. He said this as if this were good news. She no longer wants a daughter who has been with the rebels. But Kony will always take you into his family. He will always forgive you.

I knew my mother loved me, but it is true she did not know what I had done. What if he was right?

Do you know Kony? the rebel said.

I have not seen him.

Kony is very wise. He crossed himself on each shoulder and waited for me to say something.

I have heard it, I said. We heard many things, that Kony had three spirits in him, that he could not die. That he had eighteen wives. Perhaps my face did not look convinced.

You do not believe in Kony?

I said I did.

Kony is very handsome, he said. Kony will lead us to heaven.

He told me to go back to washing, and when he left I had that dizzy feeling. I knew my mother loved me. Even when we might fight, even when she did not understand me, I knew there was love. I did not believe this rebel in the striped shirt, but he was making me think of my mother turned against me. Even not believing something can make small rips in you. With the rebels I thought there was not more to be ripped in me, but there was. There always is more if you are living. That my mother would not want me was a new worry I had not imagined I would ever have.

We were told Kony wanted to meet the girls from St. Mary's so we were gathered together. By now not all of us were together. We had been separated a few times and now some had come together again, but not all were in Sudan. Janet was not with us, and for a long time we had no news. Theresa was not there or Beatrice. We learned they had escaped but were never certain if they were alive. We found Judith again. She wore a dark T-shirt with a torn collar, and around her waist I saw she now had Sister Giulia's sweater. The scar in her neck was healed, but now there was a bandage on her hand. We laughed how she always had a bandage. So this is what we would laugh at—bandages and being hurt. Charlotte, however, was not laughing. She had new unhappy eyes.

They took us to Kony. His compound was in a place with trees of soft thin shadows. Guards in camouflage pants stood by the doorway of the biggest house, with new thatch on the roof. We stood outside for a while, then a few of us at a time were taken inside.

I went in with Agnes, Judith, Charlotte and Lily. Our eyes adjusted to the dimness and we saw a man in a white cowboy hat sitting on a canvas folding chair. Women sat on the ground nearby and rebels stood behind with guns and machetes in leather holders. The man in the chair I recognized, he was the one in the striped shirt who had spoken to me by the river, the one who said Kony is very handsome. This was Kony, this small man not at all big. His hair this time was to his shoulders with many thin braids and over the wide-set eyes were yellow aviator sunglasses. Come in, he said.

More girls entered till we were all there. Louise was behind us.

Come near, he said. We moved. So these are the girls of St. Mary's, he said, tipping back his head to observe us through those yellow glasses. Do you know the Pope is talking about you?

We had heard this, but did not answer. The rebels did not really want you to speak.

What would make you so special for the Pope to know of you? Kony looked at the guards and the women near him. He had a sort of bulge above his eyes. They shook their heads. Special treatment was bad according to the rebels.

Do we treat you badly? he said to us.

This we did not answer either.

No, he said. We treat you well. We have brought you here because it is the will of God. I am only following the will of God. Who would hear God's words and not follow them?

Kony told us we were not captives here. No, we belonged here because we had sin in us. God sent his sinners to Kony and his mission was to cleanse us. He told us how he would save us, told us about the will of God. The women near him dipped their heads.

Then he said, Those who escape are like women with two vaginas, one in front and one in back. From the back, the wife of one man. From the front, the wife of another.

My eyes got used to the darkness and I could make out the shapes of cages against the walls. They had animals in them. I saw chameleons and snakes. Other animals hung on the walls, dead. I saw a couple of turtles on the floor but could not tell if they were alive or not.

You must listen to what Kony says to you and remember it. You are to be my ministers. He changed to speaking in Lor.

How old are you? He pointed to Charlotte in front of him.

Fourteen, she said, keeping her head down. She had a gap in her teeth which made her lisp.

How are you treated? he said. His voice louder.

Charlotte's eyes shifted side to side. I am treated well.

Kony nodded and stood up from his low chair. And you? He stepped near Judith. How are you treated? He pointed to the bandage on her hand as if to show she was looked after.

I am treated well, Judith said in a hoarse voice.

Kony walked along the line of us. He stopped at me.

Kony has seen this one before, he said. What is your name?

I told him it was Marie.

I felt the girls beside me flinch, hearing the lie, but they knew not to show anything.

One of the guards said, They call her Esther.

Which is your name? Kony did smile.

Esther Marie, I said. Marie was never my name, but it helped to have a lie against Kony.

Kony remembers your face, he said, proud, but he did not remember from when. Do you know Kony?

I know you are Kony.

Perhaps it was in another life, he said. He looked at Agnes beside me. You are?

Agnes.

He looked at Agnes a longer time. He looked to her feet and again to her face. Agnes had nice legs and nice skin.

This one, he said, pointing to her and turning around to the soldiers. Bring tonight, he said. He sat down again. Agnes's face did not move, but I saw the fear in her tight mouth. Her gaze slid in my direction.

This is my friend, I said. Somehow I dared to speak.

Kony turned around. Did you say something, Esther Marie? He showed us he remembered my name, even though it was not my real one.

In another life we were sisters, I said. Maybe you knew us then. We would stay with you.

His look was of interest. No one comes except when invited by Kony, he said with a warning voice. This is a rule. Perhaps you did not know this rule.

I shook my head a small bit.

But maybe you will come too. He set his hands on the arms of his chair. You will come if I wish it.

Two soldiers came for Agnes. I saw them make her stand up. They were looking around. I waited. When they spotted me they indicated that I also was to come as well.

It was a different hut that we were brought to then that night, a smaller one. Kerosene lamps sat on the floor on polished dirt of the first room and in the next room Kony was sitting on a mattress on the ground. There was a mirror on the wall, and a flashlight sat on a stump. Kony did not have a hat on and his head looked big on a small body like Howdy Doody. I cannot say I was not scared, but I was there for Agnes and it is easier to be brave when you are doing it for someone besides yourself.

Come this way, he said. Out of the past life into this one. Soon when we are dead we will be in another life. I know I will die. If I don't die I am not the son of God. God created me just as he created death.

So it was how Kony spoke.

Sit here. Do you know that when you are chosen by Kony you are lucky. Kony sees women because women are the bearers of his children.

I thought how luck was the same thing as being special and how no one was supposed to be special, but I did not argue this.

Women are also the portals of the devil, he said. He put his hands on the chest of Agnes. They are one way facing this direction—he felt her chest on one side—and another way facing another. He moved her that way. Agnes looked not at him. For this reason we must watch the women as they move among us, he said, staring all over her body.

He kept one hand on Agnes, then looked at me. He touched my arm and made a circle with his fingers and ran it down to my wrist. I see you have a bracelet, he said.

I did not speak. My nonni had given it to me, the last thing I owned. It was a silver band with a space for putting on and taking off.

See, we do not take your bracelet from you. He moved my hand, smiling at how kind he was and put it onto his lap. He looked at Agnes. Take off your skirt.

I floated up. I hardly knew I was being laid down. I didn't feel anything touching my mouth, I didn't feel hands pushing. Agnes and I looked at each other's eyes just one time, not to see what was happening, but to say, I am here. Do not worry. Then we looked away to be respectful.

Sometimes we heard jackals in the night and now and then saw a wild boar traveling by with his family, all their tails up at an angle. But there were not many animals among us. We would find a rabbit some-times, a few birds hiding in the trees. There were more animals in Kony's house than in the bush.

It turned out I could shoot. We were given guns for practice and I would hit that can in the middle many times. One time before practice we saw a dik-dik darting through the trees. We did not see them often, small gazelle-like animals with pale fur and pale spots. The rebels said if I could shoot that dik-dik I would go free. I did not believe it, but I would try anyway. I like all animals and do not like to see them die. I do not kill spiders. Maybe I would not care about a grub worm, but that is all. I shot and missed and then I shot and hit that dik-dik. The rebels laughed, everyone was surprised. They said, Maybe this girl is useful.

Girls are not often given guns to carry but after that I was taken back into Uganda when they went on raids. I thought about not shooting so well, so they would not take me, then I had the idea that it might offer me the chance to escape. So I kept shooting.

One raid brought us again near the village of Gwere. This was the village of my grandmother, my father's family. We were walking, getting closer and closer to this area I knew from visiting. My family was nearby. My grandparents were there, my two aunts, my cousins. Please, I prayed, don't let us find the village. Protect my family. I thought of my cousin Caleb, who would sit with piles of chips growing between his feet carving wooden spoons and animals which he sold in the market.

We crossed the main road and all was quiet there. Everyone must be hiding, I hoped. At the bus stop by a concrete slab there was no one. Good, they have heard we are coming. I did not show I knew this place. I asked a guard, Where are we going? Would I have said such a thing at another time? No. He hit my shoulder with his gun. That blow made me feel safe.

We crossed the field where I played with my cousins. On one side are three rocks where we used to make a house and shred flowers for petal soup. I saw Caleb kiss a girl there. We came near huts out of sight belong-ing to neighbors where I had spent days and nights. My aunt Anastasia's hut was farther along after the village. The rebels would go on and off the path and soon they turned off again, walking through thick growth to another footpath where they chose to stay walking. This narrow path was the one to my aunt's.

I saw objects littered in the grass. A plastic bracelet snapped open, the bottom rubber of a sneaker, a cardboard cereal box dotted with gray mold. Then came burnt things: a blackened soda can, a plastic fork with melted prongs, a pink towel singed with a hard foamy edge. I walked by eggshells full of ashes. A magazine was fanned open and stiff, as if dipped in black cement. The rebels at the front of the line must have come to the clearing because the walking stopped. Ahead were shouts and clapping. This meant we were about to raid. Would I see my family killed? Would I have to kill them?

We moved forward and I saw why there were no people anywhere. The huts were no longer. In their places were shallow burnt pits with all the ground black and straw like black wire.

My aunt's hut was farther on, not in sight. We turned away from that place and the rebels led us the other way, so I did not see if her house was still there. I supposed it was not. The rebels would burn dwellings when they were angry to find people gone. Maybe this had happened. Later I learned that my family had escaped and were safe, even if others had not been so fortunate.

Did God see where we were?
I wondered.
Did God see into Sudan? Louise said there was too much evil in the camps so God would not look at us anymore. What kind of God is that? I would wonder. Then I stopped wondering.

I tried instead to stay alive. I am alive now and can breathe and that is as much as I know. Why one person should die this day and another be permitted to live, who knows it? If I ask the questions now, I still do not have an answer.

If God was watching Sudan, then he was allowing for these things to be so. In that case, I say, God let us down. He forgot the children of the north. He forgot Tabitha, the girl from Arum, in the red ruffled shirt. She was even looking at the rebels without hate, you saw no hate in her eyes. And what happened to her? She was tied to a tree till the rope sank into her skin.

You see these things, and it is hard to think God is good.

Still I prayed. You get into the habit of praying. It comes when things are hard, so what can I tell you? At first I prayed to God, then soon I was praying not even to God, just to no one. It was just prayers going out to the air. I prayed for us girls to escape. I prayed to see my mother again, prayed to be able to fight again with my sisters, prayed to greet my father. I thought I would be happier this time when I saw him. I prayed to be with my Philip. I would think, please please please. That was a prayer.

And I had to start praying for Agnes. She was not always well and I worried she would become more sick. After a while I saw my prayers were not helping and I said to myself, I must do something. Then I remembered this man Chunga. And I had an idea of a thing I might do, more than just pray.

Chunga looked as mean as he was which is not always the case. Kony for instance did not appear mean in his looks, he appeared maybe he would be kind. But this Chunga had a face like a bulldog and short legs of muscles and dangerous red eyes. He carried anger in his shaking cheeks. He was with us sometimes, then would go with another group, but when he was there, he liked to stand over us with a bad look in his red eyes. He carried a gun wrapped around the handle with silver duct tape. You are not the type for me, he said, and kicked me a little with his dirty sneaker. But you I like, he said, and touched Lily's cheek. The commander Lily was wife to was not there at the time. Chunga pulled her to him. We looked to Louise, and when Louise made no sign we knew there was nothing to be done. So he took Lily off.

At these times you are relieved not to be picked. I say this because I know it is not right, even if you cannot help the feeling. You are glad it is not you. You are not proud of this, but so it is.

We think it was Chunga who gave Lily the AIDS. But who knows it. Chunga kept two rebels near him, one in a purple windbreaker with a fat nose, the other with a bony face and yellow beads around his neck. He would talk to them and we would listen to his big talk. He did not care if we were hearing. Who were we?

He said, If I have not seen blood in a while I get a headache. He grinned at us, with shining eyes. Maybe he was drunk. Even with the rule of no drinking, the rebels would be drunk in the day. Chunga said he was a better fighter than Kony. One day he said, Kony's time is over.

I was not the only one hearing him, others of us were listening also. You must not say anything against Kony, but Chunga did not believe any of us would repeat it. How would we have the chance to do it?

He said, I had a vision in *my* dream. Maybe Kony would like to hear how the spirits are now speaking to Chunga. Maybe he would like to hear what they are saying to me. He laughed, meaning it was bad news.

Kony never liked to hear if he was in someone's dreams. Only what happened in his own dreams he wanted to know. Once, another person gave Kony a prediction and after that, Kony was arrested in Khartoum from the bad luck.

We would hear Chunga speak this way against Kony. If Kony knew of it Chunga would not be alive. I saved the thought, and that thought came back to me when I was looking for it. I thought, I will try.

No one could meet with Kony unless he requested it, but I did not let this prevent me. Why would I want to go to Kony? One reason, for the sake of Agnes. Each time I returned after raids Agnes was more sick. Then this time her hair had become reddish straw, and on her face were scabs like fingerprints.

I am as selfish as anyone. But to think of Agnes I would not be thinking only of myself. Thinking of her I felt better. Thinking of her I had a mission. I went to the rebel named Ricky. He was not rude to the girls of St. Mary's and would talk with us when no one saw. He had been with the rebels a long time, but was only seventeen. I had asked him, Why do you take us from our families?

Kony wants a big family, he said. If you want your family big you must have many children. On a string around his neck Ricky carried a vial of water. In battles the water would tell you what to do.

What about your real family? Where is your mother?

His face did not move. My mother is dead.

I told him I wanted to see Kony.

He believed I was making a joke.

No. I have something important to tell him, I said.

What could you know of important things? He was taking a pebble out of his boot, but I saw he was listening.

Bring me and see. Maybe he will thank you for it.

He put on his boot. I don't know, he said.

After this for some days I would see Ricky near the fire or passing by while we dug roots. He said nothing. But other rebels were nearby. Once I was able to ask, Will you take me? He shrugged, but I saw his interest. The next time I had a chance I said, I see you are not able to go to Kony. He looked at me, then seemed to look inside himself. There was more interest in his eye.

Finally, while we were collecting firewood, he came to me. We will go to Kony, he announced.

Now?

When I say.

We didn't always know what day it was, but sometimes I would see the date on the watch of a rebel. I was surprised to find that more days had passed since our abduction than I would have guessed. Time was longer, not shorter.

Finally the day came and Ricky said, Now we go. Greg Lotti was away and this may have allowed for it. I walked in front of Ricky. He said, If this is a trick you will be sorry.

It is not a trick.

Anyone can say something and make it sound true. Saying it makes something exist which did not exist before. Once the words are said, it becomes real, whether true or not.

After a short walk of an hour we arrived to Rubanga Tek at another different hut. Children were pushing each other around outside and women nearby hit them. Ricky approached a guard. This girl wants to see Kony. The guard stared at him. He wore a brown football shirt with gold numbers.

I undestood then that Ricky had not arranged it. We were just coming in this way and it made me worried. The guard entered the hut. When he came out he went to talk with the women, forgetting us. We waited. The guard looked at us, not caring.

Finally, Ricky went again to him. Can we see Kony? he said.

Kony refuses to see you, the guard said. What? Does this girl belong to you?

Ricky frowned, as if he were concentrating on a serious matter, but I saw he was embarrassed. I had to think quickly.

I am returning this to Kony, I said. I slipped my bracelet from my wrist and held it out. So far I had kept this one thing of my past life.

The guard took it, knowing I was lying. He would take that bracelet perhaps for himself, who knows. He returned to the hut and we stood waiting. A shout came from the hut and Ricky looked at me with worried eyes. What would happen now?

You come, the guard said, his gold thirty-nine in the door.

He was not holding the bracelet. We entered the dim hut and waited for our eyes to adjust to the darkness to see the people there. Kony was the only one sitting on a chair. There were two guards holding guns and two officers with braid on their shirts, one with gray ruffled hair often with Kony. The women sat with children in their arms, Kony's children. I saw a St. Mary's girl there, Helen. She was holding a child. I did not show I knew her.

Who must see Kony?

She has said it, Ricky said, and stepped away from me, not to be blamed.

Seeing Kony's face again made my body split apart from me. He wore a baseball hat and beneath the brim I saw impatience in his face. I felt I would not succeed.

Kony remembers this one. You are one of the girls of Aboke. Again you invite yourself. A woman's vagina must be watched carefully or the devil will enter her.

The women nodded.

So you are having a child, he said and nodded, sure of it.

No, I said. I remembered his thin braids slapping my shoulder like tassels. I bent to my knee in front of him. I have danger to report to Kony.

Kony smiled all around, as if this was preposterous.

Go on.

A rebel is saying things against Kony. I spoke quietly, not looking at him.

Women leave now, he said. Those on the floor rose up and took the children away. Helen did not look at me. She was a girl I always liked but had never made friends with at school. She kept apart from most girls, but I admired her. At this moment I even had the thought of how I had missed my chance to be a friend of Helen.

Who is this man? Kony was no longer smiling.

The one they call Chunga. And I told him what I knew.

Kony turned to his commander with the gray hair. Do you know this Chunga?

The man nodded, looking at me. He is from Kotito.

What do we know of him?

Sometimes he is not right in the head, the commander said.

He is against Kony?

It is possible.

I looked at them now. I thought, Am I watching to see if I would have a man killed?

Bring this man Chunga to Kony, he said. Where is he?

The soldier whispered to the other officer, who was wearing a khaki shirt and had a narrow beard on his jaw. When the soldier stepped back, the officer said, He maybe is with Omona in Nebbi.

Can he not come from Nebbi, then? Kony said.

Yes.

Then he will.

This girl can go, Kony said. I hope you speak the truth.

May I have a blessing? I said.

He looked confused. Are you sick?

In Sudan there were many sick among us and we were sometimes given medicine. For diarrhea you were given dead water—stream water that has been boiled, so it is no longer alive—mixed with shea oil. You would take three sips for the Holy Trinity and get better. But this medicine did not help for the AIDS. Nothing would help but Kony's blessing. Maybe I did not believe it, but Agnes did.

It is for my friend, I said.

The rebels did not speak of AIDS. If you had AIDS they might let you escape. Or they would paint a white cross on you and if the cross fell off, it revealed that you were HIV positive. In this case you were to be bathed in a river, and if he was nearby Kony prayed over you. If he was not, a controller or technician would pray. As you left the river you were not to look back or you would not be cured.

Kony's head dropped back on his shoulders and his eyes rolled up. He made a strange gurgling sound. One knee was going up and down fast. Some people said Kony did not sleep. Some said he used drugs. When I looked at him I had the reminder of his wet mouth and other unpleasant things he did to the girl on the bed who was me. I looked away.

Finally he said, If you are right about this Chunga, Kony will bless your friend. Who is she?

One called Agnes.

He turned to the man with the narrow beard. Kony will remember this, he said. The man nodded, but he was watching me with unhelpful eyes.

We left that hut.

It was possible I was with child then, but how did he know it? In any case, it was to be the child of Greg Lotti.

Some days passed and we heard the news Chunga was dead. We heard that his lips were cut off, then he was executed by a firing squad.

Kony did not come to give Agnes a blessing. She was by now always lying down. She might stir the pot cooking over the fire, but was too weak for jobs in the bush. Then some time later Kony came to our camp, and when the sick ones were brought to the river Agnes was also brought. So he gave Agnes a blessing after all without knowing it. The river was like a sheet of tin, and the children were made to walk into it. Kony poured the water on Agnes out of a jerry can. It splashed on her three times.

A week later, a group going to Uganda decided that Agnes would travel with them. She should no longer be in Sudan. Agnes was crying, knowing she was too weak to make the journey. I told her she would be going in the direction of home and this was her chance to escape. Maybe they would let her go and she might be home at last. I told her she was lucky. She was even too weak to argue, she only cried.

The morning she left I gave her a kerchief and a water bottle. I am following after you soon, I whispered.

I watched Agnes go with the group straggling away. One girl we knew, Lisa, walked beside her, holding up her arm. Agnes looked back at me with an unhappy face. I could still see the old Agnes inside that face, but it did not show on the outside. Then she faced forward, walking. I tried to feel hopeful for her, but like everything with the rebels it had gone dull—the hope I mean. I was sorry she was leaving me. I worried she would not make it.

I waited for the chance that she might look back again, but I did not get that chance.

It was not long before it showed, that baby in me. My monthly bleeding had stopped for many months, but this happened in the bush with many of us girls. So when my stomach started to become wide as I was also becoming more thin, I had to believe it. Soon I felt the small feet pushing against me inside and had to ask myself, Do I hate this baby? Was it his fault his father was a rebel? I put my hands against the hard places pressing and whispered, Your one and only mother is here.

Still, I did not feel easy. I carried around this stomach. Sometimes pregnant girls also got released and sent back. What good was a girl who was pregnant? But we were to give Kony's family more children. Lotti made it as if he had the decision. I will not send Mummy home, he said.

I could sleep alone though. They stay away from you when you are pregnant. Once a rebel was walking close behind me, as if I were making an invitation to him. I was not, but he kept walking near and muttering things. When he stepped in front and saw my belly he moved away, no longer bothering me.

*

The rainy season is not yet here but it begins sometimes to rain. Last night the roof of our dormitory was drumming with the sound. On the top bunk I felt it near me, in my head. The sound of rain is a comforting sound. I remember at least when it seemed that way to me.

Turns out I have learned nothing.

VI

Refuge

12 / Hospitality in Lacor

GREEN BUSH SPREAD on either side of the road like rumpled fabric spread out to dry. The light was low and the red melted road deserted. At one point the white Toyota came to a fork and idled there, hesitating. Harry turned it onto the rough road, toward the north.

A figure appeared and they pulled over. An old man limped toward the driver's window, holding a gnarled stick with gnarled knuckles. Was this the right road to Gulu?

The man gazed at the road behind them and gazed at the road ahead. He stared at it for some time. At last he spoke in Swahili: When you reach Kanudini, after Aber . . . his voice trailed off. His bottom jaw swiveled, arranging the few teeth he had. Then—

Everyone in the truck waited, his voice was hoarse as a preacher's—Then you ask the people there.

They reached Gulu in early evening. The town was peaceful. An abandoned tank sunk into a dirt lot had children scrambling over it like a jungle gym.

They drove down an unpaved alley of towering eucalyptus smelling of mint. A boy walked toward them, herding a few goats with a stick.

Jane said, It's like a dream.

Above drooping leaves the evening sun was cracked in a marble sky.

It was a one-story house. In the open door stood a handsome man with silver hair. He wore a white shirt, khaki pants and work boots. He looked past the woman standing on his darkening doorstep, handing him a torn piece of napkin, to a white truck ticking quietly in his driveway scattered with pine needles. The passenger door was open and another woman with bracelets glinting on her upper arm had a long leg extended out of it.

He looked down at the bit of napkin. How many are you? he said. His Italian accent matched the dark skin and bluish shade around his eyes. I have no idea who wrote this note, but will assume it's someone I once knew.

Jane explained about their trip and said she hoped he might suggest a place to stay.

You can stay here tonight, he said. If you can assure me your being here will help the people, I won't turn you away. His manner was not insistent, but smooth and natural and perhaps fatigued. I have two guest rooms. The girls stay in one, the boys in the other. Where are you all from?

The passengers in the truck came straggling forward.

There's a pool in back, if you'd like a swim. Jane looked toward a dark stand of tangled trees amazed a pool lay there. I have work to do at the hospital. I eat dinner at seven if you would like to join me.

The man led them into a wide entranceway with a skylight above. The back of a low sofa with wooden arms sectioned off a living room holding other simple chairs. On the walls were framed silhouettes of African figures and carved totems of local art. The floors were wooden with small rugs. The house looked clean and unlived in.

Don had a call to make and followed the doctor back down the driveway to the high wall of the hospital complex they'd passed on their way in. Wish me luck getting through, Don said, and rolled his eyes at Jane, in case she wasn't aware of how far at the ends of the earth they were.

The pool was painted a black green and sat in a rectangle of concrete surrounded by uncut grass which could not be described as a lawn. With the trees hovering it was like being in a swimming hole in the woods.

Weird to be in a pool here, no? Jane said, treading water in the deep end.

A lot is weird here, Pierre said, looking happy.

The water felt wonderful and clean.

Shut up and enjoy it, for God's sakes, Lana said. It's heaven. She kicked hard and dove underwater and her arms pushed out fanlike into wide breaststrokes. She broke the surface, gulped for air then slid under again.

Harry sat at the edge with his feet dipped in. The high grass came to his shoulders.

Not coming in? Jane said.

Didn't bring my suit.

Neither did we.

The swimmers were all in their underwear. Jane did some brisk laps. Again Harry was the figure of restraint: swimming here was maybe inappropriate. She swam hard till her arms ached. She floated underwater where it was very peaceful. When she came up, Harry was no longer sitting and she just caught his figure disappearing around the corner of the house. With his departure the pool lost much of its allure.

In the shallow end Lana and Pierre had their arms around each other and were swishing in half-circles, whispering. Jane went under again and in the mute water remembered the nuns talking about another sister who'd recently had a heart attack: She just jumped a little and died. She went home. That's how they put it.

If only death were so gentle, Jane thought. She broke up through the surface.

Don stood above in silhouette. How's the goddamn water? he bellowed. Lana looked over, exposing her throat and smiling, staying draped around Pierre.

It's marvelous, she said. We're loving it.

*

Carlo Marciano's kitchen was small and beige with bare counters and a Formica table in the middle with two chairs, like a kitchenette in a motel. For Lacor, this was deluxe. A glass bowl with packets of sugar sat beside a coffeemaker. Lana suggested getting the rice out of the car, but Dr. Marciano, gracious and unsmiling, said he had a good supply of spaghetti if that would satisfy them, and filled a pot with water and set it on a burner. He took a head of lettuce out of the refrigerator and Lana took it as if she were a nurse at an operating table, knowing her job.

The doctor offered his guests water and took jelly glasses from the cabinet. He directed the men to get chairs from the dining room. Lana chopped the lettuce and sprinkled on oil and lemon. They ate on plastic plates the color of Band-Aids, elbow to elbow around the table.

The doctor answered questions about his life. He'd been in Lacor for over forty years now. He and his wife, Medka, also Italian and also a doctor, came in 1956. At the time, there was only one small clinic in Gulu. They ended up starting the hospital here, assisted by various NGOs, till it grew into the largest rural hospital of its kind in Northern Africa.

It has also served from time to time as a refugee camp, he said. As it does at the moment. Even with guests crowded at his table, he had the air of a man accustomed to eating alone and speaking little. He had no superfluous gestures or social tics. He was a man ruled by duty. Jane felt as if she were dining with Abraham Lincoln.

Ten years ago, he told them, his wife operated on a patient who'd been wounded in a battle. You see, there have always been conflicts here. They say it's a different war, but it's the same war. My wife was removing shrapnel; shrapnel is very hard to remove. During the operation she cut her finger on a sharp steel edge and became infected with AIDS. She died five years later.

The girls stared at the doctor's face.

We had to hide that she was sick, he said. If you are infected you are barred from practice. So we told no one. She was still performing operations just days before she died. Medka was a very good doctor.

The boys looked down at their empty plates.

I still think, he went on in an even tone, that she is behind me as I walk down the hallway. I think she's in the other room while I am making dinner. Then I remember.

There was silence. Dr. Marciano had a face of acceptance.

Lana's eyes were full of tears, but her voice was steady when she broke the silence. She finished the work she had to do, she said.

The doctor's mouth turned down as if to say, Perhaps.

They finished their spaghetti and did the dishes. Dr. Marciano cut slices of oranges and set them on a plate.

Hey, Harry said, lifting his glass of water. Cheers for letting us stay.

The only reason you are here is because I welcome the opportunity to entertain ladies, he said. He pushed back his chair, nearly bowing. Now I must go to bed.

Everyone stood and thanked him and after he left sat back down.

I need a drink, Lana whispered.

We have that wine in the truck.

I'll get it, Pierre said. He stood and trailed his hand over Lana's shoulders as he left.

That man is a saint, Jane said.

Pierre? Don looked disgusted.

No, you idiot, Lana said. Her voice had too much earth in it to sound harsh. Our doctor.

They all went outside and sat on a small wooden deck off the kitchen. Pierre pulled out the tab from the square carton and poured wine into paper cups. Harry refused a drink.

His wife, Jane said.

I know, Lana said. One dark painted toe pushed around the anklet on her leg.

Don was watching the toe. So what's the boy girl separation about? he said, sort of yawning.

Harry gave him a half-look and jumped off the porch to disappear in the dark garden.

You are not worrying about this, Pierre said.

Don, Lana said.

Jane remained quiet, having been thinking along the same lines and mortified to be aligned in any way with Don.

What's everyone so fucking touchy about? Don said.

*

Jane went down into the gathered darkness and found Harry on a bench swing suspended beneath a spreading tree by two thick ropes. Her feet kicked through papery leaves. Can I sit? she said.

He made a neutral noise in the back of his throat, gazing toward the Toyota in the driveway, as if at a ghostly sign that he would eventually get out of here. Jane had a familiar superfluous feeling.

We travel all the way here to fight with each other, he said.

I know. She sat beside him, feeling a wall between them. Longing to connect, she searched for something direct, but only managed a complaint. I do wish we could stay together, though.

His face jerked in her direction but he didn't look at her. There are other ways to be with a person, he said. Sex isn't the only one.

She felt it as a slap.

Look at us, he went on. People don't know how to get along with each other. He was picking apart a seed or a leaf, barely addressing her. No wonder there are wars. It's why I'd rather be on my own.

The alarm of his rejection vibrated through her body, rousing her. It was nearly refreshing it was so straightforward.

Aren't you a little young to decide that already? she said.

I'm older than all of you. Harry half smiled.

Must get lonely, she said.

It's always lonely. Either way.

A ball of fury gathered in her, with both pain and energy in it. She had the urge to argue him out of this. He had to believe people could save each other. If she could convince him of that, then he wouldn't have this power to cancel her out. It seemed crucial that he be on her side.

Harry looked up. Jane did, too. The sky showed between the scalloped trees. They're coming in, he said.

She saw clouds blowing, lit by a weak moon, blotting out tiny stars. The clouds?

The people. Hear them?

She heard wind. Then realized no leaves or trees were moving.

They must be coming in for the night.

Harry nudged her and stood. His touch with the back of his knuckle was quick and unthinking, but she was grateful for it. It meant, Follow me. *You. Follow me.* She did, behind him to a thin bank of trees that separated the doctor's property from the main road. Through spaces in the black leaves they could see a topaz light from the hospital gates and the topaz-colored road. Harry pushed forward, holding back branches for Jane. His arm near her filled her with a sharp longing. She wanted to give him something. No, she wanted him to give her something. But what and where? She scanned herself internally. In her body, of course. The longing seemed lodged there. But, as he'd just now pointed out, that wasn't the only way. The desire to keep him close, to be near his confidence was overwhelming.

There must be something the matter with her.

She followed him, feeling thoroughly unwelcome. His back was to her. She'd hardly even had him and already he was going. He was pretty nearly gone. She had expected it. Hell, she had probably engineered it.

Would he ever again lift her off the floor? Had he ever even done it? It seemed a vision now, hardly real. She wished to be back there, forever lifted, instead of being here now, with irritable people, in a world where steel shrapnel cut the fingers of good doctors and killed them.

Harry parted some saplings to reveal a crowd of figures moving quietly toward the hospital gates. There were hundreds of people. They carried bedrolls under arms or bundles balanced on heads. Children walked quickly, holding plastic bags. Jane felt a sort of vertigo. The people showed no outward signs of distress. In fact, funneling through the white gates at the entrance, they looked not unlike workers arriving for night shift at a factory, or a crowd heading into the stadium for a Saturday evening baseball game. It was a daily activity to vacate their villages to sleep in the safety of the hospital walls. The windy sound Jane heard was the sound of their feet, scores of bare feet and flip-flops and sneakers shuffling over the dirt.

They watched in silence. Abruptly Harry stepped around her. I'm turning in, he said, and little twigs sprung out poking her as he left and headed back to the house.

*

Jane's mattress was narrow and hard, made with a clean sheet and a thin blanket tucked in tight. Lana, on the other bed, was already asleep on her side, a still silhouette with a dip at the waist. Jane kicked her sheets down in the humid air.

She felt a tightness in her throat. She could still hear the rustling sound through the screen windows and the image of the upright figures casting long shadows in the gate's light made the ache in her throat suddenly burst and thin tears pour down her temples. Her breath was shallow and silent. She did not cry easily, she had not cried here till now. With these tears came an ominous alert to a further sadness it seemed she would never reach. At least she was feeling the top layer. Then the faces of the girls at St. Mary's came to her again—was that only yesterday?—in the chairs under the tree with their soft voices saying, *They beat him until he stopped moving* and nodding mildly, *That girl is dead now.* She imagined the girls tied in a line with rope, a young boy firing an automatic gun he could barely lift. Superimposed over all of it, or behind it, was the image of Harry sleeping, arms embracing a pillow, somewhere nearby in the house. Even thinking of these things, she could still be thinking of him. All thoughts, however, led at this hour of the night to the same conclusion: the world was a messed-up place and one was powerless to make it right and she, Jane, was just one more hopeless thing in it.

Then the image came of Dr. Marciano standing at his clean counter, shaking water from a tea bag before handing a cup to Lana. She pictured him in an examination room, focusing on a patient with his dutiful profile. She pictured him sitting in bed beside his wife, discussing something in the cool low tones of people with mutual respect, and her hot tears stopped and a trapdoor closed against the bottomless feeling.

She saw the wind blowing by Harry's arm in the car window and remembered, oddly, a moment in a short story by Chekhov when the narrator, traveling in a carriage, sees how life is after all truly beautiful and only painful when we forget, as he puts it, our human dignity and the higher aims of our existence. Her tears had loosened the strap across her throat and in its place was a band of warmth.

All was still. The rustling outside had stopped. She did not have peace of mind but some relief had descended over her, so exhaustion could take hold and sleep finally come.

The sun had not risen and the road was dark red. In the deep rosy light Jane felt as if she were still dreaming. She and Pierre had gotten up early to film the crowd departing.

The first few figures appeared between the pale columns of the gate. Maybe they wore a change of clothes, maybe they wore what they had slept in. Very soon more figures emerged, till a stream of people were kicking up a low cloud of dust, splitting in two directions, one toward town, the other to the bush. No one spoke; it was a silent departure. Now and then a rooster crowed. As the light came up, faces showed, some fresh and washed, some puffy with sleep. Some faces regarded Jane with suspicion, or curiosity. Most ignored her altogether. An old woman moved slowly, leaning on a young girl in a pinafore.

There were women in neat skirts carrying handbags, headed to jobs; a sideburned man, bare-chested, his yellow shirt flapping. A muscular man swung by on an aluminum crutch. Some boys threw stones, arching their backs as they dodged away. A thin woman in a long kanga balanced a mat on her head, and held the hands of two children. Girls in blue uniforms walked four abreast. A woman smacked a boy's head as he ran by, both continuing without expression.

The sky was light pink over the black bank of trees. When the sun appeared it threw long shadows behind the stragglers heading east to town. The air lightened, there was a cloudless sky and everyone was gone.

That was beautiful, Pierre said, lowering his camera.

And terrible.

Yes, terrible, too.

You want to see my mama? A boy of about nine or ten stood in front of Jane, thumb up as if hitching a ride. His black T-shirt fell off one shoulder and in white letters was printed *Bad to the Bone*.

Your mama? Where is she?

In my village.

Where's that?

Just here. He pointed beside them, to a field where the sun picked up stiff tufts of yellow hay and a narrow path wobbled through it.

Jane looked for Pierre. He was already coming forward, unsurprised. All right, she said.

They followed a path as thin and curving as a fat snake. Were you sleeping at the hospital? she asked him.

Yes, the boy said. We fear the rebels.

What's your name?

It is Jonathan.

After five minutes' walking through thin trees and low bush, Jane asked how far away it was.

Just here, he said.

Jane looked back at Pierre. Was he worried?

Motivated fellow, he said and shrugged.

After ten more minutes, We are close?

Just this way.

What is the name of your village?

It is Rusalem.

They walked fifteen more minutes till they arrived at a hut—a proper village never appeared—with the usual smooth dirt in front. A pantless child sat spread-legged against a log, gazing up at the strangers with the serenity of one meditating on a mountaintop. Trees encroached as if listening in.

My sis-tah, Jonathan said. Another child stepped into the clearing. That one, too, he said, and waved her off dismissively. I will find my mother.

He vanished into the dark entryway beneath a thatched roof. A woman appeared with him in the doorway; she was very small, hardly larger than her son. She wore an ankle-length kanga so faded the pattern was gone, and a buttoned-up green sweater. Her head scarf was rolled at the crown.

Hello, Jane said. Jambo.

Jambo, the woman whispered. She looked at her son, not at the strangers.

She has made eleven children, Jonathan said.

Really, Jane said. The woman looked fifteen years old.

Nine are still alive.

Pierre beamed at the woman as if she were greeting them at a large party. Would she mind if he took some pictures of her house? he said. Of her? Jane saw that the camera's red light was already lit, filming. The woman shook her head.

Please. This is okay, Jonathan said with a solemn tone. You are welcome.

Jane and Pierre ducked into the hut. It was dark and smelled of smoke. The floor space was the size of a large round table and the mud walls nubbly with bark and twigs. A tall person could stand only in the center where Pierre now stooped. An oval of light lit the threshold, but the rest of the hut was dark.

Here is where we cook. Jonathan indicated an ashy smudge at his bare feet. His mother was sitting outside, knees sideways, face turned away, murmuring in another language. We have been finding flies to cook, he said.

Flies?

In the frying pan.

Is that what she's saying?

No. She says, I do not find food for my children today. He shrugged dismissively.

Sometimes we eat dirt, he added brightly, and urged them back outside. Another boy appeared and kicked the stick the little girl was grinding into the dirt. The stick flew off and she crawled after it. The boy kicked her.

This is my brother. Jonathan wedged himself between his siblings. Stop now.

Where did you learn such good English, Jonathan?

I learn it at school.

No school today?

His arms spread out. I am with my mother today.

And your father?

He is not alive. He was killed in a rebel attack.

Oh. Jane was again at a loss.

I was hiding just there, he said, jerking his head in no particular direction. My father would not do as they told him, so they cut him with a panga. When we got to him he was dead.

That's terrible, she said. What could one say?

The rebels also abducted my brothers, Jonathan went on in a bland voice. The other children, we were hiding with my mother. He paused to say something in an impatient tone to his brother, who was straddling a log. The brother turned his shoulder away, frowning.

When was that?

Three years ago. We have heard my brothers are alive, he said.

I hope they escape, Jane said.

Yes. He crossed his arms thoughtfully. We hope it. Keith is very strong. He would be making a good soldier now. He has probably killed many people. The other one, Paul, maybe he is not such a good soldier.

Jane noticed Pierre in the doorway, folding something and jamming it into a gap of sticks. Money. Pierre's gaze dropped to the side, the signal to go.

Jane thanked Jonathan. If you wanted to walk back with us, we could give you some food, she said.

Asante, he said. I stay with my mother. Perhaps if the rebels come then I am here.

Jane wondered what she could leave them with. Pierre had left money. She had only jewelry, her hoop earrings worth nothing, her necklace, no. The dragonfly was from her sister, a family thing. She needed her watch. There was the Maasai bracelet from Harry. He'd given it to her so recently she'd hardly owned it yet. She unsnapped the leather with the red and green beads. There were bracelets like this all over the place. She could get another.

Here, she said, handing it to Jonathan's mother. I think it is an old one.

The woman took the bracelet and held it limply, barely looking at it. Immediately Jane saw it had little value and immediately regretted letting it go. But what did it matter in the larger scheme of things?

Returning on the worn path with Pierre, Jane felt a dullness in her forehead, as if something were shut off. On the driveway they ran into Dr. Marciano in short white shirtsleeves on the way to work.

Come to the hospital and we'll give you a tour, he said, not stopping.

No one at the house was up yet. Jane extracted a crushed cereal box from the back of the truck, and she and Pierre ate bowls of cornflakes, leaning against the counter in the kitchen. It occurred to Jane how little she knew about Pierre. She asked him where he grew up. Algeria, he said. She could feel it as a physical change, to be talking about something not here. He told her he'd lived down the street from a bordello, not a particularly seedy one, it looked like a neighborhood hotel where he watched men coming and going, and women sitting in the windows by curtains.

That's how, Pierre said, I was initiated into voyeurism, and women. Women still appear that way to me now, inviting in their windows, creating an atmosphere in the space around them. Men are always charging forward, hurrying. But women seem to cultivate the space they are in. It's very appealing. It makes you want to join them.

Makes me wish I were a woman. Jane laughed.

Certainly better than being a man, he said.

Don entered the kitchen like the punch line of a joke. Jane and Pierre avoided each other's eyes.

Anyone else sleep like shit? he said. He opened the fridge, then closed it immediately remembering where he was. So what horrors are we subjecting ourselves to today? he said.

Inside the whitewashed walls was a sprawling complex of buildings. A nurse in a pink lab uniform and a small paper-cup hat introduced herself as Bridget and told them Dr. Marciano was operating all morning. You are most welcome to see our hospital, she said.

The five visitors followed her white sandals snapping her heels lazily. Her hands swung around her wide hips as if trailing in water. They passed doorways open to empty rooms with no beds, to rooms with empty beds, then to rooms filled with beds and patients in them. Jane walked beside Harry, feeling love. They stepped outside under a tin roof to a walkway which extended past a courtyard to a structure with a massive pink façade of flaking paint. The old hospital we do not use, Bridget said. It is in need of repairs.

She steered them back inside, down another hallway, green on the lower half, beige on the upper. Lana hung back, pulling Pierre's arm.

Jane watched her stroll down the cracked walkway beside a rusted turquoise railing as Pierre, who had his camera up, filmed her from behind.

The others continued behind Bridget till she stopped at a doorway. Here there are sisters, she said. They looked in. In one bed sat two girls of about eleven, looking back at them without surprise.

What's the matter with them? Don said, forever subtle.

This one is healing, Bridget said. She pulled back the sheet of the girl nearest her. One leg was a stump, bandaged, with a rusty stain at its rounded end.

That's okay. Jane put up her hand. Bridget looked perplexed.

We don't need to see it, Harry explained.

Is her sister hurt too? Jane said.

No, her sister stays to keep her company.

The tour continued. Jane was mesmerized by everything. Each step seemed to take her deeper into a true life she had not known before. Each detail was savored.

Where're Lana and Pierre? Don said, moving impatiently, nodding at the doorways. He swiveled his head to see if Lana had returned. The trip had long ago stopped being what he expected.

Through a door at the end of the hall they exited to a courtyard blinding in the morning sun. The air smelled of burning wood. Some families had set up small camps in shaded areas and were tending fires inside rings of rocks. A pregnant woman wafted by in a filmy white robe. Men with bandages sat in low chairs beside women stirring pots. Children ran, looping. A woman in a yellow turban chopped orange fruit on a hubcap. The ground was a white dust, fine as powder in a compact. There was little sign that the night before this ground had been covered with a lumpy rug of hundreds of sleeping people, curved against each other, lying side by side. On rainy nights, Bridget told them, they slept on the walkways or in the halls, and the hospital handed out plastic sheets to cover them or make lean-tos with. A small girl in a shredded purple dress stood frozen, watching Jane and Harry, her face opening like a flower as they passed.

They continued into another building much like the first, went through it, and eventually reached the final courtyard. Women there sat in the shade of a far wall; children circled a dribbling faucet. Behind the wall was a dark density of trees.

Bridget thanked them and said she must be getting back to work. They could find their way out. It is a pleasure to have this visit, she said, and walked off, hands swinging.

The sun was high and white. Don patted his pockets for his sunglasses. I don't know about you, he said, but shouldn't Pierre be getting this shit?

In each place they had come, Jane felt the field of her being tilled and turned over. Don Block looked the same here as he'd be anywhere, head tipped back, hand in his pocket jiggling change. His manner said, No matter where you put me I will remain this way. Even in a hospital refugee camp I am a man impatient with the idiot late for our lunch meeting.

They're in the old wing, Jane said to be rid of him.

His sneakers made small explosions of dust as he hurried off. Jane sat at the edge of a dry fountain in the center of the courtyard and wrote in the green notebook. Harry sat beside her. She didn't look at him, but liked him near. Here among the wounded and displaced she was relieved of herself and having him there felt in balance with the world.

A boy rolled a de-spoked bicycle by them leaping back and forth through it.

You're very skillful, Jane said.

Harry spoke in Swahili. The boy did a double take, surprised. The boy chatted with him for a while then left, energized by Harry.

I gave your bracelet away, she said, still writing.

You what?

This morning. To a woman with nine children who was eating fried flies.

Oh.

Will you get me another? she said lightly.

No.

She kept writing. I thought she could sell it, she said, justifying herself. She wanted to keep the balance. She felt him looking at her and glanced up. His face was near, an expression sizing her up. His face told her she was not to be trusted measuring the worth of things.

She bent back to her notes, focusing attention on the page, not him. Sorry, she muttered.

Forget it, Jane, he said. His tone was mild and unreadable, and she pretended to believe he didn't care.

Out of the corner of her eye she saw Don, a light blue blur crossing far off, the only hurrying figure in this place of slowly moving things. His head reared back when he spotted them and his long arms rose into in an exaggerated shrug of *What the hell?*

Someone's ready to go, Jane said, and stood. She took the reason to move.

They caught up with Don on the road back to the house. They had planned to go into Gulu to find a hotel.

Is everything okay? Jane said.

Fucking great, Don said.

What's the matter?

I found them balling back there.

Jane nearly laughed. What?

Well, maybe they were finished by the time I got there. But they'd been recently going at it, that much was clear.

Harry showed no sign of listening.

Wow, Jane said.

Yes, Don said. That's what I thought. He imitated a girl's voice: Wow. He turned to Harry instinctively walking behind and shouted, What's with you people here?

What? Harry said.

You people.

What people?

You! Don screamed. Here!

Harry calmly shook his head, walking on.

Here! Here! His hands waved in the air.

Jane saw he meant nothing less than all of Africa.

13 / The You File

WHO SAID you choose your life?

You have gone away and new things steer you. Wind, hands. Some cruel, some kind. There is madness in the dark and madness in the morning with the smell of smoke.

You wade in the water, walk on your knees. Sometimes they take your hand and bind you. No one looks you in the eye. You listen to what they say, some is true, some not.

You meet yourself before falling asleep. You may have been gone from yourself all day but you are there when you close your eyes. You lie on the leaf of yourself and sail into dreams. People there fly. You may not be able to steer, but at least you are able to bear it.

You are a child again and the powerless world expands around you. Some days you say, It will be all right. Other days, It is too much to bear, no one can bear this. Then people do, they bear it.

There are always others worse off.

14 / What Comes Back to Me

SINCE RETURNING, I have the feeling that my life has a hole in it and now I am missing that hole.

I have sharp pains at night and before sunrise the fluid breaks. I am brought to a hut and lie on the straw mat with pain all day. Louise is in the doorway, then gone. The woman tells me, calm, unsurprised, It will be all right, but her face is worn out, and when she checks between my legs, she shakes her head. Lotti, I hear, is nearby, but not appearing. I want to get away from the pains but have nowhere to go. My body is not ready to push that baby out. At night tight straps squeeze me, like knives. Another woman puts her hand inside, saying the baby does not sit right. She tries to turn it, with the other hand on my stomach.

·

So it went for a day and night. I ate nothing, drank water. Maybe I will die this way, I thought. In the morning the worn-out woman returned. Now we must push. It was like being attacked from inside. Did hours pass or minutes? Who knows. The feet came first, then one arm was out and they were moving me around to pull that baby out. They were frowning, shifting me. They didn't want to break the arm.

Then the baby came out at last. It was a dark color, not moving, its neck was choked. It had been that way for some time.

She doesn't need to see this baby, the woman said. It was taken away and buried. Perhaps it passed by Greg Lotti on its way. I thought at least there was not another person to join the rebels. But my feelings—they did not appear to me.

These things come back to me: In Sudan, washing clothes in plastic buckets after a battle, rebels nearby laughing and passing around a bottle, I washed blood from a small skirt. When we poured blood from gum boots it sat like red glass on the dust, then sank in, more slowly than water.

There was a girl named Doris who gave me a pain. She would say we were abducted because we were sinful. Kony's tipu told him to punish us because we are Acholi. Look at what we did, for instance, at Bucoro.

I saw Agnes showing interest. Agnes, I said. Do not listen to this one.

We were shaken awake in the night and made to get up and steered to a clearing where others were gathered. Kony wanted to speak with us, a spirit had woken him telling him it was time to pray. We knelt and bowed our heads. Kony prayed in the name of Jesus, he prayed in the name of Muhammad. He prayed in the name of Alice Lakwena. He was the father who would lead us and all his family to the glory of the resurrection and we must pray for the sinning we'd done.

I was beside Doris but she was not even listening. She was looking toward the rebels and I saw she loved one of them. I turned to see Ricky, that one who had taken me to Kony, the one with no mother.

*

In Sudan, in a dry riverbed. A group of rebels arrived. We were some distance away in the shade and saw them crouching in lumps on the sandy ground, praying. Sometimes when they prayed, it meant they were going to kill you. They were praying for your soul. But not this time.

When they were finished, Louise looked at me, meaning there was something of interest there. The group was picking up their guns and there among the figures was Philip. His back was to us, but I knew it to be him. I did not know he had been taken. He wore camouflage pants, a dark T-shirt with a gun strap across his back, and a camouflage hat with flaps over the ears. You would only have a gun when they believed you were with them.

I waited to see if he would turn. I could not know what would happen, for me or him. I did not know if he would come near. Then Philip moved from that place and we could not see the whole ditch and I could no longer see him. Some rebels climbed out of the riverbed and came toward us. A group of children was following behind and there was Philip, pushing some children to stay in line. He pointed his gun toward us in the shade and it seemed as if I met his eyes, so my heart was pounding. When he looked easily away, I thought we were too much in the shade to be seen.

I was weaving roof thatch and my grass was in a tangle. They came near us and then Philip was there, close by. I kept my head down but my eyes were seeing everything. The children walked near and he too was near. He looked at us girls sitting among the thatch and saw me and passed by.

When a person you love moves by you with flat eyes that will not see you, it is a shock to believe it.

So this life goes. You suffer and think nothing new can come to you, then a new suffering comes you had not imagined.

I saw Philip one more time after that. We were in Uganda after a raid in a place with other rebels, preparing food. I brought some sorgham to the children and found Philip sitting there among them. His head was shaved with a white scar on the side. He had no gun, but still wore camouflage pants. This time he saw me and frowned.

Do I know you? he said.

Philip, I said. It's Esther. Was he teasing me? He used to tease so much. His voice was regular. I handed him a banana leaf with sorghum on it. He accepted it and dropped it splat on the ground. He began mixing the sorghum in the dirt, then ate it off his fingers. He stared at me. Mother is angry, he said.

What? I watched him eat the dirt.

You did not come and she needs you to take the baby. He's been crying, crying. Philip rolled his eyes. Can you at least do that?

What baby?

Go on. She will whip you.

Philip, there is no baby. We are not home.

She was everywhere, screaming for you. She needs help with the baby! he said. Another rebel came over and waved me away. He was not surprised to see Philip eating dirt.

Afterward, when I returned, I said these things to Louise. Esther, she said, Philip has gone mad.

Later we learned that Philip was hit in the head by a fragment in battle and afterward was not the same.

What else comes back to me: We are stealing food. Most villages we come to are deserted. We sleep in the empty huts, then continue on.

A week after she left we found Agnes.

We were moving to another camp and had been walking for some time when we came to a place with a very bad smell. We knew by now the smell of death. The rebels walked us away from this smell, and one went looking there. I saw a red cloth in the grasses and my body knew it was terrible. The rebel called out and they did not worry if we also moved closer. Then I saw it was Agnes. She lay facedown with her arms and legs out at angles and dirt creased in her red shirt. These arms and hands of Agnes's, I thought, they had held me. Her face was sideways to us with eyelids so swollen it did not look like her face.

The rebels stood over her, saying this and that, then deciding nothing. They said, Let us go.

We got back in line. Louise hooked her finger in mine, then dropped it right away. We did not look, but when someone touches you, you don't always need the eyes. Eyes may go deep but touching goes another deep place.

Later when I was apart making my toilet I had a feeling which had not visited me in some time, of needing to weep with my whole heart. I was there weeping, but no sound came. Agnes was my best friend in the world.

Will anyone know the pain I am enduring? I thought. Then, Why would it matter that they did? What difference would it make?

Each of us will all die one day. Some of us before others. The first time you meet death, it is a surprise. Up to that moment you have not believed it possible. You know it is there, but do not know it close-up until it takes away forever someone you love.

For a while I moved about as a ghost.

The man was so drunk you could not tell if that was why he stumbled around or if it was because he had no arms. The rebels were laughing at him as if at a clown. He had foam around his mouth and kept moving as if he had to get somewhere, as if there were someplace he could possibly make it to.

My heart by then was hard. I had a cruel feeling and did not try to get rid of it. If you were stone, nothing would hurt you.

I say this now because I am ashamed for it. I felt shame then and I feel shame now. It winds deeper and deeper inside you so it will not come out.

Helen heard them at night by the fire say they were going to test the river with us. All night we listened to the water rushing from the recent rain. The lazy one with no front teeth, Olet, said, If they can make it across, then we will follow.

That morning we went to the water. A girl, Mary, was beside me. She was not one of the Aboke girls, but she was now also a wife to Greg Lotti. I found her one day in the dark corner of the hut where I stayed with him. Greg Lotti had ordered it. She was a tiny thing and looked at me with popping-out eyes so I might explain what would happen. I could not explain. Rebels were nearby. I told her with my eyes, This is how it is here. She stayed near me, quiet as a cat for some days, and so I was her friend. She was eleven.

At the river Mary whispered she could not swim. Her village had no river, so how could she ever learn? The river was swollen with ropes of brown water rushing by. She was frightened to cross. I told her, You hold on to me. Mary was small, so I could help her.

We gathered at a place the animals had smoothed. Stones jutted into the water and made a still round pool apart from the moving hump of river. First we were made to pour water over our heads to protect us. Then we were put in a line and given a rope and told to hold that rope. Greg Lotti was standing back with the others. He had cut himself on his chin and there was blood on his face, perhaps from shaving. He looked for a second, then not again.

They said to Louise, You with the long legs, you go first. Then you, you go next.

The one with the missing teeth said to me, Go.

I did not believe it would be all right. The water was cold at first then warmer. It came to my knees and when we hit the moving part swirled up to my ribs. Mary held the rope with one hand, but at the fast water dropped the rope and held me with both hands. She was, however, very light. We did not speak. Her fingers were digging into me. I did not mind. The rope did not always stay stretched tight, and when loose it was not so easy to hold. I did not trust that rope. You must let the person in front of you stay ahead to keep it tight or there would be spaces and you did not stay close. Instead I trusted my feet. In fast water if you keep one foot on the ground before lifting the other the water will not push you over.

I took slow steps. Water pressed at my side, curled around me and continued past. Mary clung on the side downstream, protected. Her legs did not reach, so I had the weight like an animal hugging me, but water makes a person lighter. I thought perhaps it would be okay.

In this way, we crossed the river, or did not, for not everyone made it across.

A person ahead of us splashed over and pulled the rope so another behind her fell, pulling others. I too went over into the water and quickly stood. But coming up, Mary was not with me. I reached my arms and did not find her.

The rebels were shouting from the shore as if we were meaning to make trouble. We saw a girl floating away. She grabbed a branch at the other side. It was Helen. This was before I saw her at Kony's, before she saved herself to become one of his wives. Some girls who had reached the other side waded to that branch to get her. I looked farther down the river and saw a dark head being carried away. It was in the middle, not reaching the other side, not grabbing on to anything. The ball was in sight on the surface then it disappeared. The rebels noticed and shouted. Bring her back! they said. But no one was near. No one did. Maybe the river would push her to the side far enough away so she could escape. Maybe this would be lucky for Mary. I hoped this, but we did not see her again.

I am allowed one night to go home. I visit and think my mother will each minute come around the corner, but of course she does not. Neighbors come and everyone looks at me. My father sits in his chair, pats my head and drinks his beer. Aunt Karen makes the food my mother would make: chicken in sauce, rice, plantains. At the table my father passes me a bowl of rice, already looking to the salt. I don't know if he is pained for my sake, or his, unable to see me as the same daughter as before. I am there, but I do not feel among them. A gray curtain comes down and I am apart with only myself.

Even now I do not lose the urge to escape. Even if I know I have returned I am still in the habit of thinking of escape.

In the bush you never forgot that one day you might have the chance. This life perhaps would not go on forever. Each day you wondered, Is this the day? And you would answer, Not yet, not today. You waited for the right day. You learned you had more patience than you thought. Somehow patience came. You might not feel patience in you, yet it was there. At least, you told yourself, I am alive.

Then at last the day arrived.

Before sleep Louise whispered, We are moving tomorrow. She heard them talking by the fire. I was sitting away, because a girl who is in her period must sit far from the fire. She also must not touch anything that a rebel will touch. For those days I could sleep near the girls. That night Greg Lotti was in another place and no other rebel was bothering me so I was rested. Whenever we moved, there was the chance, even a small chance, so each time before we moved we would ask, Is this the time of my chance?

I whispered to Louise, I think this is the time.

How do you know it?

We are near a place we know.

Tomorrow will you take the chance with me? Louise's head lay on the pillow of her arm, not answering. In the dark I saw the darker holes of her eyes open. She shook her head.

I am not sure, she whispered.

Maybe in the morning you will think it.

We spoke no more. Would this really be the day? I was not sure myself, but I would be ready.

In the morning Louise showed she was still not sure. Louise was careful and we looked to her, but this day I thought, I must listen to Esther.

We left that place and walked and soon stopped at another place. Some girls went to make their toilet and I went with them. A guard was just there near us, and there was the shouting that we move. The girls left with the guard to join the others and I stayed sitting on my heels, still. If someone had looked back or called to me I would have stood up, but no one looked back. No one called. I saw them walking in pieces between the trees, I heard their voices grow soft. I heard someone saying, Tomorrow we will . . . Then it was silent.

I stayed crouching with my heart pounding in my knees. Soon it was long enough so that if I was discovered it would be known I was trying to escape. And so began the adventure of my life. I stood and walked quickly in the direction opposite from the rebels.

Soon I was running. I ran for a long time to be far away. I might stop for a moment and listen to hear anything then I would run again. One time I heard a voice. I looked in the direction across a field and saw an old woman walking with a child. I lowered myself in the grass. I was breathing hard from running and the green blades of grass were touching my eyebrows. It seemed as if the grass was friendly to me, not outside of myself, but part of me. Each blade touched me, supporting me in my venture.

For the next three days I did not know if I would live or die.

I had little idea where I was going, but aimed to the south. I was hungry those days, but that did not worry me. I was used to hunger, I was not used to being free. Walking on my own, I could go wherever I chose. I had my freedom back, even if I would not survive it.

When the leaves darkened I looked for a place to sleep. This tree had thorns and another was not so far off the ground. The sky was now growing dark and I had to choose. I came near a trunk split into two thick branches which tilted beside each other with a triangle at their meeting where a person could sit. This would be my tree, the first place I would spend the night alone in a year and a half.

I climbed up. The two branches were near enough so I could rest across them and not fall out, but not so close that I could relax completely. It seemed that if I fell asleep I might fall through. So I leaned back and closed my eyes, not to sleep, only rest. I woke with a jerk, thinking myself falling. But I wasn't falling. In the darkness the leaves were ticking in the silence. I could make out a dusty bush with a smaller bush beside it and a dead branch sticking out which looked like a spear. What if they find me? I wondered. Then I thought, No one in the world knows if I am alive or dead.

Then I must have fallen asleep, because my eyes opened to branches against a lightening sky. I had made it through my first free night. I slipped down to the ground.

I walked south, at least I thought south. The farther that way, the farther from encountering the rebels. I walked all morning and kept away from villages, worried they would not welcome me.

In the middle of the day I came to a place with fewer trees and open brush. I heard a baby crying. I followed the sound and saw down a slope at a low dry place a woman sitting, her head draped over with a kanga of purple and yellow. I approached, stepping on loud twigs so she would not be surprised. When I was near she turned and I saw it was not a woman, but a girl. She covered the baby's face with the kanga to protect it.

Please, do not hurt us. I suppose I did not look so clean.

I will not hurt you.

You are a rebel, she said. I saw now she was very young.

No. I have escaped from the rebels.

She frowned. You look like a rebel.

Yes, I was with them, but I am escaping now. I am trying to go home. I felt a trembling inside as I said these words.

The baby was crying in a thin slow way, and the girl bounced it near her chest, hiding it from me. My baby is sick, she said. I am afraid for her.

Let me see.

Still frowning at me, she pulled the cloth away. The baby's eyes were closed and there was a white crust around the mouth.

This baby needs water, I said. Can you feed her?

I am unable, she said, as if it were my fault. When the kanga slipped back from her forehead I saw her hair was thin and in tufts. She was not so well either.

Do you know this place? I said.

She looked at me, her eyes a little crossed, not answering.

Let us find water, I said. I started in the direction I had been taking.

I cannot go that way. Her eyes rolled off a little. I began to see she might be crazy. By now I had seen enough crazy people. I thought of Philip, how he did not look crazy right away. She stood and tucked the cloth behind her ears to keep the kanga on. It had green plums and a yellow vine. The baby was strapped close to her chest in a bundle, and it stopped crying when she stood.

I have not spoken to anyone since escaping, I said. Even if she was crazy I would say it aloud. She walked behind me, not interested. This made it easier to speak.

I have been gone a long time, I said. It made me dizzy to realize it.

Every now and then this girl dipped down, almost kneeling, and snatched at the tops of grass and threw the seeds over her shoulder. She concentrated on doing this, as if it was a dance.

I am Esther. What is your name?

Do you think my baby will die? she said.

Not if we get water, I said. But how was I to know?

Do you think water is this way? she said, bending her knee like she was genuflecting in church. When she faced me I saw she had no upper teeth. I thought then it might be better to go in the opposite direction, away from this girl.

We got to a hilltop and saw trickles of smoke rising out of the floor of trees and a dark area where the trees made a hole. We headed for the dark area and arrived at a shallow pool of water with dirt polished around it. I drank from the cup of my hands and the girl drank water and poured it from her mouth into the baby's mouth. Water spilled over their chins. The baby coughed.

I told her I was choosing now to go an opposite way. You go to the village there, I said, and pointed to where we had seen smoke. They will help you.

She looked up as I was leaving. I see the baby flying with you, she said.

What? I looked into her crazy eyes.

There, she said, pointing above my shoulder. Is it a boy or a girl?

I felt pain in my stomach.

A girl, she decided.

Yes, I said. It was hard to speak.

She shrugged as if none of this was surprising. This one, she said, she will guide you home.

The pain in my stomach seemed to become something warm and for the first time I thought of my baby as a thing I might have loved. It made me feel lighter, even if it was sad. My baby was with me, a maleika in the air. I continued on.

That night I slept not in a tree but under one. I had not passed any animals. I thought, maybe this place looked familiar. I made a pile of leaves and lay on them and covered myself with more leaves and felt hungry. In the morning I woke. A rooster called far away. People were nearby.

Things might completely change from one minute to another. I learned this the night of October ninth when my life changed forever. I woke this morning alone in the world and soon after was united again with mankind.

Something was clicking. I stepped onto a wide path and saw an old man pushing a bicycle. He had a mattress flopped over the handlebars. I moved behind a tree and the man saw me. It was only one instant but I saw his face and he was not afraid of me.

He greeted me and offered to walk with me. I felt gratitude for his kindness. He understood I was just a girl.

I woke this morning and remembered something I thought forgotten, a time they caught a man on a bicycle and cut off his foot. If you are on a bicycle the rebels think you may be delivering news. The man's wife came out and they told her to eat that foot.

You do not forget such things, even when they are not appearing. They are just in the back of your mind, waiting.

Sometimes I want to hit myself with stones.

The camp in the morning is pale yellow. I am watching, waiting for something I cannot name. I try to think of what I know and I cannot find it. Life is there before me but not close enough for my hand to reach it. My heart is suffocating.

VII

Gulu

15 / Love with Harry

THEY CHECKED IN to the Exciting Hotel, a group of stucco cottages blackened by mold. Reception had a façade featuring a yellow painted sun emerging from a line of rotting plastic bags. Lana stood at the counter between Pierre and Don, boot heel at a tilt, and asked for a room of her own. Flies buzzed them. A sort of lounge area loomed in deeper darkness.

A few streets away they found Caffè Roma and sat near the door in a sort of porch area surrounded by windows barred with grating of white hoops. The waitress took their orders with a tenderness implying pity, and they ate a late lunch of chicken wings in thin dark gravy and something called boo with peanut sauce.

After lunch Jane and Pierre walked through town in the ochre dust. It was still and hot. Thoughts of Harry drifted to Jane. *What do you have on under there?* Up on the concrete porches shop doors were shut for the afternoon. A hair salon sign was a hand-painted, yellow checkerboard of different hairdos. On some heads, green hair was arranged in a patchwork of braids like planted fields, on others, blue hair sculpted into heart-shaped puffs. Pierre was taking pictures. Look at this, he said, zeroing in on a tattered bit of ribbon around a rusty pole.

At the end of a street a man stood on a pile of garbage the size of a small hut, picking through it.

They walked loosely apart. A bony-legged brown dog trotted past with the rare attitude of no interest in the white people.

They passed a beggar sitting behind bony knees with a few coins on the ground near his toes, and farther along a boy passed out, having slid off a step with white glue caked around his nostrils. He was probably with the rebels, Pierre said. And now this. He stood looking for a long time, then snapped a picture of the boy's fingers, curled in sleep.

Jane carried her notebook but kept it closed. Sometimes I wonder what I'm doing here, she said.

Reporting your story I would say, said Pierre. He was lying on the ground on his side now, his camera jammed against his nose, squishing it, as he clicked, near some rusted cans.

What do you see there?

It's fantastic, he answered mysteriously.

I mean here on the planet.

You just want to be free, he said. His cheek pressed the dusty ground beside his camera. You have a wild spirit.

If anyone back home had said such a thing it would have been met with mockery. But here was mercifully not *back home.* Sometimes you needed another person to say something out loud. How did Pierre see it? She didn't think she showed. Maybe she showed to Harry. *Come here, take this off.* Maybe she showed in bed. It was where she felt most herself, there or away from people altogether.

Knowing oneself was like smoke wafting into air. Other people might show you the stranger of yourself. The likelihood she'd forget Pierre saying this was high. Clarity was harder to keep than puzzlement. But she would not, however, forget this. It would turn out to return to her: the hot afternoon in Gulu when Pierre said, You just want to be free. Each time it came like a steadying hand.

Look at this. Pierre stood in a yard of hard dirt sunk with fossils of plastic caps and glass shards. Above the doorway of an abandoned house a faded painting was visible in the peeling concrete. Two carefree figures on surfboards rode a curling green wave. More faded, in pink and green, were the words *Surf Club*.

One can always dream, Jane said.

C'est fantastique. Pierre snapped pictures, then stepped through the doorless doorway to an empty blue floor with two broken chairs tangled in a corner.

They came out to a boy standing at the edge of the yard with a doubtful face, holding up small baggies of popcorn. He wore a choker of white beads and a tank top that would fit a large man.

Jane asked him how much.

One shilling.

I'll take them all. She rummaged around in her bag.

There is tipu here, the boy said.

The Surf Club? She smiled, delighted. Really?

He nodded solemnly. His stance declared he wasn't going any nearer. The joki is there.

Should we be worried? she said, giving him a fifty-shilling coin.

He didn't seem to hear, or understand, more concerned with her gross overpayment. Asante, he said, and nearly tossed the little bags to her, hurrying away before she saw her mistake.

Don would say you're going to disrupt the country's economy, Pierre said.

Did you hear it's haunted?

Everything old is. The ancestors here stay around. Pierre walked past her, his expression already opening to something new. He was gazing toward the long alley of eucalyptus trees. Look at that. He shook his head. The sunlight cut through the trees in dusty swords. Beauty is everywhere, he said.

The loveliness of sleeping beside Harry cast a spell over the day.

He was lovely. His shoulders were lovely and wide and his skin was lovely and firm and it was lovely against her skin and his shoulders around her let her feel the particular muscle a man has in his arms. She liked how he was led by his body, not his mind.

The loveliness of bed sometimes overrode all else. She lapsed into day-dreams, scanning the images of the nights to relive the sensations, which were even stronger with the layer of reflection added to them. He was moving in to kiss her. Maybe he was reconsidering, studying her mouth. No, he was looking, he came closer. Still he didn't kiss her, making her heart thump in its gigantic room. Sleeping, she lay against the raft of him. Inside, he had a secret and maybe if she were close enough she would learn it.

Her mind emptied *through* the body, through Harry. She fell into a fugue, replaying his hands anchoring her waist, his shoulder pinning her chin. He twisted her wrist. His mouth covered her mouth.

One could point to a difference in our ages, she said.

Yes, I'm too old for you. He tapped her forehead.

He asked her, Don't you miss your family?

Sometimes, she said. It sounded dismissive, which she didn't intend. I mean, sure, she said with a different tone.

What about your country?

No. That sounded spoiled. I miss my friends, she tried.

Why just friends?

Because I love them?

You asking me?

Because I love them.

People aren't loved when you are away from them, he said.

That's not true.

You haven't even given it any thought.

She felt the sting of him being right.

You disagree with me before you've even thought about it, he said.

My friends matter to me, she said.

How do you love people you aren't with?

From afar? She smiled.

I miss my family when I don't see them. My sister lives in Ireland. It's too far away.

You don't choose your family, Jane said.

Isn't that the point? Harry said.

Maybe some people are better off without their family, she said.

Harry didn't speak for a moment. You show me one, he said.

How does it feel to be so sure about everything? she said.

You tell me, Harry said.

He told her about a girlfriend who did Reiki therapy. She taught him the technique and he turned out to have a knack for it and when he drove her to the hospital where she volunteered he ended up treating patients, too. He laid his hands on their arms or stomach or head and concentrated on the warmth and energy moving out of his fingers into them, and it seemed to give them relief. One time he had an old man in intensive care whom he worked on for fifteen minutes, and when Harry stood to leave he fainted. He'd drained himself.

He told her about one time in the locker room being teased by an older boy for being small. He was facing the ceiling, speaking freely not looking at her. It made me shy, he said.

Kids are mean, Jane said.

Thing is, I still believe him. It made an impression on me.

But you know it's not true, right? She smiled, not at him, but because she was hearing about something from inside Harry.

He remained grave. No, I don't.

A normal kind person might have said, You are fine, you are more than fine, but she found herself strangely blocked, as if reassurance would be a knee-jerk denial of that wound to his younger self.

Instead she glided onto him to reassure him with her body, the reassurance she trusted. She felt him distant, as if his shadow were walking away up a hill.

They were napping on the low bed at the Exciting Hotel, lying on their sides facing the same way. She was cupped behind him, her arm along his side. A cobra was chewing a small furry animal. When the cobra saw her it dropped the animal and lunged through the air toward her neck.

She woke. She turned abruptly onto her back and crossed her hands over a fluttering chest.

Harry's low eyes appeared over his shoulder. What is it?

Sorry. She stared up. Bad dream.

He kept his head turned, maybe waiting, maybe not waiting.

She didn't look at him. The thought of looking in his eyes was terrifying. I just got . . . She sat up quickly and looked for her shoes.

The town had come back to life when Jane walked past the flapping kangas and sputtering exhaust pipes in early evening. She followed the map in her World Vision booklet to the red star indicating the location of the largest rehabilitation center in the north. An entranceway was open in a high chain-link fence that bordered a neighborhood of lean-tos. In a denuded yard a small boy with a withered leg was wheeling around on a stick, showing how adept he was. She entered a cement building with a narrow sidewalk around it one step up and found a woman in a blue tie-dyed dress at an empty desk. She made an appointment with her to visit the next day.

Back at the Exciting Hotel she picked up her key where Harry had left it at the desk and saw across an empty lounge Don in silhouette at the bar.

She walked over. Here's somebody, she said. Everyone else has disappeared.

Don laughed, not happily.

What is it? Jane said.

Must've not had enough to drink yet, he said.

That's not like you, Don.

I'm trying to be not like me. He shook his short glass in small circles. Don't you think that's a good idea? I think it's a good plan.

Is it working?

Lana's found a soldier, he said. In a deeper part of the room, near a dusty window, Jane saw Lana throwing darts at a tire, watched by a man in uniform.

Have you seen Harry?

Fuck Harry.

Oh. Pierre?

Fuck Pierre. Or maybe you have, too. He lifted his glass. Another one, my friend. The bartender, a man with long holes in his ears, carried a bottle over and poured. Want one? Don said, drawing his face back as if to take in Jane.

No, thanks. I think I'll let you be miserable all by yourself.

Or you could fuck me, Don said.

What?

Why not?

Jesus, Don.

I find you attractive.

Well, thanks.

What? Not young enough for you?

She regarded him with lowered lids.

Everybody else fucks everybody else here, he said. Why shouldn't we? His attention turned back to Lana's dark figure in front of the window, standing very straight, concentrating on her aim. The soldier in full dress sat on the arm of a chair, swigging beer, watching her.

You know, when you're propositioning someone it helps if you look at the person, Jane said.

I was looking at you, he said. So what do you say?

Boy, I am tempted. She turned to go.

Don shook his head. You don't know who you are, he said.

In the morning, when they arrived at the gates of the rehabilitation center they found a funeral taking place.

Behind the chain-link fence hundreds of children sat knee to knee in the yard. Hands shielded their eyes from the sun. Except for a few coughs, it was silent, unusual to see so many children without a lot of noise.

At the far end of the yard in spotty shade, a table held a small coffin covered with a white sheet and yellow and orange frangipani blossoms arranged in the shape of a cross. Behind on a bench sat a line of adults in good clothes. A priest in a white robe held a big candle and spoke in Lor. Then he switched to English. The boy will rise together with Jesus, he said. After his blessing a man in a crisp khaki shirt stepped forward. This turned out to be the director of the center. He spoke of a boy named Danny. The boy had been with them for three weeks after returning from eighteen months with the rebels.

Danny was a much-beloved boy here, the director said. He liked to bake. Just last week he was baking bread with cook Carlton. Everyone ate that bread.

Jane and the others stood at the back, against the fence. Pierre's camera hung untouched at his hip, but Don was snapping away with his Nikon, the clicks sounding loud in the silence.

Today, the director said, we bid Danny goodbye. We will see him again when we arrive in heaven.

Four men on the bench stood. One wore a suit, the others were in button-up shirts. Each took a corner of the coffin and lifted it. The director waded into the crowd of children, trying to plow a passageway toward the gate. Children pulled their knees to the side, but they were too close and he made little progress.

We shall stand, he decided.

Everyone rose, and the white coffin moved over the sea of round dark heads. The faces of the children turned and Jane looked from one to the next. Each one had seen and experienced horror. Out of the silence came a woman's howl. No one turned, but soon all observed a woman in a dark green dress with squared sleeves being urged forward, without hurry, by two other women. Her green hat was tipped forward above a sobbing face.

The adults followed the coffin through the gate. The crowd of children loosened and some noticed the white visitors. Some gazes were direct and curious, some wounded. But most were blank.

Danny now goes home to Achar, where he will finally be at rest, the director said.

Jane looked at Lana. His village, she whispered.

Another announcement, the director called out. Today there will be no disco. In memory of our friend Danny.

Later they learned Danny's village was twenty-five kilometers away and they were walking. They've probably never even been in a car, Lana said.

We are sorry you have arrived on such a day, said the director, leading them to the administrator's office. But we will hide our sadness.

Barbara, the woman Jane had made the appointment with, was behind her desk in the same blue tie-dyed dress, as if she hadn't moved.

She wore hundreds of thin braids pulled into a bun and had a reassuring presence. She invited them to sit. Jane took the one chair. Stacks of pamphlets were slid sideways against a wall. *Helping Children in Distress, Development Manual 2.*

After trauma there is difficulty having fun, Barbara said. So we try to play games with the children. You see they become withdrawn. They do not tell you their inner thoughts. And they have aggressive behavior, because they have been taught to kill. Sometimes they are unable to think for themselves. We try to help them make decisions again.

How many counselors do you have for all these children?

Here there are three.

How many children have returned? Jane said.

We are not certain. Some numbers place it at ten thousand.

Children abducted? Lana said, shocked.

No, children who escaped back.

Don was standing by the one window, arms impatiently folded. How long are people going let this go on? he said.

Eleven years is elapsing, Barbara said calmly.

But how do you put up with it? Don said, dropping his arms. Jane was surprised to see anger in his face.

One learns to have resilience, she said mildly. If you are too sympathetic you cannot work. If you are looking at the children as human beings, every day you will be breaking. Then she glanced out the window. Her face looked healthy and inspiring. This boy Danny, he is the first one to die, she said. And her smooth face cracked into tears.

They walked through the girls' dorm. Above the doors were written *Star Room, Sparkle, Nimaro,* meaning friendship. Inside the walls were painted tomato or turquoise, and the floor was covered with gray-and-black wool blankets on foam mattresses. A pink plastic purse hung on a peeling wall. In one room a girl lay alone on her side facing away, a hand cupping the back of her neck.

Often they are tired, Barbara explained.

In the kitchen three cooks were chopping potatoes. They are given hot food, Barbara said. Horsemeat, cabbage, cowpeas, dried fish, meal. For lunch and breakfast there were food bars, a shredded cookie packed tight made of vegetable fat, sugar, protein, wheat and milk. Families nearby had once been bringing home-cooked dishes, but with the increase in cholera it was no longer permitted. The boys slept in another house. There were four times as many boys as girls. The rebels abducted the same number of girls, but the boys had more opportunity to escape.

They stayed visiting all afternoon.

Jane and Lana sat outside with the girls as they crocheted doilies. Jane scanned for girls who spoke English. Their soft voices whispered of target practice and gun drills. One said they used SP 90s.

No, said a girl in a dotted-Swiss pinafore. We used B10s. The gun was so heavy I was afraid it would shoot.

Across the yard came a burst of laughter. Jane looked over to Harry in his white hat surrounded by laughing boys. They were slapping each other with soft hands and rocking backward.

Jane had the feeling, which came rarely, of being in the place you are meant to be.

Barbara brought over a girl named Yolanda. She had been taken twice. After the first escape she got married, then she was taken again. When she escaped the second time, her husband would not take her back. He said it was because she had been raped.

But you were a wife to a rebel the first time, Jane said, not getting it.

Barbara explained. Sometimes the girls are given a husband, so they are forced to be a wife. They have no choice. Then, other times, they are raped.

But it is force in both cases, Jane said.

One time the girl is a wife, Barbara said patiently. The other time there is violence. Yolanda nodded, as if this explained it well.

Pierre had his tripod set in front of the desk where a boy in a red University of Nebraska T-shirt was speaking just above a whisper. His brother had tried to protect him when the rebels came. His head dropped down. They killed his brother. The boy's head and arms began to tremble. His head lowered till it was resting on the wooden desk. That's okay, Jane said.

The boy was led away, and the director explained that when this boy,

Victor, returned, word was sent to his parents. Victor waited five days before he heard his parents were coming, then two days for them to walk there. The director greeted them when they arrived and Victor's father embraced him with tears, but the mother stood aside with arms crossed over her dress. Victor said he wanted to come home, but he was told he must stay the required period of rehabilitation. Then I will come? Victor said. His mother would not face him. His father bent down to him. Yes, he said, looking uncertainly at his wife. This mother was very religious, the director said, and Victor had broken commandments.

How old is Victor?

Nine.

Another interviewee was brought in, a strapping young man, big as a football player. For three years Thomas had been a soldier to Kony, in his inner circle and had seen Kony close up. He was eighteen now. Thomas's handsome face was still as a mask. When he spoke his lips hardly moved. Don was leaning in the doorway, listening, unusually spellbound. In a dull voice Thomas described Kony's camps.

At the center was the yard with a border of sticks and branches that sometimes sprouted trees. Kony had them draw a map of Uganda on the ground with the location of the other barracks, the Nile River, and a half-moon, though there was no explanation for the half-moon. Before entering the yard, where God emphasized his power, you must be bathed and have no blood on you. Quarreling was not permitted; one had to keep a clean heart. On guard duty you could not have sex. When you first became a soldier you were not to have sex for two years. Each day they prayed in the yard. Wherever they were, they prayed three times a day, in the evening in song. Some prayer sessions lasted an hour, perhaps three. They prayed for those possessed by the devil, for a sterile woman, an impotent man. They prayed for the Uganda People's Defence Force, their enemy, to confuse them so they would not fire on the rebels. They would also set guns on top of a hot stove to learn of the danger to their soldiers.

How did that help? Jane said, scribbling notes, even though the camera was rolling.

The guns going off would tell them which weapon would hurt a rebel, he said.

Jane nodded, baffled. She asked about the voices who spoke to Kony.

The tipu called Who Are You would alert Kony that the spirits wanted to speak, and would make an appointment for, say, one o'clock. This tipu was a rude one, Thomas said, and very much complained. The secretary set up a table with a glass of water and the Bible, and Kony would sit in a white gown. He dipped his fingers in a glass and slumped down and a spirit would come into him. Three spirits maybe came at a time. Thomas showed no signs of wonder or pain or disturbance at these things. It appeared he was surprised by nothing.

How many spirits in all? Jane said.

Thirteen. They did not appear together, only two or three minutes for each. For Malia, Kony's voice was that of a woman. She was from Sudan and gave the military advice. Many were from other countries.

Pierre and Don exchanged a look. This was crazier than they had imagined.

The American spirit, Thomas went on, was Zinky Brinky. He was an intelligence officer who decided the court martial. Sinaska was the one passing messages to God, and King Bruce controlled the stone bombs.

Stone bombs?

Yes. When you draw a white cross on a stone so it will not explode.

Oh, she said.

There was an Italian doctor who gave medical advice—Must be our Dr. Marciano, Jane said—and the Chinese Willing Hing Sue, who established schedules. He also performed miracles, like lifting soldiers into the air during battle. The chairman was Juma Oris. His unpleasant voice made the rules for behavior. No smoking or drinking. One must respect the trees and anthills, for they were superior to us. Do not kill an unarmed person.

Were these rules kept to? Jane said.

No, he said.

In a year or so the spirits were predicted to stop speaking to Kony. Soon the Americans would fight him, Kony said, be unable to defeat him, and then join him. Then everyone in the LRA would become young again and each have ten children, for only children would emerge from the bush, with all the adults dead. The LRA would then fight SWW, the silent world war.

The listeners stared with dazed expressions.

But, Thomas said, his face brightening, wanting perhaps to end on a positive note, Kony told us peace would one day come to Uganda. And when it does, five hundred people will die of happiness.

They left when it was time for the children's dinner. Jane walked slowly to the gate, not eager to find the guilt waiting for her when she left. A boy caught up to her and handed her a piece of paper. It was not a boy she had spoken to. He had protruding front teeth, and his T-shirt said *Hard Rock Cafe* in rainbowed letters. His drawing was of a girl with a skirt to her knees and short boots and a bag with a shoulder strap and water bottle sticking out. Is this me? Jane said.

He stared at her. People here often just stood near without having to talk. For me? Thank you, she said. He kept staring, not waiting for anything. She put the drawing in her bag and took out the water bottle. Here, she said. He took it with both hands, looking at her, not at the bottle. The bottle didn't seem to matter.

They stumbled back to Caffè Roma for a dinner of curry and beer. When their stupor wore off, they commenced bickering.

Why was Don snapping pictures during the funeral? Lana wanted to know. Her hair, curled in the humidity, stuck to her temples. Don seemed genuinely surprised. It was an incredible scene, he said. When the mother started weeping? Exactly, Lana said. I thought we were here to document this, he said. She pointed out that Pierre wasn't shooting. Then, said Don, he missed out. It's like being a vulture, Lana said. Feeding off their suffering.

We are trying to help, Jane said in a small voice. At least, that's the idea.

If you don't have the stomach for it, Don said, you shouldn't be here.

Have the stomach for it? Lana said. No one should have the stomach for this. Her cold eye indicated she was including him in this.

Harry placed his napkin on his plate and stood up. I'm done.

Suddenly everyone around the table looked deflated. Tomorrow they were leaving Gulu. They were able to move on from this place. As Harry walked out the screen door, Jane felt a trapdoor open at her feet.

Does anyone have dental floss? Don said. I have goat in my teeth.

＊

In the morning they packed. Harry bunched his clothes into balls and stuffed them into his knapsack.

Is something the matter? Jane said.

We're not going to make it, he said.

For a split second she thought maybe he meant the trip and the story, but her tingling face knew otherwise.

We're not? She tried to sound relaxed. She had envisioned this moment. Is that what people meant by being prepared? It didn't seem to help.

It's not the best situation, he said.

No, she said. She wasn't sure which part of the situation he was referring to, but felt helpless to defend any of it.

She turned to her bag and started folding again what she had already folded. She waited for him to say more, but nothing came. After a while she said, Maybe when we get back . . . He turned his face to the side to show he was listening, but his back stayed to her. We could . . . But she didn't know how to finish.

16 / Stone Trees

ONE DAY Simon comes to me after washing.

I heard you lost your mother, he says. I also lost mine.

A rough boy came a few days ago. He had been with the rebels a long time. Simon saw this boy Zachary kill his mother and father. Mr. Charles and Nurse Nancy suggested a meeting with this boy so there might be forgiveness. Simon had to shake his hand. Mr. Charles said we have been forced to do many bad things, but this is a good thing. Now Simon must sleep in the tent with the person who killed his parents.

I still have a father, I said.

He nods. Then he asks me why I am not kicking the ball with him and the boys. I tell him I do not feel like it. Maybe I am angry. Maybe I do not like being told to do anything. He said he heard I was fast running. Maybe I am, but to him I said, I am not.

He kept his arms crossed and looked, not believing me.

Each time I see Simon I feel a pull coming from him. I do not always like it and sometimes I do like it. Some faces shine from inside and Simon has that. I am always turning to see where he is. Perhaps the pull from Simon will take me somewhere, I am thinking.

I point to his leg. How is it?

He shrugs. He has no worry in his face either.

We must try reconciliation also. Captured rebels have been brought to GUSCO and we are invited to go and greet them if we choose it. Six of us girls from St. Mary's are taken to Gulu. Janet and Carol come and Judith is there, coming from her home. I have not seen Judith till today. We embrace.

She says, I see you and so I am thinking of Agnes. She takes my hand with her soft fingers and we say nothing more. Such are our reunions.

Suffering has not passed through Carol and she holds it in her face and will not smile. We can look however and understand one another. When Carol was in Sudan at Rubanga Tek she was wife to one they call Doctor. After he died she was kept alone for ninety days before she could be wife to another.

We girls are stone trees walking into the yard. No one says what is in her heart. Maybe we do not even know it.

We see Geoff D'Amillo, the husband of Janet. He sits outside the building on the concrete with his half-leg out and his mouth sagging, very old. He is the father of her child. Janet believes we are blessed in life, and being with the rebels did not change her belief. Some girls are changed and not others. She named her child Miracle. She stands for a time with us then goes to Geoff D'Amillo.

You are a cruel girl, he says when he sees her. You left me.

Janet lays her arm on his shoulder, keeping her face turned away.

You are not looking well, he says. She does not move her arm off, but also still does not look at him. This is the way she forgives. I see other rebels there I have seen before. I look through them. I remember what they did. I might find a kind spot in myself but I do not try.

I dream there is a wedding, my wedding. For five days I wear a different dress each day, one white with red trim, another striped, another long and blue with open shoulders. But I do not have a wedding dress. The groom maybe is Philip, maybe someone old, but I do not find him. In one room there are all the sweets and pastries and wedding cake and I want to go into that room, but it is empty and I must not be the only one.

Today I was playing with Janet's son. I was chasing him. Miracle just learned to walk and looks back over his shoulder screaming, happy to be chased. When I bang my feet it startles him and he jumps with fright followed by the happiest smile in the world. Children like to be scared. For a moment his happiness cuts me like a sliver. He was not trying, but I get it from him. Happiness used to come to me from swimming in the river or seeing the sky turn green before it might rain, but happiness from people is most strong. For a moment I thought Janet maybe was right, that it would be okay. I thought, maybe I am not hard as stone.

Then immediately a dark cloud came to my brain, telling me to remember something. It was Agnes I was supposed to remember. I saw her with red earth caked in her shirt and her arms at wrong angles. Some people are so gentle; that was Agnes. I see her chin ducking when she would slap her hand on me, laughing, and I feel that soft hand. So, happiness makes me remember what is gone. But even if it hurts me I would keep thinking of Agnes. The Acholi have a saying, *Poyo too pe rweny.* Death is a scar that never heals.

We are preparing the dingi dingi dance. When the drumming starts I am not always wanting to dance, but after a small while beside the other girls, I find the beat comes into me and am taken along. We dance side to side with our hips and back to front with our arms. You point your foot forward, then back, stamping heels on the ground, shuffling forward. Our shoulders move like so and our hips shake like leaves rolling. The front dancer blows a whistle and we turn, tipping forward. When we are dancing I let go of thoughts.

There is one morning the mothers come. They come to hear news brought by the recent ones returned. After breakfast Nurse Nancy takes me to them, sitting on the benches by the office, waiting. I see Lily's mother holding a baby in a sling, and Marie Joseph, the mother of Helen, with her hair in a roll above her forehead. Pere Ben, Charlotte's father, is there also, wearing a jacket with no buttons. I see Abigail's mother in a dress of brown and orange pattern with creased triangles at the shoulders, dressed up for her visit. I do not see Agnes's mother. She would have heard about Agnes from someone returned before me. Grace Dollo is standing with them. She smiles secretly at me.

They all ask, Where are our girls?

I sit beside Nurse Nancy. One speak, then another, Nurse Nancy says.

Marie Joseph takes my hands. Esther. God bless you. We all bless you. And we bless your mother.

Do not hurry her, Pere Ben says. Their faces are sad and worried, except for Grace Dollo, who watches, making sure everything is said.

We are all in Sudan, I tell them.

All the girls of St. Mary's?

Yes, we are kept together there.

We have heard this, Marie Joseph says. That you are together. And Helen, she is there? With Kony?

She is a wife to Kony, I say softly.

Marie Joseph nods with a strong frown. Pere Ben says, Yes we have heard this.

Charlotte, his daughter, she was once a wife to Kony, but I do not say it. Maybe he knows it. If she returns, they will learn it. Maybe it is better if they do not know it now.

One at a time they speak. Grace introduces them. Here is the mother of Linda Ollo-Ollo. Do you know this girl Linda? She was not a St. Mary's girl. Say hello to Lily Nyeko's mother. She's here to discover what you know of Lily.

Yes, Lily is there. In the Jebelin Camp.

And she is well? She keeps her hands on the baby, who makes no sound.

Yes, I say. Mrs. Nyeko turns her ear to me, asking me again, thinking I am lying. She has probably heard Lily has the AIDS sickness. Grace says, We want to know it, Esther.

Sometimes she is not so well, I say. Must we say everything?

Charlotte was moved to Aruu Camp after leaving Kony. I say she was moved. I say I have seen this girl Linda Ollo-Ollo. She has a daughter named Sparkle. I tell Mrs. Ollo-Ollo, a wide-faced woman with plastic earrings and a plastic necklace. She smiles with tears in her eyes.

I think of my mother. When she would come with the other mothers, what would they say about me? That I was still alive. That my baby was not. Being alive is the only news a parent wants to hear.

Abigail's mother sat listening till her turn. She was not a big woman, but suddenly she took up a lot of space in front of me. And my Abigail?

I do not look in her direction. I am looking at the hem of my shirt and making pleats with it. It is a new white T-shirt. God help me, I whisper.

Abigail's mother seems to come near. What?

I shake my head and see her face out of the corner of my eye, frightened.

What can you tell us? says Nurse Nancy. I look at her. You can say it.

I cannot. Nurse Nancy whispers in my ear. Is she wounded? I shake my head. Is it sickness? I concentrate on my shirt. Is she dead? I look at her eyes. Nurse Nancy faces Abigail's mother. It is bad news, she says.

Abigail's mother's face jerks as if someone has hit her. No, she says.

I stay looking down. I do not want to tell this story.

She turns to the mothers beside her. What is she saying? No one answers.

Nurse Nancy touches my arm with one finger, as if more would be too much force. Esther, tell us.

She tried to escape, I begin. Behind them Grace is nodding at me.

Abigail's mother takes my fingers off from pleating my shirt and holds them, not hard, but not softly. And what?

Grace comes forward. Florence, she says, and puts her arm around the creased wings of Abigail's mother's shoulders.

Abigail's mother says, Tell me. I look to Nurse Nancy. My hand is being clutched by Abigail's mother. Esther, she says, please.

How can I say it? A rebel named Mali tried to get Abigail to go with him and she refused, so later he came back and forced himself on her. She was crying so hard afterward she told us she would escape now. Even to die would be better, she said. We saw she was not thinking carefully. She was not waiting for the right time. That evening when we went to fetch water, Abigail bolted into the bush. She ran, without knowing where she was or caring if they saw. So they caught her right away. I do not tell this to Abigail's mother. One day I maybe will have to say it. But now . . .

Please, Esther. In the name of Abigail.

I whisper into my lap. Abigail tried to run away and was caught. So they killed her.

Abigail's mother starts rocking back and forth. She shakes her head, saying, No no no. Grace is still holding her and helps her stand and leads her away to the van which brought them. Nurse Nancy pats my leg. It is okay, she says.

This is what people say. I wonder when anyone might say, It is not okay.

That ache in my throat gets no better. It feels like a boulder blocking a cave and it aches, that boulder in my throat.

VIII

***

Air Pocket

17 / The You File

YOU WAKE in the morning, shattered. Your dreams batter you like rapids, people trying to kill you, waiting in the woods. You are lost and the road is strange. You are late, you are weeping. You shut your eyes, holding down the saucer of your soul. Help, you say, not praying to God, but you keep saying it anyway. Help. Help me. Sometimes you even say, Help me, God.

Something stays with you, floating over your shoulder, not leaving. Perhaps it will never leave.

You hear someone's voice then see her face turning, saying your name. She is wondering where you are and where you have been. You do not know what to tell her. You are not sure. You are less and less sure. All you can say which is honest and true is, Here. I am here.

18 / Dusty Ground

THE WHITE TRUCK drove out of Gulu town. Their last stop would be Kiryandongo Camp, an hour south in the countryside. In the cab there was a wrung-out air, as if each person were hiding under his or her own cloak of shame.

Don looked deflated, all his air let out. He had stopped criticizing their every move. Lana was wrapped in a white Ethiopian scarf, attached to no lover. Pierre's camera, shielding his face, was aimed away from them, out the window. No music played, no one argued, no one cried out when the truck slammed the potholes with a spine-crushing blow. Jane felt the eyes of the children fixed on a wall in her brain. Harry drove with a distant gaze, as if he were already gone ahead.

Everyone agreed to keep it a short visit so they could make it back to Kampala that night. Jane wondered if anyone else still even wanted to stop. Pierre perhaps, the others had had enough. They wanted to get back to Nairobi as soon as possible.

The turnoff to a rough road came in the middle of nowhere.

Here, Jane said from the back. She reached to touch Harry's shoulder. He didn't flinch but a coolness received her and she took the hand back. A flush of humiliation spread through her body, the body that had been so mixed up with his.

The road was deeply rutted and they bounced on it gently, at one point scraping the ground with a metal screech felt in their feet. Shit, Harry said mildly, not stopping. No comment was added.

They crossed a wet patch of road bordering a marsh and came around a corner to an empty parking area at the end of a barren field. A spindly goal sat tipped in a triangle at one end.

A man in khakis and a dark polo shirt greeted them. Charles Oringu was in charge of the camp. Please, you are welcome, he said. He had been expecting them. Come this way. Harry got out of the car and, after taking off his hat, disappeared under the car. Jane walked away. Here she would be able to stop thinking of where he was and what he was doing.

Past shedlike buildings were a couple of huts and a cloud of smoke hanging over an open kitchen area where a few figures in aprons stood by black pots. Chickens wheeled by, flapping their wings in the dust. A large tree spread near an open-roofed structure, and behind it in the distance the white sheet of a tent appeared like a drive-in screen. Jane saw children sitting in the shade, and more children farther off, washing dishes in plastic buckets.

THE JOURNALISTS COME as we were told. Journalists have been here before, but not for myself. I see them while we are cleaning our dishes at the spout.

They get out of a white truck which has a cover over the back. There are three men and two women. One man is underneath the truck with his feet sticking out. Then they walk over like people you see in magazines with sunglasses and bags over their shoulders, some wearing hats, some carrying cameras. One woman is small. The taller one we learn, she is from Kenya. She has on long necklaces and a leather cap with silver charms pinned to it and a fringed skirt. She is crouching down to one boy, Adam, talking with him in Swahili. He does not talk back, but she keeps smiling. They are looking at his palms. The smaller woman has a gray army hat on and a light-colored ponytail and a blue dress above her ankles. She carries a straw basket with a finger loop like those we get at the market. One man has dark hair covered by a kerchief and holds a camera. The biggest man is the most white with a light pink shirt and skin like sand. He does not look at the children, but walks about in clean sneakers, looking over Mr. Charles's head as if there were something more to see. Behind them comes the last man from under the car. His hair is to his shoulders and he has on a white hat. His pants are rolled up and his brown shirt is untucked and his hands hold nothing. He walks separate from the others and goes to another place and sits on a stump in the shade, near boys playing choro in the dirt.

Later this is the one who goes to the bicycle repair and makes a parachute with a figure hanging from it. He is also African from Kenya. When you drop this figure from a tree branch or high place it would sail off in the wind. The boys learn to make more of these parachutes with bits of cloth, so after the journalists leave we will remember that one from Kenya.

The others first disappear into Mr. Charles's office. Then they have a tour. We see them by the tent, standing.

We are under the tree, crocheting, when Christine comes walking to us, bringing the smaller lady beside her. Who will talk to her? we wonder. Janet whispers to me, God will provide.

Christine tells us, This lady has come from America. She wants to hear how it is with us. If this is okay, we will help her know it.

No one says anything, but no one says no. Some keep working their needles. Emily is staring up.

The lady in the gray hat bends down to us, sitting on her heels. The man in the kerchief comes behind her, floating his camera in front of him, away from his face.

My name is Jane and this is Pierre.

She says she wants to tell people outside of Uganda what is happening here. She hopes it will help.

Christine repeats this in Acholi, but we all know what she says. The lady takes out of her basket a notebook like the ones we use at St. Mary's, with a green-and-white-flecked cover and blue spine.

She asks who understands English and Emily's arm shoots up. Some other hands go up. Not mine. The lady asks Emily her name and how long she is here and where she is from and how long she was with the rebels. She writes the answers in her notebook with a black pen. Sometimes she is writing without looking at the paper, keeping her face to us with her pen moving, listening. As she is listening she is also looking. I see her look at Carol, who will not look back. I see her spot a new girl, Paulette. She wears a dress with a ruffled collar and is showing a big stomach. The lady moves there by Paulette, who stops crocheting when she is near, keeping her long neck bowed down. What's your name?

Paulette looks to Christine, worried.

This one is Paulette, Christine says. We have welcomed her a week ago.

Does she know when the baby's coming? the lady says to Christine, but looking at Paulette's doily. Paulette answers so softly you can barely hear.

Christine answers, The baby will come perhaps in a month or so.

How old is she?

Fifteen.

And this is the baby of a rebel?

Christine nods, but asks her anyway and Paulette says yes.

Do you have a name picked out?

Paulette's face suddenly has many thoughts on it. She gives a long answer to Christine in Lor. Christine listens, tapping a twig on her chin, then, taking a breath, says, If it is a boy he will be Komakech, which means *I am unfortunate.* If it is a girl, Alimochan: *I have suffered on this earth.*

The lady looks to the man with the camera, and lifts her chin to make him come near. Is it okay if we film her? the lady says.

Christine translates to Paulette who listens, frozen. Maybe it is okay, Christine says.

The man steps around some girls, smiling at them. Paulette does not move when the lady asks where her village is and when she was taken. We know that Paulette's parents have not come yet, but Christine does not say it. The man points the round black circle of the camera at Paulette.

She does not want it, I say.

What? The lady turns to me. The camera?

She is frightened.

The lady glances up to the man who lowers his camera right away. Then I see his face and the most blue eyes I have ever seen, not dark blue, but blue like the sky. I'm so sorry, the lady says to Paulette. Will you tell her? She turns to Christine. Thank you.

Then she speaks to me. Thanks for telling us that. What's your name? I am Esther.

Oh, she says, and moves near to touch my arm, which makes me jump. She takes back her hand and puts it flat in her lap. Sorry, she says. I was just— What's your last name?

Akello.

Yes. She smiles. Grace Dollo? You know her? She told me to find you here. She said, You look for Esther Akello. And here you are. I've found you.

I felt a surprise in me too. I looked down from her face. Against her skin, she had on a short necklace with a silver charm on it, a flower maybe or a propeller from an airplane.

I see you're not crocheting. She took off her hat. Her hair was the color of bread. Would you come talk to me?

Christine moved near and said that I did not choose to talk.

Really? The lady looked to my face see if this was true.

I would not speak as they were always telling us to do. I was thinking, Why say these things when I want to forget them? I do not want these stories to be my life forever. I want another life. So I did not answer.

That's too bad, the lady said. But she did not turn away from me, she waited. She still watched me. The sisters at St. Mary's are also white-skinned, and seeing her made me think of them. I would have liked to hear you, Esther, she said.

Perhaps I would be stubborn forever. Or I could change. Maybe this was the time of my chance.

I sat up. I said, It is okay, then.

Christine looked surprised. The lady did not look surprised. She had a smile.

We moved to a place apart from the girls, where the camera was put on a triangle. The lady from America took her sunglasses off.

Shall we start at the beginning or the end? she said. The eyes in front of me were gray and a stranger's eyes, but when she said this I felt she was not a stranger. She was like the sisters.

The end? I did not understand.

Where you are now. Here. The camera was up on black legs just going by itself. The man sat below it, cross-legged.

Perhaps the beginning, I said.

Good. Tell me the beginning.

Maybe I would tell this story again, maybe this was the one and only time, but my words, they were going in the camera.

I began, They came for us in the night. . . .

The lady watched me as I spoke. I looked at her hair, I looked at her shoulder, then down at her basket. She listened with her mouth closed. Sometimes I looked to the empty football field and saw a dust devil swirl up like a rope unwinding. I saw the girls past the kitchen in their dancing costumes with the woman from Kenya. They were making steps with her. I might look down at my hands, but in my head I was seeing again where I had been. And I told her all these things I have told to you.

———

AT FIRST THIS girl Esther spoke so softly Jane thought she'd been wrong to use the camera. She had a square forehead and round cheeks and a forceful look in her eye, despite her bland delivery. She spoke as if discovering things.

Marching away that night, she said in her gentle voice, we could not believe what was happening to us. Now I am here and I ask myself, Was I really there?

Her body and face were very still, and her hands sat holding each other in the lap of her white T-shirt. She chose her words carefully, focusing, and now Jane saw she was not being reluctant, but methodical. This girl had been back only a couple of weeks. Now and then she nodded to herself for reassurance, as if to say, Yes, that's right, that's how it was. She looked into her lap, she looked at Jane with a frown. She glanced off now and then and her eyes ticked back and forth, scanning the inside of her brain. She told her story without self-consciousness, not trying to impress. But Jane was impressed. She was glad the camera was recording so she did not need to take notes. Jane listened and nodded and asked small questions. Yes, she said, go on. All her attention was taken listening to Esther Akello.

I did not want to hit her, she was saying. None of us want to hit her. Esther's cheeks started to shake in a twitchy way and Jane saw she was having difficulty moving her mouth. But I did. We beat that girl. We killed her. I killed her. She bit the inside of her mouth. You are the first I have told this to.

The molecules in the air seemed to rearrange themselves around Jane. The part of her recording this story thought how no one could hear this and not be moved and want to help. The part of her unaccustomed to reporting felt a sort of repulsion intruding on this private distress. Pierre sat on the ground beside the tripod, with his arm extended, holding out the small mic, looking down, letting the camera witness.

Esther pressed the side of her face with a flat palm to still it. Her fingers trembled.

You can stop whenever you want, Jane said.

It is okay. Esther frowned deeply, rubbing her face, seeing something new, putting a hard glint in her eye.

One day we were made to cross a river.

Yes?

It was a terrible day.

What happened?

Esther told the story of losing Mary.

That is a terrible day, Jane said.

I WAS REMEMBERING new things. I remembered how on the day we crossed the river I was not so upset. I told the lady this. I did not feel bad, I said. I would lie to say I did. I felt just tiredness.

It was hard to say it.

Yes, she said.

I wished we had saved that girl Mary, but when she disappeared I did not care so much.

The lady looked away from me. I noticed the change because her face had been toward mine so far. She was seeing I was a bad person.

THE FACE WAS so wracked with sorrow Jane glanced away, to give her privacy. What could she say? She looked in Pierre's direction. His gaze met hers and she saw tears in his eyes. She turned back to Esther.

That happens, she said. It's okay.

It is hard to know it, Esther said. Her look seemed to plead to Jane, needing to be convinced.

Jane stood up.

THE LADY CAME and sat beside me. You were surviving, she said. Her arm moved around me.

I hoped to let this comfort me.

Sometimes when you worry about other people it doesn't help you survive. It sounds to me as if you have been very brave, Esther.

A spear came into me. I did not see I was brave. Maybe I had lived, but I knew I was bad. The thought I was brave was a new thought. I looked at her blue dress beside me. She comforted me with her arm. I had never touched against a white person this way. We remained there. Soon we were talking to one another.

JANE KNEW she was crossing a line. The journalistic code barred involvement. The foreign element of yourself altered the scene and the integrity of truth.

Too bad, she thought, I won't only listen. She no longer was the neutral recorder. Listening to Esther had taken her past that. She wasn't a journalist anyway and they could have her integrity. When she put her arm around her, Esther did not jump away as she had the first time. She smelled sweetly of sweat.

Esther was looking down at her hands, still shaking. I have done terrible things, she said.

Yes, Jane said. She was breathing in a deliberate way to keep from crying. She remembered in reading about trauma how it was important not to contradict a person in recovery. You cannot take away what has happened, you cannot take away the bad feelings about it. Reassuring a person it wasn't their fault does not help. The last thing she, or anyone else for that matter, needs is to be told how you ought not to feel something, or that what had happened was not as bad as it felt.

Esther's head was tipped frozenly forward. Jane kept her arm around her. Her head was close and soon resting on Jane's shoulder. Jane felt the faint trembling.

But you're not doing terrible things now, Jane said. You are yourself again. No one is controlling you now. She did not use a cheering-up tone. She was just stating facts.

I am hoping this, Esther said. She spoke from the back of her throat so weakly it sounded like the squeaks of a small animal. Then she started to mumble. Jane couldn't make out the words. Whatever she was saying needed to come out. She moved her hand on Esther's shoulder now and then, encouraging her. Maybe the camera would pick up her words, maybe not. They were beyond words now. Esther's head leaned more heavily and Jane felt the close-cropped hair against her chin.

Yes, Jane said. Yes. And Esther muttered on.

———

THE MAN REACHED UP and turned the camera off and the lady stayed sitting with me. We stayed there for some time. I was being cleared out, not in a hollow way, but a filled-up way. That ache in my throat had dropped and now spread across my chest. The feeling of her arms was like sleeping in a safe place without needing to know where you are.

She said she had met Sister Giulia. Had she told me that? No. Sister Giulia was well. She had been to St. Mary's and spoke with Teresa and

Beatrice and Sharon. Up close the lady's hair in places was the color of corn silk. I looked at her necklace. She saw me looking and touched it.

It's a dragonfly, she said. My sister and I give them to each other. We used to swim in a pond that had hundreds of dragonflies where we grew up and so we like them.

Yes, I said. I like to see them also.

It was a coincidence, but I said so because I really do like them.

She touched the charm, trying to see it. Dragonflies barely walk, she said, but flying they are one of the fastest insects in the world. Which is funny.

I looked at her white fingers. Yes.

And other funny things. Their eyes touch each other.

My own eyes felt there were stones on them; I was feeling a change happening.

They can propel themselves in different directions, she said. Up, down, forward, back, side to side. Unlike other flies.

I have watched them do this, I said.

In some places dragonflies stand for strength and courage. Like you have, Esther, she said. She was looking at my mouth. I looked at hers. There was a crooked tooth. I looked in front of us to her blue skirt.

I would like to give it to you, she said. You will take it?

I stayed still, waiting. Was this allowed? She took her arm away from me and reached to the back of her neck and unhitched it and brought it out like a hammock between us. Her gray eyes had the question for me. Yes?

I was surprised. It is okay, I said.

Here, let me put it.

Fastening it, her fingers touched the back of my neck like an insect herself. She let go and the silver chain and the charm now lay on my T-shirt. I looked down, but the charm was high under my chin, so I could see only a part. I felt where it was and felt the sharp silver wings. Thank you, I said.

You are very welcome. Thank you.

I thought, I wonder how long I will keep this necklace before it is lost.

They also stand for happiness, she said. Her voice caught. The word *happiness* made us both look away.

We saw Christine and Emily approaching from across the yard. Emily would speak next, and the lady pushed herself up with her hands and stood to greet her.

THE VISITORS WERE INVITED to sit on benches under a feathery acacia at the edge of a circle of packed dirt. At one side girls stood in a cluster of long royal-blue skirts with pleated yellow peplums and halters crisscrossing strong backs. Each ankle had a yellow fringe wrapped around it. A few boys in T-shirts were poised beside drums stretched with animal skin, or holding hollow gourds the color of army helmets.

The drumming began and the gourds started clacking. The girls shuffled forward in lines—their feet going heel-toe, heel-toe. They took short steps, then hammered their heels double-time. Shoulders rippled like cloth. In the front of a line, a girl biting a whistle blew a sharp note and everyone turned, shuffling in a different direction. Another whistle and their torsos tipped forward, heads to the side, extended and hovering, seemingly disconnected from the body wavering behind. An elbow jutted up and pumped up and down birdlike, all in sync. The dancers' faces were placid. They appeared hypnotized, gyrating their hips in minute circles and stamping madly, sending off puffs of dust. Jane watched, transfixed by the beauty and overtaken by the beat. She thought, everyone should always be dancing. She spotted Esther. She was moving in a solid way, head level, shoulders twitching, in perfect time with the other girls, and like them with a faraway look.

One girl broke from the line and sashayed to where a group of boys stood bobbing. She danced near and stopped in front of a boy, selecting him to step forward. She shuffled in a circle around him, keeping a chin affixed to her shoulder, not meeting his eye. When he reached out to touch her sash she immediately turned and danced back to her line.

Another girl danced over to the visitors and took Lana's hand. Another reached for Harry, but he shook his head, keeping his elbows on his knees. Lana kicked off her sandals and moved into the circle, stamping her feet, her fringed skirt shaking. She rolled her hips, not as rapidly as the girls, but in the same motion. Her long arms stretched out. The dancers watched her, clapping, and for the first time Jane saw the faces of all the girls smiling.

———

THE LADY CAME to bid me goodbye. I know you will be fine, Esther Akello, she said. She thanked me and we shook hands.

I touched my dragonfly and she nodded. I watched her leather sandals walking away. They were white from being covered with our dust.

Holly and I stood as Mr. Charles accompanied them to the truck. I watched them but kept seeing Mary's head in the river appearing then disappearing. Since dancing the blood under my skin was moving like a big chain twisting through my body. I felt my own head as if it would explode.

———

THE VISITORS DRIFTED toward the parking area.

Lana held the hand of one of the dancers. You leave Lana here with me, said the girl.

Jane was the last to say goodbye to Charles Oringu. You tell them how it is in Africa, he said.

Yes I will. Thank you for having us.

Thank you. We will be very grateful to Mr. Don for his contribution, he said.

His what?

He has been very generous. Jane looked over to Don by the open door of the truck, brushing white dust off the rear of his pants. Five thousand dollars is a great deal for us here and will do much to help the children. He bowed a little to her, making her feel ashamed.

Sitting behind in the truck she found that the back of Don's head had a new look to it. Harry's arm, stretched across the seat back, was different too, not hers anymore, maybe more beautiful.

Driving away, Jane saw Esther walking with another girl, their fingers hooked together. Then they separated and Esther moved off on her own.

The truck passed a marsh lit orange in the late sun, dipped deeply to one side and stopped. Harry revved the accelerator a couple of times without enthusiasm. He got out, and Jane saw in his face he knew they were stuck. Both right wheels were sunk in soft mud. He and Don tried rocking the truck, then kicking stones and soil to fill the puddle.

People appeared from out of nowhere. At first they stood, watching, then without being asked, bent to their knees and dug with their hands. Don and Harry planted their shoulders against the fender and when the wheels spun were sprayed with mud. Someone offered a flimsy piece of cardboard which was slipped under the wheel, and that miraculously gave it the traction to move.

They drove away from waving figures. Jane and Lana climbed out the windows onto the roof and sat in the hot wind, watching a low apricot sun in the haze. At the main road, Harry stopped to let them in, but they stayed up there. The land spread around them, an open world. Jane felt the pulse of the music in her thighs through the roof. It had the sound of the other life they were returning to, which would be different now.

When would they leave her? When would she stop thinking of them? She would write about the children and eventually they would retreat to a place in the back of her mind. She would need to stop thinking about them and eventually would. They would stop being foremost in her mind, as they were now. She was already ashamed of abandoning them, but there it was. Recognizing it did not make her any less helpless before it. She thought of the girl Esther and of her fierce eye frowning and her soft voice and being next to her arm to arm. The truck picked up speed on the main road and Jane felt the sky expanding in her.

They pulled over at a dusty lot to a yellow shed that had pictures of fruit and milk bottles on the side. Pierre went in and emerged with bags and handed warm beer and bananas up to the roof. Both were delicious. They bumped back onto the road. The sun was now shocking-pink and transparent just above the trees. Jane and Lana stayed on the roof in the thick, hot wind. Harry handed them beers from the driver's window. Jane wasn't ready to get back in. She and Lana stayed out as long as there was light.

They would definitely be driving back in the dark now.

*

The night was black and the road undefined. There were no streetlights or lit windows. Now and then they passed a bare bulb on a pole
lighting a closed door. Shadowy figures were seen for a moment, then
would disappear. A few darted across the street, picked out by the farthest
headlights.

Do these people want to die? Don said. His tone was not dismissive,
but genuine with wonder.

Farther south more cars appeared, often with no headlights themselves. One massive truck barreled out of the blackness straight for them.
Harry swerved, face steely, the others poised and alert. No one said it, but
they were all relying on Harry. Lana and Pierre clutched hands. Jane sat
lightly in her seat, her arm against Lana's, bracing herself inwardly, but
she felt it as a distant fear. In the wake of all they'd seen and heard this
fear seemed really rather small.

IX

Spiral

19 / Where I Went

AFTER THE JOURNALISTS LEFT I went to my bed and lay on the top bunk.

I was full, like a barrel. I got down from my bed and thought, I will walk to a place behind the tents where I went other times alone. So I went there. It was near dinnertime and the birds were coming out to sing, but I heard little outside the silence in me. I had the face of the lady from America in front of me and thought again of what I had said today. I stood by a tree I knew. My whole body was an ache. I touched that tree and lay myself against it. It was like being close to a person and for that reason you cry on them. I coughed and a sob came out of me like a cork popping from that barrel. I bent to the ground and my crying began. It rolled throughout like a storm. There was not enough space in me to keep it.

My face was sideways on the dirt. I forgot where I was, hardly even a person curled into a ball. My hand hit the ground and the sobbing went on and I pounded more. I did not feel my fist. I also banged my head, then I hit at my head, beating myself. I beat myself as we did that girl from Gulu, the one we killed. My chest was breaking apart. A chunk split off and another wave of crying came and when I thought there was no more to break another piece would crack off. I could not breathe. I gasped at air. I thought of Janet saying, the heart is endless like God is endless, and I thought, My heart will be endlessly breaking. I wondered, even as I cried, How will this stop? It had to stop. Did it not?

I may die from it, I thought. I had survived many things, but now I would die of this. I even wished I would die and the wishing made more tears come.

Then my fist was limp beside my face and it was quiet. Some time passed, I don't know how long.

I must have moved closer to the tree, because later I woke close to it. Ants were moving on my leg. The boulder in my throat was gone and instead I felt a space open in me. The space was soft. I sat up and brushed my shirt. I sat for a while. The bush had a few evening sounds but was more quiet.

When I stood up I had a feeling of peace. This was new. I walked without any other feeling back to camp. Dinner had been served and the children were sitting at the tables. Janet and Holly looked at me troubled, but I answered them with a peaceful face. I sat with them on the bench and listened. The sound of everyone talking was like a pretty song. People were like bells, each one ringing his or her own special sound.

After that day, when I see a person cry I see they are on their way to feeling better. Since that day I cried my heart onto the ground I am feeling a change might come to me.

I remember the lady from America and the journalists who were here. I remember they had been our friends.

This morning we are under the tree with some girls doing crochet. It is sunny and not so dusty after rain last night. The air is fresh. Simon is by himself on the playing field, kicking a ball with his crooked leg. Beside me Holly shakes bugs from her yarn. She is making yellow socks. She has no baby in mind, but says there will always be a baby coming to someone. Yellow works for a boy as well as a girl. She may offer them to Paulette, the new girl.

More boys run onto the field.

What are you watching out there? Emily says.

I do not answer. A few boys run around with Simon. It is not time yet for football or shop. It is still free time. Simon's face turns toward the shade where we are and maybe he can see me. I think he finds my eye.

He starts running and does a little *one-two-three* move with the football, which ought to be wobbly with his warped leg, but he is like a goat, keeping his balance. When he kicks it to another boy, he bends low to the side. I feel the pull.

The last time I ran hard was when I was escaping. My arms hug my solid legs, my chin is on my knees. The girls, heads bent, talk like insects humming on a hot day. When Simon runs he dips from side to side, not showing on his face that it is hard for him. The ball is kicked hard and comes sailing off the field and rolls behind our tree where we sit. Simon runs toward it, running toward us. No girls notice, they are talking, and I do not know why, but I stand up and walk to the ball stopped against a dried-out log. I become someone else for a minute, someone happy. I put my foot on that ball.

Esther! Simon calls. Kick it!

I toe it with my sandal.

Pass! Come on! Here!

I pick it up to throw it. No, I say to myself. I pull back my foot and kick it. It goes sailing up higher than any of us thought. It goes to the other side of the field nearly to the marsh. Simon turns to chase it.

Do I stay? No. Do I walk back to the shade and sit? No. I run onto that field.

I run with the boys. I chase one with the ball and catch him and kick the ball from his feet. I am faster than some of them, I feel even faster than myself.

In the morning we wake and find Carol not in her bunk. Holly said she heard some movement in the night of her leaving. A search for her begins.

Later they find her in the marsh, drowned with her face in shallow water.

Her parents do not come. They tell us her parents are dead. We do not believe it. Carol knew her parents were not taking her back. She did not want to live more. Are we surprised? No.

We understand. Some of me goes with her now she is dead. I let Carol take that part away, the part that would want to die. Instead I would want to live.

The next day while everyone is drawing I pick up a blue pencil and piece of paper and think maybe I will draw this day. I will not draw so much, but something. I put lines, making a river and trees beside it and waves bumpy in it. In the middle I make a round shape. I draw myself, watching. I feel Simon over my shoulder.

What is this, he says. A snake?

A river, I say. This was a girl named Mary.

He looks at my picture, not speaking. I do not want him to speak. Then he takes it from my hands. Maybe I will show you how to draw a tree, he says.

Much time passes and still we do not hear anything from the lady from America so we do not know if she has explained our story. I begin to think of the future. I think maybe I would like to be a teacher.

20 / Don't Go

I'M NOT WITH THIS anymore, he said.

They were in Harry's room off the long downstairs hall. He lay on the bed that was his bed as a boy, a single mattress against the wall. One arm was tucked under his head on a pillow without a pillowcase, the other lay inert by his side. Jane sat near his inert hand. He was keeping his arms to himself, arms which at another time would have been pulling Jane over to him.

When I'm done with something, he said, that's it.

His words struck like a bolt. She felt she was no longer sitting on the bed, but hovering above it.

She looked at his face, then away. Looking at him was not better, it was harder.

Okay, she said. On the floor by her feet was a straw rug with woven giraffes. She wasn't going to fight it. How could she anyway? What could she say?

Should I go? she said.

No. He frowned. You stay. But I think I'm going to go flying with Andy. Go on a mission.

She waited.

There's this place we've been wanting to check out.

Oh?

He didn't say anything.

Where? she said.

In Marsabit.

She nodded. She had no idea where that was. There was silence. When? She said it as a double question, as if asking if she could ask.

Tomorrow.

She kept nodding. You should, she said. That'll be good. And I should get to work.

His parents were leaving for a week, but she could stay in the guesthouse, he said, or whichever house she wanted. She said that would be great. She could start on the story with her impressions fresh. She didn't say it would be good to concentrate on something other than him. Was it really okay with his parents?

Totally cool, he said. I'll make sure with my mom.

She sat up and took a breath, not to look downcast. How long? she said, and immediately tried again with lightness. I mean, when will you be back?

He shrugged. He didn't need to tell her these things now. It wasn't her business so much anymore. She stood, releasing him.

Not too long, he said.

They'd gotten back to Nairobi that afternoon. Pierre was unceremoniously dropped off at a friend's empty house in Karen, and when they stopped at Lana's there were no invitations to come in for a drink or have dinner later. Don sauntered toward the cottage, carrying bags, and Lana stood at the truck window. She reached into the cab and her hand warmly pressed Jane and Harry, acknowledging the value of the trip. Then she sighed. Now how I am going to get rid of Don?

Jane returned with Harry to his house where she'd left some of her things. They unpacked the truck and threw out the trash in bins in the garage. Harry led her and her bag through the kitchen past a large living room set off by steps, with wide couches of no arms and a massive stone fireplace. A two-story glass window overlooked a lawn ending in dark woods topped with the bluish peaks of the Ngong Hills above. The last room at the end of the wing was his sister's unused room. Emma had been living in Ireland for some years with her husband and children, having moved to where it was safer to raise a family. On one wall was a woodblock portrait of Mandela, and in a frame a photograph of young Emma and Harry cuddling a cheetah. The big house felt particularly solid and polished after the last two weeks.

Jane unpacked her black bag, pawing through flattened dirty clothes. She came across the oversized brown linen shirt Harry sometimes wore. She went back down the hall to his room. Here, she said. This is more you now.

He folded his arms, as if refusing it. Don't you want a shirt that's me? He was smiling.

No, I want you to have a shirt that's me.

He took it and brought it to his nose. It smells like you, he said. I won't wash it, just smell it now and then.

The smell will go away.

I won't smell it all the time. He was trying to make her smile. With an effort she kept her face bright.

He looked at her face, assessing it, the way he looked at the sky. I'm going, he said. But I'm also not going.

The air darkened as she took a bath. She didn't feel the loss of him yet, but knew it was coming and braced herself. She couldn't tell how big or small the impact would be. She'd wait to find out. He was still nearby, so she didn't have to feel him gone. He was under the same roof and her body knew it and felt reassured.

She lay in the water, trying to find more reassurance.

Okay, she thought. Okay. It'll be okay. *Okay* was the most reassuring word she could come up with. It's what she'd said to the girl Esther. It will be okay. It was the reassuring thing one said.

There was always life. At least I'm alive. At least she was still here. But here with herself, the reasons to be alive came flashing and they had to do with Harry. Those were the bright things in her. She allowed herself to note them and felt again the small shocks they gave, when he'd pulled her down the hall the rainy night in the Mara, with the loud mud and the warmth of his skin through his wet shirt. She thought of the night on the road back to Naivasha watching through the black windshield as he scooped up the body and carried it like a lover out of the headlights.

Her throat thickened.

She might be saying Okay, but No is what she was feeling. Yes, she had said to him, but inside she was refusing it, not ready to let him go. She would have to think of another perspective. One could manage most anything with the right perspective.

She zoomed into the future to picture him there. If he were in the future, then it meant he would not have gone.

Years would go by and she would still know him. They would always know one another. Some people you met and knew they would always be in your life, and hadn't she known he was one of those people?

Way off in the future she would let him know how he had mattered to her.

She could tell him then, after she'd proven it with time, not now when it might seem she was asking for something back.

He would be married by then. His wife would be a great girl. She would be a flier too. They'd have two kids, or three, and live in a tree house or by the sea. And one night when she was visiting them, because she would always come back to Africa and he would be one of the reasons why, late some night when she was sitting with her old friend Harry, she would tell him without any drama how it had been for her back then, that is, now. She would not be causing any mischief, because she would have a husband too and they would all be friends and she would not want anything from him—only that he know, for the record, how he had added an important thing to her life. How, with him, she had found a new part of herself. To describe it now might look as if she were being dramatic. She had a fear of overdoing it, and appearing needy. So she would wait. She would easily wait for years, it would be all right to say, By the way, this is how much you meant to me. And this is how grateful I am for the new bit of life you gave me so long ago, lifting me out of a dead place where I'd been wasting for a long time. Maybe she would say she'd loved him.

He might say, I didn't know. Or he might say, I was too young to know it. Or maybe he'd say, in his direct Harry way, Yes, I knew.

He might even add, I wasn't where you were yet.

And she would say she had known that.

What she might say would wait and prove itself over time. Important things lasted and could wait.

There was little food in the kitchen but they located a box of spaghetti. Harry grated some rock-hard Parmesan he found sweating in the bread box. They drank Tusker from bottles and their conversation was oddly polite, as if they were just meeting, which in a way they were, being with each other in a new way. They ate at an old butcher block in the middle of the kitchen which unlike the other kitchens she'd seen in Karen houses looked twenty years old and scuffed. Usually one did not go into the kitchen, it being the staff's domain. The rest of Harry's parents' house was polished with dark wood floors, but the kitchen looked lived-in and worn. When she asked, Harry told her about the school he went to in Langata where nearly all the students were white. His best friend growing up didn't go to the school, but lived here, on the other side of the garage, in the staff's quarters. Edgar was their servant Priscilla's son. But when he was older he didn't mix much outside the white Africans. Harry said that basically he had two friends who weren't white which was a pretty pathetic percentage.

As they were doing the dishes, Harry's parents returned in the back door, looking weathered and tan. Harry introduced them again to Jane, wiping her soapy hands. I read your book, his mother, Sheila, said. I liked it. She had short hair and looked nothing like Harry, with a slender face and thin neck. Harry's father, Joe, had a beard and wore a plaid shirt, looking like a Peace Corps worker. They'd been out to dinner and were leaving early in the morning for a week in the north to inspect some cattle. Joe said he was done in and going to bed and mildly left the room. The master bedroom was far off, in another wing of the house Jane hadn't seen.

Good trip? his mother said, picking up mail on the counter and glancing through it. She wore shorts and a sleeveless collared shirt.

Harry nodded. It was hectic, he said.

I bet.

Harry draped his arm over his mother's shoulder, only slightly below his. He mentioned Jane staying in the guesthouse while they were gone, and Sheila said that was fine, her thoughts elsewhere.

She patted Harry's back as she turned to go. Have good flights, she said, distracted.

You too, Harry said.

Oh. She stopped in the doorway, not turning around. Make sure Priscilla knows Jane is here.

After she'd gone, he said, They work too hard. But it's good.

The television was in a small room off the long hall near the kitchen. Jane lay stomach-down on the rug looking through a book about Baron Blixen with black-and-white photographs of stylish white people standing beside dead wildlife or dressed in flapper outfits beside palm fronds. Harry turned on the TV. The sound was grating; she had been so far from it for weeks. The news was on: riots in East Kenya, blurry shots of people running through rising dust. An ad came on for a floor cleaner with white tile floors and yellow cartoon sparkles. Harry switched the channel. A turbaned woman was singing an African song, then two women in chairs were talking to each other. He stopped at a movie, a cheesy horror movie from the seventies. He slumped down, accepting it with a slack face. Jane tried ignoring him, and focused on the big-hatted men and carefree women on safari in laced boots and jodphurs. She would have liked to be blank now, too.

On the screen a girl with flipped-back hair was running past a pool at night. A boy scrambled over a fence. He landed and paused, his polo shirt tucked into high-belted pants. A wall of fatigue hit Jane. She knew she should go to bed. She was not looking forward to standing and walking back to the guest room. The movie flickered on. Someone screamed. There was a man in a mask. Another girl in shorts was making something in a blender, so she didn't hear the scream.

Jane wondered if she might write him a note later and slip it into his knapsack, so he'd find it on his trip, setting up camp wherever that was. He would have it and think of her and maybe miss her. She would say, I told you I would wave goodbye. Or maybe not.

There was a loud banging on the door in the kitchen, echoing down the hall.

What the fuck, Harry said blandly and stood. He did not look alarmed. Maybe it's Andy, he muttered, leaving the room.

His sneakers slapped down the hall. She pushed herself up and reached for the TV dial to turn down the sound, muting an ad for potato crisps. Maybe they could still stay together tonight in the same bed, chastely or not. Their time together had been short but full, strange and disorienting. They could at least still hold each other. Immediately she realized, No. Harry wasn't like she was, wanting to cut corners. He was decisive and would stick to his word. *When I'm done with something that's it,* he had said. She would be like Harry then, a person of her word. She would accept this is how it was.

She heard a male voice in the kitchen speaking Swahili, an African voice, not Andy's. The voice sounded upset.

She hoisted herself off the rug, feeling thick and tired. Coming down the hall she met Harry's silhouette. Something's going on, he said, and turned around. She followed him into the kitchen where a young man in a blue buttoned shirt stood by the sink.

This is Murray. He says the askari's gone.

Harry had opened a cabinet and was feeling around inside.

Murray nodded with a worried face. He was the younger brother of Harry's childhood friend Edgar.

Some guys were down by the gate, Harry said, closing the cabinet, not finding what he was after.

Should you call the police?

Harry shook his head as if to say, Who really knows what's going on, if anything. I'll just go see, he said. The police are imbeciles anyway.

He looked Jane square in the face and held her shoulders. I want you to lock the door, he said. Come here, like this. He slid a thick bar across the door frame above the doorknob. And don't let anyone in.

Okay.

Come on, Murray. Where's Priscilla?

She is not here. This day she has gone to Kibera.

For the night? Harry sounded surprised. They stepped down to the driveway. Habari ya Edgar? he said, and before Jane could hear the answer she had shut the door and drawn the bolt.

The window over the kitchen sink faced the wing of the house with no view, so Jane went back down the hall to a laundry room where a window over the drier faced the driveway spotlit from the garage roof and the staff's quarters beyond. Through heavy grating in front of the glass she watched Harry and Murray walk past the white truck parked past the garage door and out of the area lit by the spotlight. She saw them in shadow on the grass in front of the servants' quarters and at the end of the lawn disappearing into the dark stand of pole-like trees. The woods ran along the winding driveway; they were taking a shortcut. Through the leaves' ragged screen of black lace glowed a topaz streetlight at the end of the driveway where it met the Ndege Road.

She felt for a latch and opened the window like a door. Warm air came through the grate and the very distant sound of voices. They didn't sound confrontational. She tried to make out Harry's voice, but it was too faint to tell. Then the voices got louder and were shouting. Was one Harry? She knelt up on the drier and pulled herself to the grate. There was a loud crack, and for an instant she thought it was her knee denting the drier then immediately realized the sound came from outside and an electric jolt in her body told her before her mind did that it was a gunshot. She froze. The air seemed to change into something solid, forming around the fact that something terrible had just happened.

She pulled herself near the bars. Harry! she screamed. Harry! She was screaming at nothing, and nothing answered.

She jumped off the drier and ran down the hall toward the phone. Footsteps came padding out of the deeper darkness of the house, and

Sheila appeared in a loose sleeveless shirt and pajama pants to her shins. She held a wooden stick with a round ball on the end. What is it? she said firmly and fast, managing to sound both urgent and calm.

Harry went down to the gate—

Joe! Sheila called, not taking her eyes off Jane. Joe! Then to Jane, What happened?

Jane told her. I was about to call the police.

Joe hurried by them, shirtless, his neck tan, his torso pale. I've got it, he said. Sheila and Jane followed him to the kitchen.

Sheila opened a cabinet different from the one Harry had opened and took out a flashlight. She pulled back the bolt on the door and hurried down the steps through the open doorway. Jane saw the beam of the flashlight bobbing up and down and the stick in her hand as she ran toward the trees.

Harry! she called. Harry! A voice answered. Murray! she screamed. Uko wapi? Where are you? Hapa, came the distant reply. Here. The flashlight flickered like heat lightning across the tree trunks.

Joe hung up the phone on its small table outside the kitchen door. Police are coming, he said. He should have woken us up, he continued in a tremulous voice. He opened a drawer and took out a knife.

Jane stood useless. Murray said the askari had gone, Jane found herself saying. *Murray.* Why was she even saying the name Murray? She didn't know Murray.

Joe shoved his feet into a pair of canvas shoes by the door and grabbed a jacket from a crowded hook. Lock the door after me, he said. Apparently this is what the guest was told. Jane stood in the doorway and watched Harry's father hurry toward the trees and meet a figure emerging from the darkness. It was Murray.

Mama says you will call the ambulance, he said.

Jesus God, Joe said, wheeling around. You go back with Mama, he said, and Murray turned around. Jane stood aside as Joe rushed past her to the phone. He dialed. Bloody hell! he said. He hung up and dialed again. His body was turning side to side, wanting to move but tethered to the coiled line.

Jane stepped outside down the kitchen step. Her throat was pounding. She walked crunching the gravel. Past the garage in the staff house a door was open to a yellow hallway and she saw a woman standing on the grass, the backs of her legs and the hem of a dress picked out in the light from the door.

Priscilla?

The person's head turned slowly. No, came a soft voice. Priscilla is not he-ah tonight.

They both jumped, startled by another shot. It seemed to be farther off, down Ndege Road. Joe came tearing past her, jacket flaps open. Sheila! he screamed. Answer me!

Her voice screamed back. Get the car!

Joe spun back around and went through the garage side door. The pleated garage door went clattering up. A motor started and a big square car backed out, lurched forward in a tight turn and skidded off down the gravel. Jane followed it, jogging behind the red lights floating down the driveway. At the turn it became dark and she kept running blindly. Around the corner she came in sight of the end of the driveway and the brownish streetlight past it. On the ground the flashlight made a triangle of light, picking up pebbles in the dirt.

Beside the flashlight was Sheila's seated silhouette. Across her lap was a body. The car pulled up and its headlights shone on Sheila bent over Harry. Her arms and shirt were stained dark with blood.

The car door flipped open and Joe was out. He crouched down in front of them, then ran back to the car and returned with a towel. He tucked it gently under Harry's head. Jane got close enough to see half of Harry's face covered with blood. Help us, Sheila said.

They lifted Harry and carried him to the car. Sheila, not letting go of his shoulder, backed awkwardly into the back seat while Joe and Jane held his legs. They placed him down carefully, stretched across the seat, resting on Sheila.

We are not waiting for the ambulance, Sheila said. Come on. The towel had fallen and Jane picked it up. It was dark and wet. Sheila took it and made a pillow for Harry in her lap.

Murray, unlock us. Murray grabbed a key hanging from the rearview mirror and unlocked the padlock at the gate, unwrapped the chain and swung back the gate.

Joe spoke to him in Swahili, telling him to go back to the house. Jane, he said, get in. Jane got in the front seat.

Come on, Sheila said. Hurry.

The car swung onto the Karen Road and met a pair of headlights coming toward them. It was a police car with an unlit light on the roof. Joe rolled down his window, not stopping, just slowing down. Our son is badly injured, we're taking him to the hospital.

The policeman started to answer but whatever he said was lost as they drove past.

Another police car appeared behind the first. Jane watched the cars pull up to the gate where Murray was locking up, looking tentative.

One's turning around, Jane said. The second car zoomed after them, catching up. The policeman called out the window, Follow us. The car sped ahead.

Sheila looked up for a moment, checking that Joe was going fast enough, then turned back down toward Harry. She muttered, You're going to be okay, Harry. We're getting you to the hospital. Just stay with us, my darling. We're getting help. My darling, you've been shot. Then she added with disbelief, Someone shot you.

In a different voice she said, to the front seat, He has a pulse.

No one else was in that car. There was only Harry with his mother cradling his head and her low voice murmuring. You're going to be all right. We're going to get you fixed. Don't worry. Listen. I'm right here. Dad's taking us. It's going to be fine. Just hang in there.

The ride was endless. Then when they arrived at the hospital, it seemed to have taken only a minute. The car swooped to the emergency entrance. Joe ran in and came out with two orderlies in white pushing a stretcher on clanging wheels. The unmoving body in a gray T-shirt was lifted by strangers out of the car and laid onto the stretcher. One of Harry's sneakers was gone and his foot bare. In the yellow light Jane saw half his face smeared dark red and the other half the color of white stone with an eye closed in it. Joe and Sheila stood with their hips close to the stretcher.

I'll park the car, Jane said. Joe's head nodded, without looking in her direction. The stretcher jangled inside.

Jane got behind the wheel of the big car. Her foot couldn't reach the pedal. She groped under the seat for a latch to pull the seat forward and felt rusted rods and sharp seat supports. She found a lever, but nothing budged. She perched at the edge of the seat and gripped the steering wheel and started the motor. When she released the clutch, the car jumped forward, hit the curb and stalled. She started it again and backed up in a series of jerks, finally stuttering into a dark parking area with the sign *Staff Parking Only*. A road led her one way past the entrance and away from the hospital. It was quickly dark. At the first side road she did an inefficient three-point turn, hoping no cars would come, and drove back to a different hospital entrance where she found another parking area with few cars and no people in sight. She parked and turned off the motor. She got out. Her body felt stripped inside. Normally she would have been on guard in a deserted place like this at night, but normal fear was replaced by a larger terror.

She headed for the creamy light of the emergency entrance. Her thoughts seemed both shattered in pieces and finely focused. Please God, she thought. Please God, she said out loud. She did not believe in God, but if he did exist, this was how it would feel to have him nearby, as if everything were clear.

There was no one at the first counter behind a glass window. The interior of the hospital looked like the 1950s with wooden chairs cushioned in green leatherette and yellowed walls with brown trim and aluminum ashtray stands. A plastic clock said it was ten of twelve. At the next window without glass she found a person. The woman had light-colored cheekbones as if they'd been bleached. Jane asked her where she could find Harry O'Day. The woman glanced at the sheet beside her elbow. This patient has just now been taken to intensive care, she said. It is this way.

This patient. He was alive. He's still here, she said to herself, and caught herself. *Still here.* It implied it wouldn't last.

*

Jane sat in the waiting area of the ICU. An older man in a Hawaiian shirt arrived, apparently a doctor. He went into the nurses' station and used the phone, then entered the double doors. A couple around Joe and Sheila's age came into the waiting room. The woman had long white hair, belted trousers and silver bracelets on both forearms. She walked directly to Jane. You are here for Harry? How is he?

Alive, was all Jane could say. I'm Diana, she said. And this is Lorenzo. The man beside her had drooping eyelids, combed-back hair and wore red Moroccan slippers. He bowed and shook Jane's hand. So we wait, Diana said.

The next time the automatic doors swung open, Joe stepped out with the man in the Hawaiian shirt, their friend Dr. Ross. Dr. Ross spoke. Harry was on life support. He'd been shot in the left side of his face and a bullet was lodged in his brain. There was no point trying to remove the bullet. He's alive, Dr. Ross said. But the brain is no longer working.

Andy arrived, hurrying down the hall, long hair swinging and sneakers springy. Joe brought him through the automatic doors. Some time later, he came out.

His face told Jane it was unspeakable. Still, she asked him, How is it? Bad, he said.

They sat together. Jane realized that this must have been the hospital where Harry had done Reiki with his girlfriend. He was in the same intensive care unit as the man who made him faint.

When the sky grew light in the upper windows of the room, Jane and Andy left the hospital. They drove back to Karen in the O'Days' car with Andy at the wheel. He was not a talker and Jane was glad to be beside a silent person. She kept dropping into sleep, then jerking awake.

Hey, Andy said. Take some shut-eye. She was asleep when they arrived at the house. They collected the things Sheila and Joe had asked for—clothes, an address book, paper and pens. Jane called Lana, waking her, then Andy made a number of phone calls. Jane went to Harry's room and stood in the doorway. She looked to see if there was anything she could bring him. She thought, Will he ever come back here? At the corner of a low bookshelf she saw a chess trophy. It had his name on it. She had no idea he played chess. When she went back to the kitchen Andy was gone. She sat at the butcher block where she'd sat the night before with Harry. This can't be happening, she said to herself. In times of trauma, one just thought clichés.

Andy walked in from outside. He'd been next door talking to Murray. On the drive back to the hospital he told her what Murray had said.

Something's not right about the story, Andy said. But you never get the whole story here. Murray did recognize one of the guys last night. He said he knew his cousin, whatever that means.

The morning traffic into Nairobi was heavy and slow. They stopped and started. Off the side of the road stood half-built concrete structures in abandoned construction sites. A tissuey dust hung in the early sun, the air was loud with engines. The paths along the road were full of people, a woman balancing a plastic basin on her head, a man in a heavy overcoat, children in green uniforms with their white socks pulled up, all of them unaware of Harry.

This wasn't supposed to happen here, Jane said. We just returned from a war zone.

This is a war zone, Andy said. Haven't you noticed?

They passed a man walking quickly along the path, a soiled white T-shirt fluttering above his bare ass.

Yikes, Jane said. They both laughed shallowly. It was strange to laugh.

They drove through the timeless morning.

You know Harry sort of broke it off with me last night, she said. She thought she should report this to someone. She also thought, Could that have been only last night?

Yeah. Andy nodded. I know. His face had signs of fatigue, but he was nonetheless placid, one of those people mild and stalwart in a crisis.

He told you?

Yeah. When we were planning the trip.

She wasn't sure whether she wanted to hear more or not, but didn't stop to decide. What did he say?

He said you always had too many people around. You were never alone.

It was a shock to hear he thought that. It had not occurred to her he would care. As usual Harry had noticed an important thing. She didn't know him as well as she thought. That's true, she said. I had no idea.

He liked you, though, Andy said.

She caught the past tense and in a split second wondered if he was thinking of Harry that way or just the change with Jane.

Harry hadn't exactly said it to her. Suddenly it was important that things be said out loud. He did?

Yes. He told me right off when he met you. When you went up to the Ngongs? He was trying to decide if he should go up north to work with the cows. Or I could stay, he said, and go back to Lana's and kiss that girl Jane.

People kept arriving in the waiting room. It occurred to Jane how probably more bad things than good happened in waiting rooms.

Lana came sweeping down the hall in a linen duster and leather boots with Pierre beside her. The area around Pierre's eyes looked scorched. Lana hugged Jane and her face cracked into unabashed tears. Later she sat uncharacteristically still with a brown scarf across her shoulders and an inward gaze, as if meditating with open eyes. Pierre kept leaving to smoke despite the ashtray stands everywhere. Two young men with tangled hair and both wearing torn shorts sat with Andy, other paragliders. One had a cast on his arm. Other people Harry's age turned up: a blond girl with dreadlocks talking to everyone in a whisper, smiling and grasping their hands. Meeting Jane, she gave her a kiss. I've heard about you, she said and raised one eyebrow. A pair of dark-skinned women arrived. It was Priscilla with her sister Rose, the woman Jane had seen outside the staff house in the dark.

Everyone spoke in low voices. What was being done? They were seeing if . . . they were just . . . no, no decision had been made . . . wasn't breathing on his own . . . brain activity . . . had Sheila slept? . . . Emma was flying in from Ireland . . . once Emma got here, well, then . . . the police had caught one of the guys, not the one who did the shooting . . . what had happened to the askari? . . . what Murray said was . . .

They sat in the waiting room, piecing together facts. The facts kept Harry close.

Murray was home with his aunt and younger cousins when he heard noise at the gate. He opened the door and listened and heard voices down at the road. His aunt told him to leave it alone. Stay: Kaa hapa. Wacha.

But he wanted to see what was going on. In the trees he stopped when he heard banging on the fence. The askari was not there. The fence was high with barbed wire curling on top so he could not see who was behind it. Then a figure could be seen at the gate, banging on it with a club. He looked drunk. Murray ran back to the house and got Harry. When he and Harry returned, all was silent. The road was empty. Harry asked him how many had been there, maybe doubting him, and Murray said three. But they are now gone, Murray said.

Then they were not. A wide dark silhouette came forward out of the blackness across the street, three figures making one brown shadow on the road.

Harry held his hand up. Jambo, he said, but the hand was saying, Keep back. Hakuna shida hapa, he said: No trouble here. He was not shouting, Murray said. Not angry. Everyone could picture that with Harry. Leave us alone, eh? he said.

Murray said their eyes looked full of drugs. They were not so young, but they were not old. Open the gate, one said, swinging a stick. This one wore an army coat. Another in a cap was cradling his stomach. Murray saw why. He was holding a gun, it glinted in the streetlight. He thought Harry must have seen it also, but Harry kept speaking.

No, Bwana, we do not open. He held the lock as if to say, This stays so. Go on, Harry said. Nothing for you here. Murray tried to alert him to the gun, but Harry was not looking his way.

The one in the middle stepped forward and lifted the gun. The two on either side stepped away. The man's face was very hard. Murray turned and ran. While running, he heard the shot and was too frightened to look back right away. He hid in the trees and watched the figures as they ran down the road, away from town. After they were gone he hurried back to Harry.

Why would they shoot and then run? Where had they gotten a gun? Stolen from the police probably . . . there'd been a robbery at the station a week ago . . . robbing the police station . . . only in Africa! . . . but in Kenya that's where you find a gun . . . or from a park manager . . . but this wasn't a shotgun . . . odd Priscilla was away, she was always home . . . maybe they thought no one was in the house . . . Sheila and Joe had first planned to leave that day but changed it to a day later . . . was it an inside job? . . . they often were . . . but it wouldn't have been Priscilla . . . she really was family . . . but there was that brother who'd been in and out of trouble . . . The police suggested it was a drug deal gone wrong . . . yes, less responsibility for them . . . maybe Harry owed money, they said . . . it didn't look like a robbery . . . why would they just shoot a person when they weren't even inside the property? Because it was Nairobi, that's why. . . .

Down the hall Harry's heart kept beating while the sorting of these facts—the intruders, the gun, what Murray did—was the chorus being sung around what were very likely Harry's last hours on the planet.

Pierre lay stretched out over three chairs, resting his head on Lana's lap. They were talking to each other and she was laughing. Then he was laughing, too. No, they weren't laughing. They were crying.

In the afternoon, more people. Yuri, the artist Jane had met that first day she'd met Harry, came, frowning in a linen shirt spattered with paint. He spoke in a booming voice, refusing to give reverence to disaster. With him was a small-nosed woman with a camera around her neck and a firm mouth suggesting she took herself very seriously.

Jane listened to the woman named Diana who liked to talk and had a lot of opinions. Oh, spare me the free spirit, she said. A free spirit's just an idiot who doesn't want to face reality. Our Harry's better than that. I mean, honestly, what's the point if you spend all your time trying to avoid the way things are? You miss out on life. Harry knows what's what. Always has.

Jane was grateful for the present tense. A young woman in white go-go boots and a sheath dress came in with a small child, whom she set up on the floor with crayons and drawing paper. When the daughter showed her the picture she'd drawn the woman started to cry. The daughter was not alarmed in the least. Jane told Lana what had happened with Harry, before the shooting. Lana nodded, listening. She rubbed Jane's arm, looking off. That hardly mattered now.

Later she moved the hair away from Jane's face. Come on, now, she said.

I know, Jane said. But she didn't, she knew nothing.

Sheila appeared, and everyone looked up and went still. Lana squeezed Jane's hand, not letting go. Sheila was the compass in this new world of the waiting room. She was no longer in the sleeveless top with her son's blood on it, she had on a collared shirt and a denim skirt to her knees. She looked at everyone, unsmiling, though her mouth was stretched in a stiff semblance of a smile. Then she saw Priscilla. She crossed the waiting room and Priscilla stood and they embraced.

What the hell happened? Sheila said. Everyone pretended not to listen.

We do not know it yet, Priscilla said. How is he?

It is not good, Sheila said, holding on to Priscilla's shoulders. Not good at all. And Murray? Sheila said. How is he?

Priscilla looked down and shook her head.

In the late afternoon Joe emerged. He was handed a Styrofoam cup of soup with a spoon sticking out and held it while talking to Dr. Ross. After a while he set the cup down still full on a chrome cigarette pedestal and walked out of the waiting room down the yellow linoleum hall toward the exit. The news spread in whispers he was going to the airport.

An hour later he returned with Emma, yet another family member with no resemblance to Harry. She was milky-skinned with shiny apricot hair and a long chin. She wore a blue blazer over a flowered dress, an outfit from another world. In the waiting room she greeted Priscilla, hugging her for a long time. Diana stood and embraced her, and the woman with the little girl surrounded her. Andy stood when Emma noticed him and she shook her head, as if refusing this. Seeing him was the closest to seeing Harry. She pressed her cheek against Andy's plaid shirt, shutting her eyes, then turned back to her father. With his arm around her, she walked to the double doors. Joe pressed the square black button on the right, the buzzer went off and they pushed through.

Jane knew who it was right away when Rosalie arrived. She was small, as Harry had said, with a child's body and a woman's heart-shaped face, blue eyes wide apart, dark hair and a cherry red lipsticked mouth. She wore a cute 1950s dress and blue sandals and was accompanied by a very tall fellow with a beard who stood near, guarding her. Seeing her, Jane had an unsettled physical anxiety and was mortified that jealousy could visit her under these circumstances.

The dreadlocked girl—Kira, was it?—engulfed Rosalie in her arms. Lana said hello next, putting her hands on Rosalie's small shoulders, looking down with a meaningful stare. Rosalie held the stare on her end and they shook their heads. Then Rosalie sat down and took out some rosary beads. Her red mouth moved in a small way, praying. Now and then she spoke to her boyfriend, who bent down so his ear was at the level of her vivid red mouth.

One by one they were allowed in. One by one they saw Harry. A person returned to the waiting room and everyone's eyes shifted as the next person stood and headed to the doorway to be buzzed in. Not everyone chose to go. Lana said she didn't want to see Harry that way. She didn't think he would want it.

Pierre came out and walked directly to Jane. He looked angry and rubbed the top of her head as if she were good luck. She stood. He fished around in his shirt pocket and turned to go for a smoke.

Jane went to the doors and pressed the buzzer. They opened. Inside seemed sealed off with a low hum of machines. She walked past some closed doors and some doors open where she saw heads sunk back on beds with tucked sheets and plastic masks over faces and bare arms sprouting clear wires leading to metal poles. Lit screens in boxes sprouted a maze of tangled wires.

She came to number 207. The door was nearly closed, but not all the way.

Inside was a bed and machines humming and screens blinking green numbers and colored lines and someone who resembled Harry propped against a pillow. Half his face was covered with a white bandage and plastic tubes went into one nostril and the eye that showed was slightly open with a dark unseeing pupil gazing in the direction of her hands. Jane felt a sob leap to her throat and covered her mouth to stop it. Her eyes filled with tears and heat spread in her face.

Sheila sat in a chair on the other side of the bed with an arm alongside Harry. She looked at Jane with a blank face, blank with shock, yet managed with one slow blink to corroborate the horror of what Jane was seeing. Sheila removed her arm, returning it to her lap, and glanced toward the window to give Jane privacy.

Harry, Jane said. She had to concentrate to stay steady. She felt a sea rising in her, but could keep it down if she refused to fathom what was before her. She looked at him, forcing herself to take in his face, and felt fury that he was here, the part of grief that storms and rails, and tried to stay with that outrage not to fall apart here in front of his mother. The heat in Jane's cheeks seemed to be expanding her head, till it felt huge, like a balloon hovering on top of her body.

She tried to find words. Harry was all that came.

We're all here, she said. Harry. His hands lay on the covers. She put her hand over the hand near her. It wasn't cold, but it wasn't so warm either. It was not Harry's warm hand. Maybe he could feel her warmth now. They said that without his brain he wasn't aware of anything, but maybe his body could feel something or someone there. His body had been how Harry experienced the world. The side of his face had the same shape as before, but the features were not the same. His mouth was open slightly with the lower lip drooping. It wasn't Harry's mouth. Maybe this was still his hand, but Harry wasn't here anymore. She covered his hand, and concentrated on giving him heat.

After everyone had seen Harry, Sheila and Dr. Ross entered the waiting room. Sheila stepped forward. Now I want you all to leave, she said. Her head turned a little to the side, not meeting anyone's eyes. One hand clasped an elbow. It's time to go.

Diana stood. What's happened? She had a deep, direct voice.

We're taking him off the machine, Sheila said.

Behind her Joe came through the doors, looking shrunken. He faced everyone, but appeared to see no one.

Lana gripped Jane's arm like a claw. The dreadlocked girl, cross-legged on the floor, was rocking back and forth with closed eyes. Faces waited, blank. How did one receive such news?

Sheila continued, They don't know how long he'll last when he's taken off. We will stay with him, just his family. And Andy. You all don't need to stay.

No one moved.

Finally Diana went to Sheila and hugged her. Sheila stood stiffly, arms down. Diana muttered something and Sheila wiped tears off her cheeks, looking past Diana's shoulder. People turned away, not to watch. They picked up their backpacks or newspapers, gathered the little piles they'd made of coffee cups and wrappers. They all filed by Sheila and Joe with quick or slow goodbyes and straggled off reluctantly down the hall.

One woman remained sitting in the waiting room.

Priscilla, Sheila said. You go, too.

Priscilla shook her head. I'm staying.

Sheila dropped her chin. She shrugged. Some things you let go.

Lana locked Jane's arm in hers as they walked out. I think now we must go do something really fun, she said.

In the parking lot they saw Rosalie walking with the tall boyfriend. Jane left Lana and caught up to them and introduced herself.

Hi, Rosalie said, mild and reserved. The boyfriend looked down at them, as if deciding if he should walk on or not.

I was a new friend of Harry's, Jane said. He told me about you.

Rosalie looked at her, waiting. Jane wanted to add, He really loved you, but the boyfriend had not walked on and was still there holding her hand, and Jane didn't have the nerve. Maybe another time, she thought. Though she caught herself believing in other times.

I just wanted to say hello before I left.

Thank you, Rosalie said. Her graceful hand gestured upward. This is Cal.

Cheers, Cal said. Where are you from? He had a cheerful high voice, not what she expected to come out of the tall, bearded figure.

New York. America.

So you heading home? he said.

Behind him, Jane saw Lana waving from the roll bar of the roofless Land Rover, showing her where she was parked. The wave was like a lighthouse beam.

No, Jane said. I'm staying awhile.

They gathered at the top of the Ngongs on a slanted field. Jane recognized the place, just down the ridge from where they'd gone for sundowners that first night she met Harry. A long line of motorcycles were parked tilted in the tall grass beside the mud-splattered Land Rovers and dented cars.

A great pyre of branches and logs and palm trunks had been arranged in the Rendille fashion, like a wide tepee. There were feathers and flowers decorating it, a few green wreaths. Someone said the fire for cremation needed to be built in a particular way. For a body to burn the fire had to be very hot with a sustaining flame. The pale coffin was carried by Harry's father and Andy and Emma and Emma's husband and set tilted on the pile. Before it was lit people stepped forward and spoke and read, their voices thin in the open air. The colorful crowd stood very still, women in long skirts and wide necklaces with bare shoulders, the men in patterned shirts and oilskin hats. Some rubbed their eyes. Others hugged themselves, sobbing.

Music played on a tape player. A Beethoven symphony, then Pink Floyd. Joe and Andy and Emma lit the pyre in spots near the ground and the flames started crackling right away. Soon a churning ball of smoke hid the pale coffin from view. Smoke billowed in one direction then swept in another as if pushed by a hand, blowing out over the valley and vanishing in a sheet. Then the wind swung it back over the people standing in their colors. Some turned their backs to the smoke, some covered their faces, some ignored it and stared at the fire. At one point the sound of an airplane engine could be heard and a white Cessna appeared, wavering in the soft sky, sputtering unevenly as it drew near and swooped down to buzz the crowd. The plane circled away, then came back again, diving low through the smoke. It was an old girlfriend of Harry's, Helen, who then landed nearby, arriving, as some guests noted, late as usual.

The fire snapped and grew hot and people stepped back, with faces that looked insulted or ruined. Jane found Rosalie in a flowery tea dress, for a moment unattended by her boyfriend, and told her what she might not have the chance to say again. Rosalie's face was utterly transformed by a flash of joy. Any jealousy Jane had felt completely vanished.

Jane walked away from the crowd, going the short distance to where they'd been sprawled that evening on the striped cloth drinking Lana's vodka, watching the sunset obscured by haze. It was less than three weeks ago. Time had many versions. She remembered how they were all leaning on each other. She stood on the spot. A small tremor shook her and it came back to her how Harry had been leaning on her shins, this stranger she'd just met, leaning so naturally on her bare legs. She'd forgotten that. She remembered him leaping out of his truck that day, him looking at her coldly, remembered their necks slumped in the back seat returning to Nairobi and him saying he liked old, but she had forgotten him leaning on her as if assuming they were already friends. It disturbed her she'd forgotten it, a young man she didn't know leaning on her. She considered herself good at storing away things to savor. Keeping them in mind helped carry you through the loss of them. That was a good point of memory.

Well now she had him leaning against her shins. Something new had appeared. She would have to reflect more. Any new things about Harry would now come from reflection. She would review the days. She had him flying over her head at the edge of the escarpment, had him driving her up the steep white hill with his strong hands wrestling the steering wheel. He was waiting in the shade with his hat brim down. She had his body sleeping around her body in the tent of their mosquito net. She had it again and again, each time the thought came to her.

X

Flight

21 / Perhaps It Is Better Not to Know Some Things

IF AGNES DID NOT come back, at least Louise did.

It was more than a year after I left Kiryandongo that Louise made her escape and finally returned.

When I heard this news I had real gladness. I even remembered the rebels as if there was something good that might have been there.

I had by then gone back to St. Mary's. I remained in school for a while and tried to study, but it was difficult. The air sometimes thickened and bothered me, and I found it hard to concentrate or do well. So I made the decision to come home to my father's house and help with my brother and sisters. Aunt Karen is there and it is not so bad always. Soon I will be going to another boarding school, in Kampala, but not just yet.

Louise was taken to Kiryandongo and I arranged to go as soon as it was possible.

Aunt Karen accompanied me. She got us a lift from the medical van bringing supplies from Kampala. The van stopped at our clinic in Lira where my mother had been a nurse, then continued north to the hospital at Lacor. We traveled on a sunny day and the shadows were sharp black shapes under trees and also under the people walking the red paths beside the road. The van dropped us at the sign for Kiryandongo Camp and we walked the road.

Aunt Karen wore her wedge shoes with tan straps, showing her pale heels, and the soles picked up a layer of red mud, making them higher. I wore a new dark blue dress with spaces cut at the shoulders which I made from one I had seen in my dream. At home I was sewing very much. I also made the top Aunt Karen was wearing, a striped blazer with short sleeves.

We arrived back to this place where I had lived. The trees even stood alert to greet us. I thought of Simon. He had returned to his people in Nebbi, and I sometimes received news of him from there.

I thought of the journalists who had walked across this ground. We had learned of the murder in Kenya and were sorry to hear this news about those who had been our friends.

In the yard was Nurse Nancy leaving the office, her hair flying out as always, maybe longer. She held her arms toward me. Esther, it is you, she said. I am waiting for my letter. I had told her I would maybe be sending letters. I do think of doing it.

We have come to see Louise, I said.

She nodded with closed eyes. I take you.

We approached a group in the shade. One stood. My friend Louise. She looked taller and thinner and had on a new skirt with a swirl of colors and a black shirt.

Our arms went around each other.

Close to her face I said, You are back.

Louise nodded.

You are back. I liked to say it.

Her mouth opened but she said nothing. She did not smile. Her head had been shaved and the hair was smooth. Let us sit there, I said, and we went to the smoothed dirt by a hut, a new one I had not seen. Aunt Karen sat with us. She was a little apart, while Louise and I sat close with legs bent to the side.

I have brought you plasters, I said. They were in the medical van and I knew the camp could use them, so why not?

Louise accepted them. That is okay, she whispered. She put her foot out in a thin flip-flop to show me it was covered on the bottom with plasters. It was the nearest I got to a smile from her.

It is a while before you are accustomed to being back, I told her. She touched the skin showing on my shoulder. I smiled. It will change, I said. She showed what interest she could. Her face was calm, as it is when you return, because you are blank. Behind your face there is still fright you have learned to hide and which may go away or may not. Louise's face reminded me that I am not as I was when I first returned. That other life remains in me, but it is not up in the front.

I asked Louise where were her children, her two sons, and she told me they remained in the medical clinic in Gulu. Here or there, her face seemed to say, I accept what it is.

Some girls passed by with Christine. She greeted me with a sliding hand. You looking sharp, she said. She was in a white T-shirt, and her pearl earrings stood out against her dark skin. I thought of how she had gone to nursing school in Kampala, but it had not worked out so she had returned here to Kiryandongo. Sometimes there is difficulty going back to the usual life. Christine and the girls sat with us. One beside Christine had a bandage over her ear. I recognized none of these girls, but we were all sisters.

We have seen you in the papers, Louise, Aunt Karen said.

Louise looked to her as if at something too bright. It was from her mother's efforts that Louise was known. By now Grace had been written about in Denmark, in the United States, in Germany. When Louise returned a week ago, Grace had brought a journalist there to see her and they had taken pictures. We had all seen the story. Was Louise looking forward to moving home? Aunt Karen said. Louise nodded yes. What do you think of your mother's work?

She has worked hard for us, Louise said in a soft voice. After being with the rebels you learn to say the easy thing. I now saw Aunt Karen had come with me this day because Louise was famous and she liked being near someone famous.

What do you think of what your mother did? Aunt Karen said, sitting straight up; she smoothed that jacket I made for her. My aunt can be a troublemaker. She may not mean to, I am not sure, but she always is speaking of things which might bother a person hearing them.

For us? Louise said. I am happy. Her voice was light as air, her shoulders as solid as before. She started to scratch a pebble in the dirt.

Nurse Nancy appeared from behind the hut. Mama Grace has looked after all the children taken by tongo tongo, she said. She sat down and patted the knee of the girl with a bandaged ear, saying hello. We are very proud of her.

So you understand her decisions? Aunt Karen said to Louise. Some might not agree. With Nurse Nancy here, Aunt Karen felt she had an audience.

What decisions? Louise whispered.

Aunt Karen took a breath. Well . . . she began as if unsure, but I knew my aunt, she was not unsure. She looked with a questioning face at Nurse Nancy who nodded at her to continue. When she met with the rebels.

I thought about stopping my aunt from talking, but now Louise was looking directly at her. She was not blank, she was frowning. She did not want to speak of this. Her cheekbones made her face look triangular. My mother made the decisions she wanted, Louise said. She said it in an automatic way.

I was comforted. So she knows it, I thought. I felt shame for Aunt Karen and stayed quiet, facing away. There was no one on the football field.

But Aunt Karen was not done. So you know the story?

Louise's face was a mask, as if she heard nothing.

Which one? Christine said, showing interest. In Sudan?

We all knew this, when they killed the girl Regina after she spoke to Pere Ben. Many rebels blamed the St. Mary's girls for it.

No, Aunt Karen said. Not that one. Her meeting with Gregory Oti.

Louise's gaze remained down. She was not interested, I could see that.

At the Surf Club in Gulu, Aunt Karen said. It is lived in by a tipu. She explained for the other girls.

Some believe that, I said. But this did not stop her from talking.

You know it, Aunt Karen said, speaking to Nurse Nancy.

Nurse Nancy nodded. Yes, we have heard the story.

Well, I knew it straight from my sister, who knew it from Serena, Aunt Karen said. Serena was at the meeting with your mother, Louise.

We knew Serena. She was the mother of Jackline and, like my mother, no longer alive. Serena was Grace's best friend, who died some time ago, before her daughter returned.

Louise does not know it? Christine said, now recognizing the mischief of my aunt. She placed her hands flat on her lap and observed them, thinking.

No one said anything. We were all thinking of Louise and of the story she did not know. I had the feeling of remembering an old dream, an old nightmare. She felt our thoughts, and perhaps our waiting.

So she said, Tell me.

It was a secret meeting, Aunt Karen said. But it is not a secret now. She looked at me as if I were arguing with her. Everyone knows it, Esther.

And she told us what had happened.

No one looked at anyone. We were all looking inside our heads.

The meeting was arranged by that same doctor who treated Kony. This time the doctor did not promise Kony. No one anyway believed Kony would appear in Gulu. He offered a commander. Grace hoped for Mariano Lagira who perhaps might be generous again.

Other parents went also to the Surf Club. Esther's mother Edith had even been there, waiting at the abandoned house. The doctor arrived and said everyone must leave. But Grace, he said. Aunt Karen told us he had brought Kony's second in command, Gregory Oti. We knew Oti. He was a very bad man, fat, with low eyelids and an uneven mouth. I have seen him once beat a boy with a bicycle chain.

Soldiers accompanied Oti that day, carrying guns. The soldiers entered the house and allowed Serena to stand by the door. No one else.

Louise was scratching that pebble in the dirt, listening. We were all listening. Aunt Karen had started to tell it and was going to keep telling it. Your mother showed no fear, Aunt Karen said. A mother has no fear if she is thinking of her children.

*

There were two chairs in the room, facing each other. Gregory Oti sat first, a big man with creases in his fat neck. The soldiers stood behind and Grace had a view of Serena by the door.

We will have tea, Gregory Oti said. A soldier, not with a gun, brought two tin cups of tea and handed them to the commander and Grace.

Gregory Oti leaned back on the small chair. You have been making problems for us, he said, smiling.

Grace sat on the edge of her seat. We want our children back, she said.

Oti's smile shrank. We look after our children as our own family, he said. Do not think the girls are unhappy. They are happy, they are very happy. He took a sip from his cup.

Mariano Lagira let the girls of St. Mary's go, Grace said.

These girls are Kony's family now.

No, I am her family. I am her mother.

I am not an unreasonable man, he said vaguely. You have made a group, isn't this so?

Yes. We call it We Are Concerned.

Yes. Oti swiveled his head, as if not wanting to hear it. I see.

You know our wish, she said. Then an odd thing happened; she recognized this man as someone she had gone to school with. She had known his sister. But she did not say this.

Someone had placed plastic bags on the chairs, and hers was sliding beneath her. Serena saw she was becoming angry and knew Grace's temper and gave her a warning look. Grace dropped her shoulders a little.

We ask you to please release our daughters and all the children, she said more softly. A glance at Serena. Please, in the name of God.

We have heard you, he said. He sighed. Sometimes we release girls. He shrugged as if he was tired of talking about this already.

You will give us our girls?

Gregory Oti made a noise in his throat, like a buffalo before charging. But he did not want to hurry. He finished his tea and held out his cup to be taken by the small soldier.

This is our wish, Grace said.

Then his face was angry. We have heard it, he repeated.

Grace was silent.

The Aboke girls, they are receiving a lot of attention, he said. You have been the cause of army attacks on the children, you know.

No, Grace said. That could not be so.

I have seen it, he said, leaving his mouth open. And now we hear the Pope speaking of the Aboke girls. He stared at Grace with his low-lidded eyes, as if this were proof she was damaging.

The Pope has spoken on their behalf, she admitted. And on behalf of all the children.

Oti set his feet down. Kony does not like this. There was a pause, apparently in honor of Kony. Then Oti went on, This makes trouble for him. When Kony only wants to keep his mind on saving his people.

Grace chose not to debate the truth of this.

But there may be a way, he said. He smiled. Your daughter, what is her name?

Louise. Dollo Louise. Grace was not encouraged by the smile.

Yes, I have seen all the girls, he said, waving his hand dismissively. I say this to you from Kony. He tucked his hand into his belt. I am a man of my word and I offer you this agreement if you will receive it. I will give you your daughter Louisa—

Louise, Grace said softly.

—and in exchange you will stop speaking against Kony and stop making trouble for the rebels. You and your group will remain silent.

Grace stared at him.

He untucked his hand and held his palms out, as if to say, How can you refuse?

You must release all the girls, Grace said. All the children.

Oti sat forward, hands on his knees, shaking his head. You are not understanding. I give you your daughter. You are then silent.

Grace thought of the children. Later she told these thoughts to Serena. She also thought of the mothers. She thought of Pere Ben who had just then lost his job, working instead to bring his Charlotte back. She saw the different houses where the parents would meet and make their plans. She saw one mother named Florence making soup and crying at the stove for her daughter Helen. The mothers were banded together. She would not forget all the mothers.

Grace held the tin cup in her hand. It was still full of tea. She hadn't been able to drink. The brownish liquid had a slick of oil on the surface and was swirling as if with the movement of the planet, and she kept her head bowed, thinking.

The girls, she said, they are one. She began to shake her head from side to side, and her wide curls touched her cheeks. I cannot take one without the others.

Oti straightened his shoulders. This woman was a fool, he was thinking. Then we do not agree, he said, and stood up. Serena said he looked relieved.

The meeting was over. This was easier for Oti. It would not have been so easy to release only one of the Aboke girls. He was not sorry.

Grace stood also. I know you, she said. Your sister was Angelica.

Gregory Oti had stopped looking at her. Perhaps. But it was as if he were deaf. He was already leaving. His soldiers led the way out the door.

Aunt Karen finished talking.

Nurse Nancy spoke. She inquired of Louise, Can you understand why your mother did this?

Louise's face was blank, but this was usual: a blank face.

Why not just take Louise anyway? Christine said. Then she would at least have Louise back.

Maybe she knew they would punish the other girls, said Nurse Nancy. If she broke her agreement.

They were punishing us in any event, said the girl with the bandaged ear.

I had the strange feeling of everything tilting, and said nothing. We were quiet. We were thinking about this, we were thinking about many things.

Louise stood up. My mother was thinking of all the children, she said, and walked just there, as if to go to the toilet.

When she was gone I looked at Aunt Karen. I had been learning to accept Aunt Karen, but now I wanted to stop learning. Why do you tell her this? I said.

Aunt Karen rubbed her neck. I thought she knew it.

But you see now she did not.

Perhaps it is better not to know some things, Christine said, though she did not sound certain.

The girl with the bandage on her ear, sitting beside her, spoke again: I think it is better to know it.

Nurse Nancy patted her leg again for saying this. We hope this, she said.

Louise returned and sat near me. The others were talking and so Louise and I talked separate. I told her news of Janet and Jessica. I told her I would make her a dress. I did not tell her how one day inside you just say, Enough. I could only stay near her from now on and not leave. She blinked slowly, not ready to believe this new life.

She was facing across the yard and her eyes noticed something far away. I saw why. Her mother was now there, arriving from the road. Grace walked quickly, her brown and yellow dress rippling as she walked. She carried a full straw bag. Louise stood and they embraced softly.

Esther, she said, smiling at me. You are here.

I have come for Louise.

They sat and we all felt the story we had heard. Grace said she had seen the boys in Gulu and they will be fine. Then she asked the new girls what their names were and asked Nurse Nancy about a trip she had taken and talked about being on TV. Louise listened, but she did not look at her mother. She was looking in the distance at nothing we could see.

Much time has passed since that time. Helen, the last one of us, she is still not back. We pray and think of her every day.

22 / Where I Didn't Go

IN HER DREAMS he was always dead. He appeared, but dead. He didn't seem upset. He explained nothing about where he'd been or how he'd come back and was unmoved by any emotion shown him.

Then, in one dream, he was alive again. He was sitting in a chair in his parents' tall living room with the Ngongs out the huge window behind, telling her it had all been a mistake. She fell across his lap and started to cry. There's so much I have to tell you, she said, weeping. When she woke she had a strap across her chest, making it difficult to breathe, and the grief felt like actual poison streaming into her heart.

She stayed in Kenya with no plans to return. She had a dread of going back to familiar things that knew nothing of Harry and nothing of where she'd been and what she'd seen. She had no urge to see the people she knew and to try splitting herself back into an old life when she felt she'd been turned inside out here and was thoroughly changed.

Pierre was offered a long assignment in Afghanistan and he took it eagerly. He'd been subletting an English journalist's empty cottage, so Jane sublet his sublet and moved in. It was two rooms with padlocked French doors and bars over every window.

She rode the English journalist's bicycle around Langata. Lana's cottage was ten minutes away on the dirt back roads and three minutes through the woods. There were more dinner parties with wine flowing, more long candles burning down to white coins, more people appearing, then leaving.

She worked on the story. It absorbed her.

In a daze, she pondered the usual questions that come with loss. Death steers one toward wonder. What is life after all? Are we made of what we think? Or of what we have done? Is our final measure of life the images and impressions we leave in living minds? Or how engaged life felt to us? Or is it all only dust?

One afternoon Jane bicycled to Lana's and found Beryl visiting with the four children. Her husband was still not in evidence. The children played in Lana's scooped-out garden, throwing water from buckets, running along low tree branches. Seeing Beryl had the effect of resurrecting Harry, and Jane's previous suspicion toward her was replaced with an intense unbidden affection, though Beryl herself had not altered in the least. That evening they all lay outside on large velvet cushions around a fire. The children swooped in the dusk, gravitating toward the fire as the flames grew brighter and night fell. The fire cast its spell and wonder showed on all the golden faces.

Jane stared at the twisting flames and the black wood shimmering into blocks of glowing coal. Loss turned one alert to beauty and tenderness. She felt it like a balm, the generosity emanating from Lana, Beryl's loose bravery, looking after her children on her own. The wonder coming to Jane seemed new, but maybe wonder always seemed fresh and new, and that's what wonder was. Who am I? she thought not with anxiety, but with wonder. What good do I do?

Lana and Beryl were chuckling over old stories, the time a hippo charged the Jeep, the time their mum dumped them at the orphanage to go on safari with a lover.

Beryl's daughter Tess was braiding Jane's hair with fingers soft as insects. Jane wondered if she would ever look after a child. She wondered what would it be like if Harry were there beside her on the pillow. She could picture him coming out of the darkness, throwing a log on the fire and sending sparks flying. She remembered another thing she'd forgotten. Around a fire on the McAlistairs' lawn when they were dancing, Harry had come running out of the darkness and leapt over the fire. He seemed to hang in the air longer than a normal person, skimming the flames. It came to her again, the feeling he particularly gave her, that she was an altogether better person. He was connected to something good and solid and through him she was connected too. She could get to there with him in mind. On her own it was harder. People said that it had to be all in you, that you couldn't depend on other people to make you better, but that wasn't true. It was only through people that you learned how to be better.

The women talked and the children fell asleep. Little Tess, with her long tangled hair, had curled up next to Jane and was breathing into her shoulder, in the abandon of sleep, trusting that anybody around this fire with her mother nearby was safe.

Jane wrote the story. In those times of asking herself what she was doing with her life she would fall onto the raft of work and float on the belief that the work would carry her. It was mostly true.

This time when she finished the story, it didn't leave her.

Usually when she was done writing a piece not only would she have worn out her interest in it, but she would have to strain to keep hold of what had compelled her about it in the first place.

. But that didn't happen with this story. Perhaps it was Harry. Perhaps it was because, unlike her other work, this story was real. In any event the images of the trip continued to throw themselves up like screens between her and the world in front of her. The trip was not fading, but becoming richer. It wasn't growing lighter, it was getting heavier. It took on the weight of memory.

She couldn't bring Harry back. *The dead don't come back.* She repeated this to herself. Despite how obvious and ironclad it was, she still needed to repeat it to believe it. She would not hold him again. She would not tell him the things she had been waiting to say. She had thought there was time, then time for him stopped. How was she to know time would stop?

For a long time it remained impossible to believe.

In the months and years that followed, she also continued to say to herself: I have him forever. Sometimes this felt good and was reassuring. Sometimes it even felt true. But whenever she actually pictured Harry where he was now, it was harder to keep the good feeling.

The dead Harry looked back at her from where he was with all the other dead people. His attitude was decidedly not, I am with you forever. He appeared calm, speechless and apart. His being seemed to express itself in a straightforward way. He did not even say it, but his being did. It said, I am not with you. I am not where you are. I am not alive. I am somewhere else entirely forever.

The only thing to do with loss is to bear it.

The question still pressed on: What to do? It was imperative that she do something, and that it be good.

She thought of the children. Harry would always be mixed in with them. She might do something more for the children. Maybe there was more to be written about them. She couldn't take away what had happened. What had been done to the girl Esther Akello, that couldn't be changed. You couldn't pull the sorrow out of people. It was in them for as long as it lasted, showing in their faces, in the slow blink of their eyes. You could not take away what had been done and lend them good fortune. She couldn't switch places with them. And would she anyway?

No, Jane couldn't live anyone else's life but her own. Though, looking back, she saw she had been trying hard.

She kept thinking, What is my life? What to do?

So many things in this world were cracked and sad, and still a glow-ing showed through and moments came when everything was lit and love happened. Every tree stood where it belonged, each bird had per-fect feathers folded against its tiny body, each holding a heart beating madly. Life was a vibration of light and dark, and love illuminated that life. Then darkness descended and your heart was ripped apart. So that was part of it, a requirement of the miracle. Death stayed, lurking in the shadow of beauty. In the bargain, life both had meaning and had none. So, she kept thinking, what to do? What to do?

A pressure in her would not stop asking. There were not many things she could make better, not many things she could change. And yet . . . and yet . . . sparks of possibility still shot out. Unasked for, they came and ran-domly flew up.

———

Notes and Acknowledgments

The abduction of the girls from St. Mary's College of Aboke, Uganda, is based on real-life events that occurred in the early-morning hours of October 10, 1996, following Independence Day on October 9. Sister Giulia's story is based on that of Sister Rachele Fassera, a nun of the Comboni Order, who followed the rebels into the bush to retrieve all but thirty of her girls. The author acknowledges her experience and the telling of it as an integral part of this book. Of the real thirty girls of St. Mary's, four died in captivity and the remaining twenty-six eventually escaped to freedom. In fact, the girls were held much longer than those depicted in this novel—many staying with the rebels up to eight or ten years. The last girl of St. Mary's, Catherine Ajok, returned after being away for thirteen years. She had with her a baby boy.

CAAFIG

"Child soldiers" is a vastly misused term. Children who have been abducted are not technically child soldiers, which describes children conscripted into the established armed forces of a country. A more precise acronym exists, though it's rather unwieldy: CAAFIG. Children Associated with Armed Forces in Groups.

LRA

The Lord's Resistance Army was named in 1994. In 1986, when Yoweri Museveni became president of Uganda he ousted Acholi soldiers from the army. They formed a group in the north, Uganda People's Democratic Army, which was galvanized by a healer named Alice Lakwena, who took control after being visited by a spirit at Murchison Falls. The tipu took the unlikely figure of a ninety-year-old Italian World War II veteran who had drowned there while visiting the tourist site. In 1987, Alice Lakwena led an attack on Kampala, which failed, after which she was forced out of the country. She was purportedly a relative of Joseph Kony's, sometimes called an aunt, sometimes a cousin. Kony took over the LRA in 1989.

An estimated thirty thousand children were abducted by 2012. The LRA in 2011 consisted of about six hundred people, four hundred of them children. By 2012, the numbers had dwindled to a couple of hundred. Since then Kony and the LRA have left Uganda, continuing their activities first in Rwanda and now disappeared in Congo.

—————

THE AUTHOR WISHES particularly to thank Melanie Thernstrom for her article "Charlotte, Grace, Janet and Caroline Come Home" (*New York Times Magazine*, May 8, 2005), from which she shamelessly lifted details and wove them into fiction in the name of telling a version of the story of these girls. She also acknowledges threads gathered from the following work:

The Scars of Death, Children Abducted by the Lord's Resistance Army in Uganda, based on research conducted by Rosa Ehrenreich, edited by Yodon Thonden and Lois Whitman (1997, Human Rights Watch).

The Anguish of Northern Uganda by Robert Gersony.

"Post Traumatic Stress Disorder Among Former Child Soldiers Attending a Rehabilitative Service and Primary School Education in Northern Uganda" by Emilio Ovuga, Thomas O. Oyok, and E. B. Moro, *African Health Sciences,* September 2008.

"Report of Religious Beliefs of Joseph Kony's Lord's Resistance Army," 2005, compiled by Lt. Col. Richard W. Skow, an American defense attaché to the U.S. Embassy (with contributions by Brigadier Kenneth Bama, Dr. Ray Amiro, and Major Jackson Achana, LRA technician to 1994 acting peace coordinator).

For more on the nonfiction terrain of this particular story, you might look at "This We Came to Know Afterward," published by the author initially in *McSweeney's* (Winter 2000) and subsequently in *The Best American Travel Writing 2001,* edited by Paul Theroux and Jason Wilson (Houghton Mifflin).

If it had not been for Angelina Auytum, head of the Concerned Parents Association in Uganda, and her efforts to inform the world of the plight of the abducted children, the author might never have learned of it, never come to know more about it, and never have written this book. Many thanks go to her.

And finally to Jordan Pavlin, beloved editor, for her incomparable attentions and care, the author is forever grateful.

A NOTE ON THE TYPE

This book was set in Granjon, a type named for Robert Granjon, a type cutter and printer active in Antwerp, Lyons, Rome, and Paris from 1523 to 1590. Linotype Granjon was designed by George W. Jones, who based his drawings on a face used by Claude Garamond (ca. 1480–1561) in his beautiful French books.

Composed by North Market Street Graphics,
Lancaster, Pennsylvania

Printed and bound by Berryville Graphics,
Berryville, Virginia

Designed by Cassandra J. Pappas